LIES SECRECY, AND DECEPTIONS UNLOCKED

Written by ~Theodora Higgenbotham

GOD IS A PROMISE KEEPER

"We have been the recipients of the choicest bounties of heaven ... We have grown in numbers, wealth and power as no other nation has ever grown. But we have forgotten God. We have become too proud to pray to the God that made us.

~Abraham Lincoln ~

.

ISBN:10:0692691227

ISBN-13: 9780692691229

Content

Dedication

First, I thank God, who gives dreams. I obeyed the dream seven steps and the final step said, I would become an author. To God goes all the glory.

Larry Higgenbotham, my heart, who does not fully understand my unceasing passion to write. Yet, when my old computer sizzled, I received a much timely and unexpected gift--a new lap top to continue my writing.

Erin my daughter ,and happy encourager, and **Lawrence Nolan,** my son, my sunshine. I love you both more than words could ever express.

Gail and Dave Martin, (Zion Powell Campus), prophesied on December 31, 2014, *Three more books yet to be written and more blessings from God yet to be revealed. To both, my love and God's blessings.*

Zion Christian Fellowship Family, Pastor Jim Baker, and Elders. Six years ago you opened your hearts to me and adopted me as Zion's Momma Dora. Continue to cover me with your prayers.

Acknowledgements

Betty Cattrell, words can never express how I feel about you, my dear sister in Christ Jesus.

Editor, April White Stephens, my niece and my life line. I love you.

Cover, William D. Alford, my nephew and graphic designer. I love you, and I thank you.

Senior Pastor Jim Baker and Pastor Sean O'Rourke, I thank you for your prayers and support.

Zion Christian Fellowship (Powell, Ohio) prophetic and ministry teams, continue to seep and pour out into God's people. I am forever grateful for your prayers.

"**When the final plan** *God has given to you in a dream you had in your teen years is completed, then your latter shall be greater than the former.*" Those were prophetic words spoken to me by then **Youth Pastor Wayne A. Moore**~ 2009. Now, Senior Pastor 2014, Greater Christ Temple, Columbus, Ohio.

Evangelists Charlotte Moore ~ "2008. God said, it's time to write."

Faith

"Your faith begins to move, to act, when the power of God Supernaturally empties you of doubt and fills you with a knowing. You come into a state of knowing that you know that you know. In that instant you cannot doubt." ~**Oral Roberts**

Jesus Stands Ready

Today. Jesus stands ready to hear your cry and to answer prayer for you. He is interested in every detail of your life. He knows you better than you know yourself. ~ **Kathryn Kuhlman**

Emotions

"Feeling is a voice of the body; reasoning is the voice of the mind; conscience is the voice of the spirit."

Psalm 119:105-112

The Message (MSG)

By your words I can see where I'm going; they throw
a beam of light on my dark path.
I've committed myself and I'll never turn back from
living by your righteous order.
Everything's falling apart on me, GOD;
put me together again with your Word.
Festoon me with your finest sayings,
GOD; teach me your holy rules.
My life is as close as my own hands,
but I don't forget what you have revealed.
The wicked do their best to throw me off track, but I
don't swerve an inch from your course. I inherited
your book on living; it's mine forever—what a gift!
And how happy it makes me! I concentrate on doing
exactly what you say, I always have and always will.

Prologue

Woodrow Hugh Parks, eldest son of the late Pastor Samuel Parks, left his mother's, Ida Parks, home driven by smothering flames of intense hostility for anyone who dared to question his motives. And the one who he loved the most just did.

Suppressing the urge to harm his mother, Woodrow pushed open and slammed his mother's front door with a loud *bam!* He momentarily paused when he stepped outside onto her large back porch and felt the storm's thunderous shock waves and the fierceness of the wind blowing. He heard the thunder roar, and saw lightening guided by a fearsome blast of brilliant light that flashed around him. Yet, he stood undisturbed. He put his head back and an eerie laughter followed by abominable cursing erupted from his mouth as his ill-fated soul looked into the foreboding sky and soaked up the stormy sky's tears.

He hastily put on his black, rain repellent coat and hurried down the steps. Walking quickly through the downpour towards his car, he heard his name being called. "Woodrow!"

He looked back and saw his mother standing in the doorway, shouting to him through the loud thunderous storm. "Son, I have more to say to you. I am not finished."

"You may not be, but I am mother," he answered back with bitterness. He continued to shout, "You have nothing more to say that I wish to hear."

Woody hurriedly opened his car door and heard a loud gasp. He turned to look back and saw his mother had followed him and had fallen off the steps into the slushy mud. "Woodrow, Woodrow!" She cried, "Stop! Son, you have gone too far!"

Through the torrential rain he saw his mother's trembling outstretched hands, beckoning, for him to come back. He saw her light blue dress soaking up the tears from both her eyes and the stormy skies.

His inner phantom hissed, '*Ida hasn't seen anything, for the worst is yet to come.'* As Woodrow's mother sat up, she blinked her eyes and when she opened them again, she saw flashes of lightening encircling her beloved son, and through the thunderous booms her son stood undaunted and fearless.

While he glanced back at his mother an eerie smile spread on his mouth and a raspy groan escaped and he heard his inner phantom voice, *Have I, Mother? Have we gone too far?*

Seethed in his phantom's anger and with intense, uncontrolled bitterness he screamed, "Mom, we've just begun. After all, I am unlike my natural father, but like the one who has become my father. I have become the pawn he uses to deceive, and we have many deceptions, lies and secrets yet to be revealed."

Leave Ida. Go!

With restraint, he fought the demonic interference in his mind telling him to shut his mouth and leave his beloved mother sitting in the mud.

Overriding, his master's command, Woody walked

back to his mother. His large, muscular, 6'6 body towered over his mother. He stooped and sat back on his heels and when he said,

"Mom," He heard his voice quiver and he whispered, "you and Dad taught me well. I know the Bible's words like I know my name, and to me..."

He stood, and groaned loudly, and turned his back away from his mother's love-filled eyes, and said in a low nasal scornful tone, "Those are just written words Mom, words, and nothing more. I know Apostle Peter wrote, 'be sober minded; be watchful for your adversary the devil prowls around like a roaring lion, seeking someone to devour.' But Mom," he turned fully to her with fists clenched and hollered, "Look! Really look at me Mom! Can't you see? It's me, your son? And that prowling, roaring lion is my master?" He shook his head vigorously and through the thunderous boom and with loud laughter he shouted, "I'm his!"

An unexpected, uncontrolled throbbing seeped from his heart, and the rain's heavy downpour covered his tears. Woodrow sighed, refastened his coat to protect his expensive suit, turned to his mother and lifted her from the mud-covered ground.

His mother embraced her son's neck and whispered into his ear, "I love you." Feeling the warmth of her love, he averted his eyes, and inhaled, then slowly exhaled.

He gently put her down and pulled away from her embrace, trying to control his own thoughts and not listen to his phantom master's voice telling him to not yield to his love for his mother.

In doing so, he knew it would cause him to reveal the many too many- revolting secrets that had been inaccessible for years. Buried deep inside the ill-fated, locked chambers of his heart.

Tears gathered in his eyes and his hardened heart's dam broke. The familiar controlling inner phantom screamed, '*Don't do it! Walk away, now!*'

However, Woodrow's desire to reveal the truth to the one he truly loved over-ruled his phantom controller's screaming inner order.

Woody stepped closer to his mom, with their faces separated by inches, he spoke, "Mom, I have never told you this, when I was twelve years old, I was overpowered by an elusive spirit by …" He heard, '*Shut your mouth!*

Woody suddenly grabbed his head, and groaned loudly as he struggled in opposition to his inner phantom's voice commanding him to *shut up*, refusing his command Woody continued, ..."b-b-b-by playing this magical board game at the home of my middle - school friend, Willie, a spirit inside the board told me I would fully belong to him when I turned twenty. That spirit kept its word! I now belong to whatever it is, and it has become my consuming adversary.

Heavy tears mingled with the rain, trickled down his face. Woody struggled for breath. In his mind he heard the phantom's cursing and fuming, and finally Woody screamed, "Mom, it has already devoured me! Even if I wanted to, I can't turn back! I am its prisoner, and it shows no mercy. I'm his."

Chapter 1, The End to the Beginning

Regaining consciousness, a young man laid face-up on the hardened ground. He opened his eyes and stared into the impenetrable darkness that overlaid his aching body like sheets of heavy steel.

Throughout the cold night he breathed in vile stenches, and heard heart - wrenching moans and groans that sent chills down his spine. Disheartened, confused and unable to help himself, he fitfully slept, terrified, right through the unyielding darkness.

From sleep he is awaken with hearing the sound of relentless buzzing. Unable to move his body he shook his head vigorously trying to protect himself with his uninjured hand from their explosive stings that caused his whole body to convulse.

Move, he screamed to himself, *come on move!*

The nameless stranger's face, chest, and arms throbbed from the sweltering heat that burned his exposed skin, and from being pricked continuously with what felt like little needles.

Lying there in anguish, he felt the movement of buzzing flies entering in and out of his partly opened parched mouth. He lifted his uninjured left hand to brush away the onslaught of painful buzzing pricks he felt to his singed forehead.

He unintentionally scraped a huge bump and it erupted; out squirted a wet, foul - tasting, smelly, burning liquid that flowed down his face. Immediately, his skinned, bruised face was assaulted by hundreds of unrelenting buzzing pricks that hit with persistency stinging his dry swollen tongue.

From his forehead he felt hot liquid dribbling down his face, seeping onto his cracked lips and into his partly opened parched mouth as the stinging, buzzing insects repeatedly pricked his face, tongue and exposed chest.

His mind obscured, yet he heard what sounded like a whistle being blown and a commanding voice that shouted, *Move, move, move!*

The stranger placed his one strong left hand onto the mushy ground to push himself up, but collapsed from the persistent pain pulsating throughout his body. Laying there he heard; *move, move, move.*

Exhausted, his mind confused, and fearful. The young stranger mustered all of his will power to withstand the onslaught of persistent pain as he shifted his weight, flipped over and sat up. As he sat he felt the fierce heat

Through his swollen eye and with his shrouded mind he asked himself, *where am I?*

The young stranger lifted his mud-caked bloody hands to his face then wiped his fingers across his tattered yellow shirt that clung to his massive chiseled body. He noticed his silk shirt was also soaked with sweat and blood, and reeked with foulness.

Again he heard the return of the familiar alarming buzzing sounds and conditioned his mind to receive their relentless stings that forcefully stabbed his tormented body

He willed his mind to move his body, but with each move he thought his intestine were being twisted and ripped apart, and felt as if a fiery dagger was being trust in and out of his right leg.

The combined effects of the sun's heat, his dislocated shoulder, injured right leg, cracked ribs, and the unrelenting stinging of the buzzing intruders and flies tortured his entire body. He watched helplessly, petrified as various insects leapt off his soiled pants and onto his exposed raw chest and into his dry opened mouth.

Move or die!

The young stranger set sights on a nearby grassy area with trees. He gathered all his strength to will his body to lie down and to roll over to the area.

Roll, roll, roll, roll!

Once there, he instinctively flipped his injured body again and buried his face into the soft, moist, shady, green grass, and found instant comfort and solitude from the stage of the bee's and little nips from the flies. His dark blue suit jacket protected his back from their stings, and he slept.

Before long, he awoke laying on his stomach. His mouth had soaked in the grass's moisture, and was no longer dry. He moved his head to the side and opened his unprotected eyes.

Through his narrow vision he saw the sun going down and the bees leaving. Defenseless and weary, he recalled words that were etched into his memory. *Move or die.* Tears gathered in his eyes. The young, nameless stranger placed his lips on the wet ground, sucked in the grass's moisture and swallowed. Feeling the need to roll over, the young stranger clenched his teeth revealing their beautiful whiteness. He prepared his mind and body to accept the onslaught of coming pain when he planted the toes of his blue alligator shoes into the soft green grass and commanded his tormented body to flip onto its back.

Exhausted, he slept. When he awakened he was under the shade of a large broken branch of an uprooted tree.

He saw smashed cars and many different types of vehicles, destroyed or on fire.

Observing this horrendous view caused his heart to beat rapidly as salty tears flowed and seeped into the cuts and stung the open wounds on his face. He struggled to control his emotions by taking in small gasps of air, and then inhaling deeply, which caused his stomach to retch as he tried to explain the stench to himself from the various unrecognizable, unpleasant odors.

For the first time, he noticed that he wasn't alone. He saw many strangers like him, they also sat or stood disoriented, and with agonized faces; they too were like living, stationary zombies and like him they were also in a state of panic and gave him quizzical glances. It felt like he was watching a science fiction film, but this was real. He saw bits and pieces of flesh strewn in wet pool of blood as far as his eyes could see there were so many, too many bodies to count. Some were mangled, some barely alive. Many of those bodies were covered with rodents and insects, and their tormented bodies howled in pain from the stinging bees and both the large rodents gnawing on their flesh as they laid powerless, grieving in incessant torment.

The young, nameless stranger noticed the circumference of the tree he was near. He believed it to be a great source for shelter and decided to move his body. With each torturous push, his leg muscles throbbed and his shoulder burned.

Move or die, move or die, move, move, move! He slammed his strong back against the huge broken, branch, and felt the tree's thorns prickle the back of his head and its needles penetrate his suit jacket.

Using his uninjured hand he scooted forward and saw a few inches down some bark had fallen off the tree. Slowly he pushed with his aching shoulder and throbbing legs until he reached the smoothest part of the tree.

Depleted, he closed his eyes and slept. A few hours later he opened his swollen eyes and once again he squinted into pure blackness. He looked up, where the scorching sun once shone, he was now embraced by a moonless, starless, black, ill-omened sky.

With the chilliness of the night and his mind void of all memory; he sat in an awkward, painful position and closed his eyes. Too weary to move, he dozed.

At the break of dawn the young stranger was jolted awake by a forceful, painful stab to his leg and saw movement inside his pants leg. He felt an acute tearing, biting into his wounded leg.

He screamed, and began to whimper like a small helpless, frightened child. He again felt the salty tears stinging the cuts on his face as his caged heart pounded rapidly against his ribs. His hands flailed, trying to beat out what was gnawing on his leg.

Finally, he saw scurrying out from his pant leg a small black mouse leaving behind blood, oozing through his dark blue silk trousers.

Using his strong fingers, he punctured holes into his pant leg to expose his wound and he saw the small teeth marks.

Engaged with his own heart wrenching self-pity, he became less concerned about himself and more frightened when he heard a woman's ear-piercing, pitiful cry. "Help me, somebody, help me please. Help me!"

The stranger's head turned toward the sound and he saw the form of a small frame that approached and stopped in front of him. He looked up and saw an attractive, bedraggled woman. Her face was bruised, cut and swollen, she too was covered with mud. Her green eyes were reddened from crying.

Her long fiery red hair was matted with mud and blood. He watched as she awkwardly stumbled toward him. In her hands, she clutched a small football against her heart.

Standing in front of him, the young woman collapsed onto her knees. Broken with grief, she extended her hands in a pleading position toward the young, nameless stranger and she cried, "Help, please, help me, please ... help me, I can't find my son. My son is missing and ... my baby." The woman placed both hands on her abdomen and looked down and with extreme agony she whispered, "My unborn baby, she was a girl, now, she's gone; my son, my husband, my daughter, they all ... vanished."

Grief-stricken and broken with pain, the young woman sobbed. Instinctively, the nameless stranger extended his arms to her and she - heartbroken and overcome by grief accepted his comfort and allowed him to cradle her. While he rocked her, the young woman continued to clutch the football to her heart, and told the stranger her story.

"I'm seven months pregnant and my baby." The woman handed the stranger a small brown football. The stranger hesitated for a moment, but accepted her son's football and as he gripped the brown leather ball he heard once again the words, *Move or die, move, move! ... Those words.*

Puzzled, the stranger looked up, he saw her again place both hands to her abdomen and whisper, "She isn't ... my baby, she isn't inside me anymore.

She isn't here; she ... she vanished."

The woman pulled away from him, took hold of the oversized dress and held it out. "See, do you see?" She shrieked, "My unborn baby was taken out of me! My baby and my beautiful son, they're gone. My son just turned five. His name is Joseph."

The woman stood and turned her body in circles calling out her missing son's name. "Joseph! ... Joseph!"

She stopped calling Joseph's name to look at the nameless stranger. Through her tears she told him. "Joseph can't hear me, can he? I know he isn't here anymore, so why am I calling his name?" The young woman reached down and gently removed the football from the stranger's grip

She held out the small brown rubber football, and choked back her tears as she continued her story.

"My family, we were in the car and I turned to hand this to my Joseph, this ... .football, when he vanished. You know my husband was driving the car and he also vanished; my husband was a faithful Christian."

Those three words. *A faithful Christian,* tormented the nameless stranger's mind.

He watched her lips move but he was not hearing her words. Finally, he focused his attention to her voice and he heard her say, "It's true, isn't it? Jesus came and they all have gone with Him."

For reasons unknown to him, the woman's words crushed the stranger's heart. She stood up and sat beside him on the log and looked into the nameless stranger's swollen eyes.

With a haunting whisper she said, "They are no more." She stood and walked away, calling. "Joseph!" The young, nameless stranger shut his eyes, inhaled, then slowly exhaled. Those words. *They are no more,* seemingly tormented his mind. He thought.

Why do her words bother me? Think. Breathe. Think. Who are you? Think, think, think! The nameless stranger lifted his throbbing head and through his squinted eye he saw an older, lanky, gray- haired man standing clutching his tablet staring at him. The young stranger noticed the older man's eyes were also enflamed from his own grief and his clothing also was tattered and wet from the blistering heat.

The gray- haired man came and sat under the tree in silence next to him. Not long afterward the young woman returned and the three of them huddled together. They remained speechless throughout the humid, oppressive day and into the dark, cold, moonless night where they slept.

Eventually, the young stranger awoke and softly yawned. He opened his swollen eyes and was thankful that the tree's large foliage shielded them from the beams of the baking sun's full strength that danced around them.

Motionless, the nameless stranger listened to the gray haired man and young woman talking. Not wanting to join in their conversation he pretended to sleep. The gray- haired man spoke.

"My wife and my four boys ages fourteen, twelve, ten, and four- and I were in the van coming home from the grocery store.

Myrtle, that's my wife's name... my precious, sweet, wife...she was driving.

Our boys were buckled in their seats and talking. I was watching a football game on my tablet when the car crashed. I looked up, and ... they... they all disappeared!"

From the corner of his eyes the nameless stranger watched the man remove his big gray handkerchief from his side pocket to wipe away his tears. He then took in a deep breath and continued.

"They were gone. Poof! In a moment and a twinkling of an eye. My babies, and my wife--gone. I've always teased Myrtle about church and God. I purposely stayed upset with her because she and my boys talked nonstop about God and their church. I told them they were too religious and they were drinking their pastor's poisonous Kool-Aid. Now, it's obviously too late for me, I wish I had drunk it all."

For some unknown reason, the woman's words crushed the nameless stranger's heart. *'My Troy was diagnosed with cancer. His doctors gave him two months to live, but he was healed by God.'* "After Troy's healing, he became a regular at the church and was saved. I loved him and gave my support and I pretended to love God as much as Troy. I raised my hands in worship and said all the right words, served on committees, and gave to the needy. However, I couldn't let go of my country club connections and my family's social status.

Troy and I argued constantly. Behind closed doors he would say, 'Honey, God sees you.' Unless you change your selfish motives, you will become one of the many who will see God and tell him all the awesome things they have done for Him in life only to hear Him say, 'I never knew you.'

Honey, do you know why He said those words? Because their everyday living did not represent Him. His Character is the Spirit of truth, and His true Spirit and their untrue spirits never connected.'

Finally, I became so tired of Troy's lectures, I stopped going to church. Not long afterwards, I had an affair. I had just asked him for a divorce and now look at me! I am all alone, while he and my precious son, and my unborn baby are in heaven."

The young woman turned to the gray- haired man and asked him. "Carlos, did it really happen? Did Jesus come?"

"Yes, it happened. Jesus came."

"After the crash and before my tablet batteries died, I was listening to the news stations, and they are saying all over the world millions were missing. They are saying the loud boom's vibrations we heard years prior caused the earth's plates to shift and many cities near water have completely vanished. Planes worldwide fell from the sky at approximately the same time.

"The United States' enemies now have control of nuclear weapons to be used by terrorists who are bent on achieving their future goals to annihilate America by any means, cruise ships, fishing boats, and Navy vessels are stranded because of missing crew members. Our military soldiers, government and intergovernmental civil service members are missing.

The gray-haired man pointed to the woman and told her. "Like you, pregnant women's babies were taken out of them and children, from newborns to age 12 have vanished.

"Untold numbers of subway trains have crashed and there are miles upon miles of vehicles that have crashed on highways all over the world.

Highways are closed because of traffic tie-ups. There's a shortage in our armed forces due to missing military men. Police and firemen have disappeared and loathsome prisoners have escaped.

"Our President, can you believe it? The President--and he vanished during his cabinet meeting and many of the President's immediate family members are missing. Graves have opened all over the world, and their bodies have disappeared. Looting is widespread. Our water is unsafe due to chemicals and oil spills. Water creatures are dying. Plagues, sickness, and disease are rapidly spreading. This chaos is pandemic.

Emotionally traumatized, the young woman sat rocking back and forth on the grass. The gray-haired man shook his head and with difficulty he told her more of his story. He paused to wipe his sweaty face and continued with his story. "I, like you, should have listened when my Myrtle talked about Jesus returning, I was cruel and ruthless with my criticisms.

I told her that the stories she heard her crazy pastor preach week after week, year after year, were like reading the children's fairy tale books. I told her I thought she was too intelligent, being a lawyer, to believe that rubbish. It sounded absurd to think that she believed that in the end, 'they all will live in heaven with the Son of God, whose name is Jesus, happily ever after. I scorned her relentlessly. I made it difficult for her to leave with the boys each Sunday by demanding a hot family breakfast.

She would lay out the kids' Sunday clothes the night before and prepare breakfast before she went to bed. I insisted that she say her prayers in the spare bedroom because her praying was keeping me awake.

I just knew she would eventually break, but her love for God kept her going. I watched her from the window, she would sit inside her car, wiping away tears that came from her aching heart after hearing my many hateful words that pierced her soul, and yet she never became cross with me. She loved me. I should have gone to church with her, but instead I stayed home being increasingly critical of her, telling her she was spending too much time at church and our kids were becoming brainwashed. I nagged her, telling her she loved being with those church folk more than with me. I taunted her, saying her pastor was controlling them with this spiritual nonsense."

The stranger heard the gray-haired man release a long heavy sigh and resume his story.

"Now, my Myrtle and my kids are gone and I am left here." Stammering, he uttered, "If... if... if what Myrtle said is right, our time is not up, there is still hope for those like us who were left behind, but it may cost us our lives.

Myrtle said to the very end the devil will use deception as the key to lock people's faith in God. He would then use their lack of faith to destroy God's people. To the very end, the devil will send out his deceived human army to pursue and to murder those who have pledged their allegiance to God and to serve Him."

The stranger listened, not fully understanding nor wanting to believe what he heard to be true. The more he listened, the greater the battle became within his mind. He thought, *who is Jesus? Who will lock people's faith? Deception? Destroy God's people? Who is God?*" The stranger's mind was captivated, riveted with questions, yet not desiring to join in with their conversation.

He moved his left hand, and then with a slight moan, he yielded and asked, "Ah ... how many days have we been here?"

"Days?" The gray-haired man replied, "Son, we've been here two days, but it seems like an eternity."

The gray haired man extended his hand toward the young man and said, "My name is Carlos, Carlos James." The woman smiled and graciously said, "My name is Susan Romans."

Then Carlos bowed his head, he again extended his hand to Susan. He held her hand, smiled and said, "Nice to meet you Susan Romans." Carlos looked over at the young man laying impassively on the grass. "And you, young man?" Carlos said, smiling, "I hate this dilemma we've found ourselves to be in and I would prefer to be in the Hawk's football stadium seeking an autograph. Nevertheless, it's an honor to meet you Cullen

Michael Sullivan." He stared at the gray-haired man thinking, *this man, Carlos, called me Cullen.* Eagerly he asked, "Sir, by what name did you call me?"

"Cullen. You are Cullen Michael Sullivan. You play for the Georgia Hawks, you are our hometown hero. You are the Hawks' star running back, and quite the ladies' man, according to the tabloids."

Hearing his name jolted his memory. His mind started to unravel its mysteries. Cullen numbly lifted his bloody, mud - caked hands and clutched his face as his sorrow intensified.

From within, an agonizing cry erupted. *No. No God, it can't be that! No. no, noooo.* Cullen's mind became a whirlwind of fear. Disregarding his pain, Cullen buried his head between his legs and curled into a fetal position and rocked back and forth.

With a fearful heart he spoke aloud, "God, I have missed your coming!"[5] He bellowed, "My family, they are all gone!

No! No, no, no! God, pleeeease! No!"

Cullen struggled to stand, and seeing this, Carlos extend his hands to help him, Cullen shouted, "No, please, no!" With sorrowful tears, Cullen looked at him and said, "I'm sorry Carlos, but please step away."

Cullen put his back against the smooth part of the tree. With his hands, he held onto a large knotty part of the branch, and with all his strength he pulled his aching body up and sat heedlessly on the thick broken branch, and was inconsolable.

Hours later, drying his tears, Cullen looked around and immediately remembered. He knew where he was. He recalled those wonderful camping days he shared in this very spot with his cousin Brie, his best friend Brad,

Grandpa Jeremiah and Uncle George, hunting and fishing in the lake a half mile away, and ... camping under the exact tree's broken branch which he now sat on.

He rubbed his left hand over the tree's rough outer bark and recognized the broken branch which he sat on as a black locust.

He knew it by its deep furrows and interlacing ridges. Cullen thought, *this bark represents my heart. I, like this tree, feel jagged and ripped apart.* Cullen's memory returned like an opened floodgate.

No longer was he in the comfort of his beautiful dark blue car driving down Interstate 65 with his cousin, Brie, and her husband, his best friend, Brad. He remembered their conversation about God's returning.

He remembered Brie expressing that she heard the blasting of the trumpet and Brie's giggling and Brad's happiness.

He remembered purposely dismissing their conversation and the invitation to repent. He recalled while driving, thinking, *they are hearing the blast of a trumpet? To me it sounds more like a loud boom*!

Then he recalled Carlos words to Susan, *The loud booms and vibrations we have heard years prior had caused earth's plates to shift and many cities near water have disappeared.*

Cullen recalled seeing Brie's face from his car's rearview mirror, shining like translucent light. And Brad's clothing was covered with jewels. Cullen's body shuddered as he shook his head, trying to get rid of the unwanted memory and not desiring to believe his recollection.

They are alive and out there somewhere. 'Cullen cupped his hands to his mouth and screamed out their names. "Brie! Brad!" He listened, and all he heard was the sound of his own voice resonating.

He felt a gentle hand on his shoulder. He turned and saw Carlos. Carlos asked, "Cullen, were Brie and your friends?" Cullen struggled to answer but couldn't. With kindheartedness Carlos said, "Cullen, you're calling them, Brad and Brie, but they can't answer you."

Cullen pulled away, turned to look into Carlos' clear blue eyes and for the first time he saw such tenderness that it reminded him of his Grandpa.

Refusing to accept his words and told Carlos, "No ... you are wrong. Brie and Brad are alive. I will go to find them."

Ignoring his pain, Cullen limped back to the branch and sat. He lowered his head and cried. Between sobs he whispered, "Brie, where are you? Please, please answer me Brie, please."

"Cullen," Carlos gently answered, "there's no need to plead for Brie to answer you anymore. She's not here, Cullen. Both Brie and Brad, they are either dead or with Jesus."

Cullen looked angrily at Carlos, loathing his words, Cullen hollered. "No, you are wrong Carlos! Jesus didn't come! My cousin and my best friend are out there! They are not dead!" Weeping, he said, "Carlos, I will go and I will find them."

Cullen slid off the jagged branch onto the grassy ground. He sat and pounded the soft green surface over and over trying to convince his mind that he didn't see Brie's shimmering face or Brad's jeweled clothing.

What he was recalling was his imagination or a nightmarish dream. He looked up into the light blue sky and saw the big white clouds and then he slowly lower his head. Through his tears and swollen eyes, he really observed what surrounded him.

The images he saw were horrendous, it was like watching a war movie. The air he smelled was thick with foul odors. He knew what he was witnessing wasn't a movie--it was real.

He looked over at Carlos who stood nearby and stuttered, "P-p- perhaps Brie and Brad are alive Carlos!"

Cullen's eyes broadened with new hope. "Carlos," he shouted, "I know! They are alive and trapped inside the car!"

Carlos shook his head back and forth and answered, "Cullen, no... No, believe me son, they aren't there."

Cullen replied angrily. "No you are wrong! Carlos, they are there!"

"Cullen. Cullen, look around, even if they were out there, how would you find them? There are too many crashed vehicles!"

Cullen pondered this for a moment, he patted his pants pocket. He then inserted his uninjured hand into his pocket and removed the car's back-up keys. He pushed the button, and heard a nearby beep. He smiled and said to Carlos, "That's how!"

Cullen found a heavy, thick, broken-off tree branch to support his injured body. Agonizingly, he limped with renewed hope toward the blaring of the horn of his smashed car. He wanted to believe that Brie and Brad were alive, that their bodies were trapped inside the car and Jesus returning wasn't true.

God, please let them be there.

Gathering courage, he looked into the car. He saw both Brad's and Brie's seat belts were still fastened. On the front and back seat he saw where Brad and Brie sat, were two brilliant gemstones.

From Brad's seat, he picked up an alexandrite stone. He lifted an amethyst stone from Brie's seat. He saw Brie's Bible, her navy blue silk scarf, and navy blue clutch purse.

Cullen lifted Brie's Bible and blue scarf and clasped them both to his heart. He took in a deep breath and whispered with anguish, *Oh God, all the preaching I have heard about your coming. I heard and knew it to be true, but I ignored it!*

In agony, he steadied his legs with his stick, and limped around the car. He stopped to scan the faces of nameless wounded people, both young and old who were sitting or lying on the blood soaked grass. The sight he saw was traumatic. He saw masses of bees--so many, too many bees--and other insects and rodents feeding on carcasses, and drinking the moist blood from living bodies.

They chewed into the flesh of the living, who were strewn around, uncovered, helpless, and screaming from being tormented. He walked distressed among disfigured, burned, miserable, hopeless and muddle- minded people who moved about like mindless zombies.

He then saw many healthy men and women scavenging among the dead or dying.

Without forewarning, Cullen felt an intense inner fear as the ground violently shook under his feet. Looking down and saw a shadow that was growing in size. With panic, he looked up and saw a menacing creature staring back.

The creature was dark and immense with a ghastly, scarred face. Its rotten mouth was horribly disfigured and dripped bloody foam. The creature had two long red fangs protruding from its enlarged, open mouth. Its eyes were the size of honeydew melons. One eye socket was oozing with living maggots, the other eye had a big hollow opening that dripped fresh blood. The demonic creature discerned Cullen's paranoias and was empowered. The creature hissed his name, *Cullen!*

Petrified by the creature's appearance, Cullen was suddenly encouraged when the creature transformed itself into a glowing, vaporous image of light. The light swirled around and around him and used telepathy to calm his emotions. Enticed by the image of beauty, Cullen found himself being lured into the image's open arms. Holding him, the creature suddenly changed. Its enormous mouth opened and reeked from its fiery breath a foul, repulsive, sulfuric odor.

Cullen's mind was overloaded with revolting, repulsive cursing unlike anything he could have ever conceived.

The creature flung Cullen body onto the ground and continued its swirling and taunted Cullen, digging and scraping away all Cullen's courage, leaving him spineless, while it seared its brutality deeper into Cullen's emotions.

Cullen, fully aware of his own frailness sat down on the hard surface powerless, trembling with paralysis he thought, *I need an angel.*

And instantly, Cullen watched the creature twirl rapidly, transforming into a beautiful radiant angel. With a faint smile of welcome relief Cullen's dread instantly diminished Believing the angel was sent by God, he allowed his mind to relax.

Supported by his stick, he stood, smiling at the angel's glowing beauty.

Without warning, the enticing angel changed into a burning, flaming, reddish image, transforming back into the oversized, horribly disfigured, scar-faced creature.

It's rotten, maggot filled mouth dripped bloody foam and its claws were enormous. As the creature overshadowed Cullen, he heard the creature's thoughts in his own mind.

An evil, sardonic laughter, along with more unrestrained, vile, belligerent language escaped from the creature's perverted mouth. It came exploding from its bleeding mouth and sputtered like hot lava out of a volcano and blackened Cullen's soul.

This profane, unearthly beast, with its filthy gigantic bird-like claws hooted as his enormous claws grasped and held Cullen's dangling, feeble, body in midair. The creature's searing words telepathically inundated Cullen's mind with terror.

Cullen Michael Hugh Sullivan, you have no more hope. Your loved ones are gone, you belong to me and will never escape the schedule death I hold for you.

The unnatural beast whirled faster and faster, dangling Cullen from its vicious claws as it continued to take pleasure in menacing and taunting Cullen's mind.

The creature's claws, torturous vile words, and hellish laughter fused Cullen's body and soul. Its blasphemous words felt like fiery arrows piercing deeper into his heart, causing him to experience stabbing sensations. Cullen heard over and over, *all your loved ones are gone.*

Then the creature's enormous, bird-like claws, lifted Cullen's limp body to his melon sized, maggot gushing eyes, and slowly hissed. *Die!*

Cullen knew the creature's thoughts were true. His best friends and his beloved family were gone, and seeing and hearing the creature's torturous telepathically words caused him dire worry. Cullen's physical agony gave way to the creature's power. Cullen sobbed loudly as he listened to the creature's victorious celebration, and he believed the creature's thoughts, "*That all his hope was gone*" Recognizing death was near, Cullen whispered the name. *Jesus.* Immediately, the creature howled, and released its grip. Cullen fell hard on the ground and with his one opened eye, he saw the creature levitating.

Cullen lay quivering with fear and with regret he remembered Brie. He recalled the car, Brie's kiss and her words, *Cullen, God told me to kiss you. He said to tell you to remember this kiss. It will be your reminder that He is in you.*

When you cry, Jesus! You will immediately feel a transformation of the 'Inner Man's' Spirit in you, and that will be His strength moving, and living inside you. God said He will be your present help! But most of all; He said to tell you, He has never stopped loving you, He will always love you, His chosen son.

Cullen stirred, he filled his heart with faith and his lungs with air and screamed, "Jesus!"

Immediately, Cullen heard what sounded like a lion's roar. The lion's roar was swift and furious, powerful and violent. So much so that it shook the ground and shattered the surrounding car windows.

The creature heard the lion's roar and began to moan, gyrate, and shriek in agony. It fell violently upon the blistering, cracked ground and curled its body, thrashing about completely out of control.

Its enormous body shuddered in fear and with claws flailing, it lashed out with several unsuccessful attempts to snatch Cullen.

Cullen moved away quickly. He kicked both legs, and used his upper body strength to put distance between him and the creature.

As Cullen watched the creature thrash about in terror, he remembered the scripture that says, *You believed that there is one God; you do well, the devils also believe, and tremble.*

'Cullen thought about his Aunt Cate teaching about the name of Jesus. *Jesus, the Son of our living God, fulfilled His Father's plan of complete emancipation and deliverance to all who believe in the power of the name of Jesus.*

His name gives victory to overcome the enemy's snares. His blood covering is our protection. And because of His death on Calvary, you have His ownership over the devil's entire realm. You have been sealed. You carry His authority. His name carries absolute power.

Cullen bravely stood, and shouted from the top of his lungs, Jesus, Jesus, Jesus!"

Cullen watched with astonishment when legions of four inched maggots that resided in the creature leapt from its melon sizes eyes.

They squealed in pain as they fell onto the hot, cracked earth, they sizzled and vanished.

The creature, now reduced in size and power, thrashed wildly in mayhem on the hot earth; writhing in torment, it shrunk into a small maggot that lay wiggling on the cracked ground.

Cullen perceived God speaking to him with reassurance. *Nevertheless you, the devil, will be thrust down to Sheol, to the recesses of the pit and those who see you will gaze at you, they will ponder over you, asking, 'Is this the man (the devil) who made the earth tremble, who shook kingdoms, who made the world like a wilderness and overthrew its cities, who did not allow his prisoners to go home?...*

Cullen lifted his right foot and stomped repeatedly on the small maggot. With each stomp, Cullen Michael Sullivan felt a spiritual liberation.

He then stepped back and where the enormous, foul - mouthed creature once stood - there was nothing. Cullen looked at the people who were nearby.

They were undisturbed by what had transpired.

The tortuous creature and the imps, Cullen thought. *Perhaps the heat caused me to hallucinate.* Immediately, Cullen felt the movement of the earth under his feet. His knees buckled and he fell onto his face and wept. It was there, with his face touching the *cool,* cracked ground, that he heard the voice of God saying, *Cullen, My son, I will honor the prayers of My faithful servants for you. I will not leave you. I will be with you from this day until the day you look up and see My second coming. Remain faithful and strong.*

For the first time in a long while Cullen heard himself pray.

From this day forward, I dedicate myself to You, I will follow Your leading and stay faithful until I see You, my God, my Lord and Savior, face to face."

Cullen stood and looked up. The sky was an azure blue, and the sun shone, glimmering brightly. He looked down to where the creature once stood and laughed. He saw his walking stick and bent over to pick it up, but he had no need for it. His body was pain free, stronger and changed from the inside out.

Cullen looked at the strangers nearby, they seemed oblivious of his presence. Cullen thought, *did I really see a demonic creature? Did I really hear a lion's roar? Did God really speak to me?'* He pondered his questions, he rapidly moved his healed legs, jogged in place and then stopped when he heard a fearsome roar. The roar of the Lion of Judah!

Joyously, Cullen shouted at the top of his lungs. "Hallelujah!" Laughing, he looked and the people around him were unaware of his presence.

He bent over to touch his toes, he rotated his body and was pain free. With a healed mind he thought ... *My car.* Cullen jogged over to his smashed car.

Once there, he picked up Brie's Bible that had fallen onto the ground, kissed it, then tucked it into his side pocket. He laughed when he picked up the gemstones, and tucked them into his side pocket.

He leaned into the car's broken window to remove the keys from the ignition.

Using the keypad, he popped opened the trunk, removed his backpack, and looked inside. He saw his pistol, valuable jewelry, some money, pain pills, clothing, several bottles of water, and a bottle of sanitizer which he squeezed out onto his filthy swollen hands.

"Yowl!" He screamed. He quickly opened a bottle of water to rinse off the blood and sweat and to stop the stinging from the sanitizer.

Afterward, he walked to the side mirror and noticed his face, his lips were split and his eyes were swollen, but he could see clearly. He felt different, inside and outside. Gone was the relentless agonizing pain to his face and body. He had been instantly healed.

Cullen tossed the backpack over his shoulder and commenced walking cautiously among the others, who like him, were left behind, but to his puzzling amazement, he was invisible to them. Laughing at this miracle, Cullen picked up his pace and jogged back to their spot.

Carlos saw Cullen jogging and ran to meet him. Carlos lifted Cullen in his strong arms, looked at him and asked, "What happened to you? You aren't limping."

Cullen replied, "I had an Apostle Paul encounter."

Susan clapped her hands and laughed when she said, "Cullen, while you were having your Apostle Paul transformation, Carlos and I were having our Moses experience.

Look around. While you were gone all the bees, rodents and insects left and the hot temperature has dropped in our spot. But look over there Cullen."

Cullen looked and just a few feet away he saw insects, rodents and bees all around the other unfortunate victims.

Where Cullen, Susan and Carlos stood, the area was miraculously protected by an invisible shield.

Cullen looked back at Carlos and Susan and with his fists pumping air, he shouted aloud, "Yes, God is with us!"

Cullen opened his gym bag, pulled out Brie's Bible and kissed it. He then wrapped her small purse and Bible in her navy blue scarf and tucked them into the inside compartment in his backpack.

Not saying another word, he gave Carlos and Susan squirts of sanitizer, two bottles of water and some pain pills. Even though his leg was healed, he used some of the water to wash away the dried blood. Using his fingers, he scraped out the dead insects and poured sanitizer into his open wound. He removed his jacket, ripped the sleeves off his yellow silk shirt, tied both sleeves together, and wrapped his pain-free, leg.

He removed a clean undershirt and put it on and he tossed one over to Carlos. Cullen reached into his bag and tossed a dress to Susan, saying,

"I found this in my cousin's suitcase, I believe you and she are the same size. You will have some privacy if you go behind this tree to change."

Cullen picked up his jacket and inside its pocket he saw the mousy gray envelope that Michael Jay, his friend, had given to him prior to driving off the church grounds. Cullen recalled Michael Jay's words, *Cullen, my Mom said for you to read this. It's very important.*

Cullen turned the envelope over, ready to open and read it, but instead he laid the envelope aside. For some unexplained reason, he suddenly felt an urgent need to bury his gym bag.

He waited until Carlos and Susan were in a deep sleep, and he looked around to see if others were watching but found they were all asleep.

He removed his wallet and the gemstones from the inside pocket and hid them inside the bag's lining.

He used sticks to dig a large hole next to the tree he sat beside, and buried his bag. He then replaced the grass and pushed the heavy log on top.

At daybreak, while Carlos and Susan slept, Cullen picked up his jacket and hastily removed the mousy gray envelope and took out the letter and he read all of threatening words from his godfather, Woody, Michael Jay's older brother.

Cullen reinserted the letter into the envelope, and placed it back into his inside jacket pocket. He rolled his jacket back into a pillow, tucking the bottle of pain pills and the extra bottles of water inside.

Cullen whispered, *I am glad he's locked away and can't get to me.* Cullen's head rested on the mock pillow and his mind replayed Woody's cold-hearted remarks.

'Cullen,

You need to know the truth concerning your parents' death. I murdered them. I put two bullet holes in your Mom and Dad's heads while they slept.

My biggest disappointments? I have two. The first is that I will not get the chance to see your face when you read that it was me, your unloving godfather who murdered my best friends, your Mom and Dad, and it was not the (planned) accident that took their lives. Your unforgiving Grandpa was right the whole time, and that brings me to my second disappointment. I wish I was able to torture your precious grandfather and watch him die a slow death.

Did he ever tell you how he injured his back? If not, I am delighted to tell you now, I did it! I cracked that old crotchety, nosey, geezer's back!

My dear godson, when I arrive in hell, and if I have the slightest chance to crawl out, I will come for you and your grandfather. Then I will torment both of you to death.

Believe me Cullen, I will come for you, dead or alive, and your precious grandpa who you love so much. When I find that old geezer, it

Letters usually end with the words, "I love you." Ha! There's no love in hell or in me, especially not for anyone with the last name, Sullivan.

With me, it is just an unending hatred. Dead or alive, I will see you and your remaining days will be hell!'

Woody.

Cullen remembered a verse he heard his grandmother quote many times. "... *As for a rogue, his weapons are evil; he devises wicked schemes to destroy the afflicted with slander...'*

As Cullen peacefully slept, his mind transported him back several years. He dreamt he was home and he heard his Grandma calling his name.

Chapter 2 Grandpa Sees and Knows

"Cullen, wake up, take your shower, get dressed, and come down to eat breakfast. It's Sunday and we have church in two hours."

"Okay Grandma."

Under his breath he murmured, *Grandma treats me like a 12-year- old. Soon, I will be playing pro ball and have my own home and will not have to listen to Grandma calling me every Sunday morning to get ready for church.'*

Stretching, Cullen thought, *Why do I let Brie and Brad talk me into coming home every weekend?*

He placed his size fifteen feet on the floor. Groaning. He shouted, "Oh God, give me strength!

After showering, he put on a pair of pants and a t-shirt and rushed down the back stairs, through the kitchen, and into the dining room where he was greeted with a smile and a quick kiss on the cheek by his beautiful, silver-haired, energetic, 80-year-old Grandmother.

"Good morning, Cullen. You are going to church, aren't you?

"Yes, Grandma, I'm going. I thought I would eat and then dress." Cullen glanced at his grandpa who had already sat down and Cullen saw that he was purposely being ignored by his 84-year-old grouchy, but loving, Grandpa Jeremiah Sullivan.

Grandpa's lanky, wrinkled hands holding the newspaper slightly below his eye, pretending to read and with a low snappish voice his grandpa said, "Good

Morning, young Mr. Sullivan. And did you have a long restful sleep?"

Cullen grinned and answered him with a quick, "Yes I did, and thank you for asking."

Cullen pulled out his chair and sat down. His eyes locked with his Grandpa's big saucer-like eyes, which were shooting darts at him from across the table.

Brace yourself Cullen, breathe, breathe, 1, 2, 3, and... "How are you feeling this morning Grandpa?" Cullen asked with a big smile.

Grandpa Jeremiah looked at Cullen and his jaw started trembling like a pit bull, ready to pounce. Grandpa grunted and slammed the newspaper down next to his red plate. Cullen, with his peripheral vision, saw his Grandpa raise his hand, and with his knotty finger he pulled his copper rimmed glasses down onto the tip of his nose. His light gray eyes stared at Cullen like shooting bullets.

Cullen heard a loud sigh, and scraping noise. He looked up and saw Grandpa Jeremiah had quickly scooted his chair out, stood and walked over to him.

Towering over Cullen, Grandpa cleared of his throat, "Harrumph!" Cullen thought to himself, *Cullen brace yourself for what was coming... 1, 2...*

"Look at me boy!"

Immediately, Cullen lifted his head to obey his grandpa's command. He saw his Grandpa's long, wrinkled hand reach out like a rattlesnake. He strike him, not so gently, on the back of his head. *Thump!*

"Ouch! Grandpa that hurt."

"Good! Someone needs to knock some sense into

that conceited, hard head of yours!"

His Grandpa's voice was harsh and Cullen knew he had every right to be irritated with him. Grandpa returned to his chair and sat. Cullen rubbed the back of his head and his grandpa spoke with edginess, "So, good morning to you also, Mr. Cullen Michael Sullivan. We are so honored to have your presence at our kitchen table on the Lord's Day."

Grandpa picked up the folded paper and rapidly tapped it against the table, then stopped and roughly unfolded and refolded it.

"Look me in the eyes son, and tell me, did you enjoy yourself at this so-called party you went to last night?"

Cullen knew there was no way to safely answer his Grandpa's question and not receive another unwanted, stinging lecture. He deciding to not obey his Grandpa's order to look at him.

Instead, Cullen lowered his head and replied. "Yes, I did Grandpa. Will you pass the butter, please?"

His grandpa passed him the butter. Taking it, Cullen quickly buttered his cold biscuit, then placed it on his red plate.

Eager to eat, he looked up. His eyes were staring into his grandpa's scowling face.

Cullen smiled broadly, and with a humorless, yet polite tone, he asked, "May I eat now Grandpa?"

"Boy don't give me that subdued Jack Kennedy smile of yours, and don't you go acting all pious with me. Yes, eat!"

Cullen picked up his fork, grabbed the platter of cold

bacon, and put several slices on his plate. He sat the platter back on the table while trying to avoid eye contact with his Grandpa's angry gray eyes. Try as he might, his grandpa wasn't giving in. Grandpa squinted and pointed his long boney finger at him, and spoke harshly when he said, "Cullen Michael Sullivan, how many times have we asked you to be home by 12:30 A.M.?"

Cullen's mind muted his Grandpa's voice and inwardly he answered. *More than I can count.*

With intensity, his grandpa clutched his fork, waving it like a weapon at Cullen, at the same time his head turned repeatedly toward the kitchen to be sure his wife, Lovetta Catherine, wasn't nearby. Believing the coast was clear, he hissed softly, "Your grandmother and I heard you coming in at 2:00 A.M!

Cullen watched his grandpa's knuckles turn white while he gripped the table, trying to control the anger he held toward his only grandson.

"Boy," he scolded, "How I would luv to beat you right now, with your smart, stupid self! I don't care if you are a big man on that thar college campus you're on."

Cullen knew his Grandpa was very upset because his southern accent always became thick when he was angry. Grandpa Jeremiah snapped his fingers, trying to recall his next words.

"What is it called Cullen?"

"What Grandpa?"

"Wait, it's coming..." Grandpa tapped his head trying to remember and said, "Umm, yeah, I got it! Yes, that, thar, that... thar, them bones of yours, sticking out of your skin under your t-shirt."

He pointed to Cullen's chisel chest and yelled, "That, thar, you call a six pack muscular body. I saw you at football practice a few weeks back showing off that wannabe- noticed-by-all body of yours, prancing about half-naked, showing everythin', and those silly girls fallin' all over you. You may be a big man at that thar campus of yours but boy in this house, I am the man!

And boy, when you step into our house, you are under our rules.

"Cullen Michael Sullivan, you know our house rules like you know your football playbook. Just as you follow that playbook, we expect you to follow our rules."

Cullen let out a heavy moan and Grandpa, hearing it said, "And, don't you bring that smart attitude in here! Do you hear me boy? Or, are you pretending to be totally deaf? I already know you are good at playing dumb."

Cullen looked cheerlessly at his grandpa. He wanted to say, *Yeah Grandpa, I hear you! I have heard those words at least a thousand times! 'Be home at 12:30 A.M!' Grandpa, look at me, take a good look. Can't you see, I'm a man? I am going to play in the NFL, the National Football League! Really, you are still giving me a 12:30 a.m. curfew? Geez, give me a break. Please!*

Grandpa watched Cullen's facial expression and seemingly was able to read Cullen's mind, which caused grandpa to become angrier and frustrated with Cullen. Grandpa rapped his knotty knuckles onto the mahogany dining room table causing Cullen to jump. He saw his grandfather's nostrils flare when he took in a deep gulp of air. With his southern dialect returning he uttered, "Cullen

Michael."

Cullen dropped his head and felt a slight pain to his chest.

"Ouch!"

Grandpa's newspaper hit Cullen's chest and landed on his empty red plate. His grandpa gave a restrained chuckled, and said, "Look at me boy when I'm talkin' to you, and don't you dare to pretend you ain't hearin' me, boy! I have tee-le-pha..., whatever it's called. I can read your mind and you want to yell back at me. Don't you boy?"

"No Grandpa, I have too much respect for you to do that sir. Grandpa's nose flared red and Cullen felt the increase of his grandpa's anger towards him. Cullen said, "I didn't mean any harm and I will do better, Grandpa."

Cullen tried to defuse the situation with a wink and a big smile, showing all of his pearly white teeth. He spoke to his grandpa in a hypocritical and dishonest, but soothing, tone.

"Grandpa, really, I am really sorry to have caused you and Grandma so much pain worrying about me. Grandpa, I heard you, I always hear you. Grandpa, please look at me; I am no longer a teenager, I am grown man."

Hearing the dissension in his voice, Grandpa hollered, "Boy! Are you tryin' to be politely disrespectful to me?"

Apologetic, Cullen replied, "No, sir, I will never be disrespectful to you, Grandpa. I love you!"

Cullen shook his head and tears began to well up in his eyes. He said, "Grandpa, please hear me. I am no longer a teenager, I am a grown man. I am sorry Grandpa, for coming in so late. We were having fun and time just slipped away."

"Harrumph." Grandpa cleared his throat and with clenched teeth he hissed, "Boy, you and I know you are sitting there with those pretend tears and with that Jack Kennedy smile, tellin' me a bald- faced lie. You know you have no intentions to obey our house rules. You haven't done it in the last two years. Ever since you started hanging out with that big, nappy head, no good for nothin', so-called godfather of yours."

Cullen quickly glanced toward the kitchen, praying his grandma didn't hear his grandpa's remarks about him hanging around Woody. Shocked with what his grandpa said, Cullen responded with, "What? What do you mean hanging out with my godfather?"

Grandpa smiled, knowing he had hit the nail directly on the head. He bobbed his head and heaved a disgusting grunt. He cleared his throat. "Harrumph." With his head still bobbing he said, "Got you! Cullen you thought I didn't know, didn't you boy?"

He reached across the kitchen table and forcefully grabbed Cullen's arm. At the same time, he too took precautionary quick glances toward the kitchen entrance, being sure Lovetta wasn't in hearing distance.

He lowered his voice, trying not to be overheard, and whispered, "Boy, that so called wannabe man, who calls himself your godfather, whose name is Woodrow Hugh Parks. He is nothin' more than a calculating, callous, killing machine. He has no morals. He ain't nothing but trouble, and is incapable of loving anyone, even his own parents."

Whoa! Wow, Grandpa, you are being too harsh."

"No Cullen, it's not harsh, it's nothin' but truth. I tried warning your mother and your father about him, but they didn't listen, just like you're not listenin'!" Grandpa clenched his teeth to help control his intense anger. He said, "Now you tell me Cullen, where are they? Where is my daughter, Sally and her husband, Mike, your mom and dad? Where are they Cullen

Lovetta, who had been quietly listening behind the door, but now she quickly rushed out to the kitchen dining area smiling; "Hello, my men. Are you two playing nice?"

Cullen noticed his Grandma was wearing her Sunday sunshine yellow apron. In her hands, she held a fresh platter of steamy hot pancakes and bacon.

She put two medium pancakes, and three strips of warm crisp bacon on Grandpa's plate. Then, onto Cullen's plate, she placed six pancakes and several strips of bacon. Still smiling, she turned their juice glasses over and poured in fresh squeezed orange juice.

She sat the pitcher of juice beside Cullen's plate and as she did, she gently patted his head.

Cullen watched his beautiful, petite grandmother as she walked over and stood beside his grandfather's chair. She glared at Grandpa Jeremiah, shaking her head back and forth. She poured a cup ofhot steaming coffee into his cup, which she let purposely spill over into his saucer.

"Yowl, Vetta, watch it! That's hot."

She smiled and said, "Oh, yes it is and I'm sorry Jeremy. It is getting a little hot in here, isn't it?"

Cullen's attention returned to his hot food but he didn't miss the glances that were being exchanged between his grandparents.

When his grandpa picked up his cup he looked over at his sweet wife and she mouthed, "Enough said, stop now!"

Grandpa sighed and relaxed his tense body against the back of the chair. He looked at his beautiful wife, with her silver gray hair pulled back in a bun and big brown eyes, and she tried to defuse his temper. Grandpa shook his head as he said, "Lovetta, you know you have spoiled that thar boy!

Here I'm trying to talk with him about coming in late and here you come, and get me all discombobulated with spilling coffee and giving me the death stare because I'm tellin' him the truth about staying out late. Now you get all upset with me, but not with him, when he's the one doing wrong. You tell me then,' Vetta. When will he start obeyin' our house rules?

Grandpa turned away from Lovetta, and faced Cullen. He blurted, "Cullen Michael Sullivan you are just like your mother and father! You're such a stubborn, hard- headed boy!"

Feeling distressed with the way the morning was going, Grandma calmly reached over and patted his hand.

With her, gentle voice she firmly said, "Jeremiah Michael Sullivan, you stop your mouth right now! This is the Lord's Day and I am not going to have this!" With her small hands she tapped on the table, and said "No, not today, it stops here, and it stops now!

This is the Lord's Day! Now close your mouths, both of you, and eat!"

Chuckling, grandfather said, "Now Vetta you know you can't eat with your mouth closed."

Shaking her head, Vetta said, "Jeremiah Sullivan, you aren't funny. Then open your mouth and eat."

Cullen watched his still beautiful grandma as she got up from the table and walked over to his strong-willed, grandpa.

She gently tapped the top of his wavy gray hair, bent down to kiss his cheek, and whispered into his ear, "I love you! Enough said, Jeremy."

She stood beside his chair and winked at Cullen. With her pleasant but stern tone, and yet with such tenderness in her voice, she said, "Jeremiah, don't be so hard on the boy. Our Cullen is a good young man. He will find his own way and he will do right." Cullen got up from his chair and pulled out his grandma's chair.

"Well, thank you my grandson."

"You are more than welcome."

Cullen sat down and winked at her. Cullen loved how his grandma always came to his rescue.

He also observed his grandpa. Whenever his grandma spoke to him, even when he was angry, his demeanor changed, he became jelly.

Grandpa sighed, and relaxed his tense body against the back of the chair. He looked at his beautiful wife, with her silver gray hair pulled back in a bun and big brown eyes. Grandpa shook his head as he said, "Lovetta, you know you have spoiled that thar boy!"

She answered, "And with your help."

Finishing breakfast, Lovetta said, "Well, my two men, it's time for us get ready for church. Now I'm leaving, so Jeremiah, behave yourself. I expect to see you upstairs getting dressed in our bedroom in five minutes."

She kissed Grandpa's forehead, excused herself, and walked out of the dining room into the kitchen.

Cullen watched her as she left, and thought to himself, "*Oh, how I love my grandma.*"

Grandpa cleared his throat and shouted out to her, "See Lovetta, see, there you go, tryin' to get me all befuddled by kissin' me!"

Cullen laughed and said, "My grandma is so special."

"Hmm, Cullen Michael Sullivan you may have your grandma all hood-winked with your so-called sweet honey talk, but boy, I know you. Cullen do you see these here eyes?" He motioned, touching his eyes, and said, "They are watching you son!"

Grandpa's boney knuckles lightly thumped the table. He hissed low, "Cullen, while you are living in this house, when I say be home at 12:00 midnight or 12:30 A.M., that's what I mean.

Cullen Michael Sullivan," Grandpa stood and pushed his chair in under the table, and said, "you haven't signed a contract yet, and, boy I'm not joking with you when I say this- shame, shame on both of you."

He come over to him, stood behind his chair, bent down, and whispered in his ear, "Thar's you and Brie, both, sinnin' on Friday and Saturday nights, and come Sunday mornin', you both pretending to love and worship under false pretenses. Shame on you."

Grandpa tapped the top of Cullen's head with his finger and said, "You both know that just ain't right! Why can't you be more like Bradford Rock III? He is free in his deceptions, or from keeping secrets. He can worship God in spirit and truth. You and your side-kick, Brie, naw, you two can't, and you know you can't do that, can you Cullen?"

"Grandpa! No, we can't, and you are right." Cullen's shoulders sagged, keeping his head down. Pretending to focus on his last bite of pancakes, he tried hard to avoid making eye contact with his grandpa when he whispered, "Yes sir, I know, it's not right."

Grandpa's mustache curled into a mischievous sneer. His gray eyes narrowed to a slit, he looked at him and muttered, "Boy, you ain't foolin' me. You have no intentions of changing." Still standing, Grandpa lifted his coffee mug to finish drinking. He placed the cup into the saucer, and said, "See boy, my coffee got all lukewarm, and I do not like lukewarm coffee. I know someone bigger than you and me and I heard when He tastes anything that's lukewarm, He will spit it out of His mouth! You would know this if you read your Bible more."

"Okay guys, seriously" Grandma called through the wall intercom, "you two need to hurry and get dressed.

Remember, it's the Lord's Day, and Jeremy dear, I want peace, so you need to stop picking on him!"

Cullen looked at Grandpa. He noticed his lips were moving, but Cullen had tuned him out. Grandpa, still vexing, interrupted Cullen's thoughts by pinching his arm.

"Ouch! Grandpa that really hurt!"

"Now I got your attention, and that pinch is just a smidgen of the hurt I hold in my heart from you not listening to me boy!

"Cullen, I don't want you to get into the kind of trouble that titanic of so-called man named Woodrow Parks is in. I don't know why you like hangin' around him?"

"Because my Mom and Dad were his best friends and he's my godfather."

Grandpa's bony finger pulled on his copper rimmed glasses, bringing them down onto the tip of his nose. He narrowed his gray eyes at Cullen and said, "Huh, that man will never be your godfather!"

Grandpa shook his head, still frustrated with him and heatedly said, "Tell me, Cullen, what's he teaching you? How to run after and disrespect women, to drink, smoke, gamble, lie, steal, and kill and to gamble, hmm. I already said gamble, didn't I boy? "Hearing the word 'gamble' caused Cullen to wince.

"Bingo! "Un-huh, I got your number. You didn't think I knew about your gamblin' did you boy?"

Grandpa's wrinkled lips curled, he got into Cullen's face, and said, "Cullen, son, these here eyes ... they see everythin' and these old ears, they hear a lot.

You had better watch yoself, or one day, sooner than you think, I reckon you gonna find yoself in a heap of trouble and all alone."

Grandma came back into the kitchen. She heard Grandpa still fussing with Cullen and said, "Jeremy, I came to get you, now hush and let Cullen go and get dressed. Both of you need to stop."

"But Vetta."

"Hush Jeremy." Not saying another word, Grandpa retreated, turned and left.

Grandma watched until Grandpa turned the corner. Grandma Vetta leaned over and whispered into Cullen's ear. "Your grandpa is right. Woodrow is your godfather in name only and he isn't your role model. You have a Heavenly Father whose name is God and His life is one you should admire and desire to emulate. God loves you very much, more than me, and that my grandson is some powerful love!" She bent to kiss his forehead. "Now go and get ready for church."

Clearing the table, grandma stopped to stare at Cullen as he walked away. She suddenly called out, "Cullen stop!"

"Grandma?"

"Cullen, Jeremy and I have confidence in you. You will make the right decision at the right time.

You are a grown man, not a boy." Grandma lowered her head, gave a wry chuckle and said, "I heard your Grandpa when he told you to read your Bible. Well, I know he had better start reading the Bible himself and stop relying on what he hears. And for you, young man, you are not so grown that I can't tell you what to do. Now go, go now and get ready for church!"

Cullen smiled and walked back to kiss his grandma's cheek, then he ran out of the dining area and up the steps, taking them three at a time. He jogged down the long hallway into his room. In his haste he left his door ajar, and sat on the bed, feeling all numb; he rubbed both hands through his short brown curly hair. His cell phonerang. He saw Woody's name on the screen when he picked it up. Reluctantly, he answered.

"Woody, whatsup?"

"Hey Cullen, my boys told me you won big last night. How much did you and Brie win?"

"How much did your lapdogs tell you I won, Woody?"

"My lapdogs! Now Cullen, you know that's wrong. But since you asked, they tell me about five grand. Ten between you and Brie, is that about right?"

"Well, Woody, if you already know how much we won, why are you calling?"

"Cullen, Cullen, don't be so rude. I'm your godfather, your best friend, man. I want to help you get more money."

"Help me? Best friend! What's your definition of a friend, Woody? Why did you really call?"

"Hey, I heard you are thinking about signing a contract for the NFL and I was thinking, if you need more money to tide you over, you know I can help you."

"What's the hook, Woody?

"Nothing major, all you have to do is a little job for me.

All I need you to run a few errands during your remaining days on your college campus. You can help me get my foot in the door and make some quick cash. Are you interested Cullen?"

Silence.

"Cullen? Cullen, are you still there?

"Yes, Woody, I am here, and the answer is no. I don't need your criminal money."

"What? Whoa! Wait!" Woody shouted. "Did I hear you correctly? You just said you didn't need my criminal money, but every weekend for two years you and your cousin have been here in my place, gambling, taking my illegal money! Now you are telling me you do not need my money! Then tell me Mr. Wonderful, why do you come?"

"Woody, Brie and I come because we did like being around you and we have fun gambling. Gambling and pushing drugs are two different things, Woody. Soon I will be signing a contract and it will be more than a few million dollars and besides, didn't Uncle George and Senator Rock warn you to stay away from me and my football career?"

"Cullen, you knew? Then Cullen, why be so harsh" I have done just that, haven't I? I stayed away from your high school and college campus. But, you are older now and about to leave to the NFL campus! You are now a grown man who's capable of making his own decisions, and besides they don't have to know. All you need to do is make the contacts, help me get my foot in the door, and I will do the rest. Come on now, you are my godson, my man, my friend, Cullen Michael Hugh Sullivan. You have my middle name. Although for some reason your Grandpa Jeremiah has dropped my name and you are called Cullen Michael.

"Man, I was your mom and dad's best friend, I loved them and you know I mean you no harm Cullen. But now, wham, bam! Man! Look at you! You're heading for the *'Big Time!'*

The National Football League. Man you are on your way! And with that being so, why not let me, your godfather, your friend, tag along! What do you say man? After all, I feel you and your cousin Brie owe me something. Over the years, you have taken away thousands of dollars from me."

Feeling frustrated with Woody's conversation, Cullen said, "Owe you something? I have to go Woody, it's getting late, and I've got to get dressed for church.

"Church. I used to go to church. My father was the pastor at 'The Word Church. It was called that before they changed its name, and my friend, judging from your silence, I can tell you didn't know that, did you?" Not waiting for an answer, Woody continued. "Man, I was just like you and Brie. I, with your mother and father, would sin all week long and into the weekends. Come Sunday morning, there we were whooping, hooting, and hollering with the other week-long and weekend sinners!

Ooowheeeew baby, we felt his spirit all over us! Hallelujah! Church! Man I forgot, today is Sunday! I know if I step into the church an earthquake would happen.

"Cullen, tell me is Pastor Wilson still preaching those sermons I used to hear my Father preach, those fairy tales that Jesus will come back one day? What did he call it? Oh yes, I remember now, he called his message, 'That Great Get- on- up Day!'

"Church! Man, church! I have a warm feeling coming overme just thinking about church. You know little bro, I just might take a chance, just to see if I can make an earthquake inside The Word Church. Just for laughs, I am coming to church today!"

Woody's comment about coming to church caused Cullen to snicker and he replied, "Yeah, Woody, you come to church. See you there."

"Bye."

Cullen disconnected, loathing the call, and tossed his cell phone onto his bed.

Cullen thought, *Grandma used to believe I was her good boy. Now she knows that six hours ago I was sitting at Woody's Place playing poker. Six hours ago, I held in my hand the last card, a straight flush which was worth thousand dollars.*

I placed my card on the table and called. Just like that I won all that money... in less than two hours.

He looked around his room and saw all of his football trophies and school pictures from pre-kindergarten until now. He saw a picture of his mom and dad on his study desk. His grandparents went to great lengths to make his wall resemble a football field. He got up from his bed and walked across the large room into his open closet. He looked at his twenty or more suits, then pushed them down to the opposite end.

He squatted down onto the floor to pull away the loose floorboard in order to retrieve the brown bag that held some of his precious winnings.

He walked back to his bed, squatted, then laid flat against the mahogany floor. With his strong legs, he pushed his head and shoulders under the bed to find the hole in his box spring to retrieve the red sock. The red sock held all the money he had won over the years at Woody's Place. Opening the sock he added to it, ten thousand dollars and the money from the brown bag.

He tossed the red sock several times in the air like a soft ball. He walked back into his closet, pulled out a large old tin can from under the floorboard, opened its lid, and inserted the sock.

He strained to put the can into the right position to replace the detached floor board. He stood, dusted his hands, put his suits back in order, then selected one. He took out his shiny, black, patent leather shoes from the shoe bag and closed the door.

When he turned around he saw Grandpa staring. Startled, as well as irritated, by seeing him in his room unannounced he shouted, "Grandpa, my door was close!"

Grandpa closed the door and shouted, "No, it was left cracked and Cullen Michael Sullivan, did I hear you say '*your* 'door! *Your* door was closed?"

Annoyed and with belligerence Cullen replied,

"Yes, *my* door, and my name is Cullen Michael Hugh Sullivan. I guess you forgot Woody is my godfather!"

"That man, as far as I am concerned… I will never recognize him as your godfather, and I need you not to be smart- mouthed and remind me that your third name is Hugh. Cullen Hugh Michael Sullivan, I have some questions to ask you. Who owns this here house, boy?"

"You do."

"Who owns the bed you are sleeping in?"

"You do."

"Who owns the car you drive? "You do."

"You do not pay rent, nor pay for what you eat here, or the water you drink and shower with. You do not pay for the lights in this here room or the clothes you are wearin' and as far as I can figure, that thar door to your bedroom is part of my house and it belongs to me.

So since I am the owner of this house, I figure I can either knock if I please or open that thar door whenever I please! Do you understand me boy?"

"But Grandpa! How long have you been standing there?"

"I said, do you understand me?"

"Yes, sir, I understand sir."

"And, to answer your question, I stood here long enuff, to see all that thar money you have in that thar red sock of yours that you won from your so-called godfather's place! Am I not correct, boy?"

"Yes, sir you are correct sir.

"Cullen you may be foolin' your Grandma, but boy, I see you for who you are, and for what you are becomin' and God really sees you. I heard about those fast women in college chasin' after you, and I wanted to see for myself. I came to your college and saw the rumors were true. I heard that cell phone ringin' in your bedroom and those girls callin' you late at night I know all about your gamblin' and winnin money at Woody's Place. From what I heard, you have won over $50,000 or more. Now I know it's true, because I have seen it with these old eyes. Cullen what are you plannin' on doing with that money?"

"Grandpa, at first I told myself that I was saving it for college. Then I got scholastic scholarships for college. I knew you and grandma put aside all the money from mom and dad's life insurance for me and I didn't need the money, but it was fun to gamble.

"Fun! Gambling is fun? Many unexplained deaths have occurred and they all have connections to Woody's Place. Yes, Cullen, you told the truth, I saw you still have the money. You didn't need money to be a big wheel on campus! Do you need clothes? No! There's nothing wrong with your clothes. You have always worn expensive clothing and suits and have over 30 pairs of shoes and counting. You get a new car every other year, and get money and to have fun is by gamblin'? Cullen, have you thought about gettin' a job? The last I heard workin' is fun and a good way to make money."

Before Cullen had a chance to answer, Grandma's voice saved him again. She tapped lightly on the door. "Jeremiah, I am ready for church."

"Comin' Lovetta."

Grandpa turned and hissed low, "Cullen we ain't finished talkin' about this. Gamblin' is not good, you can go and get yoself hurt or killed if you ain't careful. Your mom and dad are dead from gamblin' with Woody. Cullen please stay away from that good for nothin', beefy man. He's nothin' and never will be nothin'. He's not fit to be anybody's father let alone your godfather. He's nothing but bad news.

Grandpa watched in silence as Cullen hummed and nonchalantly tucked his light blue dress shirt into his black pants and buckled his belt. Grandpa, blustering, shouted, "Cullen!" Startled, Cullen jumped and responded,

"Grandpa?"

"Boy are you listening to me? Or do you think I am talkin' just to hear myself? You will learn the hard way one day. I justhope it's not too late."

Grandpa turned toward the door. He took several steps but then he abruptly turned to say,

"Boy, just because you are a robust, 6'4" star athlete, good lookin', smooth talkin' with that thar flashy, dazzling smile, sparkling light brown eyes, and that thar brown, curly hair, you may have deluded yoself to believe you caramel brownie, but boy you had better watch yoself. There are plenty of good lookin' guys like you now dead.

"Now finish gittin' yoself ready for church and leave that Woody man alone. He ain't nothin' but the devil's henchman! And boy when you get to church, leave those wild, silly girls alone. Grandpa opened Cullen's bedroom door and said, "Cullen, I will now close *my* door, to *my* room!"

Bam! Grandpa closed *his* door.

Tying his tie, Cullen thought about what Grandpa had said about Woody. He had seen his goons, Harry and Luke, in action. They were vicious.

Wild girls! What Grandpa said about leaving those wild girls alone was another thing. He thought as he put on his dark suit jacket, "*Aw shucks Grandpa, I like fast and wild women.*"

His cousin, Brie, she's the wildest. She's a daredevil, a fourth degree black belt holder. She cursed, gambled, smoked marijuana and secretly drank. But on Sunday morning when she stood behind that microphone to sing, her voice brought the house down! Her voice was a gift from God.

Cullen thought, *"I have to remember to ask Brie what happened at her house that got her all upset. Was she caught sneaking in?* Cullen knew he and Brie were guilty of being hypocrites just as grandfather said. They would gamble, drink and sin every weekend, then go to church every Sunday to sing about Jesus.

Cullen closed his grandpa's closet door and saw his reflection on the door mirror. He was 6'4", caramel complexion, brown curly hair, grayish eyes, and a strong jaw, with beautiful white teeth.

He said aloud, "Cullen Michael Hugh Sullivan you are too fine to touch!"

He quickly rushed to open *his* grandpa's heavy mahogany door and dashed down the stairs, thinking, "*Cullen, you have to get your fine self right with God one day soon.*"

When he stepped out the front door, he saw his grandparents were waiting in the swing for him. "Well, it's about time, boy. If Brie and Brad were waiting for you, you would have been as quick as greased lightning gittin' down here."

His grandpa stood, slightly bent over. As they walked down the steps he reached over and swatted Cullen lightly on his head. Grandpa stopped, took out his pocket watch, and said with a very loud grunt, "Look what you did boy, you have made us late for church."

"Jeremiah, you know it was you who made us late, it was you and no one else."

Cullen smiled as he opened the car door for his

grandma. He closed her door and got into the back seat singing.

"Grace, grace, God's grace, grace that will pardon and cleanse within; grace, grace, God's grace. Grace that is greater than all our sin!"

"Cullen?'

"Yes, Grandpa?"

"One of these days you're gonna need His grace, and I pray when you find it you will keep it."

"Jeremiah Sullivan you have said enough! Now stop! This is the Lord's Day! You just need to accept God grace for yourself and stop picking on Cullen.

God has a plan for Cullen and Lord, I know He has plans for you! Now, I just want to ride to church in peace. Do you hear me Jeremy?"

"Yes, Vetta, you are right. God does have a plan for that thar boy, if only he would listen."

"Jeremy!"

"Oh, alright Vetta, I know, God definitely has plans for me too!

As Cullen sat in the back seat smiling, he started to hum "Grace, grace, God's grace." He looked up he saw his Grandpa's gray eyes glaring at him in the car's rear-view mirror. Cullen grinned mischievously as he replayed his grandpa's words to his sweet Grandma, Vetta. *"Oh, alright, Vetta. I know, God definitely has plans for me too!*

Good-humoredly, Cullen winked and then smiled as his grandpa, who continued to give to him his un-tireless quick glances.

Wittily, Cullen pointed his fingers to his eyes and ears.

Finding this to be entertaining, Cullen continuously pointed back and forth at his grandpa teasing him in silence saying, *These eyes see and these ears hear you too.'*

Grandpa gave Cullen a hasty wink. Cullen saw his grandpa's lips curled into an unexpected impetuous smile.

Grandpa Jeremiah cleverly joined in with his grandson singing aloud. "Marvelous, infinite, matchless grace, freely bestowed on all who believe!"

Cullen heard his grandma's voice. She joined them harmonizing. They sang loud and happy. "You that are longing to see His face, ill you this moment His grace receive?

Chapter 3, Who's That Woman?

"Brie Catherine Hayes, are you up?" "I'm up Dad, and getting dressed." "Okay, hurry please."

Brie's father, George Alexander Hayes, was an Interior Designer. Her mother, Catherine Elizabeth Sullivan Hayes, was a worldwide evangelist and one of the twin daughters of Jeremiah and Lovetta.

Brie's father maintained the physique of a bodybuilder because he worked out in their home gym four days a week. He stood 6'5" tall. He was very handsome, boasting blonde colored hair and hazy green eyes. His demeanor was mild, yet stern.

Brie Hayes would begin college in the fall. She would commute daily, coming home every night because she knew her dad needed her to keep him company.

Brie also knew her father had a secret, but her father did not know she knew. It all happened a week ago, way past midnight, when she heard the sound of a car in their driveway.

Brie stretched her body and released a worrisome sigh as she sat up on the edge of her bed pondering her father's secret.

Startled, she jumped. From the other side of her closed bedroom door, she heard her father's voice jolting her from her deep thoughts.

"Brie! Are you getting ready?"

"Yes, Dad."

"Don't forget your choir robe."

"Okay, Dad."

Brie walked into her spacious closet, pushed aside her clothing and stepped on something soft. Looking down she saw her blue jeans on the floor. She recalled she had hastily removed them the night before when she jumped into her bed, pretending to be asleep when her father came into her bedroom to check on her. Brie let out a heavy sigh and bent to pick up her jeans when a wad of money dropped onto the floor. She dropped her pants and picked up the money. Holding this huge wad, she walked out of the closet and sat on the corner of her bed.

She slid off her bed onto the floor, then turned to kneel as if she were about to pray. Instead of praying, she braced her face against the box spring and felt with her fingers for what she was looking for, her money sock. It was concealed tightly in the corner of her torn box spring. She removed the sock which held thousands of dollars. She inserted the money into what she called her green money sock. Still on her knees, she rested her face against the side of the bed, and used her fingers to search again for the hole. Finding it, she securely reinserted the sock.

She placed both hands on the floor and pushed herself up. She stood and lowered herself onto the corner of her bed. Her thoughts returned to the mystery woman her Dad called Jada. Brie stood and began to get ready for church.

As she dressed she recalled the many nights she, Cullen and a few of their friends would leave their secret gambling shack called Woody's Place. Cullen always drove and dropped her off last, giving them a chance to talk. Brie stopped to ponder over the events she witnessed, which led her to discovering the secret.

She said to Cullen, "'Well cuz, we cleaned Woody out tonight.'"

Laughing, Cullen said, "'Yea, Brie, and old Woody is going to be very upset when he finds out between you and me we took away more than $20,000. Brie, our money socks are getting very heavy.'"

"Brie, why are we doing this? We don't need the money."

Brie didn't respond to Cullen's question. Instead she nervously tapped her hands on her pant legs and leaned her body sideways. She placed her right hand into her front pocket, and pulled out a roll of cash.

"Cullen, guess what?"

"What?"

"Woody asked me to be one of his special escorts for his 'so called' important clients. Woody must think I am a fool! I smoke pot, I gamble, and every now and then I will drink the strong stuff, and I know it's wrong, but that's as far as I am willing to go."

She leaned sideways and placed the money back into the front pocket of her blue jeans. She dropped her head and sat in silence.

Cullen turned his head to catch a quick glimpse of her. Knowing his cousin like he did, he knew there was more and he asked, "Brie, what else are you not telling me?"

When she looked at Cullen, tears welled up in her soft

green eyes and dripped on to her pink silk blouse. "Cullen," she said, while you were having fun with the ladies, Woody sent Luke Allen to escort me to his office." Once inside his luxurious palace, I saw Woody sitting like a king on his diamond studded chair, looking as dark as coffee and grinning just enough to show his front six teeth covered with diamond inserts."

"Was he wearing a crown?"

They both laughed, Brie answered, "No, but he probably has one locked inside one of his enormous gold plated, desk drawers."

Once the laughter stopped Cullen said, "Go ahead Brie, finish your story."

"Harry was there, and Woody ordered him out and to not come back into his office for any reason.

Woody told him to wait outside of his door until I came out. Once I came out, Harry was to escort me back to my table and leave because Woody would be finished with him.

"When Harry turned to leave, he looked at me and mouthed, 'I'm sorry.' And closed the door.

"Woody then rose from his throne, grinning, and deviously ask me to sit, but I refused. I said to him, 'let's cut through all your scheming politeness, Woody, what do you want from me?'

"He didn't hesitate in telling me. He told me, he wanted me to be his main woman.

He said if I did, he would give to me whatever I wanted and the position came with free drugs.

 Brie shifted uncomfortably in her seat and looked at

Cullen, she said, "I drink liquor, smoke cigarettes and pot, but cuz, you know I would never touch the hard stuff!"

"I know Brie, then what happened?"

"I refused his offer. Woody snorted and with a diabolical deep raspy voice he told me, 'I'm disappointed in you Miss High and Mighty Brie Hayes.' Without warning, he pounced on me and pressed his powerful body against mine, trying to pin me down. As I fought to free myself, he ordered Luke Allen to bring the needle."

"What! Brie, what did you do?"

"I kneed him in the groin, snatched the needle from Luke Allen's hand and crushed it on the floor with my foot.

He became furious and lifted his fist to strike me. I laughed at him and stopped his heavy fist from making contact with my face. He was momentarily frozen. I turned to walk away, but he was determined to assault me. He ordered Luke Allen to come back and restrain me. Luke Allen put me in a choke hold as Woody tried to force some cocaine into my nose.

"I became furious, I had enough of Woody's chicaneries. Cullen when I left Woody's throne room, both Luke Allen and Woody were on the floor and Woody was lying there with his large mouth open and hands up.

"Filled with rage, I swung open the door, and shouted at Harry, 'You want what they got?' Harry looked in, he saw them on the floor and smiled. I said to him, 'It's way past time to take out the trash.'

"Harry was amused, and he responded, 'Well done little one.' Still chuckling, Harry said, 'Brie, as you heard, I was told by Woody not to come back in his office. When you walked out, I was to escort you back to your table, and leave the club.'

"Harry closed Woody's door, offered his arm to me, and he said, 'Shall we go?'

"Walking down the steps, Harry told me, 'Woody finally got what he deserved. He beats women, and his poor wife is his punching bag. Now Woody has been repaid by a little bitty girl. I advise you and your friends to leave immediately because when Woody wakes up, he's going to be furious and out for revenge...Brie, please don't come back here.'"

"So, little cuz, that explains why you were all jitters, yelling for us to leave."

Cullen shook his head, laughed quietly and said, "I'm glad Uncle George made you take karate lessons. No one messes with Brie Hayes. Seriously Brie, 'Free money' and 'good stuff.' There's nothing free, there's always a price to pay."

"Cullen, before I lowered the boom on him, Woody said, if I came to work for him, all I would have to do is become his drop off and pick-up person, he would do the rest." She snickered, and said, "Woody told me he just needs me to help him get his foot in the door."

"Yeah right."

Brie sat silent and Cullen's eyes widened a little when he glanced at her. He thought. '*What is she thinking? No, she's not*,' and he shouted, "Brie you aren't thinking about doing what he asked."

"Uh, maybe my dear cousin."

"Brie!"

Brie snickered and said, "Just kidding. I may appear to Woody to be stupid, but I'm not! No way would I stoop that low!" "Seriously. Brie, get this! Woody also asked me months before my senior year in high school to sell drugs and to run his illegal number racket on campus. He called it 'quick money'.

Then he suggested that when I become an NFL star running back, he could use me in my new career to place bets on the game.

"Brie, Woody wanted me to do that in my junior year in college. I told Uncle George; he and Senator Jason Rock shut him down! I think he and his bodyguards were beaten up by the Senator's special bodyguards. Now, my Super Woman cuz gave them both the boot!"

"Cullen, Woody is a revengeful person. When I knocked him out, I saw that he and Luke Allen carry pistols inside their socks and around their belts. We both know Woody only loves one thing, and that's money. He doesn't care about anyone or anything, and will use anyone to get what he wants.

"Cullen... speaking of love and money, I heard Woody's woman is back. I never met her, but rumor has it she was beaten severely by Woody and he sent her away until she healed. Now she's back for more beatings. Has anyone we know seen her?"

"No, but I heard she's very attractive with supple lips, brown eyes, and legs that seem to be endless."

"Oh she's all that? Then why is she with Big Woody? Woody is a user."

"Time will tell all. Well, here's my drop spot for you cuz." Cullen let out a deep sigh when he said, "I will see you in church, in less than eight hours. Go, and I will watch until you signal me from the house."

Cullen parked his car a few houses down from Brie's parents' house and turned off the engine. Brie opened the car door, and he said to her, "It's 1:45 a.m. and I am more than late. I know Grandpa is listening for the door to open and watching the clock."

Chuckling, Brie said, "Poor Cullen."

"Okay cuz, go ahead and laugh. I don't know why I let you and Brad talk me into coming home on the weekends. I could be out having fun with my ladies with no curfew."

Hitting Cullen hard on his arm, Brie said, "One thing for sure cuz, my Dad and Mom and Grandpa and Grandma Sullivan didn't raise dimwitted fools."

"Although Brie, there's one person who thinks we are; Woodrow Hugh Parks. He thinks we are two simpletons."

They laughed. Brie tapped his arm, smiled, and winked, then she said, "I know, Cullen, and I also know that's one of the many reasons why Grandpa Jeremiah does not like him."

"You're right, Brie, and I would like to know more."

"Ummm, so do I and one day soon we will have to talk more about this."

Brie stepped out onto the sidewalk, turned and closed the door.

She leaned into the open window and said, "Cullen, I

have this awful feeling we need to be very careful with Woody. He is very cunning and vindictive."

Brie clenched her teeth trying not to show her fear. She said, "By challenging him, we might as well be putting nails in our coffins." Saying those words caused her slender body to shiver. "Cullen have you noticed Woody is seemingly getting more openly powerful and more dangerous each day? He gives me the heebie- jeebies."

Cullen laughed and said, "The what?" Brie repeated, "The heebie- jeebies!"

"Why Brie Hayes, I haven't heard you say that word since fifth grade."

In a solemn tone she said, "Cullen, I am really serious. I am becoming more uneasy being around Woody. He's getting bolder, he's made sexual advances towards me. We both just need to be careful and we must listen to Harry's warning; it's time for us to stop gambling."

Brie tapped on the roof of Cullen's car to signal goodbye. She began her ritual backwards jog, clenching her fists in victory. Cullen watched as Brie turned around and ran up her driveway. Swift as a cat she climbed their fence, dashed across the lawn and up the house's lattice. She slipped in through an open window to her bedroom on the second floor. Once inside she leaned out the window and waved.

Seeing Brie's signal, Cullen drove away, thinking about what Brie had said about

Woody becoming more dangerous each day.

Brie stepped away from the window. She looked at the clock and saw 1:50 a.m. She thought, *I had better get into bed; I will have to be in church in a few hours.* Starting to undress, she hesitated when she heard the sound of a car in their driveway .Her first thought was, *it's Mom. She surprised us by coming home.*

Brie hastily opened her bedroom door to run out, but stopped abruptly when she heard an unfamiliar voice talking with her father. Curious to who it could be coming this late, she cautiously crept down the hall and down the back stairs that led into their dimly lit kitchen. She tiptoed across the dark mahogany hardwood floor. Once there, Brie was glad to see the heavy pocket door to the front parlor was partially open and she could see into her father's office. To her surprise, she saw a strange woman with him.

The woman was standing close to her father, too close as far as Brie was concerned. The room was brightly lit and Brie could see the woman's face. She was beautiful. Her hair color was brown with curls cut very short, her skin tone was dark, and her full lips were to die for. She was at least 5'10" tall and she wore deep pink heels and a matching full length trench coat.

Brie watched as the strange woman placed her arms around her father's neck and talked to him in a seductive tone when she said his name, "George Alexander Hayes." Brie watched the woman use her long fingernails, slowly moving them up and down her father's shirt. The woman alluringly said, "I can't take my eyes off of this super ripped body of yours.

By looking at all this, it's obvious to me you are still working out." Brie saw her father step away from her to stand near his desk. The woman smiled and whispered in a tantalizing tone, "Come, baby, and sit with me." She walked provocatively, slowly sat on the black leather sofa, untied the belt to her coat and crossed her lanky legs. Smiling, she said, "George you do remember those delectable times we used to have way past the forbidden hours that even God would disapproved of?"

Brie watched this woman stand and saunter over to her father who was standing behind his desk. She seductively moved closer and pressed her body to his. She said, "Shhh, baby, you don't have to say a word. Just let my irresistible fingers do the talking."

Brie noticed the woman moving slightly away from her father. The woman opened her coat and tried tempting her father by swirling her hips. She smiled, and said laughing, "Mmmmm, you do remember all this, don't you baby? Go ahead and take a good look." The woman moved her body closer to her father. Bobbing her head, she said, "Uh-huh, yes Georgie, you do remember."

She licked her full pink lips and she cooed, "Yeah, you do remember. Look at this George. It's yours and we can still have a wonderful time, right now, here, together. Besides, your little Cate never really appreciated you. If she did, you wouldn't be here all alone and she would not be traveling all over the world preaching about Jesus."

"Jada!"

Brie's father's voice boomed out the woman's name and both Brie and Jada jumped. Her father's voice was tense. Brie had never seen him so angry. Brie's father said to Jada through clenched teeth. "Tie your coat, and leave this house!"

Jada stood up straight, not moving and smiled. Brie knew from her actions that this woman, Jada, had no intentions of leaving. She said, "Oh Georgie Porgy, have I made the baby mad talking about his little Cate?"

Jada said, "Come on, Georgie boy, don't use that tone with me." Instead of leaving, she slowly walked across the room and down on the black leather sofa and crossed her long brown legs. "You know, George, you have always been overprotective about your little Cate. Even in college, your precious Cate Sullivan never gave you the attention you deserved, and when you needed me, I was always available.

Jada cooed. "Here I am baby." She pulled her coat apart, smiled and told him, "Look, here I am, here in the flesh. I will give you all the attention you need, right now."

Jada stood, walked slowly over to his desk, took his hands, and tried to place them on her hot body. George jerked his hand away.

Frustrated with him, Jada shouted, "George, you see me? You know you are tempted, go ahead, touch me! Baby, I am standing in front of you, come on, touch me! I can be yours right now, just say the word Baby."

George seething with controlled anger said, "Jada, obviously you haven't noticed, I am no longer the man I was twenty-five years ago! I am asking you to leave Cate's and my house, now!"

Jada seemed shocked hearing his demand to leave. Jada said, "You are asking me to what?"

 George repeated, "You heard me, leave!"

In a condescending tone she said, "Don't tell me you are a true born-again Christian!"

Jada stood still as if she was stunned by his commitment to God. She placed both hands on her hips, shook her head in disbelief and shouted, "You really did give your life to Jesus!"

She stared, giving a faint mischievous smile, she sashayed closer to George. She placed her slender, brown hands on his arms and whispered, George Alexander Hayes, that's okay. Come to me. You and I know God loves and He forgives us sinners all the time." Her lips were nibbling on George's ear and she whispered, Come on Georgie baby, lets' have some fun right now and whenever we meet again you can ask for God's forgiveness again, and again, and again.

George pushed her away and he yelled, "Jada Perkins, you leave Cate's and my home now!"

Jada turned to leave, but swiveled her body unexpectedly. Her quick advance surprised Brie's father and she pressed her lips to his. Pulling away, as if he had been bitten by a rattlesnake, her father extended his arms and held out his hands in a stop position and he shouted, "No! Jada, get away from me! Get out!"

Jada smiled and walked away slowly, with her hips gyrating under her pink coat. She stopped at the door, turned again toward George, and their eyes locked.

Brie watched as Jada held opened her coat and she said, "Georgie, last time to see this baby? Here's my offering to you, just one more time. Look at me baby, you know you want this, and I don't have to leave."

"Yes, Jada, you have to leave, and no, Jada, I do not want your body. But before you go, Jada, tell me." He pointed at her and asked, "Who are you? This is not the Jada that Cate and I knew? The Jada we knew years ago would not have come here dishonoring God and Cate in our home? We have a daughter. Our daughter, Brie, is sleeping upstairs."

"Your daughter's name is Brie?"

Hearing Brie's name Jada laughed and repeated, "Your daughter's name is Brie?" She snickered and asked, "Is she George? Are you sure your little precious Brie's upstairs and sleeping?"

Her father seemed puzzled by Jada's remarks and asked, "What are you talking about?" Not waiting for a reply, and still visibly frustrated with Jada, he held both hands in the air and said, "Never mind, Jada. Just get out!"

Brie's father moved closer to Jada and in a very angry tone he snapped, "For the record, I want you to know that I love my wife.

Cate trusts me and I her. I do not know what devil has gotten into your twisted mind to make you even think I would want you or could still be interested in you? Cate is more woman than you will ever- be. Leave now! Get out of Cate's and my home and don't come back!"

George stepped in front of Jada to show her out. With his back turned from Jada, Brie had full view of her. Brie gasped when she saw Jada's open coat. Brie placed her hands over her mouth to muffle her scream. Shocked and trouble by what she heard, she was now also angered by what she had just seen. She thought, *this woman, Jada--*

Woody's woman, has disrespected my Mom in her home and then tried to seduce my father by not wearing clothes under her coat! As Jada walked towards the door, Brie noticed her father's fists and jaws were tightly clinched. Brie knew by his demeanor that he was very much disturbed as he tried to control his anger.

"He shouted "Jada Perkins!".

Jada stopped, turned to look at him, not smiling, and smugly answered, "Yes, George?"

"Are you sick? What has happened to you? This isn't the way you used to be!"

Tying her coat, she hastily snapped back, "No, George I'm not sick. Time, circumstances, and the need to survive will make one change. And by the way, George, my name is no longer Perkins. I have married someone who you know very well."

Brie's father shouted, "What kind of woman have you become? You are married! And brazenly come into my home and make a play for me! What's wrong with you, Jada?"

Brie watched Jada untying her coat. Her hips swirled as she walked toward the front door. George remained several steps behind her. Abruptly she turned, reached out, grabbed his left arm, pulled him against her naked body, and she kissed his lips.

Brie watched as her father's body stiffened. He stood frozen with his hands at his sides, but he did not try to push her away.

Jada smiled, stepped back to look at him and said, "See George? I am still alluring and I know you want me.

You can't resist me; even in college, you never could."

"I believe I just have, and our college days have been over for twenty-five years. As far as I am concerned, you are no more."

Jada placed her hands into her jacket pocket as she stood at the front door. Removing one hand from her pocket, she put her fingers to her full lips, and whispered "I am glad you really have salvation, George. You have passed this test, I give up, and I am so sorry for coming here like this. But the real question is, will my husband?"

She placed her hands back into her coat pockets, tilted her head to the side, looked him up and down and shouted, "We will see how long it will take before I wear you down." Jada said with an alluring smile, "George, you are still a hunk of a man." Jada blew him a kiss with her hand.

Brie rushed up the steps before she walked out of her father's office door. Back into her bedroom, Brie opened her window where she had a clear view of the front porch and street. She wanted to hear and see if more words or kisses would be exchanged. Brie watched as her father followed Jada down their steps. Jada turned, held his hand and said, "George, I will call you Monday."

Brie's father said, "Don't bother, I am finished with you! I will tell Cate you were here."

Brie watched as this Jada, again put her finger up to her lips, indicating to her father not to say another word. Jada reached into her coat pocket and showed him something, then slipped a piece of paper into his hand. Her father clutched the paper.

From her window, and with the help of the full moon and street lights, Brie had a great view of Jada. . She watched Jada walked slowly down their long driveway. to a car that was parked two houses away from their house. When she got into the passenger side, Brie noticed a very large man was driving. They sat together for a few minutes and then Brie saw Jada's head hit the side window. The engine started and as they drove away she knew who Jada's driver was. It was Woody.

Just as Brie was leaving the window, she heard their door open. She rushed back to the window where she saw her back outside and was sitting on the front steps. He looked up into the bright, moonlit sky, and shouted.

"God, why?" He held the piece of paper toward heaven. Brie heard her father crying. She watched and heard her father's prayed.

"God she said she needs my help. Her coming here was a pretense, she was forced to do it. She showed me her small recorder. She said, it's a matter of life or death! She needs money. Oh God, send Cate home! Please, send Cate home! I need Cate, I can't continue to do this alone. Come home please Cate. I need you! And God, I sure do need your guidance!"

Finally he stood, wiping his lips repeatedly with his handkerchief.

Slowly, he staggered up the steps, and onto the porch, and into the house. Brie waited until after she heard the door lock to move. Brie quickly, tossing her pants into the closet. She climbed hastily and quietly into bed. Moments later she heard her door creak open, she lifted her head from her pillow and pretended to be drowsy. She asked,

"Dad is something wrong?"

"No, Brie. I am just checking in on you. Goodnight Baby, I love you."

"Love you too Dad."

Her dad, leaving her bedroom door ajar, walked slowly away. She listened as his feet scuffled down the hall and the door to her parent's room opened and closed.

As Brie drifted off to sleep she thought, *how do my parents know this Jada Perkins? Did my beating Woody tonight have anything to do with this woman's unexpected, early morning visit? And the note? What did she want from her father?*

Chapter 4, Who Invited You?

Grandpa Jeremiah Sullivan pulled into the church parking lot and saw Woody. He immediately screamed, "Lordy! Lord,Vetta is that Ida Parks no good for nothin' boy Woody comin' to the house of the Lord? And what is that he's wearing? Orange and black! Aren't those the colors Halloween clowns wear?"

Woody's suit was burnt orange, he wore a lemon orange shirt attached by a black collar and an orange and black striped tie. His patent leather shoes were striped orange and black, and on his large head he wore a black derby hat with an orange band. Woody was a very dark, giant of a man who stood about six feet plus a few more inches. He weighed over 350 pounds, and very muscular. Grandpa went on to say, "Whoa, look at him Vetta, since the last time I saw him, he has become more of a huge man!

Grandpa blasted, Vetta! I believe that oversized tank thinks he's lookin' good, but that grown man is one large ugly hippo? Lord have mercy!"

Watching Woody walk, Grandpa Jeremiah teasingly said to Grandma, "Earthquake, earthquake, coming!" Then, under his breath, Grandpa chanted, "Woody, Woody two by four, can't through the bathroom door." Grandpa was relentless with his shrewdness.

"Cullen, are you listening? You had better hear me boy, that's one sewer tank of a so-called man; you had better stay away from him. He stinks, and has nothin' good left in him."

Woody saw them. He thought to himself, *'Showtime! Oh how I hate that bent over wrinkly old man.'*

Woody straightened his hat, forced a smiled and waved. Grandpa said, "Look Vetta, that gangster has the gall to wave at us?"

"No Grandpa," said Cullen, "he's not waving at you, it's me. I invited him to church."

Before Grandpa could retort, Cullen jumped out of the car to open his Grandma's door.

Woody walked over to them. Grandpa Jeremiah exited the driver's side. Woody removed his hat and politely said, "Good morning Grandma Lovetta." Looking directly at her, Woody said, "It's good to see you again."

Grandma Lovetta nodded her head and said, "It's good to see you again Woodrow, especially in God's house."

Grandpa, didn't say a word, he just glared at him and Woody scowled back. With devious cunningness he politely asked, "How is that back of yours Mr. Sullivan?"

Bam! Grandpa, slammed the car door and started to answer Woody's well-crafted remark, but Grandma Lovetta quickly intervened.

"Woodrow, I am praying you find what you need today. I know your mother, Ida, will be happy to see you."

Woodrow laughed. Unwillingly and jokingly he heard himself mimic, "I am praying you find what you need today."

Grandma Lovetta retorted, "Woodrow Hugh Parks, shame on you. Here you are standing on God's holy ground mimicking me. This is not a place for your nonsense."

"Grandma Lovetta, I'm sorry and I was just kidding. I knew what you meant."

With a devious laugh he asked, "Grandma Lovetta, do I look like I need help?"

"Yes you do. Woodrow, we all need help."

Woody placed his left hand on Cullen' shoulder. He looked at Grandma Lovetta and zapped, "I just hope the big man who's supposed to live upstairs remembers my name in a good way. How about you Cullen, you hoping the same?

"Woodrow," said Grandma Vetta, I am tired of your condescending remarks about my God. I know you know that the One you just referred to as 'the big man upstairs,' His real name is God, and yes, His Son, Jesus will remember you, and all of us for our deeds. Deeds that are good, bad and just downright ugly; we all will be judged. Woodrow, it's good seeing you again and you are welcome to come to God's house as often as you like."

"Grandma Lovetta, I have always liked you."

"I love you, Woodrow, and I am always praying for you." Grandma Vetta, lightly patted his face and she turned away and picked up her pace to catch up with Grandpa. Once she caught up, she took grabbed his arm and he said to her, "Lovetta, I don't know why you talk to that orange and black devil and you had better pray harder for that thar' Grandson of ours."

Grandma sternly replied, "It seems I need to pray for God's mercy for both of you." She tugged his arm lightly and muttered, "Especially for you honey. You have to learn how to forgive Jeremiah Sullivan."

"Vetta, you know that man is the devil's agent! He is always scheming. I will always believe he killed his dad and our kids."

Woody tipped his hat as he walked past the Sullivans, who were watching them going into the church's side entrance. After they had entered, Grandpa waved his hand back and forth across his nose and whispered, "Phew, Vetta, even expensive cologne don't cover his stench."

"Oh Jeremiah Sullivan, stop it right now with your cruel remarks. As far as our grandson's choices, I believe he will make the right decision when need be. Jeremy, Cullen will be okay."

"Yep, as you often remind me Vetta, one is responsible for one's own choices. And I choose to not forgive that murderous, scumbag devil."

"Jeremy, stop it. You really need God's help. Woodrow isn't worth you losing your place with God. Give Woodrow to God and let God deal with him, not you."

Meanwhile, through the open door to the choir room; Brie's hazel green eyes locked with Woody's dark eyes. Woody tilted his hat, smiled, blew her a kiss and walked into the sanctuary.

The opposite side door opened; in walked Brad. He noticed Brie, and saw she was trembling, he walked behind her and lightly placed his hand on her shoulder and she jumped.

"Whoa, what's wrong Brie?"

She turned, smiled, and touched Brad's face and said,

"Oh, I was just thinking ..."

"Well, I've been thinking about you." Taking her hand, he spun Brie around and then complimented her. "That's a beautiful purple silk dress you are wearing, the color of royalty, with your beauty Brie, you always take my breath away."

"Umm, I thank you, Mr. Bradford Jason Rock the Third." Brie pulled Brad toward her, kissed his cheek, straightened his tie, winked with flirting eyes, and said, "Looking good Bradford Rock. Is that a new designer suit?"

"Yep, my grandparents sent it to me as one of my graduation gifts. "She kissed his cheek again, they linked arms and walked into the prayer room.

Entering, they heard Pastor Wilson addressing the praise and worship leaders. He stopped when he saw them. He said, "Brie and Bradford, I was telling the leaders that, as always, this worship service is God's.

Time will not be an issue, when God's presence is in the house. Can I get another amen?" They all

"Also, I heard Brother Cullen invited Sister Ida's and the late Bishop Samuel Parks' son, Woodrow to church."

Brie looked at Cullen and mouthed, "What were you thinking?"

Pastor Wilson read Brie's lips and said, "I want everyone on this ministering team to keep in mind that God's house is for sinners. We were once sinners, myself included, but God! He pulled me out of the gutter and set me on His solid rock.

We all are here only by the mercy of God. Inside the

ark, the law was contained, and the law brought death. But God in flesh, as Jesus, came and sat upon the ark and gave both grace and mercy graciously. His Son's death permitted all of us to be able to come boldly to His throne room and ask for his mercy. Now let's pray.

"Father, we thank You for another Sunday. Cover all here today with Your precious blood. Have Your way Lord, and change hearts to hear Your knocking and to respond by opening their hearts. We thank you, Father. Amen."

"Oh yes!" Pastor Wilson shouted, "All praise leaders before we leave, I have asked Sis Brie to open with the song, 'Change Me.'" He again shouted, "Change me Lord!" Pastor Wilson slapped his hands together and shouted, "Can I get another Amen?

"Also our brother Woodrow Parks is here. Let's pray he finds God today. You know we all have lied, and we have secrets, and some secrets we think are well hidden, buried so deep that no one can find them. But let's not forget this truth: God sees all and He knows all. Nothing, absolutely nothing, is hidden from Him."

"Amen," they responded.

Brad opened the side door and went to his stool. Cullen sat at the keyboard and Brie went out the prayer room to find her father. Not finding him, she saw Brad's dad. Brie quickly went over to Senator Rock and lightly tugged his arm. He turned and he saw tears in her beautiful green eyes and he asked, "What is it Brie? What's wrong?"

"Mr. Rock, please tell my dad that Woody is in church today, I also see four of his bodyguards are here with him. They are not sitting with him, but they are sitting at the end of the middle pews in aisles one, three, and nine, and the other is standing in the left corner. I don't believe there will be any trouble, but they are always carrying guns and Woody has two small pistols in each sock and inside his jacket. I just wanted Dad to know."

"Brie, how do you know this?"

Not waiting for her to answer back, Senator Jason Rock nodded his head and said, "Never mind Brie, I have this. Go, I will tell your Dad."

"Thank you, Mr. Rock."

Brie turned and hurried quickly down the side aisle into the open door where Woody was waiting for her. Brie pretended not to see Woody and tried to push past him.

He stepped in front of her and showily shouted her name, "Brie, Brie Hayes! What's this?

You aren't going to speak to me? Why are you pretending you do not know me?"

He moved in closer and blurted out, "Less than six hours ago you and Cullen nearly cleaned me out gambling at my place, drinking all my liquor. You denied my job offer and left me knocked out and now I am standing in this house that has been forbidden to me to come in, and you pretending as if you don't know me?"

Brie looked around, clinched her teeth together and hissed, "Shhh, Woody, keep your voice down! I hope you are satisfied. Now excuse me, I have to go inside."

Over the loud music Woody screamed, "Brie, why do you want me to keep my voice down?"

Refusing to lower his voice and enjoying his

maliciousness, Woody moved in closer to Brie and with an angrier tone, he ranted, "Oh, oh I know why? You don't want anyone here to hear that you are a hustler in the making? No, that's not the right word. No, let me think, what's that word?" Snapping his chubby fingers, he laughed when he said, "Oh yes, and the word I wanted is charlatan. That's what you are Brie, a charlatan, imposter, pretender and a shame to your God."

Brie, not flinching shouted, "Woody go away or I..."

"Or you'll what, Brie? Are you going to use your karate skills to beat me up in here, in your Lord's house?"

"Move aside Woody Parks and let her through!"

Both Woody and Brie turned. Brie saw her father with Senator Rock and the church security guards.

Brie rushed into her father's arms and exhaled. He whispered into her ear, "Go!" Brie turned around, looked at Woody and answered back, "Yes, I am all that. I am a sham, a charlatan and much more, but God forgives us sinners all the time."

Brie walked away briskly She went into the sanctuary using the side door. Opening the door, she paused as she heard her to Woody, "Either you walk back into the church or walk out the doors, it's your choice."

"Wait, wait, wait just a minute Brother Hayes and Senator Rock! You can't put anyone out of the Lord's house. This is a church, a public domain and I thought everybody, especially all sinners were welcome here. Now being the sinner that I am," he laughed, revealing his front diamond studded teeth and continued, "I believe I will walk back into the sanctuary and listen to your beautiful, angelic daughter sing her opening song, George."

Woody brushed past Senator Rock and sauntered back into the church to take his seat.

After prayer, Brie stood to sing. She glanced nervously over at Woody, who smiled, and puckered his lips at her.

Brad noticed Woody's intimidating gestures towards Brie and Brie's reaction.

Brad came and stood next to Brie. To the congregation Brie appeared to be overtaken by God's spirit and couldn't sing, Brad held her in his arms and he sang,

"Here I am, I surrender.
Here I stand naked and undone.
I'm standing here by your mercy. Change me!
Right now!
I am ready to change. Here I am,
Here I am, Lord."

As Brad sang, Woody sat with his head down. After the song, he stood and walked out with his bodyguards following. The church security guards, Elder Jason Rock, and Brie's father walked out the door behind them.

As Woody and his bodyguards were about to exit the door, Woody turned. He smiled at Jason Rock and mouthed off saying, "You know Senator Jason Rock, your son Bradford is a godly good man. However you, Mr. High and Mighty Man of God." Woody pointed his finger angrily toward Brie's' father, and spoke directly to him with an unpleasant tone and a disturbing smile blasted,

"You, Mr. George Almighty Hayes, your nephew Cullen and your pious, beautiful daughter Brie, I have another name for them, charlatans. Both of them are brazen hypocrites!"

Woody shook his head and continued, "They both remind me of myself at that age. I, with your sister-in-law, Sally, we would sin all week, day and night, but come Sunday morning, we were here in this very church singing to your God."

He screamed while pounding his chest. "Now look at me! George Hayes, this is a warning, you had better tell those two to stay away from me and my club and tell them I want all of my money back, all they have taken from me, and mark my words, I will get it all back from them one way or the other."

George lunged at Woody and grabbed his jacket. Woody's bodyguards immediately pulled their guns. Woody, smiling at his assailant, reached up and tore George's hands off his jacket.

"George, today's date is July 5, and the number 75 is my calling number." Woody's smile slowly left his face and he said, "The number 75 tells me it's a good day for someone to die. But lucky, today's not your final day upon this glorious earth." He shoved George and shouted to his bodyguards, "Put your guns back in your holsters! There will be no blazing guns of glory today in the house of their God. Not today, but rest assured, there is a tomorrow and my guns will blaze."

Woody then took a few steps and whispered to George Hayes, "I'll begin with your precious father-in-law and go right down to any of your pathetic family members who get in my way." Woody shoved George away from him and shouted, "Consider this a warning; watch your back!"

"Woody, is that a threat?"

Woody suddenly froze, he glared into George's angry eyes and said, "You need to listen better. Don't mess with me."

Using profanity, Woody tilted his head forward and spat on the church floor as he reached for his hat he heard.

"Boss, you're in God's house."

"Shut your dang mouth, Harry."

Woody snapped his chubby fingers, and Harry, his shield, rushed to push open the church's double doors.

Woody sauntered out to his chauffeur-driven car. Pete jumped out from behind the steering wheel to open the car door and as Woody went to get in, he looked back towards the church and saw George, Jason and the security guards watching him from the church's veranda. Woody deviously curled his lips into an unkind smile, and his eyes locked with George's. Woody lowered his head and climb into his car. Once inside, Woody immediately window and shouted more profanity. As his car slowly pulled away, they heard Woody's imperiling loud laughter.

Meanwhile, Brie sat nervously waiting in the choir stand. She breathed relief when she saw her father and Brad's dad walk through the church doors.

Chapter 5, Eavesdropper

The following Monday morning, Brie heard the phone ringing. Believing it could be the woman she saw her father with, she carefully picked up the receiver from its cradle only to hear her mother's voice. Although excited to hear her voice, she managed to control her emotions as she carefully replaced the receiver into its cradle. Sometime later her father lightly knocked on her bedroom door.

"Come in,"

Her father smiled and said, "Brie your mother is on the phone."

Pretending to be surprised, Brie kicked the cover off the bed. Using her bed as a trampoline, she sprung off the bed, took the phone from her dad's hand and yelled, "Mom! Mom, hi Mom!

"Brie, I'm coming home on Wednesday."

Brie started to skip around the room with the receiver to her ear. She shouted, "You're coming home this Wednesday!"

"Yes, and I told your father that I have cancelled all of my speaking engagements."

"What? I can't believe this. Wow! Mom that's great news, but why?"

"I will tell you and your dad more when I see you. Love you."

"I love you, too. Mom, may I tell Brad?"

"Yes, Brie you may tell Brad."

"Great, and here's Dad."

Brie made quick springing leaps around the room like an eight-year-old child. She managed to quiet herself to listen to her dad's conversation with her mom. She heard her dad saying, "Yes honey. Okay. Brie and I will be there. Cate I am so anxious for you to come home.

"Bye honey."

Brie shouted, "Bye Mom!"

Brie turned and jumped into her father's arms. They laughed and hugged each other. When he placed her feet onto the floor, he pulled away and sternly said to Brie, "Honey, we need to talk later. I am going to go back to my den, I have a few things to take care of, and then we will talk."

"Okay, Dad. I know it's about Woody and my gambling. I will shower, get dressed and come down."

Brie, how did you know I wanted to talk with you about gambling? I never mention gambling to you."

"Dad, I…" He interrupted her and said, "Oh never mind Brie, you must have your mother's gift of foreknowledge." He smiled and said, "I love you, Brie. You know that, don't you?"

"Yes, Dad, I know that." He kissed her forehead and walked out.

Brie, walked silently behind him and slowly closed her bedroom door. She then walked slowly into her spacious, lavender and pink bathroom.

She showered, towel dried herself, and wrapped her big pink, fluffy towel around her body.

She used a face towel to wipe the mirror and looked at her reflection. She saw a beautiful girl with perfect white teeth, a medium light skin tone, long light brown wavy hair, and big hazel eyes. Thinking aloud she said, "Look at me, I am made in the image of God. God is holy, and here I am seeing my reflection in the mirror, I am just as unholy as I can be, and in love with a godly man like Brad. Bradford Jason the Third, the son of a United States senator, and a godly, sweet, kind and beautiful mother whose parents are close friends to my parents and grandparents."

As she brushed her hair she thought. *Brad and Cullen were both popular football players on their high school campus.*

Brad stood about 6'3", with gorgeous blue eyes, a square jaw and wavy long light brown hair that he kept tied back in a ponytail. His skin had a golden tone that seem to glow and he maintained beautiful white teeth, with a genuine smile that melted hearts.

Brad was president of the student body, and the school's Young Christian Club. He was captain of their football team, and just named class valedictorian. He was also a talented musician who skillfully played any instrument of choice, and he had a voice that only God could have anointed. After graduation Brad will go to Bible College, his aspiration is to become a Pastor. He, unlike Cullen and Brie, worshipped God with sincerity; he was steadfast and loyal. Brad was the real deal.

By all standards, to Brie, he was perfect. He was beautiful inside and out. He was in love with her but she had convinced herself that she couldn't measure up to God's requirements for Him.

She knew she could *never* become a minister's wife,

and definitely not Brad's. She was undeniably unholy.

She slowly closed the cabinet door, looked down into her gold dust sink with remorse and thought, *'God, I need a miracle, I love Brad, but I need a spiritual makeover. Change me!'*

In her mind, she found solace in believing her own lie. *'At least I'm not alone, and there are two in this house who are unholy. My dad has a secret and with mom coming home, I am wondering how long it will take her to discern his and my deceptions.'*

She voiced aloud, "Poor Daddy."

Brie brushed her teeth and slowly dressed. She purposely avoided her dad by not leaving her room because she, too, was waiting for Jada's call. Whenever the phone rang, she would quietly crawl over to the vent that sat directly over her dad's study. While lying there waiting, she chuckled when she thought about her dad's word, *'foreknowledge.'* She recalled the day she discovered the vent. She was seven years old and playing jacks when she overheard her Mom and Dad talking about her Aunt Thelma's abusive husband, and Tom, their unruly son. After that, she would often sit and listen to her parents' conversations.

The phone rang.

Brie scooted cautiously across the floor, she placed her ear to the vent and heard what she had been waiting for. Her father put Jada's call on the speaker setting because he always paced when he talked.

"George, I am not going to lie to you. My husband is in a financial bind needs and money.

I have some jewelry to sale… my mother's diamond ring and bracelet."

"Jada, if I remember correctly, your mom loved those two pieces. Before she died she gave them to you and she expected you to keep them."

"I know, George, but my husband is forcing me to sale them. Someone who works for him has been stealing, and some kids won over $20,000 dollars Saturday night in a game that was supposed to be fixed. His business isn't doing so well."

"Wait a minute. Did I hear you correctly, you said some kids won over $20,000 dollars gambling at Woody's Place?"

"Yes, they did, and I am terrified just being with him. He never sleeps, he's always talking to some invisible person. This happens off and on throughout the night.

"Woody told me that if I didn't get the money he needed he will make me and some young girls and boys prostitute ourselves. He has become a dope dealer; he's a bully and enjoys intimidating others. He believes he's invincible and he's becoming more dangerous and unpredictable each day. George, I live in fear for my life."

"I know what you mean. I had an encounter with him at church on Sunday. I saw a side of him I never witnessed before."

"Woody came to church Sunday? I am shocked! That explains why he had been in such a foul mood. He came home Sunday evening, overturned chairs and punched holes into the wall, then forced me get on my hands and knees and abused me. George, I am afraid of him. Please help me!"

 "Okay, Jada, I will get the money. But this is the last

time I will ever help you. You need to get yourself far away from Woody."

"I have tried and each time he finds me. I am his prisoner, and there's no escaping him. Woody has eyes everywhere.

"There must be a way for you to escape his hold on you. Jada, Cate still has fond memories of your days together in Bible College. She hasn't any idea about the life you are now living. I will not tell her anything about you because I have no intentions of destroying her memories."

"George, I am so sorry. Woody forced me to come to your home. He put my cell phone on recording mode and put it in my inside coat pocket. I was to seduce you. He would have used the recording as blackmail evidence against you for money." Choking back tears, she said, "When I didn't succeed that night, he began hitting me in the car, and he beat me that night."

Brie heard her Dad when he pounded his fist on his desk. He told her "Jada, I will help you, but I am curious, who gave you my private number?"

"I stole it from our old college friend, Melvin. The night you saved my life, the night you found me, Woody was angry with his cousin, Anderson, and his brother, M.J. Michael Jay, because they kept letting some kids clean him out. Those same kids in two years have won over $75,000 from him and he wants it back.

Did I hear you correctly? You said some kids won over $75.000?"

"Yes, you heard correctly."

George thought about Woody's remarks. *'The number*

75 tells me it's a good day for someone to die. But you're lucky, today's not your final day upon this glorious earth.'

George, George are you there?"

"I am, continue Jada."

"Woody was upset and when I tried to calm him down, I watched his eyes turn red with intense hate. He beat me and afterwards, he picked up a whiskey bottle and smashed it over my head. I remember his two bodyguards wrapping me in something heavy and as they started to carry me from the club I heard Woody giving instructions. He told them to dump me around the corner so when I was found they would think someone attacked me."

Brie heard Jada's crying. Listening to her story, Brie felt tears staining her own face.

"George, Woody left me to die on that filthy street."

"Jada, this is how I found you. I was driving through our old neighborhood. I had just parked my car and turned off the headlights.

Just as I was about to open my car door, the Holy Spirit guided told me to wait. A few seconds later, I saw a car slowly approaching one block away and it stopped. I saw two men getting out of the car, they looked around to see if anyone was watching. One of the men opened the car door, pulled a bag out, and left it on the curb. I waited for them to leave and I prayed that it wasn't someone I knew and loved. I had my hand on my car door to open it but I quickly ducked down on my car seat because I saw headlights approaching from my side mirror. The men doubled back twice. It's my guess they were being sure they were not seen. Finally, believing it was okay, I drove my car to the corner curb. I didn't know it was you, until I unzipped the bag, turned your body over, and saw your bloody, bruised face.

"Jada, I felt sorry for you and felt a need to help an old friend. That was it and nothing more. I knew Melvin could be trusted, so I took you to Melvin's Home for Battered Women. I gave him a check for $3,000 dollars to send you back home."

"George?"

"Yes, Jada?"

"I didn't know it was you who helped me. I found your number weeks later when Melvin asked me to come to his office. He told he was giving me donated money to help me to find safe place to stay. He said he found my sister Sharon's number in my wallet. Our conversation was interrupted when Melvin's phone rang and he had some urgent business to take care of. He walked out and I was left alone. I was walking around his office looking at pictures on his wall and I walked over to his desk.

When I looked down and I saw your name on a business card. I turned it over, and saw where you had written down your private number and I took the card.

"What Melvin was going to tell me was that he had contacted my sister and I was to go to live with her. He drove me to the airport, he bought my ticket, and then he gave me the rest of the money. Melvin had to leave because my plane was delayed. He told me to stay where I was until my flight was called. But you know me, I always do the opposite of what I am told. I had my ticket so I decided to go into the lobby to play on one of those slot machines. I had every intention to leave, George. As fate would have it, Woody's men were at the station looking for runaways when I was spotted. While gambling, I felt a pull on my arm when I turned around it was Woody.

"He took me back to his house. Once we arrived there he demanded to know who helped me, where I had been, and where I got the money to buy a ticket. He accused me of stealing from him. Out of intense anger, he picked up my purse and slammed it hard against the wall. My purse opened and the contents spilled out onto the floor. I had $2,500 dollars and your card. Woody's twisted mind believed I had been secretly meeting you, and he hatched his plan. He forced me to go to the justice of the peace and marry him. He felt that he could use our marriage as a winning ticket when he was to tell Cate about our so-called affair."

"This is how you show your appreciation for what I did? You come to my home that I share with my wife and daughter trying to seduce me? Now, you say Woody forced you to do that and he is forcing you into asking me for more money! When will it stop? Jada, you need to get away from him!"

"I know George, and I will one day, I will."

"How much more abuse are you willing to take?"

"George, you are the only one who can help me? Please, George, I need your help."

"You said you needed $75,000?"

"Yes."

"I will bring you $75,000. However, you need to promise me that you will never come to Cate's and my home again uninvited. Do you understand me Jada?"

"Yes, George, and again, I am so, so sorry!"

"Meet me at Mom Parks restaurant Crave Café on London Road in a couple of hours."

Brie heard a click as her dad disconnected the call.

Brie thought, '*Dad was looking for me the night he saved Jada? Now he knows Cullen and I were the kids Jada was talking about. Woody called me a charlatan; yes, he's right, I am a hypocrite, a pretender. I sin on Friday and Saturday nights and get up on Sunday morning, go to church and sing about God's love, mercy, and grace.*

Brie put on a little makeup, then walked slowly down the back steps through the kitchen and into the front room. She stood outside her father's office; she inhaled, and slowly exhaled. She knocked enthusiastically on his door. Not waiting for an answer, she pulled open the heavy sliding pocket doors.

Her dad stood behind his desk, he looked up at her and smiled. She watched as he placed his checkbook inside his jacket pocket.

He extended his arms for her to come to him, when she did, he took her hand and spun her around. He said, "My very beautiful daughter, you are looking so pretty in that pink dress. Want to go out for some lunch?"

Not waiting for a replied he said, "I will have to make a quick stop at the bank, and then we can eat lunch."

"Dad?"

"Yes, Brie?"

"May I call Brad to see if he can join us? And daddy," Batting her beautiful green eyes, she said, "Since

Bradford's house is along the way to the bank, perhaps, we can pick him up?"

"Umm, young lady, you've been spending more time than usual with Mr. Bradford Rock." Teasingly, he asked, "Brie, when is the wedding?"

Brie looked into her daddy's eyes, took hold of his hands and playfully disclosed, "Dad, you, Mom, Brad, and I, will have to talk more about that later!"

Puzzled by her snippety comment, he shouted, "Brie, what's going on?"

Brie winked at her dad. Not answering his question, she kissed him on his cheek, turned, and skipped out through the study and out of the double doors like a small very happy child.

Chapter 6, The Tyrant

Brie's father parked his silver-gray jeep in front of the bank. While inside, Brie told Brad all she had saw and heard between her father and Jada.

Brie's eagle greenish-brown eyes watched her father's scowling face through the bank's glass window. She saw him insert a white envelope into his inside jacket pocket. Arriving at the jeep, he appeared to be happy as he stared at his daughter and Brad through the opened window. He smiled, and asked, "What are you two up to?"

Brad hastily replied, while shaking his head, "Nothing sir." Tapping the roof of the jeep Brie's father laughed and said, "Yeah, nothing."

Brie's father hopped into the Jeep, and repeated, "Yeah, nothing." He sat behind the steering wheel and turned around to ask, "Are you hungry?"

"Ah, yes, dad,"

"Well then, it's time to get some grub."

Driving to the local Crave Cafe', Brie's father listened to Brie and Brad's light conversation about college. Using his rearview window mirror, he saw Brad holding his daughter's hands.

After her dad parked his jeep and started their walk into the restaurant, Brie noticed his demeanor changed and he became uneasy.

Entering the cafe' doors, Brie observed her father scanning the room. Brie assumed he was looking for the woman.

Her father asked the hostess for a table in the far corner. They were escorted to a section where they had a view of each person as they came and went.

When their waiter arrived, George stated, "Brad, Brie, go ahead and order whatever you want."

George reached into his front pocket, took out his silver money clip, removed a hundred dollar bill and handed it to Brad.

"Sir?"

"Take this, I may have to leave before our meals come."

"Leave, Dad? Where to?"

"Oh, don't worry Brie, it will just be for a few minutes and what I gave Brad should be enough for all three of us. Brad, give the waiter the change."

"Sir, I thank you, but I can pay for our meals." "No, Brad," I insist."

"Very well Sir, you will have at least $60.00 coming back. That's a generous tip."

George laughed and said, "I know, our waiter will be very happy." Nervously he drummed the table with his fingers and repeated, "Yep, I'm very generous

Soon the door opened and Brie saw the woman who was at their home last night. She was wearing the same pink coat. Brie spoke softly, "*I hope she's wearing more under that pink coat than she was last night.*"

"What was that Brie, I didn't hear you."

"I was thinking aloud Dad. I should have worn my pink sweater."

Brad quickly removed his jacket and draped it around Brie's shoulders. "Feeling warmer?" he asked.

"Yes, I am." Brad's and Brie's eyes locked.

"Ah, Brie and Brad is there something going on between you two that I need to know?" He gave Brad a harsh look and said, "You, young man, can't take your eyes off of my beautiful daughter."

Brad responded, "Yes sir, I meant nothing sir." George muttered, "Oh, Okay. So you say-- nothing."

During their fun light conversation and sipping on their coffee, George suddenly became uneasy. He removed a note pad from his front pocket. He jotted something down, ripped it off, folded it, then put the note pad back into his pocket and hastily gulped his coffee. Seconds later, he reached across the table and tapped Brie's hands. He said, "Honey, I'm leaving, and I may be a while."

"Dad, are you okay? Do we need to go home? You looked all flushed."

"Oh, there's nothing to worry your beautiful self about, your old dad is okay. Eat, I will be back."

Brie watched her father as he glided towards Jada's table. He quickly placed the folded note on her table, then slipped into the men's restroom.

Brie saw the woman reading the note, she stood and sauntered over to the men's restroom door.

She quickly knocked twice and then slipped out of the side door. Immediately, the restroom door opened and Brie saw her dad exit and follow Jada.

Brie grabbed Brad's hand. She hissed, "Brad look, exit door to your left" "Dad just slipped out the side door following that woman I told you about!"

Brie stood up, Brad grabbed her arm, he asked, "Brie, what are you going to do?"

"Brad! Mom isn't here to protect Dad and I have to find out what Dad is getting into! You stay here!"

"Brie?"

"Please stay. Brad, he's my dad and I'm going!"

Brie stood, rushed out the front door and trotted around the back. When she spotted them, she quickly hid behind the restaurant's huge, noisy, air conditioner. She watched them exchange a few words, and saw the woman place a small brown bag into her dad's open hand.

Her dad took the bag, looked inside it, and tucked it into his outside jacket pocket. He then reached into his inside jacket pocket, took out the white bank envelope, and handed it to Jada. She opened her purse and dropped it in. She leaned forward to kiss him, but he turned his head and walked away.

Brie sprinted to the side entrance leading into the women's restroom.

She opened the door and rushed to the sink. She turned on the water to wash her hands and to dab her face, when she reached for a paper towel, Jada shuffled in.

Brie stood very still with her head down inside the paper towel trying to become invisible.

Jada, not looking up, went into the stall. Brie walked quickly to the door but paused when she heard the woman say, "Woody, I have the money. Come and get me."

Brie exited quickly and returned to their table very irritated. Her father noticed her face was flushed and he asked, "Honey, what's wrong? Are you okay?"

"I'm okay, Dad, just hungry. Where's our order?"

Brad noticed the waiter coming towards their table and said, "Our meals are coming out, right… about… now!"

Seeing his daughter was miserable, George probed and asked, "Brie what's wrong?"

"Nothing, Dad."

"Don't tell me nothing, I am looking at you and something is wrong."

"Sir?"

George glanced at his daughter and then to Brad and answered, "Yes, Brad."

"I may have said something to upset Brie."

Their waiter finished placing Brie's and Brad's orders on the table. Then their waiter asked George, if he was ready to order.

"No, but I will have a fresh cup of coffee please."

Once the coffee was poured and their waiter was far enough away, George looked at his daughter with her head down, pushing her food from side to side and not eating, and Brad, taking small bites and quick, nervous glances at Brie.

"Brie?"

"What, Dad?"

"You aren't talking to Brad?"

"Yes Dad, and I do not want to talk with you either."

"Sir? Brie will be okay."

"No, Brad, Brie's actions concern me. Brie, talk to

me."

"Dad, I have nothing to say to you, but plenty to say to Brad."

George stood. He told them, "Look, I will leave you two here to work out this matter. I have to run a quick errand and come back."

"Brie?"

Not looking at her father Brie snapped back

, "What do you want, Dad?"

George tried to make eye contact with his daughter who sat, still pushing her untouched food and was obviously in a very foul mood.

"I am leaving. Will Brad be safe with you?"

"Not funny, Dad."

He stood, leaned over to give his daughter a kiss, but she moved her head away. He said, "Oh, she is upset. Brie, behave yourselfand don't be so hard on Brad."

George winked, and said to Brad, "Good luck son and remember she's a fourth degree, black belt holder."

Grimacing, Brad said, "Thanks for that reminder sir."

"One more thing Brad. Please stop calling me sir, my name is George."

"Yes sir. I meant to say, George, sir."

George sighed, shook his head. He looked at his daughter who sat stubbornly quiet, refusing to look up, still pushing her food around her plate. George looked at Brad, and then mouthed, "Good luck son."

He turned and slowly walked out of Crave Café.

Brad gently pulled Brie's arm. "Brie, come on honey, talk to me. What happened?"

"Brad, Dad gave that woman the bank envelope and she gave him a brown bag, dad opened it to look inside, then he tucked it in his side pocket and walked away. I then ran into the restroom to wash my face when that woman who is sitting over there," Brie angrily pointed to her, "whose name is *Jada*, came in and went directly into a stall. When I opened the door to leave, I heard her saying, 'Woody, I have the money, come and get me. I know I overheard Dad and her conversation, but this just isn't right."

"How so Brie?

Brie took a sip of coffee when someone coming in caught her attention. She grabbed Brad's hands, "Brad," she whispered, "to your left."

The restaurant door opposite from where Brie and Brad sat, opened. In walked Woodrow Hugh Parks.

He stood at the door to scan the large space when he spotted Jada. Brie noticed his color selection for today was all black… *just like his heart.* He wore a black derby hat with a black and gold mesh band on his head. His ears and nose were pierced, he wore big gold chains around his thick neck and hanging out his mouth was a wooden toothpick. All eyes were on him and it was obvious to Brie he was enjoying the attention because his movements were deliberate as he moved toward Jada. He looked and walked like a gigantic intimidator.

Once at Jada's table, he shoved it back to accommodate his size and sat.

Brie saw Jada give to him the same white envelope her dad had just given to her. As Woody counted the money, Brie watched intensely as heated words were spoken by Woody.

Jada, seemingly alarmed, stood, determined to leave; but, Woody grabbed her arm and shoved her back into the chair.

Brie couldn't make out what they were saying, but she saw Jada's body language, and it revealed she was afraid of him. Soon, Woody stood to leave. He leaned down and tried to kiss her cheek, but she pulled her face away.

It was apparent to Brie that Jada had embarrassed Woody, and that angered him. He forcibly grabbed Jada's arm, held it for a second, raised his free hand with intention to strike her, but stopped when he saw his mother coming through the door.

When Woody looked around he also saw Brie, Brad, and other customers looking and he released her arm and smirked. Jada sat quivering with her head down and her body folded up like a paper accordion doll.

Woody, looked down on her, put his hand into his pocket and tossed a few green bills on the table. Jada, stared up at him like a deer caught in the headlights, understandably too frightened to move.

Not speaking, Woody frowned as he walked slowly toward his mother's office. Moments later, Woody walked out and stopped at the restaurant's exit door. When Jada looked up he patted his jacket pocket, winked and gave her a scowling smile that showed the diamond studs inserted in his front teeth. Before walking out, he deliberately turned toward Brie and Brad; he glared with malice at Brie. He did a quick hand karate move, clasped his hands together, nodded his head, tilted his hat, and then he turned with a disgustingly triumphant, prideful, swagger-like limp out the restaurant's door.

Meanwhile, Jada sat crying softly. Moments later, she unfolded another paper napkin and used it to dry her tears. After two cups of coffee and a quick conversation with her mother-in-law. Jada stood. She left the money on the table and she walked out the restaurant's door. Brie sorrowfully shook her head. She felt Jada's pain because she too knew her fear of Woody.

Chapter 7, Homecoming

Dad, over there, to your left. Mom! I see Mom! It's Mom!

Brie jumped, waved, and screamed. "Mom, over here!"

Brie rushed into her Mother's arms, and smothered her with hugs and kisses, "Oh, Mom," she screamed, "it feels so good to feel your hugs."

Cate hugged and kissed Brie and smiled when her eyes locked with her husband's. Embracing Brie with one arm, she reached out to George with the other arm as he gently pressed a beautiful bunch of pink forget-me-not roses into her soft hands and gave her a very long kiss.

"Ow." Brie whined, "You guys are smothering me." Brie's mother and father laughed as they released her.

In a playful tone Brie said, "Ah, thank you." "Holding his wife in his arms he said, "Honey, I am so glad you are home."

"George, it's good to be home. You knew I wouldn't miss our daughter's summer graduation."

Cate began to twirl, and Brie asked, "Mom, who are you looking for?"

"Brad... Where's Brad, Brie?"

"Mom, you are worse than Dad! ... And Mom, Brad's coming by later this evening."

"Brie?"

"Mom?"

"Have you thought about whether you are going to continue to come home, live in the dorm, or get an apartment?"

"No, Mom, we are still thinking about that."

Her mom gave her a scrutinizing look that said, *I got your number,* as Cate eyeballed her daughter, she repeated, "We?"

Brie noticed her mother looking at her dad and back to her suspiciously, and was waiting for a clarification to her daughter's one-line taunting remark, "We are still thinking."

Brie quickly changed the subject by giving her mom another big hug as they continued their walk to the car.

Once settled inside the car, Cate clapped her hands three times to get their attention.

"Oh this should be good. Mom, you only clap when you have some important news. Oh no please don't tell us you're leaving right after my graduation."

"No. This is my announcement. George, Brie, I am officially finished with being a traveling evangelist!"

"What!" The two of them shouted simultaneously,

George's eyes diverted from the road and he drove the car left of center. Thankfully, no other cars were near them.

"Oh my! Was my timing wrong? Perhaps I should have saved my announcement for home."

Smiling, Cate asked, "Is everybody okay?"

"Yes we are," answered George. "Now, Cate, go ahead and tell us how you reached this great news of yours?"

"This is what happened. A week ago my secretary called to tell me that she cleared my schedule so I could come home for Brie's graduation. Then she asked if I wanted to confirm the invitations I had for the following several months, beginning next month in Maine.

When she said Maine, the Holy Spirit spoke, *'No more trips, return home, preach three times at your church and complete two coming assignments in a city not far away.'"*

"Mom, are you sure God said that?" Cate laughed and said, "Yes, Brie, I am sure!"

"Why three times? And what city?" George inquired.

"I didn't question God about the city's name or why would I preach three times George. I will just be obedient to His directions when He reveals them to me."

George pulled the car into their driveway. Cate looked at their beautiful, luxuriant, green lawn with its vibrant colorful flowers.

"George, when I left home, snow covered the ground. Now look, beauty is everywhere!"

With pulsating excitement George shouted, "Honey, we have missed you more than you can imagine!"

Pumping his fist in the air, George shouted, "Thank you Jesus! Thank God, He changed your schedule and you are home to stay! Hallelujah!" George looked up to heaven and shouted, "Thank you Jesus, for hearing my prayers!"

"Your prayers? Mr. George Alexander Hayes, so it was your prayers. You were responsible for my abrupt schedule change?"

"Guilty as charged ma'am."

 George opened the front door to their home. Once

Cate walked in, she turned to look at her husband and said, "Honey, our home is so beautiful, I really have missed being here."

Minutes later they heard the telephone ringing. Brie ran toward the phone shouting, "I will get it.

"Hello."

"Hello, Brie."

"Hi, Pastor Wilson."

"Brie, may I speak with your mother?"

"Yes. Ah, Pastor Wilson, please forgive me for being inquisitive, but how did you know Mom was home? We didn't know she was coming until two days ago and we didn't tell my grandparents she was coming."

"Brie, I was just told by the Holy Spirit to call your home and ask for Cate."

"Wow, that's awesome. Pastor Wilson, wait one moment please." Brie placed her hand over the receiver and whispered, "Mom, it' Pastor Wilson."

Smiling, Cate put the phone to her ear and said, "Pastor Wilson. Hello, it's good to hear your voice. May I ask, how did you know I was home?"

"Cate, I was walking in my garden, meditating, and the Holy Spirit told me to call your home and ask for you. I knew you were out of town but I obeyed."

"Pastor Wilson, I am wondering what God is up to?"

Brie walked out the room and took out her cell phone to call Brad. George went into the kitchen to heat some tea water. A short time later, Cate came into the kitchen still smiling. She said, "George, as you know that was Pastor Wilson. Saturday is Brie's High School graduation. Sunday morning, he is expecting out of town guests at the church and he asked me to preach Sunday morning. I asked him how he knew I was home. Now listen to this. He said he was meditating and God told him I was home, and God also told him that I am to preach two sermons at our church."

With a puzzling expression, George said, "This Sunday will be the first of three, Cate?"

Cate sat at the table, sipping her cup of hot tea. She replied, "I know, George, and I've been having these troubling dreams."

Brie interrupted them. She rushed into the kitchen, put her arms around her mother and said, "So you are speaking this Sunday. Awesome, Mom. I already called Brad and told him, now I will call Cullen." As she ran out of the kitchen, her mother shouted to her, "Brie! Tell Cullen to tell Mom and Dad I will be over later this evening."

"I will."

George looked into Cate's large brown eyes and said, "Cate, I prayed for you to come home, and it feels so good to have you here. But honey, I have to ask, are you sure God told you to stop traveling?"

Cate reached for his hands and said, "Yes, George, I am one hundred percent sure.

"Well ma'am, I am not going to lie. I am one happy man. I am so glad to have my wife here with me. Welcome home my dear."

Walking back into the kitchen Brie saw her father and mother kissing. Seeing her parents together made her happy. "Ahem." She pretended to clear her throat, and playfully she asked, "Should I leave?"

They laughed. Cate pulled a chair out from under the table for her to sit. She said, "Brie dear, come and sit here; tell us your schedule for the next three days."

"It's not much mom, I have been invited to the Nance's backyard barbecue on Friday night, and that's it." After giving her mother and father the graduation details, Brie left the kitchen.

"George can you believe our baby is graduating and going to college? My, how time flies." As she sipped her tea she said, "My dream … God didn't reveal any details to me, but you, Brie, Cullen, and an unidentified family member has been up to something that needs to be fixed. Not by me, but by God."

Cate finished her tea picked up her small makeup bag, looked into her husband's soft blue eyes and said, "George, God's timing is always important. During this period, I am going to have some testing times ahead of me, but always remember no matter what happens, I will trust God, and I love you very much."

She kissed him and said, "I am going to take a shower and lie down for a while. Later, when you are ready, I would love to go over to Mom and Dad's. Perhaps we can all go out to eat afterward."

"Okay, my dear, I will be up later. I'll call and let your parents know about dinner."

Walking down the hall, Cate passed Brie's room, she called out, "Brie, see if Brad and his parents can come."

"Come where?"

"To dinner with us, you can text him later to tell him where we are going. Tell my son-in-love I said, 'hello,' please."

Brie shouted from her bedroom, "What did you say mom? Did you say your, 'son-in-love?'?"

"Yes, I did, and you know I can't unsay what I have said."

Brie let out a nervous laugh. She hollered, "Mom, you are worse than Dad."

Later that evening, when Brie, George and Cate arrived at her parent's home, Cate said, "I see Mom and Dad have company."

Brie looked out their car window. She said, "No Mom, they do not have company, that car is Brad's. It's a graduation gift from his grandparents.

"Nice gift." Cate responded.

Brie jumped out of the car, leaving the car door open.

She rushed into her grandparents' house shouting, "Cullen! Brad! Where are you two?"

Cullen called back, "We're in the kitchen, Brie."

Entering, she jumped into Cullen's' arms and gave him a big hug, then she turned to Brad, kissed him on the lips, and cooed, "Good looking ride, a red BMW! Wow, Mr. Bradford!"

Cullen leaned back on the counter, crossed his arms, and said, "Okay, okay, what's going on between you two? I've been away for a while but tell me, what's up?"

Brie's parents and grandparents stood in silence listening, waiting for her answer.

Brad smiled and said, "Go ahead, Brie, tell them."

"Cousin Cullen, Mom and Dad, and my precious grandparents, we finally told each other how we felt."

Cullen shouted, "Duh, it has always been obvious to all of us, it was you, Brie, who were in denial."

"I know," said Brie. "I still have to clean up my act and get right with God."

With a solemn face Brad said, "Brie, I hate telling you this right now."

"What? Bradford Rock? Whoa, you aren't telling me you don't love me?"

"Brie... no, never. No, not that!"

He pulled her into his arms, he laughed and said, "No, never, Brie Hayes, I've been in love with you since first grade."

Brad held Brie's hands and told her. "What I have to tell you is, I have to leave for the next two days.

Mom and Dad have scheduled press conferences and dinner engagements, and I was asked to come. I will see you at our graduation Saturday."

Brad kissed Brie and said, "I will see you both on Saturday. Cullen, I am depending on you to watch my fourth degree black belt, wonder woman, and please... you and Brie, stay away from Woody. "Cullen, Mr. Hayes and my dad had a little persuasive talk with Woody concerning your potential NFL career."

"What! Uncle George didn't tell me that. I never told them that Woody was still pestering me about helping him pushed drugs.""

"I know. You know my father has ways to find things out. Months ago, my dad went with Brie's dad to Woody's

Place, with several security guards, when they entered, Woody's bodyguards tried to get them to leave and they shoved my dad. Dad's security guards handcuffed and arrested them. Then my dad and Mr. Hayes had a private talk with Woody.

Dad told him that if he heard he contacted you about getting you to throw a game, or to bet on games, he will close down Woody's illegal gambling house.

Woody got smart with Brie's dad and called" Brad looked at Brie, held her hands and said, "you, Brie, a few, not so admirable names, which I won't repeat. Your dad told Woody he had never liked him and he could not understand what Sally and Mike saw in him.

"Dad said Woody in rage responded, 'Just as many others have made their fatal mistake messing with me, so have you and your daughter.

Someone in your family will pay with their life.' That's when your father, Brie, knocked Woody out cold! Cullen and Brie, I love you both and felt I needed to tell you. Please, please, stay away from there. Woody is after revenge."

Brad pulled Brie into his arms and said, "Brie, please promise me, you will not go there."

"Okay, Brad, I promise."

"Cullen, please promise me that you will not take Brie, if you decide to go. But, Cullen, it would be unwise for you to do so."

Cullen nodded his head, tapped Brad's shoulder lightly with his hand and said, "I love her too, man."

 Brad kissed Brie and said, "Bye honey, I love you,

and I will see you both Saturday, at graduation. Brie, I will call you when I can."

Together, they watched as Brad drove away. And Brie asked, Hey, Cuz, what are we going to do tonight?"

"My beautiful cousin, after dinner with the family, we will come back here and play Scrabble."

"A board game?" Brie muttered. "Scrabble. We are going to play board games?"

Cullen said, "Better yet, let's get the family involved, let's play, the Jeopardy game!"

Cullen placed his arms around his cousin's neck. "Yep, Brie, that's the plan."

Cullen repeated with a light hearted sigh, "A board game and some hot buttered popcorn.

Chapter 8, I Didn't See That

It's been months, and things are back to normal. Cullen continues to come home when he can from NFL football camp. When Cullen came to town, he and Brie spent their evenings bouncing around the homes and apartments of different friends. Brad spent more time out of town with his parents and grandparents. Brie woke up half an hour later than usual, still. She heard her mother call, "Brie, I know you are tired, but you have to get up!"

"Brie..."

She felt her mother's gentle hands tickling her feet saying, "Brie, I didn't hear you moving! Get moving now! Hurry dear, we have to leave in half an hour."

Brie sat up in bed, stretching she said, "I'm sorry, Mom." "That's okay, but hurry." Brie jumped out of bed and watched as her mother closed her bedroom door.

Brie dressed quickly and grabbed her choir robe from her enormous cedar closet. She walked down their long hallway and she saw her mother and father dressed extravagantly from head to toe, wearing their Sunday's best.

Seeing her parents together made her very happy. Her dad looked at them and he playfully twirled his tan Fedora dress hat. He bent over and said, "Well, my beautiful ladies, I believe you are all ready, and looking fabulous. The car awaits us."

Cate smiled and gave him a quick kiss.

Walking out their front door, Brie was experiencing happiness mingled with a darkness which still remained when she thought about the secrets she and her father held.

Brie thought, *I know Mom knows about my gambling and drinking, but has Dad told her about Jada?*

Cate stopped on the front porch. She took George and Brie's hands and told them, "Pray for me. God has warned me that this day is going to test my faith. My prayer is that I will not fail God and I'll be obedient, even to my own hurt."

She firmly held Brie's hands, looked her in the eyes, and told her, "Brie, you are so beautiful." She locked arms with her and said, "Yes, George, we are ready."

Brie's father opened both car doors. He seated his wife and then turned around to close Brie's door. Her father sat in the driver's seat, closed his door and keyed in the number to start the engine. As he drove, everyone was quiet.

Out of the blue, Cate looked over at her husband and said, "George Hayes, do you know how much I love you?" He reached over, held her hand and placed it to his lips, kissed her hand and said, "Yes dear, I know, and, I love you too."

Cate smiled and said, "George, I've been thinking about our wedding day, when we promised to love and to cherish each other, and to share with one another everything, the good, the bad, and the ugly and Brie that also includes you,"

Brie sat silently in panic, thinking, *Mom knows our secrets! Why did she wait until now to tell us? Why today? On this Sunday when she's the speaker?* Brie thought, *should I try to change the conversation*?

"Hey, Mom."

"Yes, Brie."

"Isn't that an old movie title? "The Good, the Bad and the Ugly?"

"You know it is, Brie."

Her dad with reluctance responded to her mom's comment with, "I love you more than you will ever know. Cate, what's wrong?"

Brie was silently screaming, *Dad how stupid can you be? What are you thinking? Brie wanted to shout, Stop! Dad, what are you doing? Don't go there please, it's a trap! This is Mom! Remember? Duh! Dad, she has fasted and locked herself away to hear from God, she is now able to discern everything!* Brie sat, petrified thinking, *I was foolish enough to believe I had a secrets, but I know Mom knows all about it, she's just waiting for the right time to call me on it. But, you, my poor Dad, I can't believe you didn't tell Mom about Jada.*

"Ladies," her dad announced, "I have something for each of you that will take the scowls off of your faces."

George unlocked the glove compartment and removed two boxes. He gave one to Cate and the other to Brie. Then George said, "On the count of three, open your boxes

Brie waited for her mother to open her box. When she did Brie heard a sharp gasp escape from her mother's lips.

Brie watched when her mother touched the ring, her fingers twitched, and a strange expression appeared on her face.

Cate gazed at the ring and then to her husband and she said, "Oh my goodness, George Alexander Hayes, yellow diamond! Where did you get them? Do you remember our old college friend, Jada Perkins?

Cate touched the ring and her body shuddered when she thought, *this is Jada's diamond ring, although ... the setting is different and Jada also had a bracelet.*

"Brie, do you have a bracelet in your box?"

"Yes, ma'am."

"This ring and bracelet are Jada's mom's yellow diamonds! George, Jada inherited them when her mother died. When and how did you get these?"

Brie screamed inwardly, *Oh no, Dad!*

Her mother held the box in her hands for a moment. She inspected the three-carat, yellow, cut diamond ring and then she abruptly closed the box, placed it back into the glove compartment, and hastily closed its door.

No one was talking, Brie sat silently admiring the beautiful diamond bracelet.

She thought, *Jada… Bank… The money…The bag… The ring… The bracelet… The $75,000 was used to pay for this, Jada's jewelry.*

Brie hastily took the bracelet off and placed it back into the box. She inserted it inside the car's back pocket compartment.

Her dad finally broke the silence when he announced, "Well, we are here.

"Cate, I do have some explaining to do but know this, I was only trying to help Jada… nothing more."

Cate smiled and said, "George, I wish you had told me, but God concealed your ruse from me and I know God has to have a plan with His timing. Do you remember when I arrived home, and I said to you, 'George, God's timing is always important,' and I was going to have some testing times ahead of me, but always remember no matter what happened that I trust and love you very much?' George, this is that day."

George pulled their car into the guest parking space and parked. No one said another word. Two church greeters opened their doors. The first greeter opened Evangelist Cate Hayes' door and helped her out of the car. The second greeter retrieved the evangelist's garment bag and escorted her through the side entrance into the pastor's waiting room.

George turned and winked at his daughter. He said, "Well Brie, I'm in deep trouble. Let's go in and see what God has planned. This morning, I read from the Bible, 'For I know the plans I have for you, declares the Lord, plans to prosper you and not to harm you, plans to give you hope and a future.

"I am praying that this is the day that I hoped to come. The day when Cate's and my future is strengthened."

Chapter 9, God's Timing

Brie opened the door to the choir room and saw Pastor Wilson greeting everyone in the room and asked them to remain standing and bow their heads for prayer.

Pastor Wilson prayed:

Father, we thank You for Your presence here with us and we invite You to come into our service with Your agenda. Father we are thankful for having Your appointed friend and bondservant, Evangelist Cate here with us today. This is Your day; we stand as one, in faith, looking for signs, wonders, and miracles. We have heard Your warning booms that has shook earth and in our spirit, we know the earth's atmosphere has also shifted. God help our souls to shift. Change us to believe, obey, and yield to Your discipline! Awaken those who are spiritually asleep. Change hearts and remove all masks. Amen.

They all repeated, "Amen."

Evangelist Cate smiled and nodded her head as an indication that she agreed with Pastor Wilson's words and then she declared, "His presence is weighty." She looked over each of them, lifted her head, and closed her eyes. When she opened her mouth, out erupted power that recharged and inspired every individual in the room whose heart desired to be changed. She said, "In Matthew 24:24, it has been written, 'For false Christs and false prophets will appear and perform great signs and miracles to deceive even the elect'—if that were possible.' Many are here today because they come seeking miracles.

"Our God is a God of wonders. To him who alone does great wonders, His love endures forever.

Our magnificent God is the Creator and Sustainer of all that is, God has the power to rearrange, interrupt, briefly halt, or even suspend natural laws in order to fulfill His purposes. Today, God will do miracles. Miracles were a part of the ministries of Moses, Elijah, Elisha, Jesus and His apostles. God's miracles are to validate His purpose of confirming His true messenger's message as being from God.

"The Bible also says, 'The salvation that was given to us is very great. So surely we also will be punished if we live as if this salvation were not important.

"Today, many people are here to seek and experience the miraculous; and some will go to great lengths to have that experience. But God knows those who are sincere and I am His humble servant. Let's pray."

Evangelist Hayes prayed.

Father, we magnify the office of Your power, we all stand here today only by Your grace and mercy. We thank You for Your forgiveness of our sins, for we all have sinned and come short of Your glory. I pray we, who stand here now, will not take Your grace and mercy for granted. Father, we dedicate ourselves to You. You are the potter and we are Your clay vessels and breathing our natural life from Your Spirit! Come, come now, and have Your way in each of us. We are Yours. I am Your yielded vessel, submitted to Your will and ready to be used for Your Glory. We thank You even before we see the manifestation of Your glory unfold with Your chosen ones who are in this tabernacle today. Father, thank You for choosing us, and this congregation for Your visitation. We thank You, Father. Amen.

She said, "I am going to touch you, when I do, you will feel a transition in your spirits. It's up to you to receive God's transformation."

Not saying a word, she touched them. When she touched Brie, Brie immediately felt a calming sensation throughout her spirit, a feeling she had never experienced before.

After Cate touched everyone, she shouted with happiness, "I will say 'Father, Son, and Holy Spirit' and all together, you shall all say, 'One!' "Everybody ready?"

"Father, Son and Holy Spirit." "One!"

The sound of their voices was so penetrating that the room shook!

Pastor Wilson's voice raved, "Oh, we can feel God's powerful currents! Heaven has already invaded our sanctuary! This is the Lord's house, and miracles will happen!"

Cate stood in a trance, to all watching it was obvious she was being enveloped with God's splendor. The intensity of His presence overpowered her. Tears washed her face and her radiant face was unveiled with His glory. The sensation of the power of His Holy manifestation coming upon her caused her legs to buckle.

Pastor Wilson asked the worship leaders to start morning worship while he and his wife stayed with Cate.

The door opened and Brie looked back. She heard Pastor Wilson asking an usher to find Brie's father and bring him to the choir room. Brie stepped onto the platform; she saw people were packed inside the church like sardines in a can. Brie thought. *Like canned sardines, they are waiting for that special key that has always been attached to the can, but needed someone to remove the key, insert it into the perforated lid, and pull the lid back to reveal and release its stench. Unlike sardines, the people inside the church are God's living chosen ones; their lives can be transformed if they desire by God's power. Once that happens, they will no longer be carriers of sin's stench.*

Those who come seeking will find their spirits, souls and bodies will connect with the life-changing, anointing of sweet fragrances of heaven.

'Whoa!" Brie thought, *what's happening to me? I'm thinking like my mom.* The church atmosphere was pulsating. God's Spirit hovered, ready to invade His earthly vessels as they awaited for His manifestation that was coming, along with a demonstration of His power.

Brie looked around and saw Cullen at the drums. He was winking to the pretty girls sitting on the front row, wearing very short skirts. They, like Cullen, were unyielding to the spirit of God.

Cullen looked up and out, over the congregation. He made eye contact with Grandma and Grandpa Jeremiah. Grandma smiled and Grandpa frowned; he was apparently still upset with Cullen and with Woody's remarks. Grandpa Jeremiah, too, sat unaffected by the upwelling of heaven's presence.

Brad began playing softly on the keyboard, and the congregation became quiet. One of the ministers stood and prayed. Afterwards, another minister read. "What if some were unfaithful? Will their unfaithfulness nullify God's faithfulness?

Not at all! Let God be true, and every human being a liar. It is written: 'So that you may be proved right when you speak and prevail when you judge.' But, if our unrighteousness brings out God's righteousness more clearly, God is unjust in bringing his wrath on us?

(I am using a human argument.) Certainly not! If that were so, how could God judge the world? Someone might argue, "If my falsehood enhances God's truthfulness and so increases his glory, why I am still condemned as a sinner?" Why not say—as some slanderously claim that we say— 'Let us do evil that good may result?' Their condemnation is just! What shall we conclude then? Do we have any advantage? Not at all! For we have already made the charge that Jews and Gentiles alike are all under the power of sin."

"As it is written:

'There is no one righteous, not even one; there is no one who understands; there is no one who seeks God. We all have turned away, they have together, and become worthless; there is no one who does good, not even one. Their throats are open graves; their tongues practice deceit. The poison of vipers is on their lips. Their mouths are full of cursing and bitterness. Their feet are swift to shed blood; ruin and misery mark their ways, and the way of peace they do not know. There is no fear of God before their eyes. [i]

Brie shuddered; those words hit her like a ton of bricks. She had taken her will and non-submissiveness to church, before the presence of God, who was listening to her, watching her ungodly actions, and knew her heart, and now she was getting ready to sing a song, Brie thought,

How many times have I read and heard the message preached, 'My sacrifice, O God, is a broken spirit; a broken and contrite heart you, God, will not despise

Sorrowful tears unyieldingly came from her spirit, and began to flow through her soul. Her mind began to contemplate the meaning of the word contrite: which meant a grieving, penitent for sin. Brie stood behind the podium feeling regret for all of her wrongdoings. She held the microphone, wiped away her tears and opened the service singing with a repentant heart.

God You alone know each of our stories.
You alone see our hidden sins.
Reveal to us now.
So we can repent and change within.
Change us!
Oh God, take away all our guilt.
And change us!

Suddenly, Brie's pronoun changed. The plural, *us,* became singular, *I.* She sang her own lyrics.

I repent of my sins,
My heart is broken."

Brie lifted her hands to God; fully emancipated, she sang from her heart that knew what worshiping in spirit and truth meant.

Brie's soul was uninhibited, she was forgiven by God. Smiling and really happy, Brie moved across the platform holding the microphone to her mouth. Through her tears, she sang:

I feel You!
I feel Your presence within me.
My chains are gone!
I'm forgiven,
I'm free! I've been changed!

Brie stepped down off the platform, walked over to Jada and embraced her. Brie held Jada's hand and sang:

I am free!
I'm changed.
I'm set free,
I'm changed. I'm changed!
Look at God,
He changed me; I'm not the same.

No more gambling, no more drinking.
No more pretending to be something I'm not.
I've been set free.
God's grace and mercy has changed me
Praise God, He has changed me.
All chains have been broken! Look at God!
I am free! I am free! I'm changed!
Look to God!
He has changed me.
He will change you, and you and you.

Brie spotted Woody. Their eyes locked and she did the unthinkable. Now unbound, she ran to Woody, looked into his dark eyes, and she sang,

I am no longer the same,
My days of sinning are over.
From the inside out. God has changed me.

Brie pointed to Harry, Woody's bodyguards who sat wiping tears and continued to sing,

"He will do the same for you.

Brie turned toward her mother, who stood on the platform crying. Brad watched from behind the keyboard with tears in his eyes, laughing as Brie continued her song.

She sang:

Mom, I've been changed from within. I'm no longer the same.

Gyrating in the spirit Brie looked toward heaven and continued,

God, You've changed my mind
You've changed my heart.
I'm no longer the same.
You've set me free.
All my chains are gone.

Tears stained Cullen's face while he watched Brie's

breakthrough. He too felt as if his heart was ready to burst, but he chose to ignore God's invitation to repent. Cullen looked at Brad's face and he recalled Grandpa's words when he told him. *Bradford is free in his worshiping, free from lying, or deceptions, or from keeping secrets. He can worship God in spirit and truth.*

Cullen watched Brad as he effortlessly played heaven's melodies. It appeared to Cullen as if God's words were being downloaded into Brad's spirit, Brad played and he too sang God's prophetic lyrics.

God's presence, ignited the congregation. The people's sincere worship welcomed God's presence. His weighty glory came with wind and oil, mingled with fire.

His luminous glory filled the sanctuary.

After worship, it was time for the message. Pastor Wilson stood beside the podium and spoke a few words to the congregation. He asked them to stand and give the praise team some love. They stood to applaud when the drummer hit a beat and the keyboard player responded, and the church had a praise break!

The praise break only seemed like a few minutes, but it was actually at least twenty minutes before they finally sat down and Pastor Wilson introduced Evangelist Cate Hayes.

When she stood, she greeted the congregation and gave honor to Pastor Wilson and his wife. She thanked God for her husband and her beautiful, talented, changed, daughter, Brie. Cate lifted her hands and blew kisses towards heaven and shouted, "Thank you, Jesus!"

Then she said, "As I scan the congregation, I see

many old and new friends.

Now my eyes may be playing tricks, but was that Jada Perkins sitting on the second row that my daughter hugged? If so, please wave to me." Jada waved. Then Cate said, "Jada, you being here is an appointment from God."

Cate laughed and said, "I just mentioned your name as we drove to church. It's been more than twenty years since we last spoke and I am so happy to see you here today." Then she said, "I love you old friend, I will always love you!"

Evangelist Hayes turned and motioned for the praise team to stand. She took the microphone and she sang with such power.

> Elohim. You are God!
> With Your Words, light came With Your breath, man lives.
> Breathe on us, with the wind of Heaven.
> Send Your fire to sear our hearts.
> Then smear us with Your holy oil.
> As we surrender our will to Yours.
> For Your name is El Shad-di'.
> You are our all sufficient, Our God Almighty.
> Breathe on us.
> Consume us with the fire of heaven. Elohim!
> You're God! Elohim!
> You're Lord! Elohim!
> We worship You. Elohim!
> We praise You. Elohim!
> We adore You. Elohim!
> You are our King.
> For we surrender our will to You.

As Evangelist Hayes sang, God's presence permeated the hearts of His pursuers. God's Spirit inundated the church. Everyone there was visually overwhelmed with the weightiness of His glory, even Woody.

Evangelist Hayes spoke briefly and concluded her sermon with Revelation 4. She declared, "Holy, holy, holy is the Lord God all-powerful. He always was, He is, and He is coming."

While speaking, she noticed the ushers moving to get ready to collect the morning offering.

She stepped away from the podium and spoke briefly to Pastor Wilson. Returning to the podium she smiled and announced, "Ushers, please listen, no offering will be taken.

"People of God it's not by coincidence you are here, your presence here was appointed by God. Listen to me, please. God only wants you. He does not need your money. Today, the church does not need your money. We are here to offer you Jesus. I am here to declare God's message. I can't put anyone into heaven, nor can I put them into hell. The life you chose to live does that. Right now God is saying to you, "Examine your own hearts."

"God is offering to you, right now, salvation. His salvation is your freedom from sin. There are many Bible verses telling us about 'The judge.' My favorite scripture is, He, (Jesus) ordered us (his Apostles) to preach to the people, and solemnly to testify that this is the One (Jesus) who has been appointed by God to Judge the living and the dead.' John 5:22 says, 'For not even the Father judges anyone, but He has given all judgment to the Son,' and, John 5:27 tells us, 'He gave Him authority to execute judgment, because He is the Son of Man.'

"God himself became a man and dwelled on earth as Jesus; Jesus lived among man and He did not sin. Hebrews

4:15 says, For we do not have a high priest who is unable to empathize with our weaknesses, but we have one who has been tempted in every way, just as we are, yet He did not sin.'

"Therefore, He that did not sin as the Son of man will judge the living and the dead. Now, the Father's heart is seeking and searching for surrendering hearts to hear His Son's voice and come to Him. Our Father is love. He's offering salvation to you; His salvation is your freedom from sin.

"Yes, the Day of Judgment will come, and it is so near. Jesus Christ will return in glory and we all will stand before Him to be judged by Him. However, in this moment, the Son of God, whose name is Jesus, is knocking at your hearts. He wants to come into your soul to live in you.

"How would you recognize His knocking? Let me tell you. It's that fluttering you are now feeling coming up from your spirit into your soul. That's Him. It's that supernatural wind that's blowing and you are now feeling it; that's Him

It's the heat, His fire, you are experiencing in your body right now; it's revitalizing your spirit, that's His salve that gives comfort and relieves all pain. His oil heals all of sin's diseases."

Evangelist Hayes moved from behind the podium and stood in the aisle. She asked the congregation, "Can you feel Him?"

From the pews, many answered her questions with, "Uh-hum," and "Amen."

Evangelist Hayes walked over to the front pew and she looked at a small child sitting in the fifth pew. The little girl looked to be about the age of six. Evangelist Hayes gave her microphone to the nearby usher and signaled with her hand to the child, indicating she wanted here to place her hands over her ears. The little girl looked at her father for his approval and with his hands he signaled to his daughter, "Yes." Then the child stood.

Evangelist Hayes asked the girl's father to bring the child into the aisle. She then placed her hands on the child's ears. Evangelist Hayes stepped back to watch. The girl stood stunned. Evangelist Hayes smiled at the child's reaction, and she asked, "Did you feel that?" The little girl giggled and shook her head up and down indicating that she did. Then Evangelist Hayes told the little girl, "It's God's Spirit you are feeling. His presence is in you. Psalms 16:11 says, 'In thy presence is fullness of joy; at thy right hand there are pleasures forevermore.'"

She asked the child, "May I hold your hands?" The little child extended her hands. Evangelist Hayes held the small child's tiny hands; the child buckled and her father immediately caught her.

Evangelist Hayes spoke directly to the child. She said to her, "Baby, I know you are hearing my words. So, with your hands, signal yes, to me. The little child, still giggling, signed with her hands.

"Yes."

Evangelist Hayes exclaimed with excitement when she said, "Okay, baby, just repeat what I say, "I can hear."

The little girl repeated, "I can hear,"

"Jesus loves me."

"Jesus loves me."

The little girl, still giggling, tugged at her father's jacket. She softly said, "Daddy." Her daddy reached down and scooped his daughter into his strong arms, smothering her face with his wet tears. The little child took hold of her father's face and yelled, "Look at me Daddy! Daddy, I can hear!"

Thunderous praises erupted, and Evangelist Hayes turned and spoke to the jubilant congregation, "Every praise is to our God." She took the microphone from the hands of the usher. She told the congregation, "God just gave us a visual using this little child. God, our heavenly Father is standing in front of His mercy, seated in His throne room, looking and waiting for you to tug on His heart and call out, I need Your Spirit."

"The Bible says, 'For the Law was given through Moses; grace and truth were realized through Jesus Christ.'[32] Calvary gave us entrance into the throne room of God. The Bible also tells us, "Let us therefore come boldly to the throne of grace that we may obtain mercy and find grace to help in time of need."

"When you come with a repentant heart, God's Spirit will immediately lift you into His arms and smother you with His kisses. His tears, He will shed from rejoicing and laughing over you. His tear of joy will wash away your sins, and place you into His heart forever. The Bible says, 'Unfailing love, His grace and His truth have met together. Righteousness and peace have kissed.'"

Evangelist Hayes turned and walked up three of the

five steps when she suddenly stopped and turned back to the congregation.

With her fourth finger she pointed in all directions, shouting, "That fluttering you are feeling right now, the heat, or the prickling, the stinging, that relentless sensation you are having, it's God! You are experiencing the presence of Jesus and He's here.

"That tingling on your skin is the..." her voice rose to a higher pitch when she said, "touch of Jesus!"

She pointed to the middle row and said, "You, there, the beautiful lady in the yellow dress." A woman in the same pew pointed to herself. Evangelist Hayes said "No, not you but you are beautiful and you will be blessed.

You have been chosen by God to receive. I need the lady you are sitting next to on your left in the other yellow dress to stand.

Would you please help her to her feet? They stood. Evangelist Hayes said to her, "Sister the Spirit of God just revealed to me that you have been this blind woman's helper for many years.

I am asking you, 'Woman of God' to confirm that she is blind?" The Woman of God who helped the blind lady to her feet, moved her head up and down, indicating yes.

Evangelist Hayes then spoke directly to the blind woman. She said to her, "Remove your own glasses."

Then Evangelist Hayes started to giggle just like the little girl did before she received her healing. She said to the congregation. "God is and will be doing great miracles here this afternoon."

 To the woman who helped the blind woman stand,

Evangelist Hayes said, "Woman of God, I want you to hold out your hands in a receiving position. Get ready to receive this fireball from God. When you hold God's fire in your hands, you will feel its intense heat, yet it will not burn your hands. Once you feel the fireball on in your hands, you will immediately separate it and place the fire that is in your hands over the blind woman's eyes. When you do this, she will receive her sight. Are you ready?'

Evangelist Hayes began laughing. She looked over the congregation. She told them, "This supernatural fireball will be visible."

Evangelist Hayes again asked the Woman of God, "Are you ready?"

"Yes!"

Evangelist Hayes reached up to heaven and said, "God, I am in position to receive."

Suddenly, breaking through the church's roof and not consuming it, a supernatural fireball fell from heaven into Evangelist Hayes' extended hands and she held it! Her face glowed with the surge from the fire that she held in her hands.

Immediately, she pulled back her arm and she released the fireball towards God's chosen woman.

Evangelist Hayes yelled, "Woman of God, catch this!"

The woman stretched out her hands and caught the flaming ball. She juggled the fiery ball between her hands and as she held it, her countenance radiated.

Evangelist Hayes said to the Woman of God who held the fireball, "You are feeling like you are going to explode." Holding the fire, the Woman of God bobbed her head up and down. She felt as if she couldn't contain the joy she was experiencing. Evangelist Hayes said, "Psalms 16:11 says, 'You make known to me the path of life; you will fill me with joy in Your presence, with eternal pleasures at Your right hand.'

Evangelist Hayes spoke directly to the woman who was chosen by God to hold His fiery glory and asked, "Woman of God, do you think you can contain your joy for a moment?"

She answered her with laughter and replied with a shaky, "Yes."

Evangelist Hayes told her, "Now separate the ball of fire and place each piece onto the blind lady's eyes."

The Woman of God moved her hand back and forth, separating the fiery ball into two parts.

She then placed the flaming parts onto the blind woman's eyes. Immediately, the fire vanished. The blind woman screamed, "I can see!"

Then, throughout the congregation thunderous praise erupted.

Evangelist Hayes asked the Woman of God who held the fiery ball how long had she known this woman?"

She responded, "Seven years."

Evangelist Hayes then asked if there were any others who knew this woman whom God healed.

She told them to come and stand with her so there would not be a thought in anyone's mind that this was some sort of lie or trick. Fifteen or more people stood, each vowing they knew the blind woman. Evangelist Hayes exclaimed, "Saints, this is another God given visual. Now you know and believe God still does miracles with signs and wonders."

Evangelist Hayes walked toward the podium. She stopped to look to her old college friend, Jada, and smiled. She walked over, and touched her. Jada's head jerked back like someone who just touched a hot plate. Jada fell to the floor and crumpled into a fetal position, weeping.

Evangelist Hayes paused and looked at her, not saying a word. She looked up and out into the congregation; she extended her hands and spoke with a commanding voice as she pointed and shouted, "You, you, all of you, and even myself are having a first time experience in God!

"Woodrow. God is calling, Woodrow. He wants you to know that this day is your day for restoration." Evangelist Hayes waited, and no one stood.

She said, "I know you have to be out there amongst us because God has highlighted your name." She was adamant and relentless, turning and looking for Woodrow. She said, "Woodrow, you can hide from me, but not God, please stand. Wherever you are, please stand." Rising like a phoenix, wearing a bright red suit, Woodrow stood.

Evangelist Hayes' greeting was unfeigned when she saw him standing. She said, "Woody." She walked down to his pew

Woody stepped out to greet her. She took his hands, gave him a hug and smiled. Brie and Brad glanced at each other. Cullen's eyes began to seep tears.

Grandpa leaned over and whispered into his wife's ear, "Lovetta, look at him, Woodrow Hugh Parks, Ha!

God highlighted him! That man is nothing but the devil wearing fire."

"You stop it Jeremiah Sullivan! You're in God's house, show respect. Remember, God defeated the devil!"

Clearing his throat, Grandpa softly elbowed Grandma and whispered, "Vetta, look at him in that red suit. His name should be more like Hugh-mongous.

You get it Lovetta, humongous! Hugh-mongous liar, humongous thief, humongous dope dealer and a hugh-mongous, deceitful killer."

Grandma nudged Grandpa softly in his ribs and whispered, "Jeremy stop! And those are the very ones for our humongous God to save. Now stop your accusations and hating and pay attention, Jeremy. God is trying to help your mind."

Smiling broadly, Grandpa retorted, "Lovetta, you know that big man ain't ready to change. He loves his filthy money too much."

Grandma hissed, "Jeremiah Sullivan, please shut your mouth. Remember you're in God's house, shush now!" Grandpa shook his head and snapped, "Uh-hum, we will see, we will see."

Evangelist Hayes put the microphone down and spoke to Woody in private then she prayed for him and he walked away with tears falling. She walked back to the front and looked down on Jada, still laying on the floor. She said to the congregation, "Right now my dear friend is experiencing God's fire." She pointed to Jada, who seemed lifeless, laying on the floor covered up with a blue prayer blanket. Evangelist Hayes said, "Ummm, Jesus shed blood.

The power of the blood changes lives, not only her, but every one of you sitting here. At this moment you are feeling the charge of God's *D.E.S.* His 'Direct Everlasting Spirit' penetrating from His breath into your spirits, permeating into your souls and your bodies. Look around.

"Can you see it? His glory is tangible." Evangelist Hayes extended her hands to heaven and she declared, "Jesus Christ, the King of Glory is here. People, open up your hearts and let the King of Glory come in. Today, right now, you must choose Him. He chose you before the foundation of the world. Unfortunately, for many of you who are sitting here hearing my voice and the words that I am now speaking, that hell is bursting at the seams and overflowing with people like you who were forgiven, but chose not to receive His forgiveness. They chose to die in their sins. That does not have to be you. This is your day for salvation this is your moment, come!"

Many people rose from their seats and accepted God's invitation. As the people were coming, she uttered, "Many of you are sitting here and you are feeling God's heartbeat. You have seen His power come with demonstrations and many of you are still second-guessing God's truth.

My prayer for you right now is found in Second Timothy chapter two; Paul wrote, 'Maybe God will let them change their hearts so that they can accept the truth, because the devil has trapped them and now makes them do what he wants.' Timothy prayed they would wake up to see what was happening and free themselves' from the devil's lies, secrets and deathly deceptions.

She extending her hand and told them, "You have to

choose. Come on, come on. Jesus is waiting. Come now, in faith. Come, be free. Come!"

Evangelist Hayes' voice broke, and she cried out seemingly with deep disturbance in her soul. She bent her body over in distress. She was filled with raw emotion. She raised her hands and fixed her eyes toward the ceiling as if she had been transported into the throne room of God.

In the microphone she declared, "My Lord, our God! You are worthy to receive glory and honor. You made all things. Everything exists and was made because You wanted it." She looked around; her face glowed and gold dust fell off her robe. She exclaimed, "Come on people of the Most High God, Jesus is here! Right now! In your spirits, I know you are feeling Him moving. I can feel His power and I know you are also feeling Him. Jesus, who is the King of Glory, is here! He is the living God! Come on, come on, come on down!

The fire on the altar of God is burning, Jesus is here! Come!"

People were coming from all over. Some crying, some shouting, some dancing, they were coming to Jesus. They were coming to change their lives.

Brie gazed over the people coming. She saw her father walking down the aisle crying, and seemingly broken. Brie saw her mother step down from the podium and open her arms to embrace him. Her parents embraced in a loving hug right there in the aisle. Brie read her mother's lips, when he said, "George, I love you and I trust you, all is well" She gave him a quick kiss then returned to the podium.

From the podium, Evangelist Hayes watched as Woody stood and walked toward the exit. She made a statement directly toward Woody, which many took for themselves. She stated, "Listen, there are some terrible times coming in these last days. 2 Timothy 3, says, people will love only themselves and money more than God."

As Woody walked him phantom chided him saying, I told you not to come here, get out fast! Leave Now!

With each word Woody heard and with each step Woody took, he felt like a knife was being plunged into his heart as Evangelist Cate Hayes quoted from the Bible the written words of God. "The Bible says,

"They will be proud and boast mightily about themselves.

They will abuse others with insults and physical violence, even death.

They will turned on their mother and father.

They will be ungrateful and against all that's pleasing to God

They will have no love, and will refuse to forgive anyone.

They will have no self-control.

They will be cruel and hate what is good. They will turn against their family and friends.

They will do foolish things without thinking and will be so proud of themselves and instead of loving God, they will love sinful pleasure."

Woody stopped. He momentarily stood against the side wall of the church. He stood there weeping, watching, and listening. *What? Why are you listening to that woman's deceitful words? Get out!*

But, know this," she bent and kissed her nephew's forehead, she put the microphone down and whispered into Cullen's ear.

"Cullen Michael Sullivan, my precious, precious nephew, that kiss was from God, He said for me to tell you this… When you're in trouble, remember that kiss, then repent. His grace and power will be rekindled inside you, leading and guiding you."

Evangelist Hayes picked up the microphone and smiled at her nephew, she told him, "Cullen Michael Hugh Sullivan, God said He will always love you, and when you say His name, Jesus, He will be your immediate help."

Cullen sat crying, yet unresponsive to the call of God.

Evangelist Hayes moved to the center of the church and continued, 'They will love sinful pleasures. If you know these types of people, the word of God tells us to, 'Stay away from them! To run away from them.

If you are one of those people you need to change. This is your opportunity, this is your day, Jesus is waiting, please come."

Woody stopped, squatted down, and supported his back against the wall with his face in his hand. He felt the pull of God's grace and mercy on him, but instead of coming down, he stood to turn away.

In the microphone Evangelist Hayes continued, 'those who are evil and cheat others will become worse and worse. They will fool others, also themselves.'

I am not making up these words. Paul wrote them under the inspiration of God. Read Second Timothy chapter three yourselves and you will see I am speaking truth, and remember God's word doesn't need to be defended. His blood sealed His Words!"

Evangelist Hayes watched as one of Woody's personal bodyguard, pushed open the double doors for him to exit, and the other bodyguard, placed his hand on Woody's shoulder. She saw Woody angrily pushed his hand away and walked through the open doors. The last words Woody heard in church from Evangelist Cate Hayes were, "God loves you, but you must choose to love Him. The choice will always be yours."

As Woody walked out, he didn't know that his wife Jada stood to give her life back to God.

Evangelist Hayes watched as Jada came. She extended her arms and held her. As Evangelist Hayes held her old friend, she sang to her.

He's a God who forgives.
He's a God who doesn't keep scores.
He's a God who loves you more
Then you will ever know.
Thank You God for Your great grace.
You have wiped away all her sins.

Evangelist Hayes looked to heaven and sang.

God help her to walk, with and through your power.
God help her to walk, pleasing for You.
Leading her safely home into your glorious throne.

After singing, Evangelist Hayes, kissed her old friend's cheek and helped her back to her seat.

She turned towards the praise team and gestured for Brie to sing. When Brie took the microphone from her mother's hand, her mother hugged her. Brie felt like she was being electrocuted and crumpled onto the floor. Brad watched from the keyboard. He turned on his microphone and he sang, "He has changed me."

Evangelist Hayes looked toward the exit door that Woody left through. She then glanced at her father, who was now standing against the wall glaring at Woody as he walked out the church doors.

Through her tears Cate Hayes thought, *Woody, Dad, and Cullen, the three of them sat in the presence of God, and refused His invitation to change.*

They ignored God's invitation for freedom. All Dad had to do was forgive, and by refusing to forgive he remained bound.

Woodrow refused to let go of his evil controller who has no love for him and has captured his spirit, soul and body, and locked him in hell's prison. A prison where only Woody can unlock the door. And Cullen sat, smiling at the girls, caught up with the promise of fame and sinful pleasures. He denied God's invitation to change, believing he could come when he's ready.

Evangelist Hayes, walked back to chair with a heavy heart. She firmly held onto the chair's side arms, and fell to her knees, buried her head into the chair's seat cushion and heavily sobbed.

Chapter 10. Changing of the Guard

A few hours had passed since morning service and the Rock, Sullivan, and Hayes families met for a late dinner in a private room at the Original Steak House.

Cullen, Brie, and Brad sat together at the opposite end of the dining table and listened to the adults' laughter as they reminisced about their past. Brie, with her left shoulder, lightly bumped Cullen's shoulder. She leaned over and whispered into Cullen's left ear, "Cullen, isn't my mom the coolest Evangelist you know?"

She then put her hand over his and said, "Cullen, this morning wasn't an act. God has changed me and I have put a lot of thought into what I am going to tell you." Cullen gently held Brie's hand as he reached for his water glass. He said to her, "Wait, I need to take a drink before I hear this earth shattering news."

Cullen took a few sips of water then he told Brie, "Go ahead, tell me."

Cullen took another big gulp of water just as Brie whispered, "I am going to go to Bible College."

What?" Hearing Brie's words sent sprays of water from Cullen's mouth across the table onto his Grandma. Cullen Michael!"

Cullen jumped when he heard his name.

Cullen looked over at his grandmother. The water that had sprayed from his mouth had soaked her face and dress. He quickly stood, grabbed his napkin and rushed to his grandmother, apologizing. Grandma Vetta, instead snatched the napkin from her grandson's hand, and wipe her face.

"Cullen, what was so surging that you sprayed my face and dress with water from your mouth?"

Brie apologetically, said, "I'm sorry, Grandma Vetta, it's my fault. I just told Cullen I'm going to Bible College."

Hearing Brie's words stunned them all to silence. Cullen still too antsy to sit, shouted, "See, all of you are shocked and that's why I sprayed water on you grandma, it was Brie's fault."

Bursting with happiness, Brie's dad broke their silence. He stood, and clapped his hands, he shouted with glee, "Cate, see! I told you she would follow in your footsteps!

Brie stood, still laughing at their reaction to her news, she walked behind her mother's chair, placed her arms around her neck, and said, "I am so proud of Mom. Seeing Evangelist Cate Hayes today was as if I was watching her the first time. God working through you mom was truly amazing."

Cate stood, pulled her daughter into her arms and told her, "Brie,

I am skipping on cloud nine for you. However, there are three things I am going to tell you, and you must do them."

"What are they, Mom?"

"You must remember to keep God's words burning in your spirit, to remove yourself from anything that is

 oppositional to God's commandments, and finally, love,

even when it's not merited."

Cate embraced Brie she saw Brad watching and he smiled and gave Brie a quick wink and two thumbs up.

After hours of laughing, talking, and enjoying themselves, they finished their meals, said their goodbyes and went their separate ways.

At home, Brie changed out of her Sunday clothes and called Brad and Cullen to see if they could meet up at the park. Brie was first to arrive. Usually, she would be hiding behind the big locust tree smoking pot. Instead, she sat on the park's low stone wall, tossing rocks into the pond.

Brie looked up and saw Brad as he jogged towards her. Brad scooped her into his arms and they kissed.

Cullen jogged slowly toward them and watched. Since they were obviously unaware he was there, he cleared his throat. "Ahem. "Ahem. Okay, Brie, what's going on here? You can't keep your lips off my buddy."

Brie and Brad laughed at his remarks. Brie looked at Cullen as she held Brad's hand and told him, "We are in love."

Cullen grabbed Brad, giving him a strong hug of approval. Then he embraced Brie. Grinning, Cullen asked, "When is the wedding?"

Brie responded with a nervous giggled, "When the time comes, Cullen, you will be the second to know."

"Second?" Cullen shouted. "Really?

"Yes, my friend. You will be second."

Brie quietly moved away from them while they continued their playful bantering. She sat down on the park's bench. Tears filled her beautiful green eyes. Brad and Cullen stopped their razzing to look in Brie's direction and they became aware of her sadness and came and sat next to her; Brad tenderly lifted her chin and asked, "Brie, what's wrong?"

She looked at him, forced a slight smile and said, "Brad, I am worried about dad. I hope he will not be in too much trouble."

"What happened? Brie, why are you worried about Uncle George? Tell me, Brie what's up?"

Cullen looked to Brie for answers. Instead she murmured to Brad, "Go on, tell him."

"Cullen, I believe Brie is concerned over nothing. Months ago, Brie saw Jada kissing her dad in his study."

Cullen, being frolicsome, shouted, "What! No way! My Uncle kissed Jada, he is one lucky man!"

"Cullen!" Brie hollered, "This isn't the time for your witticisms.

"Okay, I'm sorry," Cullen gave a quirky smile and asked, "Okay tell me, where, when and why did my idol, my uncle, kiss Jada, Woody's woman?"

"Cullen," said Brad, "sit and listen and you will understand Brie's concerns."

Still feeling witty, Cullen started, "Wow..." but his puns were interrupted when Brie hand cupped his mouth and she hissed, "Cullen, be quiet. Go over there on the bench.

Just sit and listen please."

Cullen sat, smiling on the bench and Brad said to him, "You really need help man." Brad continued. "After Jada left their home…"

Cullen interjected, "Wow, Uncle George had Jada in Aunt Cate's home while she was away preaching God's word!" Cullen smiled and said with guarded admiration to his boldness, "Uncle George!"

"Cullen!" shouted Brie, "Please shut off your warped mind for a while and listen."

"Okay Brie, I was just teasing. I'll zip my lips and turn off my warped mind. I am now ready to hear the truth, because I know there has to be a good reason why that *fine woman* was in Aunt Cate's house."

"Cullen!"

"Okay, okay, Brie, I'm finished, go on, continue Brad." Cullen used his fingers to zip his mouth closed.

"The next day, Brie waited around in her room for the expected call from f Jada to her dad and that's when Brie heard Jada begging for her dad's help and for money. After the call, Mr. Hayes had to go to the bank and asked Brie if she wanted some lunch?

Brie needed someone to talk to. She asked her father if she could invite me and they picked me up at my house. On the way to the café, he stopped at the bank. While Mr. Hayes was inside the bank, Brie told me what happened.

I will not go into the details"

"Oh, man! I want to hear the details."

Brie, gave him a quick karate chop motion, and Cullen sealed his mouth for the third time.

"We went to eat and while sitting in the café Brie and I watched Jada coming through the door. Mr. Hayes also saw her; he quickly scribbled something on paper, folded it, and excused himself to go to the restroom. As he walked passed Jada, we saw him drop the folded note on her table. She read it. In a few seconds she got up from her table, walked over to the men's restroom door and knocked twice. The door opened and Mr. Hayes followed Jada out the side door.

Then Brie followed her dad outside and watched her dad give Jada the white envelope in exchange for a brownbag."

"May I ask a question Brad?"

"Yes you may Cullen."

"What was inside the white envelope?"

"$75,000."

"Okay... and what was inside the brown bag?

"Jewelry. This morning on their way to church, Brie's dad surprised them with gifts. He gave a ring to Brie's mother and a bracelet to Brie. When Brie's mother touched the stones in the ring she knew they belonged to Jada."

"So Brad, what you are saying is the brown bag contained a bracelet and a ring, and it was Jada's jewelry that Uncle George bought for $75.000."

Shaken by what he heard, Cullen stood to pace. He looked at Brie and questioned her. "Brie, this is serious, you are sure you saw Jada kissing Uncle George? Woody's woman, Jada! And Uncle George gave Jada $75,000 that you assumed was for the jewelry.

Brie what's really going on?"

"This is insane." Cullen snapped. Uncle George making out with Jada, Woody's woman! And giving her money!" Flailing his hands, Cullen angrily hissed through his teeth, "Uncle George must have lost his mind and Aunt Cate?" Cullen turned to Brie and told her, "Brie, there has to be more going on here? More than you know because what I just heard doesn't make any sense.

"Also, if Aunt Cate knew about the jewelry, *how* could she have preached knowing all of this? And God…*why* would God let her interact with Jada and with Woody and perform miracles through her? Then hours later we all met. We ate and talked together and Aunt Cate seemed happy."

"That's because she doesn't know the details. At least I think she doesn't know. Mom, she is an enigma, a discerner. She will patiently wait until you come clean if there's too much of a time lapse, she will come to you."

Brad walked over to the bench and sat next to Cullen. He told him, "Calm down Cullen. In my opinion, it's not as bad as it sounds

You see, Mr. Hayes didn't kiss her back, despite all of the flirtation and seduction from Jada in their parlor."

Brad shook his best friend's shoulder hard, and he repeated slowly, "He didn't kiss Jada back when she kissed him. Mr. Hayes told her to leave, and to never come back to their house.

Before Jada left their home, she gave him a note. The next day she called telling Mr. Hayes she needed his help.

That's when he gave her money in exchange for the jewelry."

Shaking his head, Cullen asked. "How do you know all this Brad?"

Brie, not smiling, raised her hand and said, "Me. I

listened to dad and Jada's phone conversation through the opening over my dad's study. He had their conversation on the speaker phone and I heard everything."

"Brie, "said Cullen, "I think Brad is right, it's not that bad. I should know, after all I am the experienced one here when it comes to women. Brie, Uncle George didn't kiss Jada. She kissed him. From what you and Brad just told me, Uncle George didn't do anything wrong, he was only trying to help her."

"Yeah, Cullen, "but what about the kiss?"

Through his clenched teeth Cullen said. "Brie, think. It was Jada who kissed him, your dad didn't return her kiss. Uncle George didn't respond to Jada's full luscious lips and , oh, oh, oh ... her body and her ceaseless seduction… And man that must have been God because that woman is." Interrupting him, Brie shouted, "Cullen! Stop, right now!"

"Okay Brie, but Brad you know I'm right about Jada?"

Brad put both hands up in midair and quickly expressed. "No, my friend, I am not going there with you. My Brie has her black belt."

Brie, not finding either of their remarks amusing, stated with scorn, "Funny, guys."

Dissatisfied with their reasoning, she yelled, "But I watched her kiss my dad and daddy didn't push her away!"

Simultaneously, both Cullen and Brad shouted, "That's because he was in shock!"

Cullen took hold of Brie's hands, he looked her in the eyes and said, "Brie, Uncle George is a saved man who love your mom, my Aunt Cate very much. But, cousin, if that was me, I would have yielded to her."

Displeased with his comments. Brie released Cullen hands and she told him, "You really need God's help! Cullen, will you ever change?"

"I will, Brie, one day. But, right now, don't talk salvation to me. I do know this you are worrying too much. UncleGeorge and Aunt Cate are solid."

Cullen kissed her cheek, then stood and stepped away from her. With perceptiveness he said, "Brie, Brie, no way, could it be?"

"Be what, Cullen?"

"Think about this! Jada asked for $75,000. I believe if we put together the moneywe won from Woody, it would total $75,000 or a little more with our last winnings"

Hearing that amount of money won by Brie and Cullen. Brad collapsed on the grass and sat speechless listening to Cullen's reasoning.

"Brie, I believe Woody is collecting what we have won from him over the years." He used Jada as his pawn to get to Uncle George."

"Cullen you are right. That night Jada left my parent's home, I remember the moon was bright and from my bedroom window I watched Jada getting into the passenger side of a parked car. When they pulled away, I recognized the driver. It was Woody.

"At the café, after their conversation, I ran into the restroom and as I was drying my face Jada came inside without looking around. She opened the stall door to go in and as I was leaving I heard her saying, 'Woody, I have the money.'

"Ten minutes after the call, Woody walked in."

"Cullen?" Brad said, "You believe Woody is collecting what you and Brie have won from him."

"Yes, I do."

Cullen turned toward Brie and with sadness he told her, "You know, Brie, my mother and father were Woody's best friends in college. Woody always told me that he was my godfather. When I asked Grandpa he replied angrily… now let me get Grandpa's tone right." Clearing his throat, Cullen continued, "Boy, that hippo of a so called man… he's no godfather to you. He's nothin' but a big devil; stay away from that so called, wannabe man.

"I now know that Grandpa's voice is a voice of experience.I remember when I was ten and you were six, the church was having their annual picnic. The older men were playing football. Michael Jay, and Anderson came by and Woody was with them and asked to play. I remember Grandpa was wearing a Hawk's football jersey with the number 75.

I recalled when Woody tackled Grandpa, he always hit him hard. With one hard hit, we all heard Grandpa's back crack. I was the first to get to him and I am just now remembering Woody's words to Grandpa as he lay there in the grass, squirming in agony were, 'I loathe the number 75 old man.' Grandpa was rushed to the hospital, and after surgery he had to undergo months of physical therapy. Since then, he walked with a slightly bent back and his back injury was one more reason for grandpa not to like

Woody."

Cullen released a broken heartfelt sigh and spoke words aloud that had haunted him for over 10 years. He said, "I wish I could have known my parents "

Brie noticed tears welling in his eyes. She scooted her body closer and put her arms around his waist to console him.

"Cullen, I do know a little about Aunt Sally and Uncle Michael's car accident."

"""What? You do? Tell me what you know. Our grandparents never talk about my parents."

"Neither does my mom, Cullen, but one day when I stayed overnight with our grandparents, I overheard Grandma's conversation on the phone."

Cullen lightly bumped Brie's shoulder and told her, "Brie you are a snoop, I'll have to watch myself around you."

"Funny, Cullen. Do you want to hear what I have to say?"

"Yes, cuz, I do, I just couldn't help myself. Go ahead, tell me what you overheard."

"Grandma was talking to her cousin Thelma.

Grandma told Thelma that all that week she felt something bad was going to happen to your mom and dad if they went out of town to that gambling casino with Woody. Grandma and Grandpa pleaded with Aunt Sally not to go, but Woody needed a ride, and they were set on helping him.

"Grandma told Thelma the officer in charge of investigating the accident was Grandpa's friend. He told

Grandpa that Woody told the police that your dad had drank too much and couldn't drive. Grandpa knew Woody lied because your dad never liked the taste of alcohol and Aunt Sally didn't know how to drive."

"Brie, I never knew any of that. My grandparents never talked about Mom and Dad. Grandpa always warning me that Woody could not be trusted."

"Cullen, our family is good at keeping secrets. I didn't know until fifth grade that my mom and your mom were twin sisters."

Brie continued with her story. "Grandma told Thelma, months after Aunt Sally and Uncle Mike's deaths, Woody came by the house to talk.

Woody told our grandparents that he was drinking too, but not as much as your dad and Woody was actually the one who drove. Grandpa called him a 'bold face liar' and told him he had some gall to come into his house shedding those fake tears. He told Woody that he believed he murdered his daughter and her husband for some unknown reason and Grandpa ordered Woody out of his house.

"Grandma told Thelma that she and Grandpa saw Woody's police report concerning the accident.

Woody told the investigating officer that they were ten miles from home when a wrong way driver slammed head on into their car. When Woody swerved, a second car hit them. Their car went over the guardrail and flipped multiple times. It plunged 300 feet down the side of an embankment, rolled several times and burst into flames as it came to rest near the river.

"Woody's wasn't wearing a seat belt. His car door opened and he was thrown out. Uncle Mike wasn't wearing his seat belt either. His body was thrown from the car and was never found; they believe he was washed away. Aunt Sally's body was still in the back seat of their car, she was wearing her seat belt and she was burned beyond recognition. They had to have a closed casket at her funeral. Then, many months later, Woody bought his own gambling place. Grandma told Thelma, she and Grandpa Jeremiah often wondered if Woody used the money Uncle Mike won from gambling to buy that building, but they had no proof."

Cullen's head dropped onto his chest as he released a deep mournful sigh. He said, "Brie, in one night, I lost both of my parents."

"I am so sorry, Cullen."

"That's okay, Brie. I know how my parents died now and after all these years I now know why Grandpa Jeremiah can't forgive Woody."

Brie stood. She frantically flung her hands in the air. Her innermost thoughts, which she had held back, erupted. She vented, "Cullen, Woody has always been or has become one of the most disgusting people living on earth. He was driving, and he lived? My question is how's that possible?"

Brie looked at Brad and said, "I know I just got saved, and supposed to love, but how can you love someone like Woody?"

Brie looked up to the sky and said, "God, please forgive me, but why did You let Woody live?"

"You and I saw how he treated Jada at the restaurant Brad. He doesn't care about anything or anybody. Woody's first and only love is himself and, oh, let's not forget, money, and we all just now realizing Woody is nothing but a lowlife, and he has no morals."

Cullen sat saying nothing for a long time. Brie, who was now sitting on the grass, looked at him through tear

Cullen told her, "Brie, go home. If your conscience is bothering you, then you need to talk with your dad about what you saw."

Cullen leaned over, and teasingly rubbed her head with his knuckles. He smiled and said, "Go ahead, tell your dad that you, and your detective partner, Brad, were spying on him, and Jada."

In in his own defense Brad said, "Hey man, I just sat in the café. It was Brie who did the spying."

Brie nodded her head and said, "Okay, Cullen and Brad, I am off to talk with dad, and yes, I did all the spying by myself, therefore I will take all the blame." Pouting she told them, "Some friends you two are, you are leaving me all alone and hanging me out to dry, I have to admit, I am so guilty!"

Brie looked at Cullen, she gave him a wry valiant smile and said, "I hear you Mr. Cullen Michael Sullivan.

I will do just that!"

Brie stood, released a loud sigh and said, "Well, I guess it's time for me to go home. She kissed Brad and punched Cullen on the arm. Then she started her customary backwards jog while staring at Cullen and Brad who were still sitting on the bench. She shouted, "Cullen, I still can't believe it. Woody lived! *How* is that possible?"

Chapter 11, The Boss

At early evening, the casino was lively with sounds of laughter, but when the door opened, a cold breeze was felt. A sudden chill crept over the room as the angry, defiant, tyrant himself entered with his two lapdogs, Luke Allen and Harry Brown, following.

Woodrow Hugh Parks, the owner of the newly renovated casino, walked into the dimly lit room. He stopped, and immediately all chattering ceased as Woody stood he coolly stared into the eyes of the men and women sitting around the tables; one of the servers scurried to remove his coat and take his hat.

Woody then turned and walked down the long hallway leading into his office followed by Luke and Harry, his personal bodyguards, who were right on his heels.

All head casino employees were summoned to wait for him in his office. When Woody arrived at the entrance to his office; he stopped. Harry stepped in front of him, opened the door, and stepped back. Woody walked in. When the men heard the door opening, they quickly stood.

Upon entering the room the men addressed him with, "Good afternoon, boss."

Unresponsive to their greeting, Woody approached the table and stood as Luke Allen scrambled to pull out his chair. Woody sat and his bodyguards stood behind his chair.

As he sat in silence, he icily stared at the men in the room. He then motioned Luke Allen to pull his chair out.

Luke quickly responded giving his boss more than enough space to stand.

Woody walked to the center of the room and slowly pulled his jacket back to reveal his firearms. He lingered for a few seconds, sending intimidating signals to those who worked for him. With his angry red eyes and a cynical smile curving his lips, he unhurriedly walked around the table calculatingly, glaring, and instilling fear into each man's soul.

As Woody walked, he intentionally stopped by selected men's chairs and abruptly swiveled their chairs toward him. He momentarily lingered in their faces, enjoying watching grown men squirm in fear.

Good. Woody thought, *'They know their place'*

Woody came and stood next to his baby brother, MJ. Woody smiled at him and he did not flinch. MJ looked him in his eyes and asked a question. "Woody, why are we here?"

Woody tapped his face and said, "Watch the attitude, baby brother. The ice you're standing on is very thin."

Woody sat down in his overstuffed designer leather chair at the head of the table. His chair was decadent by some standards. It was fashioned with fine gold thread that was intricately woven around the exterior. Diamonds and rubies decorated the armrest of the black leather chair. It was indeed a chair designed for someone of high stature.

With his head bowed and not looking up, Woody addressed the group in a low menacing tone. "I called this meeting to discuss the events from last Saturday."

He lifted his head and watched as his casino workers' bodies shifted positions, showing their discomfort with this topic of conversation. Seeing their reaction only fueled Woody's anger. He said, "I was informed that Cullen Sullivan and his cousin, that girl Brie Hayes, won over $10,000 apiece."

He clutched his hands together, and leaned forward. He said, "I know I informed those in charge that Brie and Cullen weren't allowed in this casino, and if they came to inform me. My question is directed to each of you sitting around this table, when they arrived, did any of you call?" Not getting a response, he put his head down and stared at Anderson's gold pocket watch that sat on the table. He turned his head and looked directly at his cousin, Anderson.

"Anderson, you were their game manager that night. Is that correct?" Anderson nodded his head, meaning, "Yes."

Angrily, Woody slammed both hands on the table, causing it to vibrate. Woody yelled, "I do not understand your nod Anderson! When I speak to you directly I expect your answer to be, Yes, sir, or no sir. Do you understand?"

Without waiting for a reply, Woody stood and walked around the table shouting at the top of his lungs,

"So Anderson, I will ask you again! Were you the game manager that night?"

Anderson rapidly replied, "Yes, sir, Mr. Woody, sir."

Woody walked over to MJ. With controlled tension in his voice he looked at him and asked, "Were you the floor manager

Woody's brother, MJ pushed out his chair, stood and saluted Woody, and said sarcastically, "Yes sir, Mr. Woody sir,

Anderson nervously stood.

MJ stood with Anderson and from the far corner of the room he said, "Take it easy man." With alarm, he asked, "What are you about to do? What's the matter with you man, are you crazy?"

Woody screamed, "Crazy? Did you say crazy? Well, my little brother, you are about to see crazy!"

Woody's eyes were blazing red as fire. He yelled, "$25,000 between Cullen and Brie!" Woody looked at Anderson and screamed, "All that money was taken from my place by some kids who were not supposed to be here and I'm not liking it!" Woody turned, walked across the room, hesitated, and then kicked over the small table in the corner.

MJ looked at Anderson in fear.

Anderson's stomach knotted.

MJ asked, "Woody, what do you mean by calling out Anderson?' Others in this room work for you besides Anderson and me."

"Well, my baby brother, you are about to find out what I mean!"

Lifting a gun from the table, Woody said, "I will tell you this… I do not intend for Cullen Sullivan or Brie Hayes to ever win in my place again.

"Also know this," staring at them, he said, "game managers and floor managers are easily replaced."

Woody banged his fist on the table and shouted, "MJ, your job is to watch everything, not drink my liquor or make out with my working girls! You see, I have suspected you and Anderson for a while. You both are stealing from me.

One is taking money and the other is giving away drinks. I am more than disturbed, I am angry. You and Anderson, my flesh and blood, are stealing from me. I know this because my books have been short."

MJ said, "Man, I am hurt. Giving away a few drinks is stealing from you? You are doing this to us? Woody there's no way Anderson and I would intentionally steal from you."

"You're hurt? What about me? I didn't know who it was, until I had video cameras installed. Now I have my proof."

"Woody?"

"Shut your mouth, Anderson."

Woody pointed his gun at Anderson and stared grimly into his eyes and said as if his heart was breaking, "You, my dear cousin, Anderson… you stole from me." Pounding on his chest, he repeated, "Me!

… Me! ... Me, of all people! It was you who stole from me!"

Woody shrugged and sighed heavily. He attached a silencer to his gun and uttered a shaky laugh as he pulled Anderson from the wall and knocked him to the floor.

Woody fell on him; his weight alone could have suffocated him. Laying on top of Anderson, Woody put the gun into his ear and said in an evil, terrifying whisper,

"No one steals from me! Do you hear me? … I said no one!"

Zing!

Those in the room heard a muffled bang followed by a lamp shattering onto the dark hardwood floor. Everyone at the table jumped but they sat there, not daring to move.

Woody rolled over to a chair, pulled himself up, and quickly grabbed Anderson from the floor, holding him by the neck. He knocked him back onto the floor. Towering over him and looking down, he began to laugh. He pointed to the lamp and said "That lamp could have been your head, smashed in and scattered like a watermelon."

Woody motioned for his bodyguards and screamed, "Pick him up!"

Holding Anderson between them, Woody walked around Harry and Luke as they supported Anderson. Woody stood in front of him and spat in his face and said, "It's too late for you my sweet cousin. You are a dead man, destined to hell."

As Woody stepped away, he saw the gold watch his dad gave to Anderson on the table. It once belonged to Anderson's father, who was Woody's father's brother; he died when Anderson was twelve.

As Anderson was being held to the wall between both bodyguards, Woody snatched Anderson's gold pocket watch from the table and grinned. Holding the watch, Woody told Anderson, "I will keep this as payment for all the money you took when Brie played at your table. I estimated it to be about $5,000."

Woody tossed the watch on his desk and it fell onto the floor. Woody turned toward Anderson and slipped on some water on the floor. He noticed Anderson had soiled his pants. Delighted in what he saw, a crooked smile formed on his face. He snatched Anderson into his arms and taunted him by saying, "Look here, guys. The poor, poor baby has peed himself. He needs his diaper changed."

Woody's employees sat stunned at the table listening to Woody's relentless, diabolical taunting of Anderson. He looked at them and hollered, "Laugh!" Like marionette puppets on a string they all nervously laughed.

Woody pointed to his workers and he warned them, "Keep your mouths shut or you or a family member will die!"

He shouted, "I will play a game now! Woody says, 'stand up.'" They stood. "Woody says, 'push in your chair.'" The legs of their chairs squealed against the hardwood floor as they simultaneously pushed their chairs in.

"Woody says, 'turn around and look at me and in unison shout, sir, yes sir, boss.'" They turned and in unison shouted, "Sir, yes sir, boss!"

With a ghastly frown, Woody hollered, "You, morons. Get out!"

They quickly rushed out the open door. Luke closed and locked the door behind them.

Woody turned to look at his cousin, covered with blood. With a sing-song tone he sang, "There were ten and now there's five, and soon the five will become three."

He ordered his two henchmen to hold Anderson.

Woody stood, staring at Anderson and not saying a word. He suddenly snatched Anderson from the arms of his henchmen and slammed his head against the wall. Anderson fell and crumpled onto the floor like a wad of paper, making pathetic, whimpering sounds. Woody, consumed with rage, spat again into his face.

MJ reached out and grabbed Woody's arm and said, "That's enough! Look here, Woody, I know you are very angry about the money won by Brie and Cullen, but you are going about this all wrong. This is insane! What will you get out of this by making examples of Anderson and me? We are your family man. We are your flesh and blood. I am your brother and I have your back but look at how you are treating me and Anderson. He's your cousin man!"

Woody did not respond. Suddenly, like a rattlesnake, he struck, screaming, "You have my back? It's more like you're using me! It's a good thing you are my brother because I could kill you too."

MJ shook his head, not believing the words he heard. He repeated, "Kill me, too? No man you must be joking. Kill me, too! You aren't planning on killing your cousin?"

Woody smiled as he said, "Watch me!"

"Woody, this is whacky. Man, no!"

Woody laughed, his eyes reddened and his skin tone darkened, He said, "Baby brother, I am whacky and look at me. Does it look or sound like I am joking? Let me tell you why I am so angry, Momma's little boy."

Woody looked at his henchmen and said, "Pick that dirt bag up and sit him on that chair." Anderson's head slumped over and blood poured from his mouth onto his pants. Woody went over to him, and lifted his head by pulling on his long, blood-soaked braids. He said to Anderson, "My dear sweet cousin, that Sunday morning, I called Cullen and I went to church with him. After church, I sent you and George Allen away and I came back here and I watched the newly installed surveillance video. I saw you, Anderson, stealing, and you, Michael, giving away my liquor." Woody let go of Anderson's braids and Anderson fell out of his chair onto the floor.

Woody walked over to his oversized desk and started pounding his chest. He shouted, "My! ... My! ... My liquor! That liquor that purchased with *my* money you gave away, Michael!"

Turning to Anderson, he pointed and said, "And on the same surveillance video I saw you, Anderson, my cousin, pocketing my cash! How much have you taken from me? Hundreds, thousands, ten thousands?" Walking over to him, he slapped Anderson's face and said, "Oh I forgot, you can't talk."

"Harry."

"Yes, boss."

"Did you get those supplies on the list Luke gave you?" "Yes, boss, I did."

Woody sat down and said to Harry, "Open the bag and take out the vinyl tarp."

Harry removed the plastic and held the tarp in his hands. Woody barked, "Cover my chair."

"Yes, boss."

Harry hastily covered Woody's prize chair while Woody rolled up his pant legs and put on the plastic rain coat. When Harry finished he said, "Chair covered boss."

Woody stood, walked back to his desk, picked up the pitcher of water, and dumped it on Anderson. He was bruised and barely alive as he looked at Woody through his swollen eyes. Woody motioned his bodyguards to handcuff his cousin to the chair he had just covered with the vinyl tarp. Anderson's head slumped and Woody patted Anderson on his face and ordered him to wake up. Anderson lifted his head and Woody told him, "Cousin you have always liked this chair, so I was thinking, you might as well enjoy your last moments on earth sitting in it. I also want you to know why you are dying. You are dying because Brie and Cullen took $20,000 from me. And you took $4,500. Plus the $500 you have tucked away in your sleeves.

Woody ripped his shirt sleeves and took out the money and counted, one, two, three, four, five hundred dollars.

Between you, Cullen and Brie you have taken $25,000. My money!

Woody walked to the corner where an aluminum bat was leaning against the wall. Woody picked it up and held it between both hands as he walked towards Anderson.

Harry shouted, "Woody, no, don't do what I think you are about to do?"

Bam! Harry hit the floor.

"Shut up, Harry! Have I given you permission to think? You know you are always expendable. Now get up, go in that corner and shut your mouth."

Harry stood and slowly backed away. Woody stared and laughed at Harry as he stood in the corner and he said to him, "Harry, my friend, I own you."

Woody took two practice swings with the aluminum baseball bat. Slowly, he rotated his body. With tension in his voice, he said to his brother, "Michael, just as Jesus died for your sins, Anderson is also dying for yours and his!"

Bam! Anderson let out a painful groan. Woody dropped the bat.

"Michael!!" Woody screamed his name as he advanced towards him. "I will now show you how I feel about you, my brother, talking with my working girls and drinking with them, and giving them my liquor. Free!"

Breathing hard, Woody shouted, "If you can't trust your own relatives, then who can you trust?"

Bam, bam! Woody hit MJ in the stomach with his fist. He said, "You didn't expect that, did you my brother?" MJ dropped to the floor.

Woody then lifted the bat to hit Anderson in the stomach. Anderson weakly said, "Woody, no man, forgive me, I am so sorry. Woody, my family needed food and I needed to pay the bills. I figured you would think Cullen and Brie had won it. I'm sorry man, please don't do this. Think about my kids and my wife."

"You can still talk! You figured I wouldn't miss my money?" Woody's laughter became even more loathsome and he answered back with a low raspy tone, "You figured all wrong, cousin!"

With tears profusely running, Anderson said, "I'm sorry man, but I had no other way of getting money for my family."

"Stealing from me was your answer? Why didn't you come to me and ask?"

"I did, and you told me no!" "Oh yes, I did, didn't I?"

Bang! Teeth flew from Anderson's mouth as the bat hit his head and knocked him out.

Woody dropped the bat, and he motioned for his bodyguards to come to him.

Woody ordered Harry to get out of his office and wait outside the door until he call for him. Harry stood, wobbling, he walked out the door.

"Luke?"

"Yes, Boss?"

"Pick up my brother from the floor, and beat him until I tell you to stop." With a vile smile, he sneered,

"I am in a killing mood, and I do not trust myself.

Woody's other bodyguards, Red, Pete and Luke began punching MJ while Woody watched. After a time, Woody raised his hand and shouted, "That's enough!"

"Luke, check Anderson."

Luke bent down to check his pulse. Woody asked, "Is he dead?"

Luke replied, "There's a slight pulse."

Anderson's body was bloody and his face was smashed. Woody picked up the bloody baseball bat, and turned to MJ, who laying on the floor and twitching with pain. Woody watched with delight and hissed, "My baby brother, you are highly blessed today because I am not going to kill you. But remember, I have the power in my hands to let you live or die. I am a liar and I could easily change my mind, and the only reason I am saving you is because of Momma."

Woody reached into his pocket and took out his money clip. He counted out $10,000 and order Luke to stuff it into Anderson's jacket pocket.

Woody hovered over Anderson and said to him, "You, however, won't live. I just stuffed $10,000 in your pocket to help that fine wife of yours pay your bills until she finds a job."

Woody squatted, and whispered into Anderson's ear. "I'll tell you what, I will take care of your pretty wife." Woody winked at Luke and Luke laughed, obviously enjoying the moment. Woody then yanked Anderson up by his braids and said, "I will put your fine wife on the street."

With a devious smile, Woody said, "Cousin, every day is a good day to die, and today isn't yours.

Woody stood, picked up the bat, and rotated it in his hands, and Bam! Bam! He laughed as he hit Anderson with his aluminum bat and he shouted, "Then again, you know I am a liar!" Bam!

Woody threw the bat across the floor and it landed near the back door. He ordered his bodyguards, "Wrap him in that vinyl tarp, and get Harry."

Woody went into the bathroom, removed his plastic raincoat, stuffed it into a plastic trash bag and washed his hands. When he returned, he saw Anderson's body inside the vinyl tarp. Woody said to Harry "Dump him in the Hayes' front yard. Luke, take MJ to his apartment. If my baby brother lives, he better keep his mouth shut. And if he dies there, it's still good."

Chapter 12, Confession

Opening her parent's front door, Brie overheard her father's apologetic voice as she watched her mother and father from the partially open door of his study.

"Honey, I am so sorry I kept this from you."

Brie listened; her mom's voice seemed very calm when she said, "George, I remember our college days. Jada had you wrapped around her little finger. All she had to do was bat those longvelvety eyelashes, and she had you. She was your first love, and me, your second. However, I never felt threatened by her even though she was on the same campus with you and I was several miles away on the Bible College campus. When I came to see you, I stayed with her in her dorm. I have always trusted you, and I still trust your love for me."

Brie's anxiety over her mom and dad's marriage was settled when she heard her mom's laughter. "George even then, Jada did everything she could to break us up. Do you remember the night of my graduation?

"Yes Cate, your parents were waiting to meet me at the restaurant and I never showed up?"

"Oh, how my Dad disliked you."

"Cate, 'disliked' is a mild description; your dad hated me. Thank God for your mom because she was his voice of reason." "Now, honey, you do know hate is a very strong word. I would say you were double disliked by my dad because, Mr. George Hayes, my dad thought you were playing his daughter for a fool."

Brie's watchful eyes appreciated and loved her dad even more. He held her mom in his arms and said, "Yes, Cate, I remember that day all too well. My parents and I were waiting for you at my dorm."

"George, do you recall why you and your parents were waiting for me and my parents in your dorm room?"

"Yes."

Her father moved away from her mom, pondering the question his wife had asked. *Do you recall why you and your parents were waiting for me and my parents in your dorm room?"*

Brie's dad sat on the edge of his desk and answered her mother's question.

"Cate, it was Jada. Woody gave me a typed note that was supposed to have been from you. The note stated that there was a last minute change and we were going to meet in my dorm room instead of the restaurant."

"George, I still recall how I begged mom and dad to wait. We waited for two hours. I was humiliated when you didn't come. I flew back home with Jada, her Mom, and my parents that evening with a broken heart."

"Cate, I recall sitting at the dorm that evening with my parents waiting for you; they left my dorm room inwardly gloating, knowing their opinions about you were factual and you were not good enough for their son.

Shortly after, they left, I heard knocking on my dorm door, and I hastily opened hoping it was you. Instead of you, it was Woody. He told me he had waited in the lobby for my parents to leave my room. He wanted to keep me occupied. He kept reminding me that my parents were right: their rich white son should have never been contemplating marriage to a little, pretty, black, church girl."

Cate got up from the sofa, and walked to the fireplace. Brie noted how beautiful her mom was. Her jet black hair that she usually wore pulled back was loose and rested past her shoulder. She was still dressed in her black and white suit and looked chic. Her mother was fifty-five years old, and could easily pass for thirty. She was shapely with beautiful light brown eyes and flawless, mahogany skin.

Her mother turned to look at her dad and gave him that beautiful, deep, two dimples smile. She told him, "George, I also have amazing recall of Jada sitting next to me on the plane, telling me what a loser you were. She explained how she had experienced the same pain when you broke up with her. Now, when I think back on that day, I realize Jada's words were repressed. She gave her words careful thought when she told me that she had talked with several other girls who had dated you."

Smiling, her mother slowly glided over to her dad, touched his arm and said, "Honey, according to Jada's recollection, you left them all with broken hearts

I recall how she so tenderly held my hands when she hesitantly said, "Cate, sweetie, I am so sorry that I had to be the one to tell you about George Alexander Hayes. There were too many girls in and out of his life, far too many to count."

Brie noticed how her father lovingly held her mother in his arms and sincerely said, "Cate, Jada lied. I only dated two women, her and you."

"I know, dear, but I remember I sat on that plane crying into tons of tissues, believing her; and all the time she was lying."

Cate pushed out of her husband's arms, held his hands and said, "The diamonds, George! Now I remember."

Cate walked about in circles and slowly recounted, "George… that was when I first saw Jada's yellow diamonds! We were on the plane. As Jada was consoling me, I saw the yellow diamond ring and bracelet she wore. I recall asking her about them. Jada told me they were her grandmother's and then her mother's." Cate hesitated to think, "Her mother gave them to Jada as a graduation gift and Jada told me she hoped to one day be able to give them to her son or daughter."

Brie, holding her breath, shifted her position in order to cautiously and quietly lay down upon the hardwood floor so that she could continue listening as her dad related his experience.

"While you were flying home, Big Woody was with me in my room at the dorm. I was packing my things to return home.

Woody told me he was tired of my sulking over you. He reminded me that you were a church girl and your mom and dad were strict parents. Woody stated that Sally resented living under your parents' 12:00 midnight curfew. He said I needed to forget you and come with him because he knew places where we could go and …" George laughed and said, "Cate, get this, Woody has never changed. He said he knew places where we could go and spend my money gambling my sorrow away. "Her father lowered his head and told her mother, "Cate, I finally had heard enough of his mouth, and I grabbed him by his collar and told him to get out of my room!" He slowly walked to the door and opened it. When he turned and stared back at me, I yelled, "I meant what I said, Get out!"

He stood in the hall, looked at me and said, "I really hate saying this, but you really love that little church girl, don't you?" "I shouted, 'Yes! I love her, and I see you hate asking? Why, Woody?'

I recall how guarded he was with his response to my questions. It seemed he had become inwardly irritated with himself because he was ready to divulge a cunning secret that would somehow impact his life. I became overly provoked by Woody. I walked to my opened door and ordered him to leave and that's when he decided to come clean. Woody told me Jada had asked him to give me the note. Woody claimed he didn't know what she had written because the envelope was sealed.

"It's really ironic isn't it, Cate? Jada dropped out of Bible College, you graduated from Bible College. Jada transferred to be with Woody. Then Woody, your sister, her husband, and I all graduated from Business College. Jada, Sally, and you were raised in a Christian home, and while Jada and Sally both knew about God, they still turned away from Him. I did not know about God until I met you and accepted Him.

"When you did, your parents were really upset. Your mother just knew your father's political career was doomed. Your father was this influential and very successful politician and businessman, who was planning to run for Governor. Then you, their only son, became a Christian. Not just a Christian, but an Apostolic believing Christian who loved this unsophisticated black southern Christian girl and secretly married her! Our marriage was totally inappropriate, shocking, embarrassing and totally unacceptable to them. Your father cut off all financial support from you and even took away your car. They tried in every way conceivable to break up our marriage. It was several years before they accepted me as their daughter-in-law."

Cate's husband walked over to her, he scooped her into his strong arms. Grinning, he said, "Look what God has given me! I have not one but two precious, precious, priceless jewels."

They kissed. When he released his wife his voice became very cynical, he said to Cate, "Then back into our lives like a bad penny came your sister and her husband, dragging their old friend, Big Man, Woodrow Parks, W.P. Woody Parks.

"Cate, Woody has always craved to be the center of attention, and was always very conniving. As I recall he was also very, very lazy. In college, Sally told me Woody paid others to do his class work. He attended classes once a week and he used study notes from her and other students. Then he would come to class and ace the exams.

Woody found what he wanted... the easy way. He went about accumulating his money by selling drugs, running numbers, and using people. Since you've been gone he has renovated this decrepit building in our old neighborhood and now calls it a casino. I heard he's into prostitution; Woody has stooped as low as he could go.

"I found something out before Jada and I exchanged the money for her diamonds. She and Woody are married and they have a three-year-old daughter. Woody does not know he has a daughter and Jada wants to keep it that way. Jada's sister, Sharon, and husband, Ray are raising Jada's daughter as their own. Woody is now using Jada- his own wife- to hustle money. What a loss, and what a big disappointment Woody has become to his mother."

"George, I am praying for God's protection and strength for Jada. She gave her life to God today, and Woody isn't going to receive that very well.

"As we all know, Sally and Woody were best friends. They did everything together. I heard Mom warning Sally so many times not to trust Woody. Dad and Mom agreed that Woody seemed to have many dark secrets and they were always warning Sally and Mike to be careful when they were with him. And Dad just didn't trust him! He believed Woody had something to do with his own father's death."

"What! This is this first you have spoken about your father believing Woody could have had something to do with his own father's death. Cate, please explain."

"George, perhaps I shouldn't have said anything but Woody's father and my dad were best friends.

I overheard my dad telling my mom that his friend was always sad. Dad always said he felt as if his friend carried a heavy burden that he couldn't unload, and he seemed to be excessively protective and concerned for Woody. When Woody's father suddenly died, my dad noted that Woody never cried. Dad said, Woody seemed almost jubilant."

Cate let out a heavy sigh and she whispered, "Woody." She walked to the window and stared, not turning around, she said, "I remember being at Sally's house that Thursday morning. Woody stopped by to see if they were still going to the big party, he needed a ride because his car was in the shop. He told Sally he had planned to make lots of money that night doing what he called, 'his thing.'" Sally told him about Mom's dream and she didn't really want to go, but Woody was relentless. And after pleading with her to take him, he wore Sally down and she said, 'Okay, Woody, when Mike comes in from work I will tell him that you need our help.'

"The weekend Sally and Mike died, I recall Mom calling Sally numerous times pleading with Sally not to go. When Sally dropped off baby Cullen at my parents' house, I stood silently in my parents' front room. I watched my mom, with tears staining her face, beg Sally and Mike not to go because she had a reoccurring dream that something bad would happen. At the same time, Dad was telling them if they were wise, they would listen to Mom and drop Woody as a friend.

Sally laughed at Dad and told Mom and Dad that they were just being overprotective of her. She felt Woody could be trusted; he was their friend and always would be. When they died in that car accident and Woody walked away unharmed, Dad never forgave him. To this day, Dad believes Woody had something to do with Mike and Sally's death.

Brie sat on the floor on the other side of the polished, dark mahogany pocket doors, listening. She was in disbelief, startled by what she was hearing. Brie watched when her father walked behind his large wooden desk; he opened the middle desk drawer, and took out a framed photo. After looking at it, he gave it to her mother and asked, "Cate, do you remember when we all posed for this picture?" Her mother gasped as she took the photo from his hands. She said, "George, this picture was in Sally and Mike's home, and when they died, Dad tossed it."

"I know Cate, I was helping him clean out their bedroom and I retrieved this one."

Brie watched as her mom paced with the picture in her hands and pondered over it for a few minutes. Finally, she said, "Yes, I remember, George. It was taken on Mike and Sally's wedding day. They were preparing to leave for their honeymoon when Dad had Mike, Sally, Jada, and me to group together for this picture."

Beaming, her mom exclaimed, "George, you were an unexpected guest.

Do you remember what happened next?" They both laughed. Her dad walked over to her mother, touched the frame and asked, "May I?"

He took the picture from Cate's hand and, smiled. He said, "Cate, your Dad wanted a picture of Mike and Sally, but you wanted a picture of Mike and Sally with you and me, and your dad adamantly said, 'No!' Then you got frustrated with your dad and you were determined to have your way, so you invited Jada. Your dad only had one flash and he gave in, and just when he was about to snap the picture, in came Woody.

"Then Sally insisted Woody should be in the picture with all of us. Your dad surrendered and he put Jada, Sally, and you in front; Mike behind Sally, Woody behind Jada, and me behind you. While focusing the camera, your dad started giggling and Sally asked, 'Dad, what are you doing?' He kept gesturing with his hands and yelling for Jada, and Woody to keep going backwards then he shouted out, 'No, stop!' He then said to me, 'You, white boy, hey boy, how about you and my daughter switch positions and you move back, just one step'. We did, and he shouted. 'No this is not right. Woody, I need you to move back, yes that's it, go back just one more, no two more steps. I am almost focused. Jada, one more step to your right and Woody, take just one more step back,' and splash! Woody fell into the pool. He couldn't swim, so Mike and I had to jump in to save him. Your dad stood next to the tree snapping pictures. Sally yelled, 'Daddy, I thought you said you only had one flash left?' Your dad responded, 'Yep, for that camera.' He continued to snap pictures and laugh hysterically while watching Mike and I drag Woody out of the pool. "When Mike and Sally left for their honeymoon your father said, 'George, you and Mike should have let that big man drown, he's no good.'"

Her father sat the picture on his desk. He said, "Cate, I took that picture from the bottom of the drawer a few weeks before Jada came to our home. Seeing all of us together and so much younger brought back memories, and that's why I found myself driving in our old neighborhood. I decided to take a drive just to reminisce.

"I remember now that it was right before dusk, I was driving slowly down Liberty Street when I thought I saw Brie and Cullen running across the street into a vacant building."

Brie placed her hands over her mouth to muffle her sudden gasp. She heard her mother ask, "Was it Brie and Cullen you saw?"

"I am 99.9 % sure it was. Your parents and I have been concerned about her and Cullen becoming mixed up with Woody for a while."

"I know. But Woody? He is a puzzle. God's word tells us that Jesus will judge men and our job is to live our lives as an example of God's character, to forgive, to judge our own actions and above all, we are told to love. But George, do you think there's any love in Woody?

"From what I have experienced being around him, I have to say no."

"George, even today when I gave to him what the Spirit of God gave to me to say to him, I felt his soul was being pulled deeper into darkness, and an evil familiar spirit had overpowered him, and it wasn't going to let him go, because Woody wanted it in his life and Woody didn't want it to leave.

"George, go ahead and tell me, what happened when you saw Brie and Cullen?"

"After an hour of waiting, I drove around the block thinking perhaps I would see them again. I recall it had rained heavily that evening and it was now dark. The old neighborhood was already abandoned with a few drifters mingling about. I wasn't going to leave so I decided to walk across the street to investigate the old abandoned buildings. That is when I heard a car speeding down the street. I quickly hid between the buildings.

I watched as the car stopped near the curve. Two men opened their doors, walked around to the trunk, opened it, pulled out a bag, and dropped it in the mud like garbage on the curb. They looked around to see if anyone was watching, got back into the car, and sped away. I remained between the buildings until the car was out of sight. I went over to see what it was, and to my surprise it was Jada. She was beaten badly, Cate, and it was sickening and my heart sank.

"I put Jada into the back seat of the jeep and drove her to Melvin's House for Battered Women. I left a $3,000 check for Jada with Melvin to help her make a change in her life. The next thing I knew, Jada was knocking at our door, asking for more help. She told me she needed $75,000. I gave it to her in exchange for the diamonds. I took the diamonds to a jeweler to have them reset. Despite the new setting, your discernment or long-term memory picked up that they were Jada's grandmother's diamonds."

Brie's dad pulled his wife into his arms, and he said, "Cate, there is one more thing I have to tell you."

Brie watched as her mother looked into her father's eyes. And her mother said, "I know, George, Jada kissed you."

George stood momentarily stunned. With a wry

nervous chuckle he asked, "When? How? Oh, yes, I know how. But Cate, then you also know Jada's kiss didn't mean a thing to me. Even so, when Jada kissed me, I didn't pull away."

Brie's mother pulled out of her dad's arms and stood, not saying another word. Her dad gazed into his wife's eyes waiting for a response, but she gave none. She stood in silence and an unexpected laughter erupted. She said to him in a teasing tone. "Well, George Alexander Hayes, did you enjoy that kiss?"

Brie, sat giggling to herself. She admired her mother even more. She loved her mother's cheerful, forgiving personality, and how she enjoyed teasing her husband.

Cate cooed, "So Mr. George Alexander Hayes, even in college, Jada was your 'Achilles heel' and you were always dazzled by her looks and she knew it. Some things never change." Cate sauntered up to her husband, put her arms around his waist and told him. "In a dream, I saw a woman kissing you." With a smile she said, "That's why God told me to cancel all engagements and come home.

I had to set my own house in order." Cate touched her lips with her finger and then with the same finger she tapped her husband's lips and teasingly said, "*After all Georgie Baby, you know you can't resist me*…. Isn't that the pet name Jada used to call you, Georgie Baby?" And your reply to her was, "*I believe I just did.*"

Shocked hearing her mother's accurate account of that night. Brie held her hands over her mouth, and her dad stood stunned. Her mother laughed and said, "Oh, George, I love you. It's been months since you have had any affection shown to you. I know it had to be your love for God and for me that restrained you from her sexual advances."

"Cate, "those words. God showed you that night Jada was in our home in a dream! Cate, the words you spoke were the exact words I said to Jada. Did you know about the jewelry?"

"No honey, God didn't show me that."

Brie watched as her mom comforted her father's troubled mind with a lingering kiss. Then she released herself from his embrace, looked into his face and said, "We had another problem. It was Brie. Brie and you were the reasons I came home. God showed me in a dream both Brie and Cullen drinking, and gambling, Brie smoking marijuana, and Woody planning to assault her. Both she and Cullen were hanging around Woody too much. And Cullen, he's becoming too much of a ladies' man. I was really worried about Brie and Cullen; ... I am still concerned about him."

"I know Cate. You just used the past tense verb, 'was'. Brie had a turnaround today. She gave her life to Jesus. She said she has changed, she's going to Bible College, and in love with Brad. Cate, we have to trust her, and our God's Spirit in her.

"Yes, you are right. Cullen, has no desire to do right. He keeps putting off his 'today' for tomorrow. Cullen knows well that his tomorrows aren't promised.

Brie quietly got up from the floor and walked quickly to her room. She sat on the edge of her bed to pray. She asked God to give her strength to make the changes needed in her life and to keep her favorite cousin safe.

From her vent she heard her parents praying. She knelt to listen to her father prayer.

"Father God, we thank You for Your love. We thank You for Your grace that taught us how to love and forgive. Cate and I are grateful for Your guidance and Your protection. Father let Your blood continue to cover and protect our daughter and nephew from evil. Let their desires be Yours, give Cullen a desire to change his ways and with Your help, Cullen will clean up his life. Place Your angels around Cullen. Give Jada the courage to walk away from her abusive relationship. Open the eyes to Woody's heart to see and to despise his evil ways, and surrender his life to you. Father, we thank You for Your protection. God give us ears to hear Your instructions and to obey You continue to guide us. Thank You, Father.

Amen.

Brie sat on her bed and cried. Moments later, she heard a light tap on her bedroom door. Cate heard her daughter crying. She opened the door and both her mom and dad walked in. Her mother sat on the edge of her bed and put her arms around Brie. She pulled her close and asked; "Brie, what's wrong?

Brie reached for tissues to wipe her tear stained face. She looked at her dad and said, "Dad, I was there."

Perplexed by her remarks, her father asked, "You were where, Brie?

"I was there. I was there sitting quietly in the front room behind the sliding doors spying on you when Jada was here, and I saw and heard everything, Dad."

"I am so sorry, Brie."

"No, Dad you haven't a thing to be sorry about. You are a good friend to her and an awesome Daddy." Her dad walked around and sat on the opposite side of her bed.

"And Dad, that night when you picked up Jada from the curb, you were right. It was Cullen and me who you saw running into the vacant building. We were going to Woody's to gamble.

"Mom and Dad, I also want you to know I am an eavesdropper. When we moved into this house I discovered if I sat near my vent I could hear your conversations."

Brie's father gave her an unemotional look and her mother sighed and replied, "I didn't know that."

Her mother's comment of '*not knowing*,' caused unrestrained laughter.

Gathering their composure, Cate said," So that explains how you were always one step ahead of your dad and me."

"Yes Mom, and ten minutes ago, I just sat outside your study as an eavesdropper, listening to you talk about Aunt Sally, Uncle Mike, Woody and Jada." Turning to her father Brie confessed, "I was there dad."

"You were where Brie?"

"When you met Jada. I hid behind the air conditioner at the restaurant. I was watching you, I saw when she tried to kiss you and you backed away."

Smiling, Cate teasingly said to George, "So you can resist her luscious lips."

"Not funny, Cate."

Profusely crying, Brie said, "Dad, I am sorry."

Her dad scooped her into his arms and said to his daughter, "Baby, you had every right to be concerned." He held her chin with his hand, he lifted her face to his and said, "Your mother andI are solid."

Brie smiled through her tears, she said, "I know you are dad. Remember? I was there, tonight, sitting on the floor listening outside your study." Brie held both parents hands, she told them, "Mom and Dad I meant it all! I have changed. My life is completely God's. No more Woody. No more gambling, no more smoking weed, no more cursing, no more drinking, and, Mom, I never lost my virginity. It's all finished! My dear sweet Cousin Cullen, whom I love more than my own life, must change and come with me, or I will have to drop him. I can't do this anymore."

Cate wrapped her arm around Brie, she said to her, "God has a plan for Cullen; and today, you stepped into your destiny." Cate gently released her daughter and asked, "Brie, is there anything else you need to tell your father and me?"

"Hmmm, no ... Mom... why? ... Mom?

Cate kissed her daughter on her cheek and said to her. "Okay then, now my precious angel, get ready for bed.

Today is the first day of your new beginning in God. Each day He gives a fresh day for new beginnings. Your past has been forgiven. Now, this hour, this day, all of your thoughts and actions are new. You are at this moment in the morning of life and new beginnings.

If God permits your life to move into high noon and then linger near the sunset, remember this; God has placed a call on your life. Stay watchful and hear God when He speaks. Be obedient to His directions so that you may help in the fulfillment of His promises and thereby you will be fulfilled. Our precious daughter, God's thoughts concerning you are written down in His book of remembrances. Make each day count, because tomorrow isn't promise to us."

"Brie."

"Yes, Daddy."

"My Miss Private Eye, you can stop your spying and eavesdropping. Come to us with your questions when you have them. Then all doubt and useless pain will be removed from your mind. We love you, Brie Katherine Hughes."

"Dad."

"Yes, Brie."

"Can we pray together? We haven't prayed together in years, because I avoided it."

"Baby that can be arranged." He held his daughter's hand and he kissed her cheek, he stood and took Cate's hand. Tears welled up in Cate's eyes as she tightly held her husband's hand. Together they bent their knees and Brie and her parents prayed.

When they finished, Brie's phone rings. Brie hastily reached for the phone, she told them, "Its Brad."

Her parents left out and closed her door. Through the closed door, she heard her Father's booming voice call out, "Tell Brad we said goodnight."

She heard her mother giggle when she shouted, "Tell my son-in- love I said goodnight."

Brie laughed nervously and she shouted back,

"What?" She thought, *does she?*

"Brad," Brie whispered, "I think Mom knows!

Chapter 13, Grace ... God is Good

Much later Cullen returned home from the park with Brad. When Cullen pulled into the driveway, he became uneasy upon seeing Grandpa Jeremiah sitting on the front porch swing, the front parlor lights on inside the house, and his grandma on the phone pacing. Cullen quickly put the car in park, worriedly got out, and hurried to the front porch.

"Grandpa what's wrong?" Grandpa placed his fingers to his lips. He snapped, "Hush." With his thumb, he pointed toward the parlor. "Just listen."

They saw grandma through the screen door. Cullen and Brad sat with Grandpa to listen to Grandma Vetta's conversation.

She said, "Thelma, of course we will."

Silence.

"We have extra bedrooms and I will fix one up for him.

Silence.

"Yes Thelma, Jeremy and I know all about that.

Silence.

"Yes Thelma, Jeremy and I know."

Silence.

"Cate and George will be able to help us, don't worry, but my heart is broken."

Silence.

"I love you too"

Silence.

"Bye."

"Oh, Thelma, please let us know if there's anything else we can do?"

Silence.

"Bye now."

Grandma Vetta stood frozen, holding the phone in her hand, they watched tears wash down her face. Grandpa slowly opened the screen door as Cullen followed behind him. Grandpa walked over to her, he gently removed the phone from her small shaky hands, and placed it back into the cradle. He pulled Grandma into his arms as she cried.

Brad's phone rang and he saw it was Brie. He answered her call. "Brie, I'm with Cullen at your grandparent's home. Grandma Vetta was on the phone talking with Thelma, now she's in tears. Get your Mom and Dad and come quickly."

From the screen door, Brad heard Grandpa when he asked, "Vetta, what happened?" Grandma Vetta's eyes filled with more tears. She took out her yellow hanky from one of the four pockets of her white house dress to dab her eyes. She gingerly sat on their brown leather, antique, conversation chair and told him, "Jeremy, you know that was Cousin Thelma on the phone. She said the police just left her home. They came to tell her that my sister is dead."

Weeping, she stood and staggered over to the huge fireplace shelves that held pictures of her loved ones. She picked up the picture of her sister, Maria, and clutched it to her heart. Through her painful heartache, Grandma

Vetta continued, "Tom is okay. He's at the hospital and physically, he will be fine."

Grandma Vetta's body began to tremble and she became unsteady on her feet. Both Grandpa and Cullen rushed to reach her. She composed her emotions and tightly held both of their hands. She said, "Jeremy, my sister is dead. Both Ben and Maria are dead."

Brad, outside the screen door, listened with tears flowing. He heard a car and saw Brie's parents pulling into the driveway. Within seconds, Brie and her parents stood with him outside the screen door, listening as Grandma Vetta continued. "Tom told the police that his mom and dad had been arguing all evening. Ben had been drinking heavily since he lost his job at the law firm a few months back, and Tom said his dad had become more and more, physically and verbally abusive toward Maria and him. Maria started taking prescribed drugs to calm her nerves and she, too, started drinking heavily.

"Ben came home last night, and as usual, he and Maria argued. Ben became extremely upset. He tossed furniture, pictures, and anything else that was available. Tom was in his bedroom listening to his music. He said he turned it up so he could drown out his father's voice. When the music stopped, he heard his mother plead for his dad to stop. He came out of his bedroom and saw his mother on the floor. Tom said, "Ben used his foot to kick and stomp Maria's small body as she laid there helpless.

"Tom told the police that his mother was black and blue and bleeding profusely from her ears and nose. Tom jumped his father from behind and tried to stop his father.

Ben flipped Tom off and angrily punched him; when he fell, his head hit the end table and knocked him out.

"Thelma said Tom told the police that when he awakened, his mother was cradling his head. She was covered with blood and in pain but still trying to comfort him. Tom said he heard the sound of a bottle being smashed against something. He looked and saw his father sitting in a chair waiting for him to wake up. When Ben saw Tom move, Ben stood, looked at him. Ben grabbed Maria by her hair and pulled her into their bedroom. Tom heard his dad hitting his mother. She was hurt and weak and pleaded for him to stop.

"Tom told the police that he managed to get up and walk to his parents' bedroom. Through the open door, he saw his dad pick Maria up in his arms and drop her onto the floor. He continued to kick her small, frail body several times in her rib cage."

Grandma's petite body shuddered and she cried softly into her handkerchief saying, "My poor, poor sister. Jeremy, what kind of animal would do such a thing?"

She held Grandpa Jeremiah's hands and said, with tears falling, "Jeremy, we all warned Maria to leave him. Ben had always been verbally abusive to her but not physical, as far as I know. We all knew it was just a matter of time before his violent nature came to the surface, yet Maria refused to leave him."

Grandma Vetta pounded her little hand on the telephone table. Through her tears, she said, "Jeremy, I knew it! It was just a matter of time. I should have went there and brought her and Tom here, but I didn't, and, now my Maria, my poor, poor, sister, has died in pain."

Grandpa placed his wrinkled but strong hand under her shoulder giving her his support. Grandma patted his hands, she continued to share what Thelma had told her.

"Thelma told me, Tom said his dad's mouth spewed abusive words as he kicked and stomped his mother. He said, Ben ordered her to get up, she tried, but couldn't. Jeremy, Thelma said Maria's body was beaten so severely she was unrecognizable.

"And poor, poor, Tom saw all this. Tom was beaten and hurt, but he managed to limp around behind his father and hit him on the head with one of Ben's college hockey trophies. Ben fell on the floor and Tom helped his mother onto her bed. He went into their bathroom to wet a wash cloth to clean the blood from her face. Tom said he watched as his dad got up from the floor still enraged, using profanity, and staggered out of the bedroom. Tom followed him very cautiously and locked the door behind him and placed chairs under the bedroom's front and side door's doorknobs. Tom said he heard his father beating on the doors, demanding to be let back in.

"Moments later, Tom heard the garage door open and the car engine start. Naturally, he thought his dad had left. He rushed out of the bedroom and locked all the doors. He returned to the room and picked up the phone to call the police, but his mom begged him not to. Tom got her to lie down and he covered her with a blanket. As she rested on the bed, he dozed in a chair beside her. Suddenly they were awakened when they heard windows being smashed. He unlocked his parents' bedroom door, picked up his mother from the bed and carried her into his bedroom. His plan was for him and his mother to escape through his bedroom window. But, Maria refused to leave, she told him to go, she would stay and try talking to Ben. Tom said he told her, 'Mom, he's insane, he tried to kill us, and we have to go now!' But Maria, she refused to leave.

"Tom took out his cell phone and called 911. After hearing his mother's weak plea for him to stop, he tossed the phone under his bed without disconnecting the call. Tom escaped just in time through his open window. He managed to get to the far ledge and pressed his body against the house. He and the 911 operator listened. Tom said he heard Ben ranting and spewing out profanity as he kicked open Tom's bedroom door.

"Tom peeked into the open window. He saw Ben holding a gun, taunting his mother with it. Maria saw Tom and she shook her head and with her eyes she warned him not to come in. She mouthed to him, 'Go.'

His father held a whiskey bottle in one hand and a gunin the other.

Fueled with anger, he hollered, 'Where are you Tom? I know you can't be far because you will not leave your momma! Come out Momma's boy, and watch me as I kill your mother and then you, and then I will die."

"Ben saw the open window and heard the police sirens. Ben said to Maria, 'He went to get his momma help? Didn't he?'

"Tom said he heard Maria pleading for Ben to put the gun away. The more she pleaded the more agitated he became. Tom said his father started crying, he told his mother, 'I'm tired of losing. I have lost all that I spent years working for, and for what? This? This house, our home that is in foreclosure? We have no money in our accounts, and no one cares about me, so why should I care?'

"Tom heard his mother's weak voice saying, 'Jesus, forgive me of my sins, and have mercy on me!' At that very instant he heard bang, bang!" Grandma's small body bent over. She was inconsolable just hearing her describe the brutality Maria and Tom endured, she felt as if a dagger had been inserted into her own heart. Grandma cried, "Jeremy, Ben killed my baby sister. My baby sister is dead."

"Lovetta, come, and lie down," "No, Jeremy, there is more."

"Thelma said, Tom came back through the window, and lifted Maria's lifeless body.

Holding her, he looked at his father and screamed, 'How could you?'

His father pointed the gun at him and Tom said he felt something hot hit him in the side of his head. He fell, still holding his mother's body. He wasn't dead, but he pretended to be. Tom said he closed his eyes, held his breath, and laid still. His father kneeled over him and said, 'I'm sorry son. I wasn't much of a father to you. You were a good boy and I made you what you have become. Forgive me. And your mother, she loved you more than her own life and I did love you. I wasn't a man anymore. I couldn't provide for you.'

"Tom not moving, heard the police knocking down

their front and back doors and he," Grandma Vetta stuttered, fighting to hold back her tears, repeated, "and he, heard Ben laugh when he said, 'Tom, God may have forgiven Maria, because she had time to repent, but you son, you didn't, I made you into a bad boy, and I will see youin hell.' He heard the click of the gun as Ben pulled the trigger."

Grandma Vetta became inconsolable. Grandpa held and rocked his precious Vetta. Cate, George, and Brie, stood behind the screen door and cried as they listened to her recount the story of Ben and Maria's death.

"Come, Vetta, come, lie down."

They watched as he walked his wife to their bedroom to rest. Cate went to the kitchen to make coffee and boil water for tea. Grandpa and George joined her.

While drinking coffee and tea they reminisced about Ben and Maria.

The phone rang and Brie answered. She covered the receiver with her hand and whispered. "It's Thelma."

Chapter 14, Grandpa's Eyes

Brie knocked.

"Come in."

"Grandma, I sorry for interrupting your rest, but Thelma is on the phone."

"Oh you are never a bother, dear." She handed the phone to her grandma and kissed her on her cheek and said. "I love you, Grandma."

"Brie, I love you more."

Grandma held the phone. She let out an anguished sigh, then she put the phone to her ear and said, "Hello, Thelma."

Brie closed her grandparents' bedroom door and joined Cullen and Brad on the front porch.

Brie heard Brad when he said, "Wow, Cullen. Tom is coming here to stay with your grandparents. Do you know when he is coming?"

"From what I gathered, any day now."

Brie walked out the front door and she sat near Brad and Cullen on the steps. She took Brad's hand and held it. Cullen said to her, "You know cuz, I am glad he's coming. I am leaving tomorrow morning for football camp. It will be great for Grandma and Grandpa to have someone staying with them."

Brad released Brie's hand and whispered, "Cullen, I know I shouldn't tell you this but I heard my mom and dad talking about Tom. Brie, your dad has used my father's connections to get Tom out of trouble more than a few times. Tom's mom and dad were alcoholics and took drugs. Tom even sold drugs and lived a gay lifestyle. I know your grandmother knows this because she was the one who approached my dad for help many times to get him out of trouble I have also heard your grandmother talking with my mother about Tom and his parents."

"What?" Cullen said, in shock. "They never told me about Tom… but why should I be surprised? They never really told me about my parent's death. When it comes to my grandparents and their secrets to protect me from harm, I am not really shocked."

Cullen stood and wiped his sweaty hands on his pants. He said. "Gee, Brad, now I am really worried. It's just like Grandma, thinking she can help Tom change. Grandpa always said, 'A leopard can't change its spots.'"

Brad, Cullen and Brie were unaware that Grandpa was listening to them. They were surprised to hear his voice when he said, "Yep, I was thinking the same thing, Cullen.

Cullen turned, he asked, "Grandpa, how long have you been listening?" Grandpa gave Cullen a wry chuckle. He said. "Long enough son. And you were right; I'm sorry that we never talked about your parents. I guess it was too painful for us."

Grandpa looked over at Brad, he smiled, and winked his eye. Brad nodded his head to give Grandpa proper respect. Brad said, 'Sir."

Grandpa cleared his throat and repeated his answer to Cullen's question again, "Long enough son." Opening the screen door he sat on the swing. They all sat in silence until Grandpa spoke. "You know, Vetta means well by inviting Tom here to live with us but a person cannot change who they are unless they have the desire to do so. I really believe we are inviting trouble into our home. I have never said no to Vetta and I have never said no to someone who needed our help."

Grandpa looked at both Brad and Brie and he winked. Brie gave Brad a worried look. Brie was thinking, *that's twice Grandpa has winked at Brad. What could that mean? Oh no, he doesn't know, or does he?* Brie heard her Grandpa saying, "Vetta and me will need help from you and Brie, and I am glad you two aren't going away to school." Hearing Grandpa's words alarmed Brie.

Cullen responded, "Grandpa, have you forgotten? Brie is staying but Brad is scheduled to leave on Monday for Bible College."

Grandpa, have you forgotten? Brie is staying and Brad is scheduled to leave Monday for Bible College."

"Uh huh," Grandpa chuckled, "Cullen I believe that was the plan. Bradford, by the way, have you told your parents?"

"Sir, tell them what?"

Cullen looked searchingly at Brie and Brad, he noticed Brie and Brad's uneasiness, and he turned to his grandpa and asked, "Tell them what, Grandpa?"

With explosive laughter Grandpa burst out, "About them goin' and getting' hitched, that's what!"

Brie rushed over to her grandpa and placed her hands over his mouth and hissed, "Grandpa, hush, please not so loud."

"What?" Shouted Cullen! "No way!"

Brie looked through the screen door to see if anyone was there and overheard Cullen and Grandpa.

"Brie, Brad, what about me being the second to know?" Cullen looked at his watch, he said, "Weren't those word spoken to me in the park just a few hours ago? ... Brie?"

Brie hurried over to Cullen, placed her hands over his mouth and whispered, "Be quiet!"

"Brie, you mean you haven't told Cullen?"

"No, Grandpa, they didn't tell me and I am deeply hurt. Is there anything else I don't know? Perhaps a little cousin on the way? No, that's impossible because my man Brad is a devote Christian and he would never …"

Waving his hands in the air, he answered his own question. "No, what am I saying? Forgive me Brad, I know you wouldn't, *would he?* Cullen shook his head and answered his own question with an inquiry when he said, "You two didn't ... Did you? Brie, Brad, I am going nuts here. Please explain because my mind is topsy-turvy and my heart is pounding overtime!"

Frustrated, Brie said, "No Grandpa, Cullen didn't know."

She looked at her cousin. She told him, "I am so sorry, Cullen."

Showing her displeasure toward her grandpa, Brie stamped her feet, feeling like a five year old who was caught in the cookie jar. She whined, "We were waiting for the right timing! Grandpa, please tell us what do you know and how did you find out?"

Grandpa winked at her and said, "These here old eyes

see a lot. I just put one and one together and got two. Yep, you two."

Grandpa sat, with obvious delight, swinging and watching Brie do the jitter bug dance. Brie pleaded, "Grandpa, stop teasing us, how did you find out?"

Grandpa said, "Okay, okay, let me give both of your minds some peace. I will tell you. Come, Brie, sit next to me" Brie sat and he placed his arms around her neck and Brad sat next to Cullen on the banister. Cullen looked at his best friend and frowned, he shook his head with disappointment with his and Brie's deceitfulness and said,

"Unbelievable."

"Cullen, don't be so hard on sneaky Bradford."

"Grandpa, that's the correct word, sneaky." Grandpa laughed and Brie shouted, "Grandpa, stop playing around and tell me please, how did you find out?"

"Brie, I just happened to be at City Hall the day you two got hitched. I went there to visit an old friend who works at the county clerk's office. I wanted to take him to lunch but he said he had to wait for Senator Rock's son and his girlfriend, they were scheduled to get married. I didn't have to hear your name since Jason only has one son, and I knew the girlfriend had to be you since Brad has been in love with my you since first grade

"I said nothing to my friend about knowing you two. We talked a few minutes and I had just walked out the door. It was perfect timing because I was about to turn the corner when I saw you and Brad get off the elevator. Brad, you and Brie didn't see me because your lips were locked. When you two went inside, you left the door ajar and I witnessed your marriage.

I ran and hid before you came out. When you both came out, I saw you. Brie, you were holding the paper and Brad here was suckin' on your lips; then, I heard Brad call you, 'Mrs. Rock.

"Yep, you two. Now if my recollection is correct that's been about..." Grandpa removed his arm from around Brie's shoulders and put his head back as if he was thinking and said, "about three weeks."

Looking at Brie, still smiling, he asked, "Isn't that correct Brie?"

Cullen, feeling discombobulated, responded, "Three weeks you two have kept this from me for three weeks?"!

"Yep, Cullen, they are two little sneaks. You heard me right. These two have been hitched for three weeks and," Grandpa patted his chest proudly said, "I am really proud of myself because I haven't told anyone, not even Vetta,

"Grandpa, I know that's true because if grandma knew she would have called my mom. Now Mom, as we know, is an enigma. I believe she knows but she will wait us out. But Grandpa, why did you choose to reveal our secret tonight?"

"That's a good question Brie, this is why. I figured Bradford and you could help me out."

"How, Grandpa Jeremiah?"

"You see Bradford, Vetta is hurtin' real bad now and I thought it's time for hearin' some good news. Hearing this news will take Vetta's mind off of Ben and Maria just for a while."

Brad walked over to Brie, held her hands and asked,

"Are you ready?" She bobbed her head indicating yes.

Brie cracked her neck moving it side to side and she smiled. She kissed her grandpa and said, "Gramps, it's been three weeks and you haven't said anything until now, wow!"

Brie stood and shook her head back and forth. She smiled and said to her beloved Grandpa. "Grandpa, I am shock. You kept this from Grandma."

"Yep, and I know I am now in trouble. But I figured it wasn't my place to tell."

Grandpa looked at Brad and said, "Bradford, I know it's very late, but before we tell them you need to call your parents and ask them to come over. Yep, Kids, I think right now seems to be a good time for all of us to hear some good news."

Cullen sat on the porch banister and smiled as he rubbed his short brown curly hair. Now he understood why Brie and Brad were flirting and kissing more in public. His not so shy little cousin and his sneaky best friend went off and got hitched. This was one he didn't see coming.

Brad and Brie walked down the steps. He dialed his mom's cell phone. On the third ring she picked up. "Hi, Mom. I know it's late, but I am over at Grandma and Grandpa Jeremiah's. Could you and Dad come over right now? It's important … Yes and no Mom. Yes something bad has happened and no, it can't wait any longer, because something good has also happened."

Silence.

"Love you too, Mom, see you and Dad soon."

Brad took Brie's hands and they walked up the steps

and moved around to the opposite side of the porch.

He looked up at Grandpa and said, "They are coming."

Brad said to Brie, "Now I know why I put your rings into my pocket this morning."

She responded with a quick kiss, "Brad, I did the same. I have your wedding band."

They embraced.

Grandpa and Cullen watched the two newlyweds.

"Cullen."

"Yes, Grandpa?"

"I am glad you have stopped that gamblin' and hangin' with that no good for nothin' Woody. He is nothin' but bad news.

Grandpa Jeremiah stood and pulled Cullen to him.

Cullen gave his Grandpa a strong hug and said, "Yes, Grandpa, for the very first time I'm listening. My gambling days are over."

Releasing his grandpa from their embrace; his grandpa sat back down on the swing and Cullen said, "Grandpa, I am concerned about Woody and Tom being together and I'm thinking there will be trouble. Trouble draws like the pull of a magnet and I'm thinking with Ben and Maria's deaths and you and Grandma inviting Tom to come to live here, that you and Grandma may be in for some rough times. Perhaps I should let go of my dream to become an NFL player, and stay home to finish my senior year at our local university."

"Absolutely not, Cullen Sullivan! Do you hear me son?"

"Yes, Grandpa, I hear you."

Grandpa pushed himself up out of the swing. As he stood, he grunted, "Lord, heal this old back!" Cullen came over and Grandpa placed his hands on Cullen's shoulder and said, "by the way Cullen, I have been meaning to tell you this; if your mom and dad were living, they would be very proud of you."

Grandpa tapped Cullen's face, smiled and told him, "I know I am, son." He then turned and walked back into the kitchen where Cate and George sat talking.

Cullen walked over to the corner of the wrap around porch. He saw Brie and Brad embracing.

"Ahem, may I interrupt?" Teasing them Cullen asked. "Are you two newlyweds ready to face the firing squad?

I know your parents will be happy, Brad. But, Brie, you have denied your mother of giving you that dream wedding she never had. And Bradford your mother will be hurt that her Bradford, her only son was so underhanded and sneaky to listen to that conniving Brie Hayes and go to the courthouse to get married."

Enjoying this moment Cullen continue his taunting, "You, Bradford Jason Rock III, are the son of a United States Senator who will one day be president of this great country. Bradford, how will your mother explain this courthouse wedding to her social club? Look what you and Brie have done. Your mother will have no wedding pictures, nothing to show.

"We know both of your dads will be high fiving and congratulating each other because for some reason they love you both as much as I do."

Brie and Brad stood on the porch listening to Cullen's teasing remarks and looking worried. Cullen laughed, jumped from the banisters and shouted, "Come here you two sneaks."

Cullen grabbed them and they hugged. He said, "I love you man, and cuz you have an awesome man here, take care of my friend or I will come and take care of you."

Brie laughed and said "Okay, Cullen fun is over. Let's focus on Tom. Cullen, Brad is worried and now so am I. We think this arrangement is going to be a disaster. Grandpa and Grandma are much older and they should be enjoying life, not inviting a keg of smoldering dynamite that may ignite and bring them unnecessary trouble into their home.

"I have heard Mr. Hayes and my dad talk about Tom. From what I heard, he is crazy and he does not need to come here."

"Brad, this is the only place he can come. He could have died but God let him live. We have to believe God has a plan."

They looked up and there stood Grandma Vetta. Brie said, "Grandma. I thought you were resting?"

"I have rested enough and needed some fresh air."

Brie rushed to open the screen door and helped her grandma over to the swing. Just as Grandma Vetta sat her small frame down, Grandpa Jeremiah walked out onto the porch.

"Vetta," he said, "I was just about to go into our bedroom to check on you and I heard your voice."

 Jeremiah sat next to his Lovetta and told her,

"George and Cate are in the kitchen do you care to join them there?"

"No Jeremy, I need some fresh air.

"Grandpa Jeremiah planted a quick kiss on her forehead and told her, "It will all be okay, Vetta.

Chapter 15 Secret Revealed

Senator Jason Rock II and his wife, Julia, drove into the Sullivan's driveway. When Grandma Vetta heard the car, she stood and walked to the edge of the porch. She asked, "Is that your parents, Brad?"

"Yes, ma'am. I called them and asked if they could come over. I hope it's okay?"

"Bradford Rock! I should swat you for asking that question. Of course it's okay."

Jason and Julia walked onto the porch and exchanged pleasantries. They all walked into the kitchen to join George and Cate. While they sat around the kitchen table, Grandpa recounted the story told by Vetta to them concerning Ben and Maria's death and their son Tom's pending visit.

Jason gave George a look of anguish. Shaking his head, he said, "George you and I know that young man's record with the law throughout adolescence until now. How old is he George?"

"Sixteen."

"Grandma Vetta and Grandpa Jeremiah, I admire you for wanting to help Tom," Jason said, "however, Tom has been in and out of trouble with the law for over seven years and I just hope when he arrives here that he doesn't get involved with Woody.

"Jason and George," said, Grandma Vetta, "it takes a village to love and save one child.

I know Tom is 16 years old, and I can only imagine

the abuse he had to withstand, but I believe God saved Tom from death for a reason and He is sending him to our home for a reason."

"Grandma Vetta," said Jason, "I wish I could share that same reasoning as you, but I just can't."

Grandpa Jeremiah sat next to his wife. He reached for her hand and said, "Jason, Vetta and we have never turned anyone away from our home who needed our help, and we will take Tom."

Grandma Vetta looked at each face around the table and she said, "I am counting on all of you for your support. Now, I hope you all understand that, don't you?"

Julia said, "Momma Vetta, we will all be here for you and Dad and for Tom."

Julia turned to her son and said, "Okay, Bradford, you also said that you had some good news to tell us. What is it son?"

Brie stepped over and stood next to Brad. Julia covered her mouth and she let out a soft gasp. Brad, holding Brie's hand, went over to Brie's parents and said, "Mr. and Mrs. Hayes, you both know I have loved Brie since first grade." Brad turned his head and he looked into Brie's father's eyes.

George's facial expression was unyielding, without encouragement towards Brad. George watched with inward delight as tiny sweat beads started to form on Brad's forehead. Brad's body shook with fear, but somehow he was able to continue. He said, "Mr. Hayes, I also know it's appropriate for the man to come to the woman's father to ask for his daughter's hand in marriage."

"Marriage!" George shouted.

He turned to look over at Brad's father and winked and said, "Jason, did I hear your son correctly? Did he say marriage?"

"Yes, George, I believe we both heard the same word, the word was marriage."

Brie came to Brad's defense, "Dad, Mr. Rock, both of you stop teasing Brad."

Brad tightly held Brie's hand. They both looked at their parents and Brie nudged and encouraged him saying, "Go ahead and tell them."

"Tell us what Brie?" shouted George.

"Boy this should be good! Grandpa hollered, Go ahead boy, spill the beans and tell them what's on your mind."

Brad said, "Mr. and Mrs. Hayes, Mom and Dad, Brie and I were married three weeks ago."

Julia gasped when she said, "Brie, how could you and Bradford have done such a thing without telling us?"

"Brad wanted to tell you, Mr. and Mrs. Rock, but I persuaded him not to because …" Brie turned to her mother and slowly repeated, "Because you and my mom would have hosted a big engagement party, which neither Brad nor I wanted."

Brad's parents sat stunned and he was shocked by his parent's reactions to their marriage. Brad looked at them and shouted. "What's wrong with you?"

"Cate?"

"Julia?"

Did you know?

"I had my suspicions, but I was waiting for Brie to tell me."

Brie turned and looked at her grandpa and mouthed, "Help."

Grandma Vetta, asked, "Jeremiah Sullivan, why is Brie asking you for help?"

Grandpa Jeremiah's hands shot up in the air and he let out a hearty belly laugh and shouted, "Don't look to me for help! You two got hitched, I wasn't involved."

Brad's dad stood and walked over to his son. He gave him a serious stare which provoked Brad to angrily shout, "What's wrong with you dad?"

Brad held Brie's hand tightly. He looked at his beloved family as they remained unresponsiveness to their news and not showing any happiness towards them. Feeling ostracized, Brad said, "Let's go Brie, this is not right." He looked at them with tears in his eyes and said, "I thought you all would be happy for us."

Jason and the others suddenly burst out in laughter. Jason pulled his son into his arms and shouted to his wife over the clapping and laughter, "See Julia? I told you he's been acting weird." Jason looked at Brie and Brad and said, "Come here you two." He gathered them both into his arms and gave a big bear hug.

Brad reached in his pocket to reveal a beautiful diamond ring and a wedding band. He placed the rings on Brie's finger

"Honey, I have had this set for months and I am so happy you finally get to wear them."

Brie reached into her skirt pocket and said, "I have had your ring for months and I am so happy to be able to put this on your finger."

She slid Brad's ring onto his finger. They kissed and the family clapped. Brie hugged her mother and said, "Mom, I am sorry to deny you and Mom Rock the joy of planning a wedding."

Cate smiled and said, "Brie Catherine Rock, you are standing there looking me in my face and not telling me the truth. You are my daughter and I know you have never like people fussing over you. However…" Cate looked at Julia and continued, "However, please give us the opportunity to have a reception."

Brie softly sighed and said, "Okay, but Mom and Mrs. Rock, you both must promise us you will keep it small."

"Only if you call Jason and me, Mom Julia and Pop Jason." "Deal," replied Brie.

Grandma looked over at Grandpa. She said, "Jeremy, this is becoming a family tradition."

"Yep, it sure is Vetta."

"Ma'am? I don't understand," said Brad.

"Well, Bradford, Cate and her sister Sally both eloped and correct me Julia if I am wrong, but I believe you and Jason eloped?

"Yes, Grandma Vetta, we did."

Grandpa clapped his hands. He then slipped up and loudly stated, "Ooooowee, I am glad everybody knows. I worked hard not to tell their secret."

Startled by his remarks, at the same time they all shouted, "What? You knew?

"Jeremiah Sullivan, you knew and you didn't tell me?"

"Now Vetta, you know if I had told you, then Cate would have known, then Julia would have, and the next thing there would have been a big wedding."

Cate said, "Daddy, I am curious, who told you? Or how did you find out?"

"Oh, Cate, you know these old eyes see a lot!" Grandpa stood and looked to his wife in an effort to evade Cate's question, he asked, "Vetta, do we still have that bottle of non-alcoholic champagne?"

"Why yes, Jeremy it's been in the fridge for three years." With laughter Grandma said, "It should be icy cold."

"Well, Vetta, I will get it. Cate will you get the special glasses from the cabinet? I will get that champagne and uncork it. It's time to celebrate."

While the women talked and celebrated; George, Grandpa, and Jason withdrew into the study and closed the door. Jason said, "George, I am still concerned about Tom, and Grandpa Jeremiah, we all know Tom is bad news and it wouldn't surprise me if he had something to do with the death of his parents. I hate thinking this way, but we have seen his arrest record. He is capable of doing so much more."

"Yes, I know Jason. But what else can we do? This young man needs a home and we are the only family that is willing to take him in. We have to be prayerful, cautious, and always on guard.

Jason said, "Grandpa, Tom staying here is asking a lot. There is a 99% chance Woody will get him hooks into him."

Grandpa let out a loud grunt.

He stood and said,

Not on my watch, because that Woodrow Parks is… is… Jason, I have too many terrible words to describe him, and, if I said them all I would have to make my bed at the altar.

Chapter 16, The Firing Squad

Cullen stood unrestricted with Brad outside Grandpa Jeremiah's den. Cullen was hesitant to knock because Brad was still nervous about his and Brie's elopement and he knew Brie's dad had a few questions for him to answer.

"Go ahead, Cullen, you knock. The firing squad awaits my arrival."

"Brad, you are my best friend, I have your back." Cullen's knuckles rapped on the closed door.

Grandpa answered, "Come on in Cullen."

Cullen entered and behind him stood Brad. Nervously, Brad said, "Sir?"

"Yes, Bradford."

"How did you know it was Cullen knocking?"

"Oh," said Grandpa, "Bradford, I have this special gift. I see everything."

"Grandpa, stop your teasing. Brad, I have a heavier knock, that's how." Cullen turned to close the door but in his haste he unknowingly left the door ajar.

Cullen stood with Brad in the center of the room and said, "Uncle George, Grandpa, and Mr. Rock, Brad and I would like to speak to all of you while we are all together."

Grandpa said, "I see you left the door ajar and that's good because it might get a little hot in here."

Senator Rock," said, Cullen "Sir, I really appreciate you warning Woody to stay away from my NFL campus

He hasn't been around and that has been a big relief."

Cullen turned towards his grandpa giving him that 'Jack Kennedy' grin. He was laughing when he said, "Grandpa, yes those old tea cup gray eyes of yours did see right. And. Uncle George, I won a lot of money gambling and I believe Woody wants it all back. When I talked with Brie she told me about the $75,000 you gave to Jada"

"George, you did what?" inquired Jason

"George, when did this happen?" asked Grandpa.

Cullen's remarks about the money set off George spewing out to Jason and Grandpa a detailed explanation about Jada, Woody and the money. Afterwards, Uncle George asked, Cullen, do you still have the money?

"Yes sir, every dollar." Looking to his Grandpa for confirmation, Cullen told them, "Grandpa saw it. It's in a sock, hidden in my bedroom."

"Cullen." Cullen turned to his grandpa and answered him with, "Sir."

"If you would have come and talked to your Grandma and me, you would have known we had money set aside for your college education. All you had to do was to show up in class and study."

Grandpa turned and directed his remarks to the Senator. "See Jason, that's what's wrong with young people today." Grandpa stared at Cullen and tapped his own head with his finger.

He continued, "Jason, they think, they know it all, and they never think about the consequences of their actions."

George sat at his desk. His peripheral vision saw Brad

sitting and fidgeting. George's eyes caught Jason's and he gave his friend a mischievous wink and with a quick head movement toward Brad, indicated his intentions to tease his son. He said, "Tell me, have you slept with my daughter?"

"What? Yes, I meant no. Sir?

"Well, Bradford, which is it? Yes or no?"

Laughing Cullen said, "Grandpa, what was it you said to me? I think it was, 'Cullen, you should be more like Bradford, he has no deceit, he is sinless.'"

"What?" Brad reacting to Cullen's statement. Brad said, "So much for having my back, best friend. I see you aren't helping me at all."

Cullen sat with his legs crossed, laughing and enjoying seeing his best friend's intense emotions. Brad turned back to George and said, "Sir, I meant to say, I would have like to… but, but no…,"

"Man, that's not the answer I wanted to hear."

"Be quiet, Cullen!"

"Okay, Grandpa, my lips are zipped."

Bradford passionately shook his head back and forth as he struggle to find the right words. He wheezed. Breathing heavily, somehow he was able to speak. "Sir, Mr. Hayes, I would never have slept with Brie without letting the family know we were married."

Brad's father walked over to his son, got into his face and asked, "Bradford tell us whose idea was it to run off and get married?

"Oh, said Cullen, "Mr. Rock, you know it had to be Brie's."

"Whose idea? Exclaimed Brad. "Dad, what do you mean whose idea was it?"

With boldness, Brad looked his dad in his eyes and said, "Brie's and my marriage was a mutual agreement. It was both of us, and Cullen you need to be quiet."

Brad looked at his dad and said, "Dad, I love Brie and she loves me. I didn't realize just how much I love her until I thought of leaving town to attend Bible College. I knew I didn't want to go without Brie."

Brad's legs felt like rubber, without tripping over his own feet he managed to hold on to the corner of the desk. He saw a tissue box and grabbed a few tissues to wipe his sweaty face. He looked at his dad, Grandpa and Brie's dad and nervously stuttered, "I, I, I can't believe this. This interrogation you are giving me. And you, Cullen, I will deal with you later, best friend. Dad, Mr. Hayes, Grandpa, you all know I have loved Brie since we moved here in first grade. I have always known I love her, and she felt the same about me but she always tried to deny it. To Brie, I have always been this obedient, perfect, Christian and that is what she tried hard not to be."

Brad drew in his breath and exhaled. He extended his hands in a begging motion toward Brie's dad, and said. "Mr. Hayes…" he then looked over to his own father. He told them both, "You must understand, Brie and I love each other so much. We talk for three to four hours on the phone several times a day. Mr. Hayes, I have always loved Brie. But I didn't know how much until a few weeks ago when I started supporting my dad by campaigning with him and Mom. I was going days without seeing Brie and it was torturous."

Brad held his hand in the air in a prayerful stance and he looked up and he said, "Thank you God. After 12 agonizing years of waiting, Brie finally admitted she felt the same about me. These last weeks in high school were a nightmare of anguish. I just couldn't study. I love her so much."

Clapping erupted from behind the door that was left ajar. Cullen knew they were there but kept quiet because he enjoyed watching his best friend being drilled. He opened the door and the women walked in.

Brad's mother walked over to her son, she gently held his face between her hands, and she kissed him and said, "Now I know the reason why your grade point average fell."

Brie rushed over to her husband. She took Brad's hand and said, "That's enough taunting my husband, just look at him, his face and hands are sweaty. Now since all this teasing is over, Brad and I have another announcement."

Cullen barked, "I knew it! Brad, you lied, and Brie, you are pregnant?"

Brie walked over and lightly jabbed Cullen on the arm and said to him, "Cullen, really! No! Everybody, relax."

Brie glared at Cullen. She said, "I am not pregnant. But I am serious about this announcement. Dad, Mom, Mr. and Mrs. Rock... Brad and I have reserved an apartment near our Bible College."

Brie went over to her grandfather and kissed his cheek. She said to him, "Thanks Grandpa, now that the truth has been told, Brad and I are free to be together."

Brie looked at her mom, took her hands and said, "Mom… " Then Brie looked back at Cullen, whose grin would set the world on fire, as he sat in the big leather chair next to the fireplace. She said to him, "Cullen, you deserve this one, this is payback my dear sweet cousin for the insinuation you have made a couple times tonight asking if I was pregnant and your statement is incorrect.

Brad and I, unlike you, are virgins."

Cullen, without smiling saw all the faces watching him and he shouted, "Whoa, that's a low hit!"

Cullen looked at his grandpa and grandma, he was ready to defend himself when he heard his grandpa saying, "Cullen, we know about you, now sit down!"

Brie winked at Cullen and said, "Got you!"

Brie enjoyed watching Cullen's distress. She smiled and mouthed to him, "I love you, cousin."

Brie continued. "Brad and I have kept God's law. Even when I was sinning. I never lost my virginity. During these weeks Brad and I could have, but we didn't yield to temptation.

Brie looked into her mother's eyes, she told her, "Mom, we haven't consummated our marriage."

Cate hugged her daughter. Brie whispered, "You knew we were married, didn't you."

Cate shook her head, indicating she did.

Cate held onto Brie hands and she walked over to Brad who was standing near his mom. She took his hands and placed Brie's hands over his, then she kissed their hands and said, "Well my Son-in-Love and my Brie, I speak for your dad and myself. Your marriage has our blessing."

"Bradford," said Cate, "You are a very fine young man who loves my daughter more than your own life." Cate turned towards the others and laughed as she shouted, "Is there anyone here who objects to this marriage? Let them speak now or forever hold their peace!"

Brie Katherine Hayes, and Bradford Rock III, again with both families blessings, I pronounce you man and wife. Brad you may now kiss your wife."

Brad smiled, and took Brie into his arms and kissed her.

"Bradford?"

"Yes, Mom."

"Jason and Brie's parents and I have talked. You and Brie will have both families' financial blessings to finish college and find a new apartment that we will furnish. As far as Brie Katherine Rock is concerned, Jason and I have always loved her."

Brad's mother and father both kissed Brie. Smiling, Julia said, "I now have a beautiful daughter. Brie, welcome to the family."

Cullen came over to Brie and he whispered in her ear, "I can't believe it, you threw me under the bus."

Brie smiled when she told Cullen, "You started it big boy." She lightly touched his chin with her finger, and said to him, "Oh how I love you, my dear, sweet cousin."

Julia looked at her watch and saw the time. She announced, "I hate to break up this happy occasion but it's 3:00 A.M... We had better leave for home."

"Mom, asked Cate, "will you be okay if we leave, or do you want me to stay with you?"

"Why no Cate, I'm okay. I have your Dad here to take care of me. Besides, Tom arrives in a few days, I have to get your room ready for him."

"Mom, that room is…"

"Yes, I know!"

Cate's mom nodded her head and gave her daughter a riveting glance with a big smile. Cate said, "Oh Mom, I didn't see that. And I will not say another word. This is God's business."

"Go home, Cate. As you know Tom will also bring my sister's ashes with him. Besides, there isn't anything else anyone can do."

"Okay, Mom. Dad, it's time for George and me to leave."

Cate looked at Cullen who was standing dejected and looking miserable. She asked him, "Cullen, are you going to hang out a little longer with Brie and Brad?"

Brad took Brie's hand, and with the other hand he shook Cullen's shoulder and told him, "Cullen, as much as Brie and I love you, my friend, you are all by yourself."

Brad shouted, "To our family, it's time for me to leave with my wife!"

They hugged everyone and Brie said, "And may I say, we will see all of you sometime tomorrow."

Brad lifted his wife into his arms, pulled her closer, and winked.

Then he said, "Maybe not."

"Well, Aunt Cate, you have your answer, my cousin

and best friend just told me I wasn't welcome to spend any more time with them tonight." Cullen gave a pretend pout when he said, "I think I'm in for the night."

Grandpa smirked, slapped Cullen on his back and said, "Thank you God for miracles.

Chapter 17, My God is Greater

Several hours later, Woody furiously stomped into the kitchen. He tossed his keys and cell phone onto the kitchen counter, and then proceeded to snatch open all the cabinet doors. Finding a mug, he roughly removed it from the shelf and slammed shut each open door.

He poured a cup of cold coffee and placed it in the microwave. He punched in 30 seconds, and noticed his badly swollen knuckles, and groaned.

He walked over to the kitchen sink, pushed back the bright yellow window curtain and saw a full blood moon.

And the sun became black as sackcloth of hair, and the moon became as blood. (*Revelation 6:12)*

His inner phantom screamed at him. *No, no, no!*

Ding. The timer sounded and so did his cell phone; Woody picked up and shouted, "Speak!"

It's done boss. No one was home at the Hayes'; Anderson's body is on the north side of their patio. When they come out for their morning paper, they will see him.

He's dead?"

"Barely alive. Boss, I seriously doubt if he lives another 10 minutes."

"Harry, I told you to be sure. I do not want him to live and tell it was me who beat him."

"I know, Boss. But I didn't want to take the risk of being seen. I am certain he will not make it"

Woody angrily mimicked, "I am certain he will not make it."

Woody was silent.

"Boss, are you there?"

"Harry, you aren't paid to think! You are paid to follow my orders, and you had better pray he's dead because if he lives, mark my words, eventually you will be a dead man."

Filled with frustration and annoyance, Woody flung his cell phone against the wall, and it separated as it fell to the floor. Woody's eyes saw splashes of blood on his hands. Even though he knew he covered his clothing, he saw Anderson's blood on his shirt and arms. He experienced a fleeting moment of anguish. He knew it was his out-of-control fury caused by the knowledge that his cousin was dying, and perhaps his brother too.

Woody picked up the separated pieces and reassembled his phone and he thought, *Is this an omen of my life? Like this phone, I am split, but there's no putting me back together.*

He placed the cell phone on the table and walked back to the kitchen sink. He put his hand on the handle with intention to turn on the spigot, but hesitated when he looked out into the ominous night sky. Again, he saw the reddish glow of the blood moon and Woody thought, *Am I safe? The only ones who know it was me who killed Anderson are my brother, who is now dying, and my employees, who fear for their own lives and their families. … They will keep their mouths closed. My one trusted bodyguard is Luke. However, I have noticed a change in Harry since he went to church and heard Cate's sermon. I am doubting his loyalty, and Jada will soon know. Too many people, too many.'*

 "Ding, ding." The timer's warning sounded, telling

him his coffee's temperature had dropped. He turned the handle, and the broken spigot sprayed hot water. Disregarding the water's heat, Woody scrubbed himself, washing away the outward remaining blood of his brother and cousin from his hands. He snatched a paper towel from its roller, dried his hands, and then pushed the microwave button for 15 seconds to rewarm his coffee.

As he sat sipping his coffee. His thoughts shifted to his family. He thought about his mother, MJ, Anderson, Anderson's children, and Gloria, Anderson's angelic, beautiful wife. He thought about the torturous lie he told Anderson about making his wife one of his working girls. He thought about the great Evangelist Cate Hayes, God's mouthpiece, and the words she privately gave to him He murmured her name. "Evangelist Catherine Hayes." Just thinking about Cate fueled Woody's inner phantom's anger. Woody screamed aloud her name. "Cate Hayes!"

He had a total recall of Evangelist Catherine Sullivan Hayes's private spoken words to him when she embraced him.

"Woody, *chaos is all around you, and it's your own making because you are refusing to let go of that controlling inner phantom. You must choose to accept God's invitation and experience his great love and total freedom from the life you are now living. You will have to pay man's penalty, but you will experience God's inner freedom, or you can choose to continue in the spiraling fall you are now in, and this fall will land you into hell. Woody, God's words, that I speak, are abrasive because that spirit you are housing has made your life threatening to others. Woody, I love you, God loves you, and that inner phantom that's feeding your mind hates you. It has no power other than what you allow it to have in you. That evil phantom inside you is not capable of love. Its final mission, that you chose to accept, is for you to kill, steal, destroy lives of others and then destroy yourself. Always remember, Woody, that there isn't any sin too dark that God's love can't forgive. His blood secured your salvation. God can save you, but you must be willing to ask God for His forgiveness with a repentant heart. Then let God's perfect mind wipe your sins away from His memory, then forgive yourself.*

Woody released a very heavy loud sigh, then in a frenzy he shouted, "The audacity she has to tell me with her sanctimonious self that her God loves me, a killer, and He can forgive my sins!" Woody heard his phantom's voice say, *I told you not to go to church to hear that Cate Hayes. I am furious with you. You disobeyed me and I want obedience. Now you must do what I order.*

Woody's inner phantom's voice was furious with Cate's words and provoked Woody to slam his coffee mug against the wooden table, causing it to shatter into many broken pieces.

Woody released a deep, tormented sigh and the spirit that possessed him spoke in a terrorizing manner. *Cate Hayes. I wonder who is going to save her daughter from me?*

Her precious Little Miss Brie thinks she can knock me out and I'm not going to get revenge? Ha. I will break her apart and leave her crippled; or perhaps kill her and then watch the great Evangelist Catherine Hayes grieve as she did for her twin sister. Then I will see if she can still talk about how big her God is and ... Jada!

He thought about Jada being at church and curled up in a ball, crying. An unexpected scornful chuckle from the darkness that Woody housed causing him to shout. "Jada! Where are you woman?" A tortuous laughter erupted, and he started his intimidating. "Hey Jada, I saw you at church, laying there on the floor all curled up in a ball. Tell me Jada, did that God of yours answer your prayers? Did he deliver you from me?"

He waited for a response and all he heard was silence. Woody's fists banged the table top and he screamed, "Jada!"

Jada did not answered.

Woody stood and wiped his hands on his pants. Feeling unsettled by her silence, he shouted, "Woman, I know you heard me calling you! Please, please, please, I am begging you woman, pleeease, don't make me come in there and drag you out here."

"Woody, I heard you. I always hear you. I am here, and I am not your slave anymore."

Momentarily stunned to silence by Jada's surprising brazen sassiness, Woody shook his head in disbelief. Regaining his bearings, he clenched and unclenched his hands and shouted, "Whoa! What did you just say to me?"

Jada stood in the kitchen entrance and she repeated with calmness. "I said, I am not your slave anymore."

"Dang woman, church must have gotten into you! He approached her shouting, "Do you know who you are talking to?"

Woody lurched forward and grabbed his wife by the neck. Pinning her to the wall, he yelled, "Now you know, the devil is here! You are standing in my house disrespecting me with that tone!"

Woody's body started to vibrate and with a terrifying grin, he touched her chin and tilted her head upward so he could look into her big brown eyes. He then struck like a cold-blooded rattlesnake. Woody backhanded Jada and the force of his hand knocked her to the floor.

"Woman!" He screamed, "Who do you think you are talking to with that tone of voice? I own you Jada! I can talk to you in any tone I wish, but you will never disrespect me! You, Jada, you will obey my master's commands and do whatever we tell you!"

He sat on his heels and put his foul mouth close to her nose and angrily hissed, "My master is your lord and master."

Woody stood and slowly walked away. He pulled out a chair from the kitchen table and straddled it as he watched his wife struggle to sit up. After several attempts, she pressed her pained body against the kitchen wall.

Woody noticed her big brown eyes were filling up with heavy tears and washing her beautiful face.

She wore a blue, satin lace gown that made her mahogany skin shimmer.

He came over to her to look into her face, admiring her beautiful full lips, and perfect features. He grinned as he continued his badgering, "Jada, you are so beautiful, most men would appreciate a woman like you, but me ... I will never be loyal nor faithful to you, and I can never be your loving husband."

A low, spiteful, coercing chuckle escaped his lips and he said, "But at this moment, I can be. Come here woman." He snatched her from the wall and said, "Don't be upset with me. Papa wants a big hug! Come on woman and give me some of your sweet kisses."

He forced Jada into his arms and tried to kiss her, but Jada struggled, refusing him of his desires.

Her actions enflamed the phantom's wanton soul. Filled with extreme rage, Woody's hands were like a cuttlefish tentacles. He punched Jada in her abdomen, yanked her into his arms and again tried to kiss her.

Jada struggled, refusing to give in to his vile desires. She was trapped and unable to free herself. She felt the pricks from the stubble on his heavy unshaven beard against her face, his heavy hands, and his body on her body, using his strength to his advantage. "Stop struggling, woman!" He smacked her face over and over.

She felt the sting of his tentacles around her neck and against her face. In pain, she fell back onto the floor. Almost immediately, the unfeeling, inhuman, cold-hearted, merciless animal was all over her. Once Woody's phantom was done assaulting her, Woody stood and stared, looking down at Jada curled up on the floor, whimpering in pain and looking like a discarded rag doll. Woody adjusted his pants. The chameleon filled with remorse and said, "Jada, I am sorry. I don't like mistreating you, I love you. It's this thing that controls me, it makes me do things like this, and say things I don't want to."

Shut up and leave this room now. Go!

Instead of obeying his controlling inner voice, Woody reached down, lifted Jada from the floor and gingerly sat her down on a kitchen chair. He soaked paper towels, came back to the chair, sat on the edge of the table and wiped away the blood that oozed from Jada's mouth. Jada started to whimper. Woody said, "Jada, I..."

I commanded you to shut your mouth and move away now!

Jada watched as Woody abruptly stopped talking, and like a controlled robotic man, stepped away from her. He began to pound his head with his heavy hands, fighting an inward battle. He was trying to control his thoughts, but he was powerless against the inner phantom. Woody turned back around to face Jada, she saw Woody's eyes had glazed over and turned cold-black and his voice changed, sounding gruff, the chameleon pointed at her and shouted, "See, this is your fault, Jada! You make us crazy like this, you are so defiant!"

Woody stood over her and watched her cry. Jada, unable to stop her whimpering, rekindled the phantom spirit with more heedless anger. Woody's phantom ordered him to pound the table and holler, "Stop it! Stop it, Jada! I am not George Hayes. He's your push over, I'm not!"

Fueled with anger, he knocked over a chair, stomped over to the kitchen sink and stared out the window. Seeing daybreak, Woody abruptly wheeled around and shouted, "Jada!"

Jada, afraid to look at him, heard an unexpected diabolical laughter piercingly penetrating the atmosphere and the phantom that possessed Woody spoke.

So, Mrs. Jada Perkins Parks, before we walked out of church Sunday morning, when that woman, Cate Hayes, touched you, we noticed you went down under the power of her God."

Jada slowly lifted her head and saw a repulsive smile that broadened when the phantom saw her reaction to his words. Woody slowly walked over to the chair where she sat. He lifted his heavy fist; Jada shielded her face believing he was going to strike her. Instead, he pounded the wooden table several times and it cracked opened. The table splitting startled Jada and she jumped with fear.

Amused by her reaction, the possessed Woody laughed and sneered, "Now Jada, where is your God? I see you are still here, under my lord and master's power."

The spirit within Woody continued its mocking with torturous words.

"Tell me, Jada Perkins Parks, can your God save you from my god?

Woody turned his muscular body in circles, pretending to be looking for Jada's God.

"Apparently, He didn't,"

Woody's phantom triumphantly giggled when it said, "Because you are still here in the flesh."

Woody's phantom boldly moved in closer to Jada's face, tilted his large head and furiously sneered, "Jada, can your God save you from me and my master?"

Then like a boa constrictor's squeezed, and the next words that escaped from Woody's phantom's deathly mouth crushed Jada's heart.

The spirit controlling Woody victoriously shouted, "Let me answer that question for you!"

Jada watched Woody's face. It was subdued with deceptive merriment as he pounded his chest. He responded, "*No*, the answer is *no*! I have a newsflash just for you." Woody moved closer. In her ear, he shouted, "Are you listening? This is a fact! Nobody, nowhere can save you from my lord and master!"

Woody, began to pace back and forth, a possessed mad- man. Then he stopped his pacing and shouted, "Listen, my dear, you belong to me. I am your god and master. So get that into that small, dodo bird, pea-brain, head of yours. Jada, you are not going to go anywhere, and if you ever try to leave again I will find you, and when I do I will kill you with my bare hands."

Tense and elated, Woody gave Jada an intimidating look and with a quick wink and contemptuous chuckle, he turned to walk away.

Jada unsteadily stood from the chair and like a phoenix rising from the ashes, she shouted, "Woody!"

He kept walking. Woody's phantom commander fanatically ordered him, *Leave! Don't turn around, don't stop! Go!*

"Woodrow Hugh Parks and that phantom spirit that's in you will listen to His Spirit that dwells in me. My Master, Jesus Christ of Nazareth, sent by God into the world to save the ones who believe and follow Him, commands you both to turn around!"

Woody's phantom twitched and turned. Woody saw Jada looking like a downtrodden bedraggled, powerless woman and he laughed.

Jada stood, unbending and with an inner boldness. She was determined to speak, knowing what she was about to tell him could be detonator to the explosive he housed within him, causing it to command Woody to kill her.

She thought, *If I die, so be it. I will be with my Lord and Master Jesus Christ.*

Jada laughed, and with a peaceful spirit she said, "Woody! I will answer you and your deceiving phantom's question. God did save me from the fury of hell on Sunday."

Jada tried to walk, but stumbled. She braced her small body against the wooden chair, and without fear.

She looked into Woody's wrathful face, into his lifeless, darkened eyes, and spoke boldly. "You asked me if my God could save me from you and that spirit that controls you. Woody that is a great question. I don't know how or when, but I know He will."

Woody impatiently replied, "Woman we have given you too many blows to the head. You are talking crazy."

The spirit within Woody jabbed at Jada. It said, "God doesn't want you! You are one of his biggest disappointments. God is disappointed with you baby because you became a slut. That's what you are to me and to him, Miss Jada."

Woody hotly spelled the word, "S-l-u-t! You are a slut and you can't return to that innocent girl you once were. Baby, those days are *over*!

Your boat has *sailed*, and baby, you missed it; you are all mine."

He looked around the kitchen as if he was seeking someone's help and said, "And may someone ... Hey, Jada, how about those angels that your God gives to watch over his people,[Psalms 91:11)] if they are here will they please help you because you are getting on my last nerve woman."

Jada moved away from the chair and limped over to the kitchen sink, staring out the window, she prayed in silence. *Come Jesus, in power and demonstration.*

Instantaneously, she felt an inner empowerment of boldness. Jada felt no pain as she turned toward Woody and she boldly asked, "Woody, who gave your phantom entry into the mind of my God to be his mouthpiece?"

Woody's body convulsed. He wanted to react but stood rigid, unable to move.

Jada proceeded with a supernatural inner courage, "How God sees me?" She laughed, "What an awesome question… How God sees me? When you look at me, you are seeing the slut. But when God looks, He sees me, His created one. The one He loves. He sees me as His redeemed one, not a slut, not that sinful promiscuous woman I was. I have been refreshed. I have changed, I have been reborn. I am once again His!

You called me a slut, but God's love stooped low, just for me and it's His mercy that saved me and not Woody's so call master."

Woody, no longer inflexible, was standing in her face in a flash. His body gyrated from anger; he lifted his hand to strike her but couldn't. He made several attempts, but felt a stronger invisible force withholding his hand. Not believing what he felt could be real, he smiled at Jada, pretending to walk away. He quickly turned and lunged towards her, but he was pushed backwards. He felt as if he hit a brick wall; he couldn't touch her. Speechless and perplexed, he walked away steaming with anger. He hissed, "Jada, I have heard enough of your nonsense, now shut up!"

"No, Woody, I will not shut up! Your so called master isn't mine! My God, my Master has given me more to say to you and that inner pitiless, merciless, heartless, lying, deceitful so called friend of yours. And my Master commands you both to listen!"

Frozen like an icicle, Woody and his phantom listened. "Woody, you have welcomed that spirit within you to possess your soul. Your temper has become more outrageous and that controlling spirit that you house enjoys exploiting you, and other people. Lately, I have observed you getting all powered up with your hurting and hating. I have seen the four of you, you and your lapdogs, Luke Allen, Harry and Pete plotting ways to attack people to their demise. That spirit that you house makes you believe that you are a big man. But here a newsflash for you both. My God is bigger, and that thing that's in you, will *never* be bigger than my God! Woody.

I read in my Bible where Jesus stated that He personally witnessed this momentous event when your phantom spirit was literally ejected with the velocity and power of lightning from God's throne. That thing you house has no power, other than what you allow him to have.[5]

You have allowed that killer within you to beat me, to let other men abuse my body for years. That phantom within you told you to wrap me inside a vinyl tarp, and dump me into a mud puddle on a dark abandoned street corner to die. Even now, if God would permit it to happen, you can pick me up, toss me around like popcorn, and I could die. But from where I stand now, that doesn't seem possible because God just protected me from your attempts to harm me. Have you noticed, Woody, I am healed! See my face?" Jada touched her face, she said, "I feel no pain." Jada twirled, "See, I can jump with no pain."

Smiling broadly, Jada continued, "Know this one fact Mr. Woodrow Hugh Parks, God has recorded everything you have said and done to me, and others like me. You can only be helped when you choose to change and ask God for His forgiveness. Otherwise, you will give an account for your twisted actions someday."

Woody, fuming with anger, shouted, "Jada, are you preaching to me?" He pointed at her and screamed, "Get out of my face, talking all crazy. Go and get dressed!"

He reached into his pants pocket, removed her car keys. He hurled her keys at her body with intentions of inflicting pain; but instead of hitting her, the keys dropped onto the floor.

Laughing, she bent to pick them up. Jada said, "And Woody have you notice, my God, He is my shield."

"Woman, take your car and your shield and go to the casino and clean my office. You will be messy after cleaning so come directly home, shower and get dressed. We have to go to Gloria's house. Anderson is dead."

Not wanting to believe what she just heard, she asked, "Did I hear you correctly? Anderson is dead? What happened?"

Woody said nothing more. He walked into the front room, sat on the couch and bent over to remove his shoes.

 Jada saw how swollen his knuckles were and

the splashes of blood on his shoes and pants bottom. She said nothing.

Woody also noticed the blood, he looked over at Jada staring at his pants and shoes. He sighed and said to her, "Keep your mouth shut."

He slowly took out his small pistols from his socks. He removed his gun holsters and placed them on the table while giving her a menacing stare. Jada turned to walk away.

"Jada!" He called, "Before you leave, I have a story to tell." Jada stopped, not looking back.

"My Mom said when I was born I had skin covering my face like a mask. The old midwives told her I was born to become evil. My mom and dad did all they could to protect me. But I was destined. Villainous is who I am. Now you are dismissed."

Before Jada could walk seven steps, Woody scornfully chuckled He called out, "Oh Jada, do not think you can ever escape me, if you try, I will hunt you down and when I find you

It will not be a happy reunion. Have you noticed, I have never disfigured your face? Your face is so beautiful, but if you try to escape me again that doll face of yours will become acidic… permanently damaged".

Unresponsive to his threat, Jada walked away hearing Woody's daunting laughter. Then he pompously commanded, "Woman, before you leave make a sandwich, pour something cold to drink, then bring it to me. Now go!"

In the bedroom, Jada was overwhelmed by God's

demonstrations of His power against Woody's inner enemy.

She was distraught about seeing blood on Woody pants and shoes, and pain- stricken when hearing from Woody's mouth that Anderson, his cousin was dead. She was concerned by seeing Woody's injured knuckles, and he showed no remorse. He was seemingly unaffected by Anderson's death, but also appeared to be delighted.

Dressed, Jada tip-toed into the front room and sat a sandwich and a glass of iced tea on the table. Her hands accidentally brushed against his guns. Her hand lingered, and she gazed at him lying on the couch with his eyes closed. She heard an evil inner voice saying to her, *Go ahead kill him, kill him. He deserves to die.*

"Every shut eye isn't asleep." Startled, Jada jumped. Not averting his eyes, he slipped his hand under his pillow, and retrieved a small pistol and pointed it at her.

"Jada, you are a dodo bird. You will never outsmart me. I am inside your mind. I will always be one step, no several steps ahead of you. Now get out!"

He put the pistol back under his pillow, turned his back away from her, and said, "Luke Allen will be waiting for you at the casino. When you leave my house, lock my door!"

Chapter 18, The Unimaginable

At Woody's Casino, Jada unlocked the door and quickly closed it behind her. She turned to flip on the casino's lights. There she stood dejectedly, observing Woody's so-called success.

She remembered Woody's first club. He bought it with $75,000 that he won gambling. It had an old dented, colorless jukebox, eight differently shaped kitchen tables, cracked, but functional, chairs, a wooden bar with twelve mismatched stools, and a broom closet he used as his office.

This club had a very large area with laser lights that when on, illuminated the dance floor. If it was normal club hours, she would see people drinking, laughing, making out in the dark corners, and hearing the whimpering of men and women who had lost their family's grocery and rent money at the gambling tables or wheels.

Instead of a wooden box bar, she saw a beautiful one sectional bar and matching leather stools; the bar was loaded with row after row of bottles of alcoholic drinks. When she turned to remove her jacket she felt a sharp pain in her stomach. She was sick from her stored up emotions of disgust with Woody and all he stood for. She hated this place because it was built on his lies and blood, mingled with secrecies and Woody's scheming deceit and disrespect towards others.

Slowly, she opened the side door to the steps leading up into Woody's office. Standing at the top of the stairs, she looked down the long corridor and saw Luke Allen guarding the entrance to Woody's office. It was unusual for him to not be with Woody.

Luke Allen was a tall, athletic, attractive bald headed, dark skinned man with lifeless dark eyes, and a mean personality, much worse than Woody. He, like Woody, was devoid of empathy, and enjoyed inflicting pain upon others.

Luke Allen sat in a chair at the door, ignoring her. When she approached him, Jada moved slowly around him, trembling; she somehow managed to insert the key into the lock. Once inside the room, Luke Allen edged his way in behind her, and coldly mumbled. "Jada, I was told to wait here for you. When you have finished cleaning this office, knock."

Not saying another word Luke Allen turned and stomped out, slamming the door. Startled by the sound of the door being slammed, Jada jumped.

The room was pitch dark. Jada dragged her feet while touching the wall for a switch cover when her foot kicked against something hard that triggered intense pain. Jada let out a loud squeal, but covered her mouth to muffle her voice as she listened to the unknown object roll across the wooden floor and stop.

Gathering her bearings, she removed her hands from her mouth and continued to touch the wall for the switch cover. Finding it, she pushed in and immediately the room was well lit. As her eyes adjusted to the light, she was startled by what she saw. She screamed and turned to run out, but bumped into Luke Allen. She smelled his foul breath when he laughed. He barked, "Clean up this mess and when you finish, knock then I will call Woody."

Not saying another word, Luke Allen slammed the door and inserted his key, locking her in. Outside the door she heard his diabolical laughter.

She saw blood! So much blood! Blood on the walls. Blood on the windows. The dark mahogany wooden floor was covered with splashes of blood. Woody's priceless jewel throne was covered with plastic and the plastic was splattered with blood. All four lamps were shattered.

She looked down. A few feet away she saw what her foot had struck, it was an aluminum baseball bat. Jada walked over to the bat. Trembling, she bent down and picked it up. The bat was covered with skin, hair, and blood. She remembered Woody had splashes of blood on his pants and shoes, then she recalled his words. *Anderson is dead.*

What she saw was beyond frightening. The bat dropped from her trembling hands onto the floor with a loud bang. Heartbroken, she shuddered and silently whispered, *Anderson.* She thought, *Could this be Anderson's blood? Did Woody kill his cousin?* She screamed. "No! God no!"

She heard the key being inserted into the lock. The door opened and Luke Allen walked in laughing. He said, "Hey doll face, I heard your scream, now you have seen what we've done."

Luke Allen held out his cell phone and told Jada, "Woody called, he instructed me to take your cell phone. Luke Allen snatched her purse, opened it to remove her cell phone, he then flung her purse against the wall. He walked over to Woody's oversized mahogany desk, removed the plastic cover, from Woody's diamond studded chair and sat down. He opened the middle gold plated drawer, took out a cigar, and inserted it into his large mouth. He looked at her and chuckled as he proceeded to yank the phone cord from the wall.

"Jada," he said, "the boss said to me, and I'll quote, 'If she gives you trouble, kill her. Then enclose and tape her body in plastic and toss her into the river.' Now Jada, I wouldn't want to do that. I like you."

Luke Allen walked over and put his large lips to Jada's neck and he whispered into her ear, "If I have to kill you, I will first have some fun!"

Jada slapped his face. He laughed. That's when she noticed how dead his eye were. They were without light, just like Woody's.

Luke Allen walked away. When he opened the door to leave, he stopped and told Jada, "I'm not like the boss, I don't beat women. Knock, when you've finished!" He closed the door with loud heinous laughter, then she heard the lock click. She was trapped.

Jada felt as if the room was spinning. In shock, she somehow managed to walk into the bathroom.

There she saw an oversized canvas bag. She opened it and inside were rubber gloves, trash bags, sponges, and several bottles of cleaning solution. Besides the bag there was a new bucket with the price tag attached, three scrub brushes, and two mops. She pulled on the rubber gloves and filled the bucket with soap, bleach, and hot water. She took out the mop and started cleaning up Anderson's blood. As she mopped, she cried. Jada moved like a mechanical robot. She pushed the mop under the desk and it felt like she was dragging something. She lifted the mop and saw what appeared to be teeth. She squatted to pick them up; she held two bloody teeth in her hand. She removed the bloody rubber gloves and unbuttoned her blouse, revealing her bra. She had sewn small pockets into the cups where she could safely hide money from Woody. She placed the teeth into a tissue and tucked them inside the bra's pockets and buttoned her blouse. She thought. *Woody told me Anderson was dead. He didn't tell me how he died. Are these Anderson's teeth?*

Jada put on another pair of rubber gloves. As Jada cleaned around Woody's desk, she noticed a photo of Brie and Cullen. Both their heads had red circles drawn around them and in the middle of each head was a large hole.

She looked again at the picture of Cullen and Brie, and she remembered Woody's words, about Cate. He had said, *Then I can watch her as she grieves. I will see how she talks about her God then!* Jada gasped. She felt cold shivers going through her body. She whispered to herself, "Woody is planning to kill the kids?"

Jada looked around the room, then she looked at the bloody mop and she thought, *No! Woody! How could you? Anderson was your cousin. He grew up with you and MJ as your brother. He has two precious children who are crazy about you and who you seem to love. Your mother loved Anderson and she thinks of Gloria as her daughter.*

As Jada cleaned the blood stained floor, the mop again

caught something hard. Jada lifted the mop and saw a gold pocket watch. She picked it up and she recognized it. It was Anderson's. She removed her second pair of plastic gloves, unbuttoned her blouse and inserted the pocket watch inside the other bra pocket. She buttoned up her blouse and put on a third fresh pair of plastic gloves while tears washed her face.

Jada felt sorrow for Gloria, her kids, MJ and Mom Parks because what she believed about Woody was the truth. Woody killed his cousin... he killed Anderson. She questioned herself as to why? What could have angered Woody so to do such a gruesome thing? She whispered, "*Woody. Why?*" Jada's question needed no answer; she knew why. She spoke aloud, "It had to be about his money.

Chapter 19, Apparition

Monday at 10:00 a.m., Jeremiah hollered, "Vetta! Cate is on the phone. She sounds pretty upset to me."

Vetta rushed into the kitchen and hastily took the phone from Jeremiah's hand and placed it to her ear.

"Cate, what's wrong dear?"

"Momma, the gardeners found Anderson's body this morning lying on our front lawn. We called the police and the ambulance brought him to the hospital near our home. George and I are here at the hospital waiting for Gloria and Mom Parks. Momma, Anderson was assaulted. He's in a coma and they aren't expecting him to live!"

"Oh, Cate! Do you want Jeremy and me to come to the hospital?" "No, Mom. I wanted you to know where we were just in case you try to call our house phone. George and I will be with Anderson's family. I will call you if there are any changes. Momma, pray."

"I will do that sweetie. Oh, Cate, we will come by later. Bye. Mom."

Cullen heard Grandma's conversation. He asked, "What happened, Grandma?"

"It seems that someone beat poor Anderson nearly to death. He's in a coma and not expected to live."

"How did Aunt Cate get involved?"

"Cate said the gardeners arrived and found Anderson's body lying on their front lawn.

They notified the police and an ambulance was called.

Now they are all at the hospital waiting."

"Anderson's body on their front lawn? Grandma, that doesn't make any sense. Anderson doesn't live near them. Why would his body be on their front lawn? I believe I will go to the hospital."

"Cullen," said Grandpa. "Your plane is scheduled to leave in an hour."

"Yes, I know Grandpa. I can leave tomorrow." "Cullen, can you do that? This is your training camp."

"Yes, Grandma, camp do not start until next Monday. I was going back early just to work out in the new football facility."

"Vetta, I would like to go with Cullen to the hospital, will you be okay?"

"Of course I will. Go. But, Jeremy, Woody will be there. Please avoid him and call me when you know something."

Arriving at the hospital, Cullen and Grandpa saw Anderson's wife and their three small kids. Not long afterward, Cullen saw Woody staggering in with Luke Allen and Harry. Woody purposely ignored Cate, George, Grandpa and Cullen and went over to his mother.

Gloria also saw Woody, and with a scowled face, she asked him, "Why Anderson?"

Woody sighed heavily. He answered, "I don't know?

"Gloria?

"Yes Woody?"

"Do the police know who beat Anderson?"

"No, Woody, not yet. They are still investigating."

Woody walked over to his mother and kissed her on

the cheek.

Woody looked around as if he was searching for someone and asked, "Mom, where's MJ?"

"Woodrow, I have tried calling Michael, but he isn't answering."

A nurse entered the waiting area and gave Anderson's belongings to Mom Parks, and handed papers to Gloria for her signature, confirming that she received her husband's belongings.

Cullen observed Mom Park's facial expression when she inserted her hand into Anderson's pockets. She stood quickly and pulled Woody and Gloria aside. She slowly opened Anderson's jacket pocket to show them what was inside.

Gloria's hands muffled her scream. She snatched the jacket from Mom Parks. Trembling, she walked to Cate and took out a roll of money and shouted, "Look!"

Mom Parks asked, "Woodrow, did you give this money to Anderson?"

"No, Mom. Perhaps Anderson won it gambling at another club."

Holding the money, Gloria, very upset, shouted, "Mom Parks, this is insane.

I can't believe this was in Anderson's pocket!" Woody stood and rushed to close the door, he grabbed the money from Gloria's hands, and sat down and counted it. He said, "$10,000."

Gloria shrugged, she shook her head in disbelief. She repeated, "$10,000!" She looked at Mom Parks then pointed at Woody. With contempt in her voice she asked,

"Mom Parks, did you hear your son?"

"Yes, Gloria, I did."

Gloria stood in Woody's face and said, "Something is wrong, isn't it, Woody? This isn't right. The investigating detective said Anderson's injuries do not appear to be from a robbery because they did not take his money."

Gloria disrespectfully looked Woody in his face, her wheels turning rapidly. She was thinking, but didn't dare to trust or repeat her thoughts. *Woody did this to my husband.* Gloria snapped, "But Woody, they did take something." Gloria quickly picked up Anderson's jacket and his pants, she searched all pockets. Not finding what she was searching for, she said, "Anderson's gold watch is missing."

Gloria walked over to Cate and took Cate's hands. She said, "Cate, I thought the detective was talking about $50.00 or less. But $10,000?"

Gloria still holding Cate's hand turned to stare out the hospital's large window that overlooked the highway.

She said, "Now I understand why the investigating officers said it looks more like a revenge beating." Releasing Cate's hand, Gloria turned and stared angrily at Woody.

She held her hostile glare directly on him when she said to Mom Parks, "Mom Parks, tell me please, what low-life brute could do this? Who would do this to our Anderson?"

Fat tears formed in Woody's eyes and washed his face. Sniveling, Woody took out a large handkerchief, wiped away his tears and blew his nose. He then stuffed his used handkerchief into his side pocket. Woody tenderly answered Gloria question. "Gloria," he said, "I haven't any idea what kind of low-life brute could have done this to my cousin." Woody stood and walked uneasily out the door to join Luke Allen and Harry in the hallway.

A period of awkward silence followed.

Grandpa Jeremiah sat thinking that *big devil trounced his cousin and he's pretending he didn't.*

Woody walked back in and he closed the door. Looked over at Gloria.

"Gloria."

"Yes, Woody?"

"Where did they find Anderson?"

"At Cate and George's house, their gardeners found him when they came to do their weekly lawn work."

"Oh."

Gloria heard Woody's nonchalant response and she went ballistic. She flailed her hands with frustration and anger. She shouted, "Oh! Oh!" Gloria's pent-up fury toward Woody spewed out. "Oh," she repeated. "That's all you have to say is 'Oh?' Your reaction to Anderson's body being found on Cate's lawn tells me you knew."

"Gloria, No! Please don't think that. I would never hurt Anderson. I love Anderson like a brother."

"Speaking of loving your brother. I will ask once more where's MJ? Woody, this makes no sense! I am shattered. I have questioned the reason why Anderson's body was found on Cate's and George's lawn? And this ... this money?"

She grabbed the money from the table. "Where did Anderson get all this money?"

Woody was about to say something when Gloria shouted, "No, not now, you sit and hear me out!"

Pounding her chest, Gloria shouted, "Now this is where I get really confused, Woody. Perhaps you can help me. I know Anderson asked you for money, but you told him no, because your business wasn't doing well. But Anderson said it was. He said you just like to hear him beg. Knowing that about you infuriates me. Is this your blood money, Woody? Did you order your two puppets, Harry and Luke Allen to beat Anderson and they went too far?"

"Gloria! No, Stop!" shouted Mom Parks.

Gloria, unwavering about her beliefs, stared at Woody. Not looking at Mom Parks, Gloria motioned with her hands for her to 'stop!' She said, "Please, Mom Parks don't. I am dog-tired of Woody's lies, and when it comes to Woody, you have blind eyes. My husband is in there fighting for his life. When Anderson left home he had nothing but a few dollars, and his gold pocket

Gloria reached down, grabbed the money from the table, and threw it on the floor. She bent down, picked up two $500 dollar bills and waved the money in Woody's face. She shouted, "Woody, Anderson had this in his pocket! Anderson had $10,000 in his pocket. You said you didn't give it to him! That is what you said, isn't it Woody? You said you didn't put this money into Anderson's pocket? When I look at your swollen knuckles I am wondering… did you beat Anderson? Woody," Gloria asked, "how did your knuckles get bruised? Anderson's body was dumped on Cate's and George's lawn and who else hate the Hayes and Sullivan's family as much as you do? Who is diabolical enough to do something like this? And if you didn't… well Woody, if you didn't… someone did.

There are so many unanswered questions, and yes, I too would like to know … where's Michael? Something is terribly wrong. There's no way he wouldn't be here. Perhaps he's dead! Woody did you order your thugs to kill your brother?"

Woody stood he shouted, "Really? Gloria, Anderson is my cousin, he's like a brother to me. I would never do something like this to him. Geez, give me a break."

Mom Parks quickly stood and rushed to Gloria, "Please, Gloria, stop it! Not now. This isn't Woodrow fault. Don't take your anger and pain out on him. Please, we need to pray and not turn on each other."

"Gloria."

"What, Woody!"

"I am so sorry I didn't give Anderson the money. But Mom is right. Now all we can do is Woody gasped, pray for Anderson." With heavy tears falling, Woody tried to control his emotions when he said, "Gloria, I didn't do that to Anderson, but we will get answers when Anderson comes out of his coma."

Cate watched and waited for the correct time to speak. Cate asked, "Do you mind if we all walk down to Anderson's room and gather around his bed for prayer?"

Everyone except Woody quietly walked to Anderson's room. Mom Parks wept when she saw Anderson's lifeless body lying on the bed. He was black and blue, with massive head injuries. The monitor slowly, continuously, beeped, measuring his vital signs. They held hands and prayed. Gloria looked around for Woody and saw him standing outside the door.

Soon, they all left Anderson's side, but Gloria noticed Woody wasn't with them. She walked back and stood silently inside the open door. She listened as Woody stood over Anderson and said with a raspy whisper, "Die."

Horrified, Gloria asked, "Woody, what was that you just said to Anderson?"

Startled he turned towards "Gloria…" He gave a wry smile, and said, "I just told Anderson, he will not die.'

"Oh, I heard you say, 'Die?'

"Gloria, please, not here. And why are you accusing me of such a monstrous thing as beating my own cousin?"

Dismissing his words, she sighed, "I have so many unanswered questions Woody and I have been very hard on you, and I am so exhausted. I know you love Anderson. Will you forgive me Woody?"

"All forgiven, Gloria, Woody said, turning back towards Anderson. "I saw his eyes fluttering, I believe he will come out of his coma. Besides, I had better get back to the club."

"Woody, where's Jada?"

"She woke up with a headache and I decided not to tell her about Anderson until we have some news. I am going to leave you here and go sit with Mom before I leave."

"Yes, you do that Woody. I am staying here with my husband."

Not long afterward, while Gloria sat next to his bed asleep in a chair, Anderson regained consciousness. He reached out and touched her hand. He whispered, "Hi. Gloria,"

Startled, she replied "Oh...Anderson."

Anderson closed his eyes and Gloria pushed the emergency button and immediately his doctor rushed in.

He spoke, he said to me, "Hi Gloria."

The doctor said, "I see his vitals are stronger, Mrs. Parks would you please step out for a moment. We will come to you soon. Anderson is a fighter."

Gloria left Anderson with his doctor and nurses. She ran to tell the others the good news. She saw Mom Parks and Woody standing in the hall. She shouted, "Anderson talked!"

Mom Parks clasped her hands, turned and shouted to the others inside the waiting room.

"Gloria said Anderson is talking!"

Woody, not giving them ample time to respond to the great news, asked, "What did he say? Did he tell you who assaulted him?"

"No, Woody, he didn't, but I believe we will know soon who did this to him."

She turned to the others and said, "This is what happened. I dozed off but I woke up when I felt a touch. I looked up and it was Anderson, he said, 'Hi Gloria'"

A short time later, Anderson's physician came into the waiting area and gave them an update on Anderson's progress. The doctor told them, "Anderson's vital signs are stronger and that's good news, and *I* expect Anderson to make a full recovery. If any of you would like to spend the night with Anderson then you are welcome to stay with him in his room. We are understaffed tonight so we will monitor him at the station. As I have stated you are welcome to stay, or you can go home. We are very confident Anderson will live."

Hearing the great news George, offered to take Gloria, Mom Park and her grandchildren back to their home or to Gloria's house. Woody gave orders to Luke Allen to take his mother, Gloria and the kids back to Gloria and Anderson's home.

Gloria walked out with them with intentions of going home, but she decided not to.

"Mom Parks," she said, "I want to stay. Will you stay with the kids?"

"Of course I will. But you need to get some rest, Gloria."

"I will. I am going to the cafeteria and get something to eat. I'll come back in Anderson's room and perhaps stretch out on the sofa.

As they all walked to the elevator, Grandpa Jeremiah eyes locked with Woody's and Grandpa Jeremiah mouthed, "You did it."

Woody slyly responded to his remarks. Using his finger as a gun, he inserted it into his mouth, then he pretended to pull the trigger.

"Woody."

With a smirk, he answered, Yes Momma?"

"Please go and check on your brother. Do you still have the key to his apartment?"

"I do, but his key is locked inside my office safe."

"Get the key and check on your brother for me please." "Anything you say Momma."

"Thanks son."

Gloria stepped off the elevator by the cafeteria and said goodbye to the Cate, George, Cullen, Grandpa, her children, Mom Parks, and she gave angry glares at Woody, Harry and Luke Allen.

Once the elevator door opened, they all went their separate ways.

Harry and Woody got into Woody's car. Woody ordered Harry to drive around the block and park his car in the alley down from the hospital. Woody ordered Harry out of the car and once the car doors closed, Woody walked around and attacked Harry. Seething with rage, he hissed through his clenched teeth, "You can't do nothin' right!"

With his injured fists, Woody knocked Harry to the ground and kicked him hard in the chest. Harry's thrashed around on the ground and his muffled whimpering caused Woody to mutter, "Get up! It's your fault that I am here.

"I have a plan. We will walk to the hospital and up to Anderson floor. I want you to go and see if that supply closet across from Anderson's room is still unlocked."

"What about the security camera outside his room?"

"I am several steps ahead of you boy. While waiting outside Anderson's room, I saw the maintenance crew working on the cameras. I heard one of them say, 'All cameras in the stairwells and outside the fourth and fifth floors are out, and the parts we need to fix the surveillance cameras will not be in until tomorrow.'"

"Yes, Boss, I will check the closet."

Harry walked quickly, to the closet to check. He promptly returned and said, "Boss, the closet is still unlocked."

"Harry, it's because of you, I am here. Watch me and follow my orders, your days with me are numbered, I have had enough of your blundering."

"Yes, Boss."

Together they stealthily tiptoed into the spacious closet. Once inside, Woody hand searched for the light switch and knocked over a few trays. Picking them up, he tossed them aside and cursed. He ordered Harry to crack the door and check to see if the hall was clear. Harry peeked out and he motioned to Woody to come. Just as Woody was about to step out, Harry saw Cate swiftly walking from the waiting room going into Anderson's room.

"Stop, Boss! It's Cate, she's going back to Anderson's room." Harry hastily closed the door.

With controlled anger, Woody hissed, "If you had done your job, then I wouldn't have to sit in this closet waiting for *that* woman to leave. Get out of here, go into the exit stairwell and wait for her to leave. Then come back to get me. And Harry once again, your days with me are numbered."

Daring not to respond to Woody's warning. Harry obediently stepped from the closet and walked toward the nearby stairwell.

As he walked he thought about Woody's threatening words, "*If you lives, mark my words, eventually you will be a dead man, your days with me are numbered."*

Defying Woody orders to wait in the stairwell, Harry decided to go into Anderson's room.

Harry knock and Cate turned and saw it was Harry. Harry opened the door and Cate said his name. Anderson's finger touched Cate's hand. Cate looked down and Anderson weakly shook his head back and forth, meaning, '*No*'.

Harry walked over to Anderson's bed. And Cate sat and said nothing. Anderson closed his eyes, pretending to sleep.

Harry said, "Evangelist Cate, I was on his way home and I wanted to see if there were any changes with Anderson." Harry looked at the 'monitor and saw Anderson's vital signs were improving, and his heart rate was increasing. He said, "Evangelist Cate, before I knocked, I heard you saying the Lord's Prayer and you telling Anderson God has forgiven him for his sins.

I am happy for Anderson. I like him, he is a very good man."

Harry turned to walk away, but stopped in the doorway. He turned and said, "Evangelist Cate, please keep my name in your prayers. Your words at church that Sunday when I was there keep turning over and over in my mind, and I really want to change. I know you have heard these words so many times. 'I will give my life to God tomorrow.' But each second in my day with Woody makes me believe my tomorrow may not come, and my death could happen any moment.

"Cate's eyes filled with tears. She shouted, "Stop

Harry, Let me pray for you and God's protection over your life."

After prayer, Harry said, "I want to accept Jesus as my Lord and Master, would you lead me to him?"

"Yes, Harry I will ...

Moment later, Harry said, Thanks Evangelist Cate, my soul feels so much lighter, and take care Evangelist Hayes and please stay alert. I know what I'm going to say may mean nothing to you, but I am really happy for Brie. He opened the door and stopped he said, "but I'm afraid for Cullen, your dad, Anderson and myself.'

Harry left Anderson's room and went into the stairwell across from Anderson's room and waited for Cate to leave.

A short time later Cate finally left.

Harry reluctantly, yet obediently knocked on the closet door and Woody walked out into Anderson's room.

"You stay here."

"Yes Boss."

Woody stood over his bed and whispered, "Anderson."

Anderson opened his one eye. Woody removed the pillow from under Anderson's head and whispered into his ear, "Now I will lay you down to sleep, and in hell you will awake. Woody put the pillow over Anderson's face. Anderson gave a weak struggled and Woody whispered, "Goodbye, my dear cousin."

The monitor sounded. Woody rushed from Anderson's room to the exit door leading into the stairwell. Using the stairwell, they went into another patient's room.

Woody pretended he had the wrong room and after having a light conversation with the patient, he and Harry got on the elevator, and stopped in the cafeteria. Woody, calmly grabbed a newspaper, sat down and sent Harry to fetch him a cup of coffee. While he sat sipping his coffee, the sound of running awakened Gloria who was asleep in the waiting room.

Gloria stood outside Anderson's room crying, staring at the closed door. Not noticing, Woody approached, at the moment when the door to Anderson's room slowly opened and the doctor stepped out and quietly told Gloria that her husband had died.

Gloria collapsed and Woody caught her. As Woody held Gloria, he felt something brushed against his shoulder. Woody turned to see who touched him and he saw and heard Anderson's spirit said, *'I love you and I forgive you.'*

Woody's body began shuddering. Gloria pulled away from his arms. She saw both tears and fear in Woody's eyes. Then Gloria felt gentle strokes on her face, she immediately felt Anderson's presence and she softly whispered his name, "Anderson."

Gloria eyes were supernaturally opened. She too saw Anderson's spirit. Anderson's appearance was indescribable. He was adorned with brilliant colorful precious stones from head to toe. Her husband flashed her his million dollar smile and turned away.

Gloria looked beyond Anderson and saw the hospital hall filled with a brilliant light, and angelic activity. Anderson turned to wave. She saw two glorious, angels lifting Anderson's spirit, and instantly, Anderson, with the angels, vanished.

Gloria stood in awe while Woody's body shook from fear. Woody let out a loud gasp, and his legs gave way beneath him.

He was terrified. For the first time in his life real tears soaked into his blue shirt.

Chapter 20, Money Socks

Later in the evening, at the Sullivan's home, their doorbell rang.

"Now, Vetta!" Grandpa Jeremiah hollered, "Who can that be this time? And why does that doorbell always ring just when I am about to have my steaming hot cup of coffee."

"Oh, Jeremy, stop your grumbling and please get the door."

Grandpa slammed the evening paper down onto the kitchen table. He pushed out his chair and as he moved towards the door he thought, *Lordy. Lordy. Lordy, have mercy. An old man can't have his hot cup of coffee without being disturbed.* He shouted, "Whoever is behind that door had better have a good reason for being there."

Opening the door, Grandpa saw Cate and George and he cheerfully shouted with a hint of sarcasm, "Well it's my beautiful daughter Cate, and George, my favorite son-in-law. Seeing you two is always a good reason for me to put down my newspaper and my steaming hot cup of coffee to answer the door, especially when you both have keys. Why didn't you use your key?"

Cate didn't answer, and her dad then noticed her demeanor wasn't right. He asked, "Now what's wrong?"

"So much Dad. I need to talk with Cullen."

"Your mother and Cullen are in the kitchen."

"Dad, I have already called Jason and Julia asked them to come here, and asked them to contact Brie and

Brad.

Why Cate? Why are you so serious?

What happened? Did Anderson die?"

"Yes, he did Dad."

Cate took hold of her father's arm and pulled him towards the kitchen, she heard the back door in the kitchen slam shut. She jumped and muffled her scream with her hands.

"Cate, what's wrong with you? Why are you acting like this?" asked her dad.

Cate heard Cullen shouting, "Grandma, look who I found in our driveway!"

Cate rushed into the kitchen; her pent-up emotions erupted when she embraced Cullen.

Brie saw her mom sobbing and asked her dad, "What's wrong with Mom? Please tell us, what has happened?"

"Brie, when Cate is able, she will tell you."

Cullen, stunned by his aunt's actions, looked at the others while he held his aunt tightly in his arms. He said, "Whoa, Aunt Cate, what's wrong?"

"Hello, hello, Grandpa, Grandma. Your front door was left ajar, I closed and locked it."

"Thank you, Jason!" hollered Grandpa, "Come into the kitchen and join us." Grandma Sullivan took out extra cups and placed a steaming pot of coffee and fresh baked raisin oatmeal cookies on the carousel. A short time later, Cate was able to sit with them. Grandma Sullivan poured Cate a cup of coffee and said, "Cate, tell us why are we gathered here?

And why are you crying and frightened for Cullen? Is this about Woody?"

"Yes it is, Mom. It's about Woody and Anderson. And yes," Cate looked directly at Cullen who was standing near the refrigerator with his arms folded. She said to him. "I am frightened for you, my nephew."

She took a few sips of her coffee and told them, "When we left the hospital last night, Anderson was out of his coma and was progressing. His doctor expected him to live. But less than an hour ago, Mother Parks called to tell us Anderson died."

Grandma Vetta reached across the table and touched her daughter's hands, she said, "Cate, I am so sorry. Anderson was such a delightful man."

Concealing his tears, Grandpa cleared his throat and his voice tightened. He said, "That's too bad, I was hoping he would pull through. I liked that boy. Anderson was kind and considerate, unlike that big, no good for nothing, fake crying cousin of his." With a strained voice Cate's dad said, "Cate, look at me."

Grandpa made eye contact with his daughter and asked, "Did you see that act he put on at the hospital? He should get one of them academy awards for best actor." Grandpa continued, "There he was, leaning on his mother and carrying on like he was in pain over Anderson's beating. Cate,it wouldn't surprise me at all if Woody didn't have something to do with this. When riding the elevator, Ida ask him to check in on his brother, and he answered, "Yes, Momma." Woody dad once told me Woody only call his mother momma when he had done something wrong. And yes, I believe he beat and killed Anderson."

Looking at Cate, Cullen, George and Cate, Grandpa asked them, "Was I the only one who saw that killer's raw, swollen knuckles?"

Grandpa looked at Cate and told her, "Yep, Cate, it wouldn't surprise me at all if Woody didn't have something to do with this."

"Now, Jeremiah Sullivan, Woody has done many unholy things, but I certainly hope he wouldn't stoop so low as to kill his own cousin."

Cate sat at the table, dabbing her eyes with her handkerchief said, "Momma, that's why I am here so early. I wanted to tell you and the others that Woody called our home this morning."

"Cate, why did that snake in the grass call you?"

"Dad, Woody called to tell me Anderson had died. Woody told me that Gloria had asked him to call me. He said Gloria wanted to know if Anderson had said anything to me before he died about who may have caused him his injuries. He said Gloria told him I was the last to see Anderson before he died. Then, approximately 30 minutes later, Mom Parks called to tell me Anderson had died. I told her I knew, she asked me how? I told her Woody had called to tell me. Mom Parks said, and I will quote her, 'That's odd, Gloria just called me. Gloria told me, Woody was with her at the hospital and being taken care of by the nursing staff because he's in shock over Anderson's death. And after I said goodbye to Gloria, I immediately called you.'"

 Cate took a long sip of her coffee and continued.

"Woody had called me before Mom Parks."

"Yep, Cate, that man has overplayed his hand. He just put the final nail into his own coffin. That big ugly, gingerbread devil is just as guilty as the cat being caught with the canaries' feathers inside its mouth."

Grandpa Jeremiah rose from his chair.

Agitated by what he heard, he began to pace in circles. Grandpa asked, "Cate tell us, were you the last one to see Anderson?"

"Yes, Dad I was, and that's what I am bothered about. When Anderson started improving, we all left Anderson's hospital room. I saw Woody and Gloria on the floor outside Anderson's room. I heard George offering to drive Ida Parks and Gloria and her kids to our house to rest. However, Woody didn't wait for his mother to answer George's offer. Woody immediately intervened and told Luke Allen to drive his mom home and to take Gloria and her children back to Gloria's house.

"I drove my own car to the hospital because George had a scheduled business meeting. George and I walked out together to the garage. George left me there in the garage because I was stopped by some of our church members and we talked for a while.

Afterward, I went to the garage attendant to get my car key. As I sat in my car, I inserted the key and started the engine started. I immediately turned it back off because the Holy Spirit decided that I should go back to Anderson's room so I did.

"When I stepped out of the elevator, I walked to the nursing station and saw only one nurse working. I informed her that I was going into Anderson's room to pray for him. When I passed the waiting room, I peeked in and I saw Gloria. The television was on and I stood over Gloria and whispered her name. She was sleeping soundly and I did not awake her. I went into Anderson's room and sat by his bed to pray.

As I sat praying aloud, Anderson opened his eyes and he looked at me, and said my name."

"Aunt Cate."

"Yes, Cullen?"

"Did Anderson say anything to you about his beating?"

"Not at first. We talked about Jesus and how God had given him this opportunity to repent of his sins. I told him he could have died, but God and His mercy had given him this chance to get his soul right. Anderson repented of his sins and he asked God for His forgiveness and vowed that he would change and live the rest of his life serving God. He asked me to read aloud Matthew 6. As I read the scriptures aloud, Anderson repeated The Lord's Prayer with me.

"When we said, 'Amen.' Anderson told me, 'Cate I have an inner peace that wasn't there before I accepted God back into my life. God has forgiven me.'

"We heard a knock and I turned and saw it was Harry. I said aloud Harry's name. I felt Anderson's finger touch my hand and I looked down.

Anderson weakly shook his head back and forth, meaning, 'no'. Harry walked over to Anderson's bed. I never moved, but watched, saying nothing. When I looked down at Anderson, I noticed Anderson had closed his eyes, pretending to sleep.

"Harry told me he was on his way home and he wanted to see if there were any changes with Anderson. Harry said to me, 'I see from the monitor Anderson's vital signs are improving and his heart rate is increasing. I heard him saying the Lord's Prayer with you and you telling him God has forgiven him for his sins. I am happy for him. Harry started to walk away, and he stopped in the doorway.

I stood and Harry turned around and he said to me, 'Evangelist Cate, please keep my name in your prayers. Your words at church Sunday keep turning over and over in my mind and I know I want to change. I know you have heard these words so many times, I will give my life to God tomorrow. But each second in my day with Woody I believe my tomorrow may not come, and my death could happen any moment.'

Harry gave me a weak smile and said, 'Take care, and I know what I'm going to say may mean nothing to you, but I am really happy for Brie… but I'm afraid for Cullen, your dad, Anderson and myself.' Harry asked me to lead him to salvation and I did. After I prayed with Harry, he left, closing the door. I looked back at Anderson and his eyes were open. I immediately stood and walked to the door, I looked both up and down the hall and I didn't see Harry. I thought perhaps he was with Gloria. Before I left his room, I went back to Anderson's bed and I touched his hand. I whispered, 'keep your eyes shut, I am going to check on Gloria and come right back.' I rushed to the waiting room and saw Gloria was still asleep. As I walked back to Anderson's room, I saw the utility closet across from his room slowly closing, however, I didn't think much of it. I went into Anderson's room and I closed his door. I walked to his bed and whispered, 'Anderson, its safe. You can open your eyes.'

"Anderson didn't respond to my voice, and I repeated, 'Anderson, I am alone. You can open your eyes.' Nonetheless, with all of my encouragement Anderson kept his eyes closed. He did not respond, so I whispered, 'Anderson, I am leaving, but I will be back.

"Anderson's injured eyes opened and he whispered, 'Cate, wait.' Anderson tried to smile and that's when I noticed his two front teeth were missing."

Grandpa, still annoyed about Woody's possible involvement with Anderson's death said, "Well Cate, at least Anderson is in heaven, and not in hell. That's where his big, nasty cousin Woody is going to go. And while we are on the subject of teeth. Did you see those diamond stud inserts that devil has implanted into his teeth? Lordy, that scoundrel is too much!"

"Jeremiah Sullivan, when are you going to forgive that man? Do you remember the true meaning to the Lord's Prayer, Jeremy? If not, I will be happy to repeat it just for you. God's word says, 'If you forgive others for their transgressions, your heavenly Father will also forgive others for their transgressions.' Your heavenly Father will also forgive you Jeremy."

"Yes, my dear Vetta,

 "Jeremy, forgiveness, is the word that connects us to

God's heart, and you are still holding this grudge against Woody and it has locked your heart. Sally and Mike have been dead for more than twenty years. Jeremy, dear, it is time for you to let go."

"Why should I, Lovetta? You have enough forgiveness forboth of us. Besides, God's word says, 'The woman sanctifies her man.'" With a smug smile, Grandpa Jeremiah said, "Lovetta, you are more than holy enough for us both."

Flustered with her husband's indifference. Lovetta shouted, "Jeremiah Sullivan, you know that is not what that scripture means! It says, "The unbelieving husband." You know you must forgive Woody!"

Grandpa stuffed his hands into his pant pockets, gave a cocky grin and quipped, "Yep, I know what that scripture means, but I choose not to forgive that calloused, calculating, murderous devil."

Cate walked over to her dad. She lovingly put her arms around his waist and told him, "Dad, you know Mom is right. You will have to let go of all this pent-up anger you have against Woody and let God have it."

Not arguing, he stared at his daughter and wife and heaved a big sigh as he thought, *Nope, no- way will I ever forgive that good-for-nothing so called man. He killed my daughter.*

Cate looked at her mom and the others and said, "There is more I need to tell!"

Then she pointed to each person around the table and told them "All of you here must promise me you will not repeat what I am going to tell you."

Receiving their promises, Cate told them, "Anderson

did talk to me. Anderson said, and I quote, 'I was wrong in what I did to Woody. I stole his money to feed my kids and to pay bills. I asked him to forgive me, but he refused. I forgive Woody for what he did to me.'"

Bang, bang, bang! They all jumped from the sudden, unexpected, loud pounding on the table. Grandpa struck the table with his fists and shouted, "See thar. See thar! I told you Woody killed that boy, just like he killed Sally, Mike, his daddy, and only God knows who else!"

"Jeremiah, you know Woody's father died from a heart attack."

"And who was there when Sam died?"

Lovetta reluctantly answered her husband's question. She whispered, "Woody."

"Lovetta, you're mumbling, so I can't hear you"

Lovetta answered, "Jeremiah, I said Woody was there when his father died."

"Lovetta, I got my thoughts and you have yours. My thoughts tell me Woody is a cold-blooded killer."

Also before Harry left Anderson's room he told me, to tell you both, Cullen and Brie, and you too dad, to watch Woody.

"Cullen and Brie why should you two have to watch Woody?" Cate said to them, "I believe I know the answer to this question, however, I want to hear from each of you, what Anderson meant when he said, 'to tell you two to watch Woody?'"

Brie stood quietly and looked at both of her parents.

She walked over to her dad, locked her elbow in his, and laid her head on his shoulder. She said, "Mom, Dad, I have to tell you something. Brad already knows."

Grandpa interrupted, "Please tell us you have knocked out those diamond studs from that lying hippo's mouth."

"Hush, Jeremy, and what you just said isn't at all amusing."

Brie forced a smile and said, "No, Grandpa."

"Ooooowee child! I am so sorry to hear that!"

"Jeremiah Sullivan, when will you quit your joking? Can't you see the girl is hurting?

Grandma Vetta stood up from the table and walked over to Brie. She placed her arms on Brie's shoulders, and said to her, "Go ahead dear, tell us."

Grandma Vetta frowned at her husband. He winked at his Lovetta and said, "Okay, Brie, I apologize for being inconsiderate and insensitive to your needs."

"Jeremiah?"

"What, Vetta? I apologized like you told me. Didn't I say it right?"

Brie exhaled noisily. She looked at her Grandpa and said, "I love you, Grandpa."

Brie looked at her Dad and told him "Dad, you also have suspected for a while that I have been gambling."

"Yes, Brie, and that's water over the dam."

"Yes, I know. But, Dad, there's more that I haven't told you."

Brie gave Cullen a quick glance and he lowered his head. Seeing this exchange between the two, Grandpa chimed in, "You meant to say, you and Cullen been gambling, didn't you?"

Brie barked back sharply, "No, Grandpa! Please forgive me for snapping at you, but I know what I am saying." With tears flowing, Brie looked at her beloved grandpa and said to him, "Grandpa, it's me, and I have won over $35,000 over the last few years at Woody's Place." Brie walked over to Cullen and he handed her a paper towel to dry her tears. Brie continued, "I didn't say anything to Cullen or anyone else about this until now. For months, while we gambled at Woody's, I noticed that each time I made money, Anderson would take a few hundred dollars and tuck them under his sleeve. He knew I saw him and he motioned for me to keep quiet.

"Grandpa, my gambling money is what you call, 'ill-gotten loot', and I want to give it all to Gloria. She will need the money to help with their household bills. I don't need it. I just liked the thrill of winning. Mom, I know what Anderson meant. I've noticed Woody becoming more domineering, aggressive, manipulative and so much more destructive. I used to like being around him, but over the years he has changed.

Woody has become an evil, self-absorbed, skimming, untrustworthy, and untruthful person."

Grandpa's sudden outburst caught them all off-guard. Breathing hard, he ranted, saying, "What is it that you have called me for years? Unforgiving!" He pointed to Brie and Cullen, saying, "You my granddaughter and you, my grandson, especially you Cullen, you tagged me as this malicious person. I am the only one who knows Woody is the incarnated devil himself. I know Vetta and Cate do not want to believe Woody killed Sally and Mike. I know with every wrinkle in my body and with every gray hair on my head that Woodrow Hugh Parks murdered them! He is evil and can't be saved, even from himself. Yes, I am just an old man, yet these old eyes see a lot. That cuttlefish has been hiding his true self beneath his grimy, filthy surface too long. The truth about him is beginning to unlock and you all will see and know Woodrow Hugh Parks' tentacles are poisonous. His mouth speaks lies and like flies caught in a tarantula's web, his web of deceit will be his self-inflicted death trap.

"Grandpa," said Brie, "I am so sorry for not believing you, your eyes did see the truth."

Brie walked over to the kitchen counter. She picked up her purse and quickly opened it. She took out her green money sock and handed it to her dad, and said, "Dad, I want to go with you and Mom to give this to Gloria. And, if it's possible, I want Woody to be present when we do this. Is there any way you can arrange this?"

"Brie, your mother, Pastor Wilson, and I are scheduled to meet with Gloria and her family tomorrow evening at Gloria's home to finalize Anderson's graveside ceremony."

"George?"

"Yes, Cate."

"Perhaps Brie can come with us." Cate turned to Brie and said, "I am certain Woody will be there. Once we are all there, you can give Gloria the money. Then Woody will not have any reason to mess with you anymore."

Grandpa looked hard at Cullen and said, "Well here I go meddling and butting in once again. Cullen do you have anything you want to say or do before you skip town?"

Cullen stared at Brie thinking about her words. After an awkward silence, he gave her a thumbs up and told her, "Brie, I am so happy for you.

You have married my best friend and your life is now committed to God. I have to keep it real though. I am a little heartbroken and I am really sorry I have lost my personal bodyguard."

Brie planted a quick kiss on Cullen's cheek and said, "Cullen you know I love you and you will always be my favorite cousin." Brie walked to her husband, put her arms around his neck and kissed him. She shouted. "Alleluia! I am free! No more tentacles around my neck from Woody. My life will be *forever* led by God's Spirit and not by the desires of my flesh."

Brie rushed over to Cullen. She placed both hands on Cullen's broad shoulders and shook them.

Laughing, she said to him, "Come on cousin do the right thing… remove Woody's tentacles."

Cullen stared into his cousin's dancing green eyes and without saying a word to her, he walked out of the kitchen. Brie turned slowly and saw the others looking quizzically at each other with distressed faces. Brie smiled and said, "I know my cousin. Cullen will do what is right."

They were sitting around the table strategizing when Cullen returned to the kitchen.

"Ahem."

They looked up and Cullen looked at Brie and smiled. All the while, he was tossing his red money sock. Not saying a word, he dumped out rolls and rolls of bills. And nonchalant announced, "$55,000 to be exact."

George's mouth dropped open from shock. He shook his head and said, "Brie, you and Cullen have been doing some serious gambling! Cate honey, I'm sorry. I guess I wasn't a great daughter sitter."

Brie poked out her lips and said, "Dad, I'm sorry! You trusted me and I was the one who deceived you."

Cullen came to his cousin's defense. "Although I am three years older than Brie, I wanted my favorite cousin's company and protection, I persuaded her to come; now, since Brie has been convicted by the Holy Spirit, I will follow her lead and give this money to Gloria."

Cate looked at her dad and jokingly asked, "Dad, do you still have that old dried up tree limb you used on Sally and my legs when we disobeyed you and Momma? I could use it right now on my daughter and nephew."

She pointed to the kitchen table and shouted, "Just look at this! $90,000 between you both! Wow, you two need to be in that whipping shed!"

They all laughed. Cate said, "Seriously, Cullen and Brie, George and I will take this money to the bank and get a cashier's check made out to Gloria and ..."Cate suddenly stopped talking. She smiled and tugged George's arm. She said, "George, you know that jewelry? Would it be okay if we gave it back to Jada? Not now, but later when she has broken free of Woody's tentacles."

George responded quickly, "Yes."

Cate laughed, as the wheels turned. "And George, you had Jada's jewelry appraised? Right?"

"Yes, Cate?"

"What was the appraisal amount?"

$100,000." George laughed and said, "Cate are you thinking what I think you are?"

"George, would it be possible to give Gloria that $100,000?"

"I believe we can easily afford that, Cate."

Jason pounded the table and shouted, "Oh what the heck! Julia and I will toss in another $100.000."

"Wow! You guys are being jovial and generous."

Brad said, "That's $290,000." Brad looked at each person and said, "Mr. and Mrs. Hayes you are giving Gloria $100,000 in cash from the jewelry that's worth $100,000 that you will keep, and not sell, to give back to Jada when she has broken free of Woody, and Brie and Cullen, you are giving up your cash, and my parents, your'$100,000 donation is an additional blessing for Gloria and her kids and deliverance for Brie and Cullen from Woody's poisonous tentacles."'

Cate took out her cell phone. She pressed her finger to her lips signaling them to keep quiet. She then punched in Gloria's number. "Hello, Gloria, this is Cate Hayes. I'm calling from my mom and dad's home. Jason, Julia, Brad, Brie and Cullen are here with me.

Would it be alright if I put you on speaker mode?" "Why yes, Cate!'

They all shouted, "Hi Gloria." "Hello, everybody."

"Gloria, I am calling to see if 8:30 p.m. tomorrow evening would be okay for us to come by."

"Why, yes Cate"

"Gloria, will it be okay if Grandpa, Grandma, Brie,

Brad Cullen, Jason and Julia come with George and me?"

"Of course, Cate."

"Gloria, Jason just passed me a note saying, he and Julia will come by later if he can't clear his calendar."

"They can come by anytime. It's always great to see Jason and his Julia."

"That's good. Then we will look forward to seeing you. I also want to tell you about my conversation with Anderson before he died."

Anderson talked with you?"

Cate heard Gloria sobbing. After Gloria composed herself, they heard her giggling. She said, "Thank God. Now I know what I saw was… never mind. I will tell all of you when you come. Love you all, and bye, Cate." Before Cate could disconnect, she heard Gloria screaming, "Mom Parks, Cate said. ..."

Replacing her cell phone into her purse, Cate pondered, then said, "You all heard when I told Gloria I wanted to tell her what Anderson said to me before he died. Her reaction to what I said tells me she didn't know Anderson had regained consciousness, and that he spoke with me. But when Woody called me this morning, he told me Gloria wanted to know what Anderson said to me. In retrospect, how would Gloria have known I was there? She was asleep."

Grandpa gave his daughter a concerned look when he said, "Cate, do you think it was wise to tell her you had a conversation with Anderson before he died? She will tell Ida, and Ida will tell Woody. Then Woody, that low-life of a wannabe man, will be at Gloria's house waiting for you."

"That's my plan, Dad. Woody will come to Gloria's desiring to hear what Anderson said to me, and then he will see Brie and Cullen telling Gloria how they won the money at his place, and the amount they have won. Besides, Dad, we all know when Anderson didn't live right, Gloria did. Gloria has always been the backbone in that family and she needs to know that Anderson was looking forward to a new life with her and their children, they all need to know Anderson gave his life to Jesus.

"So if my theory is right, both Woody and Harry were hiding inside the closet across the hall from Anderson's room, and Woody sent in Harry to see if Anderson had regained consciousness.

"Mom, Dad," said Cate, "If Woody had anything to do with his cousin's death, then he will have to live with the consequences of two judgments. The law of man and God's final judgment."

Brie said, "See Cullen, isn't your aunt an awesome woman?" Brad shouted, "Hey, she's my mother-in-law!"

Grandpa added, "Smart plan, Cate. I will be there to watch that weasel suffer!" Smiling broadly, Grandpa Jeremiah continued, "Smart? No, she is brilliant!

Jason added, "And our friend." George said, "And may I add, my wife.

Stop it!" said Cate, "You know I don't like that sort of admiration."

"Cate..."

"Yes, Mom."

"A smart and dangerous plan having Woody there. No one knows if this plan will work or backfire, and if it backfires, your plan may cause more trouble for those who have been exploited, and mistreated by Woody, especially his and our immediate family members. By the way, have they found Michael?"

"I don't believe they have, Mom."

"Mom?"

"Yes, Brie?"

"Woody carries 4 or more concealed weapons. He is a keg of smothering dynamite and no one knows when he will implode."

"Brie, we just have to trust God to send His angels to be our shields.

"It wouldn't surprise me at all if that son of the devil killed his own brother and dumped his body in the ocean."

"Jeremiah please, let it go!"

"Vetta he's capable of doing anything. Ah, you didn't see him, but on the elevator I mouthed to Woody, 'You did it.'"

Jeremiah Sullivan, you just couldn't keep your opinions to yourself. Could you? You are a pigheaded old man. Now tell us what happened?"

"Why that son of the devil put his finger into his mouth and pretended to pull the trigger. He jerked his head back, stuck out his tongue and smiled. I figure he thought that would intimidate me."

Smiling broadly, Grandpa, lifted his hands to heaven and shouted, "Thank you, Jesus! God please keep me alive so I will be there to watch that weasel suffer!"

"Jeremiah, stop it!"

"What, Vetta? I have a right to express my opinions.

Vetta, our Cate is brilliant." Grandpa leaned back on his chair, then pulled and popped his suspenders.

With an explosive chuckle, he said, "After all, she's my daughter and we Sullivans are amazing! Ain't that right, Cullen?"

Cullen had never seen his grandpa this happy. Grandpa rose from the table, grabbed Cullen's neck and gave him a big bear hug. He kissed his grandson's forehead with a sloppy kiss and told him, "I am proud of you son, getting that dirty, blood money out of my bedroom and house!"

Grandpa released Cullen, looked at his beloved wife, and shouted, "Lovetta, while the family is here, I believe this is a good time to tell Cullen our news. Let's take advantage of this joyous moment. Honey, go ahead and tell him."

"Tell me what? Asked Cullen as he moved closer to his grandma. He lifted her in his arms, and teasingly said, "Grandma, are you pregnant?"

"Put me down boy, and that's not funny, Mr. Cullen Michael Sullivan." Grandma's head swayed back and forth trying to maintain the scowl on her face, but she couldn't. She playfully tapped Cullen's face as she listened and joined in with the others' laughter.

After the laughter had died down, Grandma Vetta said, "My funny grandson… but seriously, Cullen, your Uncle George, Aunt Cate, and especially your Grandpa and I felt you weren't ready for what we are about to tell you. But after what has happened tonight, we believe you are ready to handle this additional huge responsibility you are coming into. Cullen, you did not know that we have been saving for your college education."

Cullen interrupted, "Grandma and Grandpa, I had scholarships.

I want you to use that money,"

"Thank you, Cullen, but no thanks. We don't need it. Just hush up now and listen.

"Yes, ma'am," Cullen responded with a wink. He stuffed his hands into his pant pockets and looked down at his feet.

Grandma Lovetta lifted his chin and said, "Cullen, we all here know your football skills will lead you to greatness and we all would love for you to go back to college to get that degree."

Grandma Lovetta glanced over at Jeremy, winked, and told him "Cullen, I also know you told your Grandpa that you are gambling.

Grandpa looked at Lovetta, obviously in shock by what she revealed. His mouth dropped open and his hands shot in the air. He shook his head back and forth, and said, "Vetta, I didn't tell you about the conversation I had with Cullen about his gamblin'!"

Grandma Lovetta smiled and said, "I know you didn't Jeremy." She cleared her throat, and laughter immediately erupted when she mimicked his voice. "But these old ears ain't deaf."

"Oh, Mom!" Cate swaggered over and high-fived her. Laughing, she said, "Good one, Mom!"

A short time later when all the laughter died down, Grandma Lovetta said, "Now I'm serious, Cullen. When your parents died, they had a life insurance policy.

Jeremy and I didn't need the money, so we invested all of it for you."

"George, how much does Cullen have for life?"

George smiled, rose from the table, walked over to Cullen, placed his hand on his shoulder, and said, "Cullen Michael Sullivan, son of Mike and Sally Wallace, you have a little more than a million dollars."

Clutching his head, Cullen shouted with disbelief, "What? What? What? What did you say? Did I hear you correctly, Uncle George?"

Cullen rushed to the sink and turned on the water. Using his hand as a cup, he gulped down water and dabbed his face. Brie handed him a paper towel to dry his face. Cullen muttered, "With my NFL contract and this money, I am very wealthy."

Grandpa replied, "And that's the reason Cullen why you need to stop gambling, you don't need the money and gambling is a habit that will not end well."

"Grandma and Grandpa, you are right and I haven't gambled in months and I promise you both that I will never gamble again." Cullen grabbed his grandma with his wet hands, he lifted her and danced with her around the table.

"Cullen Michael Sullivan, put me down. I am old and these old bones have danced enough." Holding tightly to his grandma, he gingerly sat her on her chair. Cullen stood holding his head, trying to contain his joy.

Grandpa got up from the table, walked over to Cullen and slapped his back. He told him, "See Cullen? You didn't need Woody's dirty, blood money. We were waiting until we thought you were mature enough to handle additional responsibility to tell you.

Seeing you give up that money just now was the sign for all of us that this is the correct time to give you this great news."

Cullen scooped his Grandparents into his long arms and gave them both kisses. Beaming with happiness, Cullen announced, "Grandma and Grandpa, do not worry, I will take care of you."

Grandpa replied, "Boy, you don't have to worry about us. Lovetta has always had a great big God looking after her and He has always been Lovetta's provider. And me? I reaped all of God's benefits being married to my sweet Vetta"

"Really, Dad?" Cate said, "You really believe you reaped Mom's blessings because you are married to her? We need to have a very serious talk really soon."

Chapter 21, A Malicious Gaze

The doorbell rang. Opening the door, Gloria welcomed her friends with smiles and hugs. From the door's entrance, they saw Ida Parks, standing and smiling with outstretched arms, shouting "Come on in, Pastor Wilson is already here."

Embracing Gloria, Cate asked, "How are you and the family doing?"

"Considering all that has happened, we are doing well. I just can't understand what happened to Anderson?"

"I know," said Cate, "when I left Anderson's bedside he was doing well… Gloria?"

"Yes, Cate?"

"Did the doctor tell you what he believed may have happened to Anderson?"

"Anderson's physician is perplexed. He said Anderson's vital signs were improving and he was doing very well. His doctor believes he died from asphyxiation."

"Asphyxiation? The physician believes Anderson choked to death?"

"Yes, Cate."

"But, Gloria, I don't …"

The doorbell rang and Gloria excused herself. Shortly, she returned to the room with Jada and Woody.

After saying their hellos, Gloria told them, "I was just telling the others that Anderson's physician believes he died from asphyxiation."

"Asphyxiation is suffocation. Is that the same as strangling, or being smothered?" asked Grandpa.

"What?" Woody's hands flailed as he shouted, "Then the police need to find out who did this to him and arrest them!"

"Gloria responded, "They are investigating, but unfortunately the surveillance cameras outside Anderson's room and inside the stairwell were malfunctioning. However, the one inside Anderson's room was functioning. They believe that video will give them the identity of my husband's killer by tomorrow."

"By tomorrow," Woody's voice faded when he whispered, "that soon."

"Woodrow. Woodrow."

"Yes, Momma."

Mom Parks chuckled.

"Why are you laughing?" asked Jada.

"Oh, it's Woodrow. I laughed because he just said, Momma. Woodrow never calls me Momma, unless he's done something wrong and..."

Interrupting his mother, Woody hastily replied, "I have done something wrong, Momma. I just regret not giving Anderson the loan he needed. If I had, perhaps he would be alive.

"Woodrow, I know you loved Anderson just as much as all of us here did and I'm certain Chief Jones and his investigators are doing all they can to find out who did this to our poor Anderson.

We just have to be patient and let them do their job. But Woodrow?"

"Yes, Mom?"

"Son, please ease your Momma's mind and tell me why you didn't give Anderson the loan?"

"Mom, I was having a financial setback. Despite what Anderson thought, and…" apologetically, Woody said, "Gloria, I didn't like Anderson begging. I just didn't have extra cash on hand to give away. If I had the money, I would have given it to him and then…" Woody began releasing tears, appearing to have a broken heart. Woody began sniveling and sobbing; he cried, "then my cousin would not be dead."

Looking at Gloria, Woody said, "Gloria, I am troubled because I may have indirectly caused my cousin's death and..." he looked to his mother and said, sniffing, "that troubles me, Mom."

"I understand, son. Come." Ida Parks pointed to the overstuffed chair next to her. With her outstretched hands she said, "Come, Woodrow, sit next to me, and try to relax." Woody stood and lumbered over to sit next to his mother.

Holding his hand, she said, "Woodrow, Gloria was waiting for all of us to come together to tell us some good news and heaven knows it's time for some good news."

Ida smoothed her dress, and said, "Go ahead Gloria, tell us your good news."

Clapping her hands, Gloria started to jump around like a young cheerleader. She cupped her hands to her mouth and yelled, "I saw Anderson's spirit!"

"You what?" Pastor Wilson shouted. "Gloria, that's amazing. Please Gloria, tell us more!"

Anderson's physician had just told me Anderson died. Hearing those words was too much pain for me and I collapsed, but Woody caught me. As Woody held me, I noticed his body began to shake and his knees knocked together. I pulled myself out of his arms and I saw tears mingled with fear in Woody's eyes. Woody let out a loud gasp, and his legs gave way beneath him. As I watched Woody lying on the floor, I felt gentle strokes to my face and I immediately felt Anderson's presence. I whispered, 'Anderson,' and instantaneously my eyes were supernaturally opened and it was then that I saw Anderson's spirit!"

Ida Parks' hand touched her heart. She gasped for air and asked, "Woodrow, did you see Anderson's spirit?"

"No, Mom, I didn't. I was only reacting to hearing about Anderson's death."

"Now, Woody, I beg to differ- I know you saw him because your face turned darker with fright. You started shaking, fell to your knees crying and the nurses helped you."

Gloria waited for Woody to tell them that her insights were correct. However, Woody looked away.

Gloria happily said, "That's okay, Woody. You can live in your world of denial. I know you saw Anderson spirit. And I." She placed her hands over her heart and continued, "I am 100% certain I saw Anderson.

"Anderson's appearance was beautiful. His garment was adorned with colorful, brilliant, precious stones, and he smiled that beautiful wide smile of his, showing all his perfect teeth and then he turned away from me. I looked to see where he was going and I saw the hospital hall fill with flashes of lightening and angelic activity. My Anderson turned towards me and waved; then, Anderson, with the angels, vanished."

Gloria walked over to Cate. She stooped down and held Cate's hands and said, "Cate, I saw Anderson's spirit with the angels before our talk on the phone. Seeing Anderson's spirit with God's angels confirmed that Anderson had repented and given his life back to God. Cate, I thank God for your being there and leading him to secure his place in God's kingdom. I can now rest in peace knowing Anderson is in heaven."

Cate smiled and kissed Gloria's cheek.

"Woody," said Cate, "to answer your question, I'm certain the police department is doing all they can do to find out who murdered Anderson."

Ida Parks said, "Who could have done this to him? Whoever it was had to be callous, calculating, cold-blooded, heartless and crude."

"Uh-huh, and inhuman and a premeditated murderer," added Grandpa Jeremiah, as his eyes locked with Woody's.

Observing this interaction between the two, Grandma Sullivan said Jeremy."

"Yes, Vetta."

"Would you pour me a cup of coffee? Please."

"Okay dear."

"Cate."

"Yes, Gloria."

 "You and Anderson talked before he died? Did

Anderson ..."

Woody interrupted Gloria and shouted, "What? Cate, you and Anderson talked! Did he tell you who did this to him?"

"Woody, don't you remember? You called my home and said Gloria asked you to call me because she wanted to know what Anderson said to me."

"What? I didn't know you talked with Anderson until you told me, and Cate I never asked Woody to call you."

"Did I say Gloria? I apologize. I meant to say Harry. Well, Cate, did Anderson say anything?"

Puzzled by Woody's comments, Gloria probed Woody further. She asked, "Woody, why would Harry want to know about Anderson?"

"Gloria," said Cate, "I believe I can answered that for Woody. I was with Anderson when Harry came into the room. Harry said he was on his way home and Woody told him to stop by to check on Anderson's progress.

"Woody, Anderson and I talked about God and how he loves unconditionally."

Cate turned to Gloria, and said, "Gloria, that's when Anderson gave his life back to God."

"Gloria."

"Yes, Mom Parks?"

"Anderson received God's grace. Grace is God's lovingkindness that forgives the sincere heart. I am waiting for my Woodrow to ask God for forgiveness for all his sins."

Woody inner phantom said, *Old woman that will never happen! I am his master.*

Woody sat, quietly sulking in the overstuffed chair, listening to his inner phantom planning tactics to find the right words to trick Cate into telling him if Anderson told her about him.

The telephone rang. Gloria excused herself to answered and returned crying. Ida rushed to her. She asked, "Gloria, what's wrong?"

"Mom Parks that was Chief Jones on the phone. The surveillance camera inside Anderson's room was also malfunctioning. Now we may never know who murdered Anderson."

Woody silently breathed out a sigh of relief hearing the news. *My inside men did their job.* He heard his mother saying, "Don't cry baby, the truth will be revealed."

Woody quickly responded, "Let's hope so Momma."

After dinner, Woody sat and listened as they celebrated Anderson's life by sharing pictures and telling stories.

"Woodrow."

"Yes, Mom?"

"I'm sure you have stories to share."

"Not now, Mom."

"Cate."

"Yes, Woody?"

"You saw how badly Anderson was beaten.

Do you know who could have done such an awful thing to him and why?"

"I have my idea, but I'm not God, Woody."

Woody's phantom released a spiteful, loud, contemptuous chuckle and blurted out, "You have your idea? You are God's prophetess aren't you? Aren't you the great Cate Hayes? God's best friend. Hasn't your best friend told you the name of Anderson's killer yet?"

"She don't need God to tell her the name of Anderson's killer!" shouted Grandpa.

"Shut your mouth old man, I wasn't talking to you."

"Woodrow!" Hollered Ida. "Stop it! What has happened to you?"

"What has happened to me? Mom, is it wrong for me to ask the one who claims to be her God's mouthpiece, the one who you all think walks on water, who killed Anderson?"

Cate calmly replied, "Mom Parks, that's okay, I do not need you or my dad to be my advocate."

Cate looked unflinching directly into Woody's dark eyes filled with malice and told him, "I am God's mouthpiece. And my God has revealed a lot to me. I do not know all the details, but as I sit here, and listen, and observe, I am beginning to put all the pieces together from the past, the present, as well as into the future. Why, Woody, does your phantom have something to reveal?"

Woody's phantom became even more aggressive as fear filled its host's quarrelsome mind. Woody screamed, "Do I…? Did I hear you correctly? Did you just ask if I have something to tell you?' Woody's inward phantom feared, *Cate knows it was you who killed Anderson. She must die.*

His look was contemptuous with forewarning. Woody stood. He put his hands into his pant pockets and touched the butt of the small pistols.

He scornfully shouted, "Oh Cate, I understand it all!

You still blame me for your sister's death. You have convinced yourself that your God is revealing to you all of my deep, dark secrets, and you, you have convinced yourself and my family that I had something to do with Anderson's death. Cate Hayes, you are nuts! You are a false prophetess, phooey, God's mouthpiece! You make me laugh."

Cate rose from her chair and walked boldly over to Woody and whispered, "My God and Master commands you to remove your hands from the pistols you have concealed in your pockets, and to do it now!"

Immediately, Woody complied. With courageous power, Cate said, "I am from God and stand in His power. I command that phantom that's in you to sit and be quiet because the One who is in me is greater than the one who is in you.to Go and sit down!" Woody's spirit complied and Woody's phantom sat.

Cate calmly turned and sat back on her chair. She looked around and noticed the others were in a trance, and had no knowledge of what had just transpired between her and Woody.

Gloria stood and walked over to Woody. Undeterred, she attacked by repeating Cate's question. "Do you have something to tell us?" She boldly asked, "Woody, did you kill my Anderson?"

"Gloria!" hollered Ida. "Stop this! You both are hurting!"

Ida pointed to Woody and said, "Woodrow, who are you? I do not recognize this person who's in front of me. You are being disrespectful to us all."

Ida looked at Cate and said, "I am sorry, Cate. Both of my children are wrong. I apologize to you for them. My son and Gloria are saying such hateful words, and such hurting accusations."

Ida looked directly at her son and told him. "You, Michael and Anderson were raised together like brothers. I know you would never do anything to intentionally harm Anderson. Now, son, apologize to Cate, Jeremiah and the others for your rudeness."

Woody gazed at Cate and Jeremiah with malevolence and he did not apologize. Jada knew Woody's forewarning gaze too well. She looked over at Cate, who sat smiling at Woody, and said, "Cate, at church last Sunday, I had a transformation in my soul. I have rededicated my life back to God and now God is giving His protection, strength and peace to me."

Brie let out a delightful high pitched squealed. She leaped from her chair, rushed over to Jada, and gave her a big, exuberant hug, and shouted.

"So did I Jada! I rededicated my life back to God. Not only that, I am now Mrs. Bradford Rock!"

Hearing Brie's announcement, kisses, hugs, and congratulations were given by Gloria, Pastor Wilson and Mom Parks, while Woody sat quietly agonizing.

"Gloria!" Ida shouted, "Put on some praise music!"

Woody defiantly said, "Mom, this isn't the time to praise, this is time to mourn Anderson's death. If you're going to start praising your God with shouting and dancing, then Jada and I are leaving."

Gloria stood, walked over to him and placed both

hands on the armrests of the chair that Woody sat on. She looked him in his dark malicious eyes and said, "This is my home and I disagree with you Woody. This is an excellent time to praise God. Anderson is rejoicing in heaven right now and not agonizing in torment residing in hell."

She kissed Woody's forehead and shouted, "Let's praise our God!"

Staring at Woody, Gloria shouted over the loud music. "Jada, do you want to leave?"

Jada looked at Woody. He mouthed to her, "Let's go!"

Jada smiled, and brazenly shouted, "Mom Parks!"

"Yes Jada!"

"If I stay, will you drive me home?"

"Why yes, I can do that!"

"Then I will stay, and Woody can go!"

Gloria grabbed Jada's hands and together they happily danced in circles. As they danced, Jada's scarf fell onto the floor. Ida bent over, picked it up, and put it around her neck and continued dancing.

Ida glanced over at her son and saw him staring spitefully at Cate, Gloria and Jada. As he glared, she came over and embraced Jada.

Ida looked over at her sulking son and said, "Now Woodrow, I see you aren't happy for Jada, and I know why; you have lost your working wife! You are wondering what you are going to do now that your wife is saved! We all know she can't work no more in that club of yours."

Not waiting for his response, Ida said, "Jada, I tell

 you what, honey. You can come to my restaurant and work

there. I can always use more help and Woodrow you will let her come."

Smothering with revengeful thoughts, Woody sat in silence.

"Well, son, since you didn't respond, I will make the decision for you. Woodrow, your wife is now working with me."

Woody gave his Mom a sinister smile and muttered. "Anything you want, Mom."

"Then that's it! Jada, come tomorrow morning at ten. You will be a new employee of Curve Café."

Jada hugged her and said, "Oh thank you, Mom Parks!" Jada's eyes locked with Woody's and his gaze was filled with forewarning.

Ida walked over and turned the praise music off.

The dancing stopped and they all looked at her. Ida smiled and then turned around to her sulking son and said, "Cate, will you please ease my son's mind. Did Anderson say anything about the people who beat him?"

"Mom Parks, Anderson just said … now let me get his words correct." Cate sighed, she told them, Anderson said, 'I was wrong in what I did. I have forgiven him for what he did.'"

"Forgiven him?" Ida turned to Woody and asked, "Son do you have any idea who is ... this him?"

Woody didn't answer; he shrugged his shoulders, indicating, he didn't know.

"Mom Parks."

"Yes, Gloria."

"All I know is the person who did it is really heartless.

Anderson's body was beaten so badly, his jaw was cracked and they knocked out his two front teeth. Mom Parks, tell me what kind of monster or insane person could have done such a thing to Anderson."

Ida looked over at Woody, whose dark stare was foreboding. She stretched out her hand for her son to come to her. When he did she held his hands and tears fell from his fiery eyes onto his black suit jacket.

Ida held him close, and kissed his cheek, and whispered, "Are you okay, son?"

"Yes Mom, I'm okay, but I'm beginning to feel that those friends of yours are thinking I am responsible for Anderson's death. Come on Mom, that's ridiculous. He's family."

"Son, they are friends and have been for many, many years. No one is thinking that. The only one who know for sure who killed Anderson is God. And He will reveal it all when He's ready."

Woody and Ida saw Brie bubbly skipping and giggling across Gloria's large living area. She grabbed Cullen's hand, and together they stood in the center of the room. Brie cheerfully shouted, "Please, everybody find a seat. Gloria, do you have tissues? If not, Mom will you get her some? And Dad, Gloria may need a catcher if she falls from her chair."

"Okay, Brie," said Ida, "Now I am curious, what is this announcement? It must be a life changer."

Brie snapped her fingers, and said, "You know, Mom Park, your words are prophetic. This announcement will be a life changer and will give freedom from worry."

Curious about this news, Woody's body stiffened and his stare became more ominous. Without hesitancy, Brie boldly looked directly at Woody. No longer stressed by his terrifying look, she said, "Woody, God has made changes in my life. Woody what was that word you called me at church? 'A charlatan.' Well, I am no longer that." Brie gave Woody a faint smile and turned to address the others. She said, "I know you all heard about Cate and George's daughter being a frequent gambler at Woody's Place, and my sinning on Friday and Saturday nights and praising God on Sunday morning, and all that." She paused and said, "Well, it was true."

She walked back over to Woody and she directed her words to him. "Woody, I am happy to announce that those gambling days are over for both Cullen and me!"

Woody smiled while thinking, *Where's my money? You and Cullen will pay me back, or somebody will die.*

Woody, hastily responded with a slightly open-handed gesture and a quick head nod.

Cullen, not hanging back, held Brie's hand and he too spoke directly to Woody. "Woody, Brie and I together have won over $90,000 in the past year at your place."

Hearing the amount, Woody's insides became mentally deranged. *$90.000,* he thought, *I only asked for $75.000. I want all my money back.* Holding pent up anger, Woody somehow managed to control his temper.

Ida chided, "Now, Cullen and Brie, you both know that was too much time spent gambling, especially for two church going young people who are ministering to others. God's word tells us that you must be serious, and not be two-faced, nor addicted to wine, or greedy for money."

"Yes, Mom Parks, you are right. Cullen and I knew all that, but all that time we didn't think about God's feelings or His Word. We were self-absorbed and enjoyed the thrill that came from winning. We were having fun."

"Um-hum, thrills, and having fun… don't you know both are temporary?"

Ida looked over to her old friends, and said, "Jeremiah and Lovetta, if we had a nickel for all the times we have heard that expression, 'Having fun.'

You know that's what's wrong with our youth. Young people today don't think about the consequences of their actions." Ida looked directly at her son and not wavering, she said, "Then there's you, Woodrow."

"Me, Mom? Why put me into this? They won money from me! I didn't put a gun to their heads and make them gamble, they came willingly! Geez, Mom, give me a break please!"

"A break! You know God's word like you know the pain you must be feeling from the wrinkles in your swollen, bruised knuckles."

Everybody looked at Woody's hands, but his mom, not noticing their stares, continued her ranting. "Brie, Cullen, and you," she pointed to her son. "Woodrow, all three of you know the Bible says, 'Whoever knows the right thing to do and fails to do it, for him it is sin.' Knowing right, and doing right, are two different things. Ida looked directly at Woodrow when she told the others, "That's what went wrong with Woodrow, and with Michael, and my poor Anderson." She shook her head, and with closed eyes she said; "Those three believed they could do whatever they pleased and they did, and they did *not* think about God's feelings or the consequences of their actions." Ida shook her head, and said with reprimanding words.

"I know I am preaching now. But children, you have to hear this. Don't you know God has feelings! He hurts when we hurt, and when we deliberately sin, it pains Him so much."

Ida turned her attention to Brie and Cullen and told them, "Our loving God, took our sins on Himself, and we received what He didn't deserved and He didn't receive. That was love, mercy and justice. Brie, you found and accepted God's grace, and Anderson found what grace and mercy was all about when he looked into the face of Jesus. Cullen, I perceive you are still straddling the fence, but God has a plan for you.

"You children must remember, God allowed Jesus to be captured and Jesus willingly died upon that cross for our freedom. God's Spirit resurrected Himself to life from the dead on the third day and caused Himself to be visible as Jesus. The One Spirit who hovered with life in the beginning, continues to hover, desiring to find a resting place in you and in me. He desires to give us His renewing Spirit of life that's wrapped in a gift called grace. His grace keeps giving, even after we sin against His law and deserve death; but instead of death, He gives life. Now, children, that's great grace."

With a big wide grin, Cullen happily replied, "Mom Parks, in a moment you and the others will see that Brie and I are so thankful for God's great grace and our freedom. And you are right, I haven't yet committed my life back to God, but I will. Mom Parks, Brie has thought about God's feelings and the consequences of her sins. She has welcomed God's Spirit and He has found a resting place in her, and that's why Brie and I have decided to give away our money that we won when gambling at Woody's to..."

Cullen turned towards Gloria and said, "To you, Gloria."

Hearing this news, Gloria lost her balance and began to fall off her chair but George caught her. Gloria sat speechless with tears flowing. While sniffling, she told them, "Anderson had $10,000 in his pocket when they found him. The night before he died, he brought home $500..."

Gloria, overwhelmed by Cullen and Brie's generosity, became inconsolable. Cate stood next to her and dispensed tissues, while the others sat and prayed silently, while waiting for Gloria to regain her composure.

A short time later Gloria preceded to say, "I never asked Anderson how he got the $500.00." Gloria looked at Woody and said, "Woody, I figured you must have given him the loan he said he was going to ask you for."

"Mom Parks," Gloria said, "I know this is gambling money, and you also know how much I hated Anderson working for Woody, but the kids and I need this money so much. With this money, I can pay for Anderson's funeral and I will have enough left to catch up with our rent and

 pay off a few bills. My question is, do you think God will

forgive me for using this money?"

"Child hush, if God didn't want you to have it, he wouldn't have protected Cullen and Brie while gambling. The Bible says, 'The wealth of the sinner is laid up for the just.'

"Woodrow?"

"Yes, Mom?"

"Did you give Anderson the $500.00?"

"Yes, I guess I did momma."

"Anderson worked for you at that sinful building you call Woody's Place for how many years?"

"Ten."

"Woodrow, do you have some type of compensation for those who work for you?"

No, Ma'am."

"Well, Woodrow ... you are always bragging about how much money you make. And each year you purchased one or two fancy cars with cash, and wear fine tailored made clothes, and gold necklaces, bracelets, rings, earrings, and now I see you have had diamond studs inserted in your front teeth… I believe I counted six? Am I correct?"

"Yes, Mom."

"Woodrow, you are always trying to give me money that I will not touch, and I believe God will forgive me just this one time. Woodrow, that money over the years I have said no to; would it be possible for you to give it to Gloria and the kids? ... Let's say ... $25,000? With the $90,000 Cullen and Brie gave, plus the $10,000 found on Anderson, and the extra $500 you loaned him; Gloria will have $125,500. Then she can get caught up on her bills, and not have to move back to Ohio. She would not have to live with her brother or work for a while, but spend time with the kids and take her time looking for a good job. Woodrow would you do that for Gloria and for your cousin's children?"

Not saying a word, Woody put his swollen hand into his inside jacket pocket, took out his checkbook and wrote out a check for $25,000.

Grandpa watched Woody writing the check. It was apparent to him that he was still angry. Grandpa Jeremiah sat chewing on his bottom lip, mulling over Woody's spiteful words that he had said earlier to Cate, Grandpa finally spoke. "Gloria, the Bible also says, 'they shall cast their silver in the streets, and their gold shall be removed: their silver and their gold shall not be able to deliver them in the day of the wrath of the Lord."

Woody, fill up with malice, ripped the check out, and handed it to Gloria, giving her a weak, but subdued smile. He irritably said, "This is for you and the kids."

He stared at Grandpa Jeremiah thinking, *a day is coming old man when I am going to cut that repulsive tongue out of your mouth and watch you die with delight.*

"Woody," said Gloria, "Cullen and Brie have given the money they won from you to me. Anderson brought home $500.00 and the $10,000 that was found in his pocket is enough. I will not accept another dime from you."

Gloria rose from her seat and went over to Woody. She leaned in and whispered into Woody's ear, "Seeing your fiery eyes tells me your soul must already be in hell. I heard what you said to Anderson. You told him, 'die.' I see your swollen raw knuckles, and I know you killed Anderson, and the truth will be known."

Gloria sat down and Cate asked, "Gloria, do you still have the$10,000 dollars?"

"Why yes, I was going to go to the bank and deposit it on Monday. Why are you asking about the money?"

"I was thinking, why not give George the $10,000, and he will give you a check for it right now. This way, you will not have to have that cash in the house."

Gloria opened her purse and handed over the $10,000. George hastily wrote her a check for $10,000 and smiled as he handed it to her, and Jada stared at the money

Woody stood and turned to walk out of the room when George called to him, "Wait! Woody, don't leave just now, there's more good news you need to hear!"

Oh how I loathe all of you right now!

Woody pressed himself against the wall. He stuffed his swollen hands into his pockets and touched the butts of his concealed weapons thinking, *I could kill all of them.* Suddenly, his fingers felt like they were on fire and he hastily removed them. Cate asked, "Woody, are your fingers on fire?"

The others were oblivious to the shrouded altercation between Gloria, Cate and Woody. George continued, "Woody, Woody, Woody."

"What?"

Snapping out of his trance, he looked at his singed fingers and answered back, "I wasn't listening."

"I was saying, Woody, that Cate and I came into

some jewelry which we don't want or need. We had it appraised and found it to be worth $100,000.

When we told our friends, Jason and Julia, about our intentions for the appraisal money, they too wanted to contribute."

George turned to Gloria and told her, "Gloria, in my hand is a cashier's check combining Brie and Cullen's winnings from Woody's Place, the money from the appraised jewelry, and Julia and Jason's gift to you.

We are more than happy to give this check to you. We know this money will help with a new beginning for you and your kids."

Gloria took the check. When she saw the large amount a loud gasp escaped from her lips. Her feet moved rapidly as she screamed, "This, this, is, is $290.000" She repeated, "This is $290,000!"

Holding the cashier's check, Gloria, with much happiness mixed with pain, leaped from her chair, and shouted, "Cate, George, Brie, and Cullen, how can I thank you?" She looked at Brad and told him, "Please tell your mom and dad thanks with all my heart." She turned to the Hayes' family and told them, "Oh my! Cate, George, Brie and Cullen, how can I ever thank you?"

She looked at Woody, who sat speechless, fuming with silent anger. "Woody, forgive me for my words to you tonight. I spoke out of anger and not love. I also know Anderson loved you, and I know he's in heaven smiling, knowing his family will be secure. Gloria put her hand over her heart, tilted her head back and shouted, "God, I thank you, I thank you, I thank you, for your unmerited, divine assistance called, Grace!"

Cate looked across the room at Jada. Jada with tears on her face put her hands on her heart and mouthed, "Thank you!"

Unexpectedly, Jada's hands shot up into the air and she shouted, "Thank you, God! Anderson is in heaven and not in hell. Gloria, our God; He is God Almighty. He is and will continue to be your Jehovah Jireh, the great provider, He supplies all your needs, and He has turned your mourning into great joy!"

Ida Parks stood with laughter. She looked at Jada and then to Woody, who stood looking obviously agitated and disgusted at his wife. Ida said, "Woodrow, it seems like we have another preacher in the house.

"And you, my dear daughter, if my math is correct, you have $300,000." Ida smiled with the others as they clapped their hands and hugged.

Over the chattering, Woody shouted, "Mom, Jada and I have to leave!"

"Nonsense, son, we are still celebrating. If you have to leave then go, but Jada can stay with me. I will take her home. Jada, come with me, let's make some fresh coffee."

Ida grabbed Jada and together they turned towards the kitchen.

Woody heard his mother say, "Whoa, what an evening," as she rapidly walked into the kitchen.

Woody sat down and watched Cate's interaction with Gloria and the Sullivan's with repulsion. He saw Brie, Pastor Wilson, Brad and Cullen as they stood chatting and he thought, *All my money… gone! Somehow, someway, I will make Cate and her old loud mouthed father cry.*

"Mom Cate."

"Yes, Brad?"

"If you don't mind. I need to take my wife and leave, we have early classes tomorrow."

Laughing, Cate replied, "My son-in-love, you don't have to ask me to take your wife home. By all means, go."

"Hey!" called Cullen, "I'm right behind you with Grandpa and Grandma. Aunt Cate my flight leaves in six hours. I will see you sometime next month."

"Love you, nephew, and Godspeed. Please keep in touch, Cullen."

"I promise, I will do better with keeping in touch."

"Cate?"

"Yes, Mom?"

"Tell Gloria goodnight for us please." "I will do just that Mom and Dad."

"Godspeed to you both and I love you."

Closing the door, George saw Woody sulking in the overstuffed chair. George walked over to him, holding Cate's hand said, "Woody, I am going into the parlor to catch the last half of the basketball game, care to join me?"

"No. I am comfortable right here."

"Okay, if you change your mind, come on in."

Cate smiled at Woody, then she and George walked down the hall. Woody watched George kiss his wife; then she went into the kitchen and he into the parlor.

In the kitchen, Cate saw Ida Parks and Jada talking. Ida asked, "Cate, where's Woodrow?"

 "Woody is sitting alone in the front room. George

invited him into the parlor to watch the game with him, but he refused."

Ida poured two cups of coffee and said, "I will go to him."

Jada watched Ida leave, then she moved closer to Cate and whispered, "Anderson told you it was Woody, didn't he?"

Not waiting for a response, Jada whispered, "Cate, thank you and thank God the kids gave that money to Gloria because Woody was planning to get it back in some diabolical way." Looking toward the door, nervously, Jada whispered, "Cate, the money Gloria gave to George had small green dots on the edge of the bills ... that money is Woody's; he marks his money with green dots. Tell George to take it to Chief Jones."

Jada glanced over her shoulders to see if Woody was nearby. She saw Woody was still talking with his mother. She quickly reached down into her bra and shoved a crumpled tissue into Cate's hand. She whispered, "Keep this!"

Woody walked into the kitchen area and Cate saw fear in Jada's eyes. Cate pretended to use the tissue that Woody saw Jada hand her and quickly dried her eyes.

Woody barked, "I need a refill, Jada!"

Cate answered, "We have one pot ready. Woody, if your fingers are hurting, I will pour you a cup."

"Forget it!" Hollered Woody, "It's getting late and we had better leave." He stomped across the kitchen, took hold of Jada's elbow, swung her around, and with snake eyes he looked angrily into Cate's face and whispered, "It's not over."

Squeezing Jada's elbow, Woody hissed. "Jada, say goodnight to your prophetess, Cate."

Jada giggled and said with happiness, "Goodnight, Prophetess Cate."

Woody yanked Jada's arm, and pushed her out of the kitchen. His mother saw him and she stopped him and said, "Woodrow, may I have a few words with you before you leave?"

Woodrow whispered into Jada's ear, "Wait here for me and stay away from Cate!"

His mother slipped her arm into his and directed him out onto the side porch to talk

Alone, she asked, "Woodrow, why are you acting like you are? Why are you mistreating your wife? Are you upset over the money the kids gave Gloria? If so, you should be glad they did. It will help Gloria and your little cousins. Woodrow, I know you are upset about Anderson's death, but son, please watch your temper. You know your blood pressure is already high. And Woodrow promise me, you will search for your brother because I know something is terribly wrong… and, Woodrow, please get some rest when you can."

Jada watched as they talked, afraid to move. She saw Cate coming toward her.

"Psst, psst, Cate."

Cate looked in her direction. Jada put her hand slightly up, and pointed towards the porch where Cate saw Woody and his mother talking.

Jada signaled Cate to step back. Cate took a few steps

back until she was hidden from Woody's view by the wall. Jada pressed her finger to her lips and whispered, "Cate, Woody is dangerous and out of control. Keep that tissue, Anderson's teeth are in it!"

Hearing the door open, Cate stepped back and remained hidden behind the wall. Cate jumped when Woody hollered, "Jada! Let's go!"

Cate watched as she remained unseen behind the wall; she saw Woody quickly kiss his mother's cheek, she heard Gloria saying goodnight to Jada and she saw Mom Parks watching as Woody and Jada walked out the opened door. Cate rushed out the door and called, "Goodnight."

Woody replied angrily, "Mom, we will see you tomorrow."

Woody's mother stood on the porch watching them leave and shouted, "Woodrow, you need to get some rest, and take your high blood pressure pills!

Your eyes are red as blood."

"Mom, I'm okay! I will see you tomorrow!"

"Woodrow?

He stopped and looked back at his mother.

"Yes, Mom?"

"You had better control that temper of yours. You just might have a heart attack or stroke. Are you listening to me son?"

Trying to control his voice, he said, "Mom, I am always listening to you. And don't worry about me, I can take care of myself."

Jada pulled away from his clutch. She ran back up the steps where Ida stood and kissed her.

The porch was well lit and when Jada kissed Ida, she saw a lot of fresh bruises on Jada's chest and neck. For the first time in her life, she felt painful disgust toward her son, and distress and compassion for Jada.

Jada ran down the steps to the sidewalk where Woody stood. Ida saw him yank her small arm and she called, "Jada!"

Jada turned and answered back. "Yes ma'am."

"You will need to dress in something very comfortable. I will come by your house and pick you up.

"I will do that, and once again, I thank you, Mom Parks."

As Jada ran down the steps toward Woody, Ida yelled, "Woodrow, you let her come. And please don't forget what I asked you to do. Check in on Michael. I know something is wrong because he would have been here."

"Mom, I've tried calling MJ. He's not answering his cell."

"Just check on him please. God knows how I worry so much about him and you.

Especially you, with your temper and all. Woodrow, promise me. You have always kept your word to me. Go by to see about your brother and tell him to call me!"

"Okay, I will Mom."

Waving, Jada happily shouted, "Thanks for the job, Mom Parks."

"You are more than welcome dear. I love you. Bye"

Ida turned and walked through the door as she left it ajar. She went inside to watch them from the partially open curtain. She saw her son jerking Jada's fragile arm and pulling her towards his car. She heard Jada's painful cries, "Ouch! Woody, you are hurting me! Let go!"

He did just that. He let go and she fell onto the sidewalk. Then he stepped away, leaving her to get up. She stood, staggered to the car, and opened her own door. Then Woody advanced toward her like a stinging bee. He slapped her face several times and mouthed a few words with his finger pointing in her face. He then walked to the front of the car and sat in the driver's seat, leaving Jada staggering and whimpering.

Ida Parks heard her son scream, "Get your butt into the car now, Jada!"

She watched as Jada obediently got into the car, closed the door and rested her throbbing head against the window. Ida heard Woody's shrieking tires as he furiously sped away.

Chapter 22.The Nightmare Within

While driving, Woody's inner phantom voice was unhampered with hatred and Jada sat fearful and listened. Woody was answering his phantom's questions and unlocked many hidden heart- wrenching secrets that had darkened his soul for too many torturous years.

He told his phantom stories about Anderson, Michael, Cullen, Brie, Cate, George, Jeremiah and his own parents.

Woody's inner phantom was very angry with his mother for suggesting he give Gloria a check for $25,000 and Gloria embarrassing him by refusing it. His phantom was angry with Anderson for stealing his money. His phantom was angry with Michael for not being loyal to him, sleeping and drinking with his working girls, and not watching his back. His phantom was angry with Cullen and Brie because they used their kind personalities to get his employees to talk and they distracted them from their jobs, and then pounced, taking all his money. $90,000 to be exact, and then giving it to Gloria.

His phantom hated Cate because of her bond with God. Her God made him an idiot when He put everyone in Gloria's room into a trance and overpowered his master. He hated George because he was married to Cate. Woody's phantom was angry with his father and mother because they both failed to tell him that his father had an identical twin brother, and he, believing his father's twin to be his father, caused him to do an unimaginable violation to both his father and his father's twin's woman.

Woody's phantom spirit loathed that nosey, loud mouth, Jeremiah Sullivan because he believed his father had told him that he had killed his twin brother Milton. He hated how Jeremiah constantly insinuated that he murdered his daughter and son-in-law. Woody pulled his car into the driveway and Jada opened her door. Woody leaned over and shoved her out onto the blacktop causing her to scrape her face, arms, hands, and knees on the asphalt. When Jada looked up, she saw Woody's cold, red eyes staring at her showing no remorse. She watched Woody's face contorting with aggressive rage as he sat behind the steering wheel. He smirked seeing her laying on the asphalt.

Jada heard an unpleasant diabolical voice coming from Woody's mouth. "Jada," it ranted, "Keep your mouth shut about what you saw in my office and what you heard while Woody drove or we will kill you too."

Woody leaned over the seat and with an eerie, ill-omened laugh he chided, "Oops, Jada, your God didn't catch you. I guess He and His kingdom of angels must be asleep. Jada in my master's kingdom there are too many of us, don't try to run away, because no one can escape my master's kingdom without experiencing his hellish torment before death, and you don't want that."

Woody's long arms reached across his black leather seat, grabbed his gold plated door handle and slammed his car door shut. Laying on the asphalt, Jada listened to the squeal of his tires when he hurriedly back out of his driveway.

Jada stood and took four shaky steps toward his house, but stopped and said to herself, *No more!* She then shouted, "No More!" Jada pointed her finger heavenwards and shouted, "Devil, My God is My Deliverer!"

Determined, bruised, and in pain, Jada limped two blocks down the sidewalk until she reached the bus stop.

Thirty minutes later, she rang a friend's doorbell. Gloria answered. She saw Jada's cracked and bruised lips, her black eyes and scraped face. She heard Jada's pitiful moan, "Help me."

Gloria grabbed Jada around her waist, and shouted, "Mom, Cate, George, help!"

They rushed into the front room and saw Jada. George scooped her into his strong arms and carried her into the den. He placed her fragile, beaten body on the leather sofa.

Ida Parks kneeled beside her and with a hoarse voice said, "Woodrow did this to you. Didn't he?"

Jada's small frame trembled as she bobbed her head, indicating that what she said was correct. Quivering, she told them, "I will not do this anymore, I can't. I am tired of being beaten and wronged. I came here hoping to get help. I am so tired of being physically and verbally abused by his sick environment for too long. Woody's mental state has debilitated and he has become more destructive to himself and others."

Ida, weeping, pulled Jada's small, shivering body into her arms. Through her tears, Ida asked Jada, "How long has this been going on?"

Jada looked into Ida's soft brown eyes to answer, but

was unable to because her dam burst and released every ounce of deep raw emotion that had been entombed from the years of physical and mental abuse.

Heartbroken, Cate sat on the floor next to her friend, wiping away her own tears. Eventually, Jada answered, "For more than 30 years."

Ida slowly released Jada from her embrace and repeated softly, "30 years?"

"Yes, for 30 years Woody has abused and misused my body."

Jada's twitching hands unbuttoned the top of her blouse. She showed them her bruised chest and turned to reveal her back which was black, blue, and red. Seeing Jada's bruises caused Ida to avert her eyes. She felt as if a dagger had been plunged into her own heart.

Jada's soft hand reached out and held Ida's trembling hands. Jada told her, "Mom Parks, Woody's mind has always been sick .... 'When we were in college, he stopped by my apartment and told me to bring my dog because he wanted to take us to the park. While driving, he told me his plans to open a nightclub, and to do so he needed money. He asked me to become his working call girl. When I refused him, he reached over and snatched my beautiful poodle, Princess, from my arms. Once we arrived at the park, he ordered me to get out of his car. He opened his door and I stood paralyzed with fear as Woody did the unimaginable. He strangled my poodle and dropped her onto the grass. Then he ordered me to pick her up and get back into the car. I refused him and he lifted me by my neck. I was suffocating and my feet were dangling. Finally, he released me and I fell onto the grass. He cursed and ordered me to stand up, pick up my dog and get my butt into the car. Shaken and in pain, I did as he ordered. I picked up my precious Princess, got into his car, and he locked me in. I cried, as I held my dead dog on my lap. He drove us to the ocean and once there, Woody yanked my Princess from my arms, opened the car doors and jerked me out. He then forced me to watch when he tossed her small body into the ocean. He turned, with this scary, unnatural smile and told me. 'Jada Perkins, the same thing will happen to your beloved mother, your sister, her husband, her kids and anyone else you love if you ever say no to anything I order you to do again. You are my property now, I own you.'

"After 30 years of being Woody's property, a few weeks ago we were married. He only married me to blackmail George."

"What? I don't understand," Ida responded with the question, "Why would Woodrow blackmail George?"

"I will explain it later, Mom Parks. Don't worry, all is well" Cate said.

Jada continued. "When I refused to continue working as a call girl, Woody beat me nearly to death then he left me laying on the floor in his casino office. While I laid there drifting in and out of consciousness, Woody berated and kicked me so many times. Before I lost complete consciousness, I heard him telling Harry and Luke what to do with my body. He told them to dump me on the street corner." Jada looked at Cate and said, "Cate that's where George found me.

"I recall being bound with tape and stuffed inside a zipped bag. I remember Luke and Harry lifting the bag, with my body inside, and tossing it into something mushy. Moments later, I tasted mud in my mouth. Then I drifted in and out of consciousness, feeling mud on my face and body. Barely alive and in intense pain, I laid there listening to the hard rain falling onto the bag and praying for God's help."

Through teary eyes, Jada looked away from Ida's grief stricken face, and stared into the fire blazing flames. She broke her gaze to look on the mantle at a framed picture of Michael, Woody, and Anderson as teenagers. The words written on the frame were, "Friends Forever."

Jada continued, "Mom Parks, when we were in college, I tried many times to get away from Woody, but he always found me. I am truly scared for Woody. He has always been greedy for money and power, but now Woody is talking to some invisible, inner phantom all the time and it controls him. Woody's temper is getting worse; he is filled with uncontrolled rage against anyone who crosses him."

Cate stood, and walked several steps toward the blazing fireplace. She stopped and said, "Jada, my dear friend, it was Woody who strong-armed you to come to our home to try to seduce George?"

Jada nodded yes. Cate walked over to Jada and held her hands. Cate sat on the hardwood floor next to her old friend and Jada looked into Cate's eyes and told her, "Cate, I thank you for forgiving me."

Jada looked at George who stood in the corner

listening and said to him, "George, I am truly sorry. Woody forced me to come to your and Cate's home. He wired me with a small tape recorder and when I came back to the car, he already knew his plan had failed. When I sat in the car he physically and verbally abused me all the way to his house. When we arrived there, he dragged me by my arms into the bedroom; there he handcuffed me naked to the bed and he beat me with his belt. During the beating, he talked to this invisible inner- phantom person, pleading with him to let him stop.

"The more Woody pleaded the angrier the phantom within Woody became. After my beating, I remained handcuffed to the bed for hours until his phantom permitted Woody to come into the bedroom to release me.

"I had been laying on the floor for hours, naked and in pain. Woody came in unlocked the handcuffs, and lifted me off the floor. He bathed me, gave me pain pills and took care of me."

"Ohhhhh!" Ida groaned as heavy tears rolled from her eyes.

Jada, with compassion, said, "I know it's difficult for you to hear this about your son and I'm so sorry Mom Parks."

"Don't worry about me and my feelings child. This is all God's timing for the truth to be revealed. Go ahead, Jada, tell us all."

Biting on her lower lip, Jada hesitated, then said, "George, after I left your and Cate's home, Woody informed me that since I failed his first plan, he knew another way to get the money he needed. He took my mother's jewelry and told me I was going to sell her ring and bracelet to you. Then he was going to get all the money that Cullen and Brie had won from him back from you.

"Cate, Woody was so furious when driving home tonight. He was angry watching Brie and Cullen give his money to Gloria. Then, when you and George announced you had the jewelry appraised and gave Gloria $100,000 Woody said, and I will quote, 'I asked for $75,000 and they got $100,000. Why didn't you, my all-knowing friend, think about us pawning the jewelry? We would have had $25,000 extra. Cate and George have so much money they can just give away a $100,000.'

"Woody became quiet and rapidly started nodding his head up and down. Seconds later, he answered his phantom, "Yes, I know the $75,000 you asked for was a token, a memorial to my two dead best friends."

Jada looked at George, who was still standing, and she said, "George, when you gave Gloria that certified check, which included $100,000 from Jason and Julia, it only helped to fuel his madness and made his phantom spirit even angrier than usual. Mom Parks, you asked Woody to write a check for $25,000. He did so grudgingly with a deceitful smile. When Gloria refused it, inwardly, he was enraged. I know you observed Woody's red eyes, but they weren't red because of high blood pressure. His eyes were red because his thoughts were filled with anger and a need for retaliation.

"Mom Parks, he couldn't punch you so once we were in his car, he took his frustrations against you out on me.

During the drive home, Woody said many appalling things about you, his father and his father's twin brother."

"His father's twin? ... Woodrow never knew his father's twin brother. Jada. Jada, my heart is breaking. I didn't know he was beating you, I'm so sorry my baby."

"Mom, you have blind eyes when it comes to Woody. Woody is sick. Right now you are the only one Woody really loves, but he is angry with you; and now, only God knows what he is really capable of.

"Cate, you and George saved your kids' lives! Woody was planning to blackmail the kids in some heartless way and if they didn't give him back his money, he would have blackmailed you, George. He had planned to reveal our so-called affair to Grandpa Jeremiah and Grandma Vetta for money by using his bogus recording of my visit to your home.

"As his final plan, Woody was going to force me to make a public video with a false statement about my and George's affair to the media that would discredit Cate's ministry."

Ida stood, walked swiftly over to the mantle, removed the picture of Anderson, Michael and Woody from its frame, ripped away Woody's image and dropped it into the fire. She came over to Jada and placed her arms around her and told her, "Woodrow isn't going to use you as his punching bag anymore. I will see to that."

"Jada?"

"Yes, Gloria?"

"I believe Woody killed Anderson. Tell me Jada, did

 he?"

"Gloria stop it! Anderson is Woodrow cousin, he was like a brother. Woodrow would never do such a thing."

Ida looked at Jada and said, "Tell her, Jada."

Jada's soft brown eyes were seeping tears. Ida's body jerked and she cried, "Jada, ... Oh no! Woodrow."

Jada hesitated, she thought about how to answer Gloria's question. Finally, she said, "Gloria, I believe he did."

Ida moaned as she grabbed her heart. Gloria, Cate and George helped her to a chair. Moments later, Ida forced herself to ask a question "Jada, do you think Woodrow has something to do with Michael being missing?

Jada responded, "Mom Parks, again, I can't be for certain, but Woody and his phantom friend and henchmen are capable of doing unimaginable things."

"Ida replied, "I am now hearing myself saying words I should have said 40 years ago, but I let my love for Woodrow blind me to his mental condition. I know this much, when all's said and done, if Woodrow killed Anderson, he will have to answer to the law of God and man. We will know for sure about his involvement with Anderson's death when we find Michael. Until then, Jada, I must hide you from Woody."

"How will you do that, Mom Parks?" asked Gloria. "Gloria, Jada is going to stay with me."

"But, Mom Parks, your house will be the first place Woody will come to."

"Gloria, you let me do the worrying. I have my

secrets too. And..." Mom Parks smiled, she patted Jada's hand and told her. "At least my grandbaby is safe!

Jada gasped! She repeated. "Grandbaby, oh God, no!" You know about my daughter?"

Jada fearfully shook her head back and forth. She screamed, "Please! No! Please!" She pleaded, "Mom please, tell me, you didn't tell Woody?"

Ida didn't respond to Jada's question. Jada pulled on Ida's arms and searched her brown eyes for an answer.

With sorrowful tears Jada again asked, "Mom Parks, does Woody know about my baby?"

"Shush child. Stop your worrying. You aren't the only one who knows how to keep secrets. No Jada, Woodrow doesn't know about your baby, and as far as I am concerned, he will never know."

"What?" Gloria screamed. "Jada, you and Woody have a baby?" "Yes, Gloria, I have a daughter. She is three years old. I was so small, no one knew I was pregnant. I was due around Christmas and I had been begging Woody for months to let me visit my sister at Christmas time. He let me go and God's timing was perfect. I gave birth to my daughter at my sister Sharon's home on Christmas Day. I have the most beautiful girl, and Cate, I named her Sally. Sally Michelle, after your twin sister Sally and her husband Mike."

"Is she still with Sharon?" asked Cate.

"Yes she is. My sister and her husband Ray are raising Sally as their own child until I am delivered from Woody's tentacles."

 Jada, not hesitating, said, "Gloria, Woody must never

know about my child. You must promise me, please promise me that you will never tell Woody. If he knew he would take her and Woody is not stable, he's crazy."

"Please, Gloria, and Mom Parks," Jada pleaded, for your granddaughter's sake, promise me, you will never tell. Woody must never know."

"I promise you," said Gloria, "I will never tell Woody. And Jada, you know I believe he killed Anderson and I will not stop pursuing the truth until Woody is either dead or locked away behind bars and waiting for the electric chair."

"Gloria, please no."

"I am sorry, Mom Parks, if my words are cruel, malicious and without forgiveness, but your son is a man without a conscious, he will even kill you if he feels cornered. He is sick."

Puzzled and still searching for answers, Jada asked, "Mom Parks, how did you find out about Little Sally?"

Ida walked to the leather couch and sat. She patted the cushion with her hands, inviting Jada, who was standing, to come and sit next to her.

Once Jada was seated, Ida said, "Jada, it was your sister, Sharon, who told me. Now that I know the rest of your secret, I will tell you mine.

Sharon called my home. She told me Woodrow had come to their home searching for you and he was calling everyday asking her if she had seen you. Sharon told me she called your secret cell phone number and you weren't answering. It was then that your sister told me how she had witnessed Woody verbally abusing you. She hadn't heard from you and she wanted to know if you were okay.

While talking, one of her kids shouted, 'Tell Aunt Jada that little Sally Michelle is getting bigger.' I thought, *that name ... Sally Michelle.* I then questioned Sharon about it, and she told me about my granddaughter. Sharon made me promise to keep your secret from Woodrow."

Ida pulled Jada into her arms, she told her, "Jada, as much as I would love to see my grandchild, I would never reveal this precious secret.

"Tonight, when you told us in front of Woodrow that you had rededicated your life to God, I was so proud of you. When you were leaving, I watched from behind the curtain. I saw Woody abusing you and I hated what I saw. It was then that I decided to kidnap you when I picked you up for work tomorrow and shelter you in a safe place. When I do this, Jada, you will not be able to go outside until Woodrow is locked away. Until then, you can talk with your sister on the phone every day and as often as you like. And one day you will be able to love and to raise your own daughter in peace.

"And my daughter, Gloria, you are right," said Ida, "Woodrow, is mentally sick and needs help. But until that day comes, I must keep Jada safe. Now, Jada, tell us, will you be able to live in isolation?"

The others stood in silence waiting for Jada to answer. Jada finally gave voice to her head nods. She repeatedly said, "Yes, yes, yes! I can live in solitude."

Cate said, "Jada, George and I will help you financially when that day for your freedom comes. Also, we still have your mother's jewelry. It's yours to one day give to your daughter, our godchild, Sally Michelle."

Jada tilted back her head and laughed wholeheartedly with tears falling; first time since meeting Woody, she felt a lightness in her soul, she felt free

Jada reached out and pulled Ida into her arms, and repeated, "Yes, Mom Parks, I can! I can! I can!

Chapter 23,Locked Out

Bang, bang, bang! Woody was at Mom Parks home at 11 a.m., Thursday morning. He yelled, "Mom, its me!!"

As Woody pounded on her front door, Mom Parks rose calmly from the sofa, pressed her finger to her lips and motioned to Jada to keep quiet.

"Just a minute, Woodrow, let me get on my robe and slippers."

Mom Parks fastened her robe, and slip her feet into her green slippers. She swiftly walked towards Jada who stood frozen with fear. Mom Parks gently pushed her into her bedroom and closed the door. Jada trembling, recalled Woody's haunting words, *if you ever run away, when I find you it will not be a happy reunion.* Just remembering his words made her anxious and fearful for herself and Mom Parks.

Mom Parks glanced around the room and observed the extra coffee cup, Jada's jacket, purse and her shoes. She tossed Jada's belongings under the sofa.

She again scanned the room, making sure she hadn't missed anything that would indicate Jada being there. Satisfied, she opened the door. Woody bolted in, gave his mother a quick kiss on her cheek and casually glanced around the room.

"Boy, your breath smells like an outhouse! Eyeballing his wrinkled clothing, his mother asked, "Why are you still wearing the same clothes you had on yesterday, and why are you surveying this room like a lion?"

"Oh it's Jada, I thought I smelled her perfume." I went to the restaurant and you nor Jada were there and I thought perhaps she was here with you." Dismissing the notion she was there with his mother, he said, "Mom, my men found Michael this morning. He's been beaten badly, and is barely alive. He's unconscious and in the ICU."

Stunned and infuriated with her son's words, she shook her head and with disbelief and shouted" "Stop. Stop. Stop! Michael's where? He's been beaten, and is barely alive? Your men found him. Are you really listening to what you have said to me? Why didn't you check on him when you left Gloria's house last night like I asked you Woodrow? How long has it been since your men found my son, your brother?"

"Mom, what difference does it make who found him or how long it's been? Michael is in the hospital, dying!

Woody's tone and his words further enraged an already smothering inner fire; she repeated Woody's words, "What difference does it make! Woodrow, it's your brother we are talking about! Woodrow Hugh

Parks, I want the truth from your lying lips right now. Do I need to repeat myself?"

"No, Mom. It's been hours since they found him."

"Hours! It's been hours and you're just telling me!"

"Mom, I didn't want to disturb you until I had some good news. Besides Anderson is being buried tomorrow, remember?"

Whop! Her hand slapped his face. She shouted, "Did you just ask, do I remember? Of course I remember, someone murdered

Anderson, and Michael is ... No Woody."

Woody hung his head, pretending to care, while tears stained his shirt. "Mom." he said, "Mom ... Michael ... may not make it."

Grief-stricken with anger, she stared in her eldest son's cold, seemingly caring, dark eyes and told him, "I will get dressed and go to Michael."

"Mom, I will wait and drive you there."

"No, Woodrow! You need to go home and clean your repulsive self up. I will drive myself to the hospital."

"No, I don't mine, I will wait for you."

Without warning, His mother angrily, barked at him, like a charging bulldog. She snapped,

"Woodrow Parks, I told you no! You heard me! Your mouth stinks!

You need to go home and clean yourself up! I will drive myself! Now you go, get out! Get out of my house. I am so upset with you right now, I can't stand to look at you! Just go!"

"Upset with me! Why, Mom?

"Woodrow, you do not know how revolting you are to me right now. You have let your own flesh and blood suffer for days. You could have stopped by his apartment on the same day we were all at the hospital watching and waiting prayerfully for Anderson to pull through. I asked you then to check on Michael. I even asked for the key to his apartment but you told me it was in your office safe. I went to Michael's apartment and was unable to gain entrance into his building. Woodrow tell me, why didn't you check on him then?"

"You know Michael likes his privacy."

"Four days! Hogwash, Woodrow, stop it! First Anderson, then Michael. Just last night I asked you to check in on your brother. It had been several days since I last saw Michael. He calls me two or three times a day. When one day went by and I had not heard from him, I knew something was wrong.

"This is the fourth day since Anderson was found and you with your selfish- self, decided to send your boys, because you were too busy, or thought yourself to be too important to give up your valuable time to check on your brother. You gave them the key and they found him and called you, and then you went over to check for yourself, and called 911. Isn't that happened Woodrow?

"Mom, I filed missing person papers two days ago."

"You did what? You filed missing person papers on Michael without first checking his apartment? Woodrow you aren't making sense."

His mom reached out, gently touched his hand and gave him a weak smile. She told her son, "Although I am upset with you Woodrow, I am glad you got your brother help."

"Mom the doctor said MJ may never come out of his coma. We may never know who killed Anderson and who is responsible for beating Michael and leaving him in his own apartment to die."

Not waiting for a response, Woody slowly moved toward the door. Ida Parks watched her son walking away and she shouted, "No.... Stop! I can't keep this inside.

"Woodrow, something is not adding up here! You know I have a feeling that this has something to do with you. God knows I pray I am wrong. I saw you shed those fake tears last night at Gloria's. I have seen your, 'I am hurting' demeanor before, especially when you have done something wrong. I have this déjà vu feeling washing over me. I've been here, I have done this. I know you and your expressions too well, I have seen how you can turn your tears on when you have done something wrong and you are afraid you will be caught."

"Whoa, stop Mom, no! Don't go there!"

"Or what, Woodrow, you will treat me the way I saw you treat Jada last night? Woodrow go, just leave!"

Woody shifted his feet. He felt uncomfortable with his mother's words and they intensified his anger toward her. It was obvious to him she was suspicious of his involvement with Anderson's death and his brother beating, and he needed to find Jada before she told her the truth about Anderson. Woody stood frozen, staring and furious.

Mom Parks walked over to the study desk and lifted the telephone receiver from its cradle. She said, "I will call Pastor Wilson, Cate and George and see if they can meet me at the hospital."

Hearing the names of Cate and George infuriated him even more. Woody's rage filled voice shouted, "Mom! Why? Why do you always call Cate and George? I can understand you calling Pastor

Wilson, but Cate and George Hayes? Can't we have some family time without them?"

His mother slammed the phone down into its cradle. Like a rattlesnake, she struck. She walked over to him and got into his chest. Woody's thundering eyes looked down on her as she angrily hissed, "Boy, don't you dare stand here in my house telling me who I can call and what to do. To me, Lovetta, Jeremiah, Cate and George are my family!"

She looked up and pointed her index finger at his face and said, "Woodrow I've had enough of your despicable, scheming ways. Go! Just go! Get out of my house! Go home, and clean yourself up. And brush those nasty teeth of yours. Get out! I have to get dressed and go to Michael."

"Okay, Mom, I was just saying. I'm sorry I made you angry. I'm leaving."

Woody walked toward the door, but stopped to look back at his Mom, who stood near the door staring defiantly at him. He said to her, "Mom, are you sure? I can wait for you."

His mother angrily shouted, "Woodrow Parks, you have done enough. Just leave. Go! I have a car. I will drive myself to the hospital."

She stood, glaring at him with her hands on her hips, daring him to say another word. Woody lifted his hands into the air, as an act of surrendering. He forced a crooked smile, and said, "I am truly sorry Mom."

He put his large hand on the doorknob, he turned and said, "Mom?"

"Woodrow?"

He gave a wry chuckle and said, "Okay, okay Mom, I am going to go home, shower, change clothes, and brush my nasty teeth. I will see you at the hospital. I need to go home to check in on Jada. You said you would pick her up to start working with you, and it's obvious you didn't because you are here."

"I was sicken by your actions last night and I was tired and didn't go to work."

"I keep calling and she isn't answering. I just hope she's not with George and Cate."

"There you go with your George and Cate lyrics. Why would it be so bad if Jada was with them? And Woodrow, if I were her, I wouldn't be at home."

"Why Mom? What have I done now that you are displeased with?"

Mom Parks walked boldly toward her oldest son and stood under his unshaven, nasty face. She said to him. "Aren't you listening? I saw you. I watched you, with Jada, last night from Gloria's window. I saw you when you pushed that small, frail girl down the sidewalk!"

Woody's fists clenched and unclenched as he stared into his mother's brown eyes. He looked up from her face, quickly scanned the room and asked, "Mom, is Jada here?"

"Stop.... Stop....Woodrow, why are you questioning me about Jada's whereabouts?

"It's her perfume, Mom. I smelled it when I came in."

She mimicked him, "'It's her perfume, Mom. I smelled it when I came in!' Mr. Bloodhound, you smelled her cologne! So what?"

"Look at the coat tree in the corner behind you. Isn't that Jada's scarf? When we were dancing, it fell onto the floor and I put it around my neck and forgot to give it back to her. I wore it home."

Woody ambled over to the coat tree, removed the scarf, sniffed it, and tucked it into his pocket. He walked out the door without responding.

Mom Parks walked behind him, closed the door and locked it. Jada slowly opened Mom Parks' bedroom door. She rushed out and gave her a firm hug.

"Thank you, Mom."

"I love you, Jada Parks."

Mom Parks sat down. She motioned for Jada to come and sit beside her.

"Jada," She said, "I have seen that the devil has taken Woody captive. He's not the same. I saw this change for the first time when he was twelve when his best friend and mother died in a house fire, then again before his dad died. After Sally and Mike's death in that car accident, he was never the same."

Tears formed in Mom Parks eyes and rolled down her face. She removed a hanky from the pocket of her robe to dry her eyes. She told Jada, "I remember when they found Sally's body." Mom Parks inhaled deeply and very slowly exhaled before continuing.

"Poor Sally. I went with Cate, Lovetta, and Jeremiah to the morgue. I saw Sally's tiny body; it was burned beyond recognition. I witnessed the pain Cate and my two dearest old friends endured. They had to have a closed casket funeral for Sally. Mikes' body was never found. Woodrow was driving their car that night and the strangest thing happened… he wasn't hurt.

"Jada, you heard Woodrow telling me Michael is in the hospital and he's in the ICU. I had better get dressed and go to see about him."

From her open bedroom, she shouted, "Jada, you may not know this but Michael is my dead sister's child. She was a close friend of Sally's husband, Michael Wallace. I raised Michael as my own son. My sister named him after her best friends', Lovetta and Jeremiah Sullivan's, son-in-law, Michael, but we called him Mike."

Mom Park let out a heavy sighed and said, "We will finish this conversation later. You heard Woody tell me that Michael is in the hospital. I have to get dress.

Jada sat thinking. She knew a part of the true story about Mike and Sally's death. She remembered the night Woody told her. Woody was sloppy drunk and feeling deeply troubled, and remorseful about his many heinous, deep, dark lies and secrets. She remembered...

The night Sally and Michael died, Woody was driving. Woody revealed to her that he had spiked Mike's two sodas, so he was too impaired to drive and Sally never learned. Mike was a brilliant card player, and had won over $75,000. Woody was amazed that somehow Mike had won a rigged game. The owner of the club was upset with Woody because Woody worked part-time for them. The game was fixed; no one was supposed to win and he wanted his money back. When the three of them left the club early that morning, Mike gave his winnings to Sally. She was trying to keep Mike from falling, while trying to hold the money bag, and it fell onto the floor. Woody picked up the bag from the floor, tucked it into his jacket pocket and helped Sally put Mike into their car. Sally sat with Mike in the back seat. Woody said they were 10 miles *from home when the car started to stall. He got out to look under the hood, when a wrong-way driver came out of nowhere and slammed head-on into their car. He said he was knocked down, yet still conscious. He watched as the car flipped multiple times. He said the car tumbled down a 300 foot embankment. Settled down near the bank of the river, and burst into flames. Sally's body was completely burned because she was buckled in her seat. Mike's body was thrown from the car and never recovered.* Jada remembered him telling her, *"I have some missing parts to this story, I will never reveal."*

Startled out of her inner thought when she heard the bedroom door opening. Jada's hands muffled her loud squeal.

"My, my, little one, you are afraid, aren't you?"

Mom Parks walked over to the end table and grabbed her keys to leave.

"Mom Parks?"

"Yes, Jada."

"How long was it after Sally and Mike's funeral that Woody really changed?"

"Immediately."

"Woody seemed to be so hurt, he didn't even attend their funeral." He stopped going to church, and two months later he opened up that god-forsaken outhouse he calls Woody's Place."

"Mom, where did he get the money to start his business?"

"Jada, I asked him that question. He told me he took out a loan. The peculiar thing was one month later, he quit his job and starting spending all of his time running his gambling house. I pray for that boy, but the more I pray the worse he gets. I have given him over to the Lord.

"I have this feeling that Woodrow is coming back here when I leave. He has keys. Before I leave, I will show you a secret place. No one alive knows about this secret. There are only two people to know what I am about to reveal to you. One was my dead husband and the other is me. Neither Michael, nor, Woodrow knows this secret. Now, listen closely and please follow my directions."

"Yes, Ma'am. I will."

"When I leave this house, I want you to just lock the door. Do not push in the dead bolt. If you do he will know you are here. Besides, Woody has keys to all locks. I always keep the side doors bolted. He smelled the expensive perfume you wear and I did not like how he was questioning me about you being here. When I leave, I want you to take a good shower and change clothes. We are about the same size, I have some dresses in my closet that you can wear. Be sure to clean up after yourself, put your clothes into a double trash bag, tie and toss the bag into the laundry chute. You and I know Woodrow's nose is like a bloodhound's. Now come with me, I will show you the secret."

Mom Parks motioned Jada to follow her into her bedroom. She went into her spacious closet. She squatted to hit a floor panel and a hidden door opened. She stood, smiled, and said, "All these old houses have secret panels and rooms. They were used to hide slaves. I would have never found this one if I hadn't been trying to find the mate to a shoe while stretched out on my stomach. As I was getting up, and I pushed down on this floor panel, and the wall opened up. Come now, follow me."

They climbed twenty steps and entered into a very large room. Jada was amazed how cleaned it was.

"See that window?"

"Yes, Ma'am."

"You can see the street from it. Woodrow always parks his car across the street so you will be able to see him from the window. After you have showered, I want you to gather all your things. I tossed your purse, shoes, and jacket under the couch. Get them and put them into that laundry bag and throw the bag down the laundry chute, then come up here and stay.

"I do not know when I will be back. That window is coated, you can see out but no one can see in, so you will be able to keep the lights on. I will come to get you when I come home."

Mom Parks walked over to a trunk. She said, "I've stored dry foods to eat. There's bottled water, instant coffee, tea, and three electric outlets over there," she said pointing to the opposite wall.

"There are flashlights in the trunk, just in case, and this bed to rest on. Look in the vacuum zipped plastic bags in the trunk for clean sheets and blankets. I also have a small television set and ear plugs, a small refrigerator with cold soda, a Bible and many other books you can read. I wouldn't use the television without ear plugs. Also, do not use the electric hot plate over there to cook anything because the aroma will penetrate through the house."

Jada looked around in total disbelief. Mom Parks saw her face, and laughed. She said, "Yes, I keep this place prepared, just as I keep my soul prepared… just in case. You never know what today or tomorrow may bring. Well, Jada, I have to go to see about Michael!"

They walked together down the steps. Mom Parks started to giggled.

"What's causing you to giggle, Mom?"

"Jada, remind me to show you the basement tomorrow."

"Oh, Yes, ma'am."

Chuckling at Jada's reaction to the hidden room, and not saying another word to her, Mom Parks kissed Jada's cheek and walked to the door. She turned and told her, "Honey, George, Cate and I will find you a safe place to live far away from Woodrow. Now take that shower, clean up behind yourself, go to that room, and stay until I come and get you. I have a feeling Woodrow is coming back here to search for you. He may think I have hidden you in the basement. Lock this door and stay alert! I don't trust my son."

When Mom Parks walked out, she waited beside the door until she heard the lock click. She walked away knowing Jada had locked her door.

Chapter 24, Tom

Early Thursday morning, the doorbell rang at the Sullivan's.

"Lordy. Lord, have mercy. Vetta it is 7:00 a.m. and I just poured my hot coffee. Now that dang doorbell rings."

"Jeremy."

"I know, I know, behave myself."

Grandpa Jeremiah got up from the kitchen table and walked through the parlor towards the front door grumbling. He shouted, "Whoever is there you had better be a family member who I am going to give you a good tongue lashing, coming here to my house at this time, and my coffee is getting cold."

Opening the door, Grandpa's eyes widened. He saw a lanky, light-skinned teenager with brown hair cut into a Mohawk, he had facial piercings, and multiple tattoos. Grandpa's first instinct was to close the door in his face. Instead, he opened his mouth and he heard himself rudely saying, "Oh Lord have mercy, what do we have here? You look like something that the cat dragged in."

Vetta whispered from behind him, "Jeremy, hush!"

The young man asked. "Is this the Sullivan's home?"

Grandpa answered, "Why, yes it is. I certainly hope you're not Tom?"

Fearfully, he slowly answered, "Yep, I'm he."

Grandma stepped in front of Grandpa, and through the screen door she greeted Tom with a million dollar welcoming smile. Grandma Vetta's uplifting and soothing voice said, "Hello, Tom."

"Hello, Auntie, I know I was to arrive next week." Through the screen he said, "Uncle Jeremiah, please accept my apology for arriving earlier than expected," Unguarded he heard himself say, "I just had to get away. Once again, I thank both of you for taking me in."

Uncle Jeremiah opened their screen door wide and Tom stepped in. He stood, turning in circles as he took in his Aunt and Uncle's spacious and beautiful home.

"Aunt Vetta, this house is amazing. My mom often spoke of your place, but standing here and seeing it ... it's breathtaking."

Grandma Vetta closed the door.

Grandpa's opinionated mind thought, *your looks are breathtaking.*

Grandpa stood in silence, gawking. Vetta's observant eyes noticed him and she nudged her husband to tell him to stop.

With a hard-hearted tone he said, "Put your bag and guitar case on the table in the corner. Ah, Tom? You need my help with the rest of your things?"

"That's it, Uncle Jeremiah. Cousin Thelma packed and stored the rest of my clothing. I have money to buy new clothes and to pay rent."

"Pay rent? Nonsense, Tom." Aunt Vette quickly replied, "You are welcome to stay here. This is your home now. You know, you were right, we weren't expecting you until next week, but we are so glad to see you."

Tom noticed and felt the pain of his uncle's heedless

apprehension toward him. Tom pushed aside his feelings and, grabbed and shook his Uncle Jeremiah's hand and said with blissfulness. "Look at you Uncle Jeremy. It's so good to see you."

"Boy stop that lie. It's good to see me." Ruthless as ever, Grandpa shrieked, "Boy, your cousin, Cullen, tried that phony politeness with me too." He pulled his wire glasses down to the tip of his nose, pointed to his eyes and said, "Boy, you see these here eyes?" He placed his wrinkled hand behind his ear and asked, "Do you see these here ears?"

Jittery, Tom answered, "Yes, sir."

"Tom, I am not stupid and I know foolishness when I see it." Grandpa continued with his uncouth, opinionated, unhinged insults. "Boy, look at all those tattoos and facial piercings. What were you thinking?"

Tom laughed and said, "That's it Uncle Jeremiah, I wasn't."

Tom, outrageously happy and not offended by his Uncle's remarks replied, "Uncle Jeremiah, you may not be happy to see me, but it's good to see you!"

"I never said I wasn't glad to see you… but I sure do hope I will be able to say I am glad to see you one day. Only time will tell."

"Jeremiah Sullivan, stop! The boy barely has his feet inside the front door and there you go being obnoxious and throwing insults. You need to stop!"

"Vetta you know my mission in life is to make these hard headed boys lives miserable until they straighten up and do right."

"Oh, Jeremy, you need to stop your quarrelsome ways!

Tom, come with me and let's get you settled in." "Now I know my coffee is ice cold, Vetta."

"Then pour yourself a cup of hot coffee." She shook her head, took hold of Tom's arm and said, "Come."

After giving Tom a tour of the house, Aunt Vetta showed him the five bedrooms upstairs. They walked down the long hall and stopped. His Aunt Vetta told him, "Across the hall is Cullen's room and this is your room. Opening the wide door, they walked in together. Aunt Vetta heard Tom's loud gasp for air, "Oh, oooo!"

His clever Aunt Vette smiled, and asked, "What's wrong, Tom?" "Auntie ... electricity? When my feet stepped into this room I felt an electric charge throughout my body."

"Ummm, and it feels good, doesn't it?"

"Yes, it does. Aunt Vette, what is it? Wow, this is fantastic, I am suddenly warm. Look, what is this forming on my arms?"

"Gold dust."

"What's gold dust?"

"Tom, I am curious, have you been talking to God?"

"Yes, I came here hoping to find God."

"Well, you have found Him." "What?"

"Tom, God found you long before your mother knew your name."72

Still confused, Tom shook his arms and watched as gold dust fell onto the carpet. Puzzled, he looked at his aunt and her smile broadened.

"Tom," she explained, "this was your cousin Cate's room. When you see her, you will see she's a continuous carrier of God's gold dust. And apparently you, my nephew, are one of God's chosen sons. His golden dust." She pressed her fingers together and continued, "is just a smidgen of His grandeur God has shared with you"

"Auntie, I don't see gold dust on you or Uncle Jeremy. Does Cullen have gold dust on him?"

"No, we don't. As I said, God has chosen you to share in His majesty."

Aunt Vetta closed the door and further explained to her bewildered nephew. "Cate calls this room her Preparation Room. Cate comes to our home to shut herself in for four to five days without eating and only drinking bottled water. She comes seeking God's agenda before she leaves for her revivals."

Tom once again turned in circles, absorbing the room's beautiful crown molding, its mahogany wooden floor and built in drawers. It had two closets large enough to be another room, two large windows with built in window blinds, one chair in the eastern corner of the room with cushions surrounding it, and an oversized bed.

The room's color palette consisted of different shades of blue, purple, red, and gold, and to Tom's amazement he had his own bathroom.

"Whew, Aunt Vetta, this is a beautiful room!"

"Thank you, Tom. George, Cate's husband, was our interior decorator. I think he did a wonderful job fixing up this old house."

Grandma Vetta stretched her arms and stood on the

tips of her toes to pat Tom's shoulder and said, "Ummm, another tall son, just like your cousin Cullen. Now go ahead and clean up, then come down into the kitchen, that's our central station. Breakfast will be ready in one hour. Cullen left very early this morning for football camp and your cousin Brie and her husband, Brad, are living nearby. They are attending Bible College in the city."

"Brie's married?"

"Why yes. Brie eloped."

Chuckling, His auntie said, "Eloping seems to have become a Sullivan trademark. I will call Brie and Brad and see if they can come by to say their hellos and welcome you."

Grandma Vetta walked over to Tom and motioned for him to stoop. When he did, she cupped his cheek and kissed him and said once again, "Welcome, Tom. We are glad you are here."

"I don't know about Uncle Jeremiah. He doesn't seem too happy."

"Oh, Tom, please pay him no mind. He treats Cullen the same way.

As he told you, it's his mission in life to make you miserable until you change. Tom, your Uncle Jeremy is a good man and loves his family."

"Thanks Auntie. I know there's concern and risk to taking me in, but I want to change and I will not disappoint you and Uncle Jeremiah."

Grandma Vetta smiled. She said, "Tom, I know you won't be a disappointment. You're a good boy and so handsome. Now unpack and get yourself ready for some good, southern style home cooking."

Unpacking his bag, Tom took out and held the urn with his mother's ashes. He held it to his heart and cried heavily. As he wiped away his tears, sniffling, he thought, Mom, your last words were "God forgive me." I sincerely hope He did.

Tom placed the urn on top of the dresser. There, he noticed a Bible. He picked it up and caressed it. He sat down on Cate's chair and instantly jumped out and shouted, "Yowl, hot!" He stood rubbing the seat of his pants as he backed away from Cate's chair.

The bed, I wonder if I can sit there. With caution, Tom placed the Bible on Cate's bed and stood somewhat fearful, he did quick taps to the bed with his fingers, and worriedly sat down. He bounced a couple of times and felt secure.

Okay good." He said. Tom went to lift the Bible and jerked his hands away. "What?" he exclaimed. No, my eyes are playing tricks on me. Is that smoke rising out of the Bible? He chuckled while thinking, *get a grip.* Tom carefully lifted the Bible and held it in his trembling hands. When he opened the black leather Bible, his eyes fell on Proverbs 30, and he began reading aloud.

"...The man declares: I'm tired, God; I'm tired, God, and I'm exhausted. Actually, I'm too stupid to be human, a man without understanding. I haven't learned wisdom, nor do I have knowledge of the holy One who has gone up to heaven and come down. Who has gathered the wind by the handful?" Who has bound up the waters in a garment? Who has established all the ends of the earth? What is this person's name and the name of this person's child— if you know it then you will know all God's words are tried, and true; a shield for those who take refuge in him. Don't add to his words, or he will correct you and show you to be a liar. Two things I ask of you; don't keep them from me before I die: Fraud and lies— keep far from me! Don't give me either poverty or wealth; give me just the food I need, or I'll be full and deny you, and say, 'Who is the Lord?' Or I'll be poor and steal, and dishonor my God's name. Don't slander a servant to his master; otherwise, the servant will curse you, and you will be guilty. There are those who curse their father and don't bless their mother."

Tom wiped tears from his eyes, his heart was broken and he knew why. He hated his father and was full of resentment toward his mother for what they had become. They used to attend church, but church gave way to the country club, social status, numerous affairs, domestic violence, and then, to nothing.

Tom continued to read. "There are those who think they are clean, but haven't washed off their own excrement. There are those—how arrogant are their eyes; how their eyebrows are raised! There are those whose teeth are swords; their jaw is a butcher's knife, ready to devour the needy from the earth, and the poor from humanity..."

Tom closed the Bible, clutched it to his heart and prayed.

"God, I now realize that even when I was doing drugs and all things wrong, You were there watching with tears of compassion protecting me from harm and desiring me to stop. But You didn't intervene, You gave me free will and I had to choose. Now, I am ready for a new beginning. I thank You for this beautiful godly, house, and my aunt and uncle. You have my permission Lord to break down the wall of self-protection I've built to keep others out. I need You God, and I invite You to come into my spirit and invade my body and soul to make changes in me. Amen."

Through teary eyes he scanned the room and saw a guitar standing in the corner. He walked over, picked it up and squatted a couple times. Not feeling any zaps, he sat down on Cate's bed, and strummed the strings. He recalled a song he learned in children's church that he had forgotten. He skillfully began to play and sing.

"Jesus loves me, still today, walking with me on my way. Wanting to give me his light and love and to come to live with him above. Jesus loves me!

He who died, wants to come and forever abide. He will wash away my sins, and, let His little child come in." (Lyric, writer unknown)

Tom, strumming the guitar and pondering the words to the child's song thought, *what's happening to me? Why am I crying? That's a kid song and why am I feeling like this?*

While Tom showered and dressed, he repeatedly hummed the same line, "He will wash away my sin and let His little child come in." *God, I'm that little child who wants to come in to your heart. God show me how*!

The intercom buzzed, "Tom, Breakfast is ready."

"Okay, Auntie, I'm coming. And thanks."

From the stairs, he smelled the welcoming aroma of love before he entered the kitchen. When he arrived he was greeted warmly by his golden cousin, Cate, and her husband, George.

Cate laughed when she said, "Tom, Mom told me you have my old room. That is a very special room, it will change you,"

"Auntie, I believe it has already happened."

Vetta glanced at her daughter and smiled. She eased over to Cate and whispered, "This is God's son, not ours."

As they ate, Tom enjoyed listening to Aunt Vetta, retelling stories about his mother.

Her stories lifted Tom's spirit. As he sat and looked around the table he recalled how much cousin George and his friend, Senator Rock, had done to help him when he was in trouble; and that was most of the time because trouble had a way of following him.

"Cousin George."

"Yes, Tom.

"I am glad you are here. I want to thank you in person. I am hoping I would also have a chance to thank Senator Rock for all you both did for me through the years when I was in trouble... which was all the time. Tom looked across the table at his Aunt Vetta.

"Aunt Vetta, thank you. Being here with you and Uncle Jeremiah is a new beginning for me. This is what I have been desiring for so long peace and genuine love. I really do hate what I have become."

Tom stared into his Uncle's eyes and told him, "Uncle Jeremiah, I'm not faking. My encased fears, shielded my pain and my determination to survive by any means is now over.

"Cousin Cate, I found Cullen's Bible and I read Proverbs 30. I prayed to God and immediately I felt an inner change."

"Tom."

He glanced over at his Aunt Vetta, and she said, "That's why I put you in Cate's room. Her room carries the residue of God's glory."

"Well, something happened to me and that's good. I'm not lying about this. Cousin Cate, while sitting on your bed just for a minute, I changed. Tom gave a weak chuckle, "I tried to sit on your chair, but my behind was zapped. I cautiously moved to see if I could sit on your bed. Do you see the gold dust on my arms, and face and my hands?"

"I do."

"Tom, I know that to be true," interjected Grandpa. "A month ago, I stepped into your room, Cate, with intentions to take your chair into the basement to sand and varnish it. Immediately, my feet started to tingle and when I touched the chair I was electrocuted."

"Dad?"

"Cate I was. Tom, my boy, I know first-hand what you said is a fact."

"Uncle Jeremy, you just said, 'Tom, my boy.'"

"I guess I did, didn't I. But these old ears are still listening to your words."

"I can understand why you want to be rough with me Uncle Jeremiah not trusting me, and not knowing what kind of havoc I could bring into your home, but ... Aunt Vetta, after seeing how my mom and dad lived and died, I don't want that for myself. I want a new life, coming here to live with you and Uncle Jeremy is what I have been desiring for so long.

"Cousin Cate."

"Yes, Tom."

"You are a preaching machine.

Laughing Cate replied, "Now I wouldn't call myself that."

"I've watched you on television and I've been to some of your church meetings. I want to be saved, and live for Jesus. I have done and seen so much. I don't want to drink, do drugs or lie and steal anymore. I don't want to become my father all over. I need help. God has given me this chance to change. He has given me you, Cousin George, Uncle and Auntie; a family that will love and support me. I have two years left in high school and I want to do something meaningful with my life. I want to have a career, get married one day, and have a family who will serve and love God like you, Cousin George. Uncle Jeremiah and Aunt Vetta.

"I…" Tom stopped to ponder. "Cousin Cate ... I have been thinking a lot since my parents died. I hate my life as it is."

Tom turned to Cousin George and said, "I loathe what I have done in my adolescent years. I have been verbally and physically abused, then tossed aside by my dad and others like him.

I need someone to help me to become a better person. I..." Tom's voice trailed off as he surrendered to his raw emotions. Tears slipped from the corners of his eyes. As he wiped them, his whole body shook and he was inconsolable.

Grandpa looked at George. Dumbfounded, Grandpa said, "Whoa, I didn't see that coming."

George smiled, scratched his head and replied. "Neither did I."

Grandma Vetta stood, came over to Tom, pulled a chair next to him and rocked him as she wiped his tears.

Meanwhile, Grandpa sat, wiping his own teary eyes.

Through sniffles, Tom apologized, "I'm sorry."

Grandpa replied, "Son, you have nothing to be sorry for. I apologize to you. You have been through a lot in life, and you needed to get out all of that thar sufferin' you have been through out of that system of yours. I'm glad we are here to help you."

"Tom?"

"Yes, Cousin Cate?"

"Please call me Cate, are you really serious about changing?"

"Yes, Cate, I am."

"Have you read the Bible story about why God sent His only Son to us?"

"Yes, I have and I read Proverbs 30 this morning and the written word impacted me. I found Cullen's Bible and his guitar in your room,"

Grandpa's hands slapped the table hard. He shouted, "See Vetta, Cullen, that boy hadn't any intentions to do right on that thar campus he's on. He purposely left his Bible here!"

"Yes Jeremy, but think. Tom found Cullen's guitar and Bible in Cates' room, and Jeremy, Cullen can find a Bible on his computer or his electronic devices."

"Cate?"

"Yes, Tom?"

"You asked if I read the Bible. The answer is yes, my mom had one. My parents used to read Bible stories to me when I was younger. Over the years, every now and then, I would see Mom reading the Bible. We used to attend church, but stopped when I turned ten years old. Dad's business took up his time, and then his club, which led to him and my mom having many affairs. That led to heavy drinking and our lives spiraled out of control. Eventually, all the choices they made led them to their deaths."

"Tom, I am so sorry," Cate said.

"Cate, I am feeling better just talking about this. A weight has been lifted. But I really need God. I have this feeling that something bad is going to happen to me while I am here. It may be days, weeks, or months from now, but I can't shake it. I need help. I don't want to die and live forever in hell, a place without an end, encased in darkness and relentless torment."

"Tom, Father God, has shown you how much He loves you, and you have seen the lies and deceptions of the evil one. What the d**evil** meant for evil, God meant for good. Come with me, we will gointo the parlor, read some scriptures, give a prayer of thanksgiving to God, and ask His Holy Spirit to fill you with His voice. When that happens, you will receive what your heart has desired, and that is a new life with renewed meaning that comes with an inner change."

"Okay, Cousin Cate." He sighed, "I meant to say Cate."

"Cate, yes! I am ready for that change."

"Mom, Dad, George, Tom and I are going into the parlor, we will return shortly."

As they walked away, Grandpa Jeremiah said, "Well, I

am surprised, I never thought that would happen."

"Jeremy, perhaps you need to spend some time sitting in Cate's chair"

"See thar George, that woman God gave me is always picking on me. I…"

In the parlor, Tom sat across from Cate. She explained, "Calvary secured our place with Jesus. Jesus told us to confess our sins and ask God for forgiveness. You have already done that.

"Now I want you to repeat what I say. Are you ready?"

With his pulse pounding, Tom shut his eyes. He said, "I am ready. I have been desiring this for a long time."

"Repeat. Father, I have already confessed my sins and I thank you for forgiving me."

Tom repeated, "Father, I have already confessed my sins and I thank you for forgiving me."

"From this day forward, I surrender my life to You and I promise I will serve You for the rest of my life."

"From this day forward, I surrender my life to You and I promise I will serve You for the rest of my life."

"Now, Tom, inhale."

Tom inhaled.

"Now slowly exhale,"

Tom slowly exhaled.

"Open your eyes, Tom."

He did, and Cate asked, "How do you feel?"

"I feel refreshed, I feel good."

Cate said, "That's called salvation. You have secured your place in God's kingdom. But there's more."

"You mean the Holy Spirit, where I speak or communicate with God in unknown tongues?"

"Yes," answered Cate, "that's it. Do you want to speak God's Holy Language?"

"Oh do I? Let's do it!"

Cate chuckled at Tom's response. She explained, "When you speak in tongues, you are taking in and receiving God's thoughts. His thoughts, His words are entering into your spirit, and when His Spirit comes into you, your inner spirit will become full of His Spirit filled words. Your inner spirit will begin to feel like a bubbling well of water on the inside. While drinking in His thoughts and you will become full. You will want more of His Spirit-filled words, but you won't be able take in more until you have released what you already have taken in. You will have to let it out.

"The Bible says, 'If anyone is thirsty, let him come to Me and drink. He who believes in Me, as the Scripture said, 'From his innermost being, that's your inner spirit, will flow rivers of living water.'*

"Tom, God is a Spirit; you can't see Him, but you will feel His Spirit churning, flowing, and permeating through your spirit, and seeping into your soul. His Holy words will come gushing out of your mouth as utterances of sounds. God said, 'For with stammering lips and another tongue will he speak to His people.'*

"Tom when you speak in tongues, you are declaring, 'the wonderful works of God. Instantaneously, a newness is felt in your spirit. You will feel His Spirit changing your heart and you will welcome Him with praises of thanksgiving, and so much joy and love as His words of utterances erupt, spewing out of your mouth and changing you from the inside out.

"The initial physical evidence that one has been baptized with the Spirit of God is, Speaking with other tongues as the Spirit of God gives utterance. *This utterance is His words just for you. It isn't a learned language like that taught in schools, but a gift from God.

Your natural mind will not understand His Holy Spirit filled thoughts, for when we speak in tongues, our soul speaks but our understanding is unfruitful.

"When you speak in tongues, you will speak directly to God. Speaking in tongues edifies you, builds up your spiritual life, and repairs, enlightens, informs, and instructs you in all of your undertakings.* When we speak in tongues, we are speaking God's answer. We receive His answers to our prayers directly from the mind of God."

Glowing with so much joy, Cate said, "Tom, isn't that encouraging? And oh, most importantly, the devil does not have entrance into God's mind, and he can't decode or translate what God is telling you. That's why the devil fights so hard for people to not understand the benefits that come with speaking to God in tongues inside their secret place. That secret place is your heart and mind, or your physical prayer closet.

If you stay there and meditate on God and His words, He will give you the interpretation of His tongues. At that time, you will pray your prayers with understanding. "We've read Psalms 103* and you saw the list of benefits that we are blessed with by our loving God.

"Tom, are you ready for this complete transformation?"

"I am ready!"

"Okay, Tom, begin to praise God in your spirit and when it's time, you will know. His words will come from your spirit, seep into your soul and erupt from your mouth. Open your mouth, speak what your spirit hears and let His words come out. What your spirit hears could be short syllables or it could be sentences. It's always in another language; it will not be English which is your learned language, or any language that you've previously learned and mastered."

Tom shut his eyes again and he began to silently praise and worship God in his spirit. Immediately, Tom's mouth begin to tremble. Without warning, God's Holy language erupted inside his spirit, permeated through his soul, and words of praises gushed out of Tom's mouth in an unknown tongue.*

The words Tom heard within his spirit came directly to him from the mouth of God. Immediately, Tom felt an inner newness. Tom's surrendered body became God's resting place.

Not long afterward, the kitchen door swung open. Tom entered into the kitchen a very happy and free young man! He rushed over and lifted his Aunt Vetta from the floor, swinging her and singing, "Jesus loves me!"

He turned and rushed to his Uncle Jeremy, and told him, "All my self- protective walls have crumbled at the foot of the Cross, and Jesus' blood has set me free from sin and from eternal death!"

"Sounds like we have another Evangelist in the house." Grandpa laughed.

"Cousin George, no more lawyers, no more trouble, I am clean!"

After the celebration died down, Vetta prepared a light lunch. As they talked, their conversation turned to Anderson's funeral.

Cate said, "Tom I would like for you to come with Mom and Dad to our friend's graveside service tomorrow afternoon. There, you will meet your cousin Brie and her husband Brad, Pastor Wilson and Mother Parks' family."

"Tom?'

"Yes, Uncle Jeremy."

"Boy, listen to me. There will be a big, ugly, coffee color, bald headed, rough around the edges, no smiling man there by the name of Woody. He's a no-good, conniving, atrocious, bloodthirsty killer. Stay away from him."

"Whew!" responded Tom. "He's all that! Okay, Uncle Jeremy, I will do just that."

Tom scraped his hand over his lower jaw and said, "You know, Uncle Jeremy, weeks ago, I would have been a magnet, drawn like a steel paperclip to this man named Woody. I would've willingly participated in any sinful acts needed to get money for my sinful habits. Now," Tom snapped his fingers and said, "Instantaneously, swiftly, my life has changed.

"Hmmm,"

Tom again scraped his hands over his chin and asked. "May I be excused?"

A short time later he rejoined his family. To their surprise, they saw he had removed his facial piercings.

"Tom!" shouted George, "What have you done? You know you don't have to do that?"

"I know, but I chose to remove my facial piercings. I never really wanted them. But the tattoos, they are permanent. I did all of this to fit in with my group of friends. I had no idea that my life would change, especially a rapid change like this" He began to sway and shouted, "Whoa! What I am feeling is indescribable."

George stood, and led him to a chair. He said, "You had better sit for a while."

Tom looked at George and told him, "This feeling is awesome, man."

"Laughing, Tom said, "Uncle Jeremy and Aunt Vette, when I stepped onto your porch, I felt this pull inside my gut. I felt like I was destined to be here. I am here with the support I have always wanted. I now have the new beginning and for the first time I can say, I'm really happy. I can say goodbye to the old me with pleasure, and hello to the new me!"

Tom chuckled. He ran his hand over his chin hairs andtouched his stiff hair and asked,

"May I be excused?"

A short time later, Tom returned without his face piercings."

"Tom, what have you done?" Exclaimed George. "You didn't have to do that?"

"Yes I did. I never wanted them. I did it to fit in with the group." Grinning, Tom asked, "Cousin George and

Uncle Jeremy, do you think you can take me to the barber shop and the mall?"

Uncle Jeremy's response was, "Vetta ... for the first time in my life I am speechless."

"Say what?" Responded Vetta. "Now, we all know that's a miracle."

After the laughter died down, George answered Tom's question. "Tom, we will be happy to take you to the mall and to our barber shop.

Chapter 25, Michael

Looking at the monitor, Ida Park's gently touched the deep vicious cuts on her son's face and her fingers lovingly stroked his black curls. She looked at the monitor and saw her son's heart beat was very slow. She whispered, "Michael, Michael, baby. What happened? Did Woodrow do this to you?"

"Mrs. Parks."

"Yes."

"I need to change his catheter. It will take a few minutes.

Will you please step out?"

While waiting, Ida paced and thought about the question she had asked Michael. *Did Woodrow do this?* She recalled the scripture. *There is nothing concealed that will not be disclosed, or hidden that will not be known.*

"Mrs. Parks, you can come back in."

"Thank you."

Ida stood next to Michael's bed. She watched in silence as the nurse adjusted his IV bag. Nurse Eleanor turned to leave and stopped to say, "Mrs. Parks, if you need me, just push this button and I will `come immediately."

"If I need you, I will do just that. I thank you."

"You are more than welcome. May I bring you something cold to drink, or a cup of hot tea or coffee?"

"No thank you, I'm fine."

"Very well. Now Mrs. Parks remember, if you need anything, please let me know."

"I will and thank you again."

"You are more than welcome, Ma'am."

Nurse Eleanor left Michael's room, closing the door behind her.

Ida looked down at her son, and asked, "Michael, is there anything too hard for God? His specialty is making the impossible, possible."

Ida momentarily stopped talking and tilted her head upward and she prayed.

"God, the doctor said Michael has bleeding in the brain that will impact his ability to walk and speak. Father, open his ears to hear and his heart to understand the words I speak. Transform his brain functioning that he will be able to ask for forgiveness

Ida's hands lingered on his swollen cut lips, and her teary eyes looked at her son's swollen head, and again she touched his scarred, bruised face. Crying and through sniffles, she told him, "Michael, you are my baby. When it was time for my sister to give life to you, God looked around at all the unique different embryos that He had created." Dabbing her teary eyes, she continued, "God had in mind that each embryo's body would become His dwelling place and welcome His glorious Spirit. Your body was selected by God to become that special habitation where His Spirit could house His glory and find rest. God looked at you, and He spoke these words, 'Michael White Parks' spirit come, and dwell within my Spirit, and together we will become one.' Michael, God redeemed your soul.

He loves you and His love will never leave you. You are His.

"God said you are His, Michael. My son, please, please understand and hear, God said it and His words are established and they can't be altered. Yes, the devil also heard what God said. He saw God's love and commitment to you, and the devil became jealous because he lost all of that. He lost God's love when he decided to rebel against God. With his rebellion, he sealed his eternal destination in hell. The devil is determined to destroy you too since he's lost. But he is a liar. The Bible says, 'The devil, was a murderer from the beginning, not holding to the truth, for there is no truth in him. When he lies, he speaks his native language, for he is a liar, and the father of lies.'

"Michael, do you remember the scripture in Roman 12:1-2? It's about the transformed mind? I remember...you wrote a song about transformation." Ida lifted her head, thinking about the song and said, "Now let me see if I can still remember the lyrics and tune"... She sang,

"Here am I Lord, on my face.
You see my soul, and its disgrace.
I'm in need of Your redeeming grace.
Transform my mind to run this race.
Here I am Lord, on my face.
I'm in need of Your consuming grace.
Here am I, here am I. Lord.
Here am I
In need of Your perfect grace.
Transform my mind.
To hear your thoughts.
Transform my heart.
To love as You.

Transform my spirit.
To live in You.
Here am I Lord,
Here am I.
Here am I on my face,
Thanking You for Your infinite grace."

"That song and your voice is beautiful."

Ida stood and saw Michael's evening nurse had been listening. She was an attractive, tall, young nurse with an angelic face and smile. Ida read the name on her badge, and told her. "Thank you, Nurse Angela. Michael wrote those lyrics; he used to be a worship leader."

"Mrs. Parks, I am a Christian and I believe Michael heard you. I believe your son is asking God in his spirit for that change right now. I believe Michael's mind and heart sung to God while you sang his lyrics, and I have to believe God is listening."

Nurse Angela held Ida's hand and said, "Mrs. Parks, it's time to change Michael's head bandages. If you like, you can stay"

"No, and I thank you Nurse Angela, I have to leave. We are planning my nephew's funeral services today."

"Oh, my condolences to you and your family. We will take care of Michael and I will be here when you come back."

Once outside Michael's room, Ida took out her cell phone and dialed Cate's number. The phone rang several times before she heard Cate's voice."

"Hello." "Cate, it's me."

Ida turned toward the entrance hallway, and caught a

glimpse of Luke Allen before he swiftly dodged behind the wall.

"Hello, hello, hello, Mom, Mom Parks, are you there? What's happening?" Cate questioned.

"Ah, I am sorry, Cate. I had a distraction."

"Are you okay? Do you need me?"

"No ... Perhaps later but not right now. I'm at the hospital with Michael."

Choking back her tears, she told Cate, "Woodrow's men found Michael in his apartment. He was severely beaten, his head is massive, and he has bleeding in the brain, and Cate... my Michael is in a coma.

"Cate ... I have this sickening awakening… that Woodrow, my Woodrow – Woodrow Hugh Parks is responsible for this. I hate to think that my son would do something so ... so inhumane and outrageously monstrous as this to his cousin and brother.

"Excuse me, Cate, please stay on the line."

Ida placed her cell phone into her jacket pocket, removed a handkerchief that was tucked into her dress sleeve, and dabbed her tears. She quickly walked down the hall. Through the tinted window of the hospital's waiting room, she saw Luke Allen and Woody getting into Woody's car, but they were not moving.

She placed the phone back to her ear and her voice cracked when she said, "Cate, Woodrow has always been different, and now he's a lost enigma. One minute he's completely thick-skinned and insensitive, and the next minute he's moved to tears and acting vulnerable. His behavior is as if he has dual personalities.

The biggest problem is he thinks he's invincible. He believes his gambling club is his throne and his bodyguard are his puppets."

Ida stopped to suck in air. She sighed heavily, and said, "Cate, I had planned on meeting all of you at the funeral home, but I have decided to stay here with Michael. I will call Gloria to let her "Okay, Mom Parks. Stay strong. We will come by later to see and pray for Michael. Oh, how is Jada?"

"Jada is safe."

"Mom Parks, we are praying for God's protection for you, Jada, and all of us who are connected to Woody's ongoing revengeful saga. Please be careful. Woody will become much more dangerous."

"I will dear. Bye, Cate."

Ida punched the red exit button on her cell phone. She rushed to the nurses' station where she saw Nurse Angela.

"Excuse me, Nurse Angela."

"Mrs. Parks, how may I help you?"

"Would you call your administrator and ask him or her to contact the investigating officer who was in charge of Anderson Parks' case? He was in the same room that my son is in now, room 7.

I would like to talk with him concerning my son, Michael Jay White Parks. Please inform them that I am asking for security guards to be placed at my son's door because I have concerns for his life."

"Okay Mrs. Parks, right away."

After thirty minutes, there was a knock on the door.

"Come in."

"Please forgive me," Mrs. Parks said to the officer standing inside the room. "I was told that the chief of police was coming and not the same investigating officer I saw when Anderson died."

"No need to apologize. I get that all the time. My name is Chief Jones and you are right, I am the same investigating officer for your late nephew Anderson. We met briefly in the waiting room.

He walked over to Michael's bed and examined Michael's injured body. Moments later, he asked, "Is Michael your other son?"

"Yes, he is."

"You are concerned for Michael's safety? Why?

"See for yourself. He has the same markings on his face and body as Anderson. Anderson was doing well, as you know, and someone entered this same room and killed him. Do you have a suspect?

"As of now, all of our evidence is circumstantial. But I will assure you, Mrs. Parks that security measures for Michael will be taken immediately."

"Thank you, Chief Jones."

"Mrs. Parks, may I have you cell number in case I need to contact you?"

"Yes, it's 554-557-5575."

"Thank you, and, Mrs. Parks, stay safe."

"I will, and thanks again."

Ida Parks walked Chief Jones out the door, and returned to Michael's bedside.

"Michael, did you hear that? Investigator Chief Jones

will place security guards outside your door. You are going to be guarded 24/7. Woodrow, nor Luke Allen, Red, Pete or Harry will come inside your room without someone being present. They will not be left alone with you. You will be safe."

An hour later, Ida heard a knock on the door, she turned and saw Chief Jones with the two police officers assigned as Michael's bodyguards.

Chapter 26, Graveyard Showdown

During the conclusion of Anderson's graveside service, Pastor Wilson gave the final remarks,

"In sure and certain hope of the resurrection to eternal life through our Lord Jesus Christ. We commend to our Almighty God our brother Anderson. We commit his body to the ground; earth to earth, ashes to ashes, dust to dust. May the Lord bless him and keep him, may the Lord make His face to shine upon him and be gracious unto him and give himpeace. Amen."

With the passage of time, everyone had walked away with the exception of Ida Parks. She stood alone, grieving with her head bowed at Anderson's grave, when Woody approached.

"Mom, have you seen Jada?

"What? No good afternoon, Mom, or Mom, how are you? Or how is Michael? ... No, my self-centered, self-absorbed, son's first words are, 'Have you seen Jada?' Woodrow, if I had, I would never tell you."

Knowing his mother wouldn't lie, he watched her reactions to his direct question with eyes of an eagle, searching for truth. He again asked, "Mom, have you seen Jada?"

"And again, I will not answer your question Woodrow. My prayer is that she gets far away from you. You do not deserve her, or any other woman."

"Mom, have you seen Jada?"

Through clenched teeth, his mother asked,

"Woodrow! Have you seen your brother? He has blood

clots and is bleeding in the brain. That may impact his ability to walk and speak. He's in a coma, fighting for his life! But you," Ida spoke harshly, scrutinizing her self-absorbed son with scorn, "you are asking me if I have seen Jada? You stand here in my face without any concern for Michael or Gloria, Anderson and their kids. Woodrow are you capable of caring about anyone other than yourself? Did you care about Anderson or about Gloria and Anderson's kids, and since I have your attention, tell me Woodrow, did you kill Anderson? Did you beat your brother? Answer my questions and I will answer yours."

Woodrow's face tightened and he angrily looked away without responding. His mother turned to leave him standing at Anderson's graveside when Pastor Wilson approached.

"Hello, Pastor Wilson," said Ida. "That was a wonderful homecoming eulogy for our Anderson."

"Sister Ida, Anderson was a delightful young man. I am beyond thrilled to know he repented, found God's forgiveness, and experienced God's unadulterated, pure love before he died. And he was seen by Gloria being escorted to heaven by God's angels … Hallelujah … My, my, my, my, and oowheeeew! What a loving, gracious God we have."

"I can say amen to that Pastor."

Woody felt a hot, heavy hand on his shoulder and he pulled away. Pastor Wilson said, "Woody, I was glad to see you in church a few weeks ago. Please do not let it be your last time coming."

 Woody smirked and said, "That was my last time

coming."

"Woodrow!"

"What Mom? I am telling the truth and that's what you are all about--truth. Isn't that right mom? It is written in that book you read and love, 'The truth shall make you free.'"

"Woodrow, my Bible that I read and love says, 'If you abide in my word, you are truly my disciples, and you will know the truth, and the truth will set you free*.'"

Pastor Wilson said, "Woody, I can perceive that the load you are carrying is too heavy, and it is suffocating you. Son, God is your only help. He's waiting for you to call out to Him."

"Well, Pastor Wilson, excuse my candor, but that will never happen! And I wish I could say it was nice seeing and talking with you, but I can't."

With straightforwardness Pastor Wilson responded, "Please don't excuse my candor, I will tell you, you are lost and without hope unless you repent."

Woody's phantom enjoying this jostling with words, replied, "And with candor, Pastor Wilson, I will tell you that my repentance to your god will never happen and I have nothing else to say to you."

"Nor I to you. May God have mercy on your soul."

"With a loud snort, Woody replied, "Please stop?"

Woody swung around to talk with his mother, but he saw her talking with her family, Cate's family.

Woody stood alone. He lowered his head pretending to be paying homage to his cousin, but he was listening in on Cate's conversation. Cate said, "Brie this is your changed cousin Tom. And Tom, this is Brie's husband, Brad."

"It's great to finally meet you. I have heard so much about you both."

Brad grabbed Tom and hugged him. He shouted "Welcome to the family of God. Man, to tell the truth, we were all worried about your coming to live with Brie's grandparents. But no one saw what happened to you coming."

Brie asked. "Tom, when will you register for school?"

"Your mom and dad will take me to your old high school on Monday to enroll. I am excited about starting school and making new friends."

"It's a beautiful campus with wonderful teachers."

"Hey, Tom. You have plans?"

"No Brad, just hanging with my Aunt and Uncle."

"Well, that's about to change. After Anderson's repast, Brie and I are going over to the church to meet some of the youth. They are auditioning for the band guitarist for our worship team. Would you like to come with us?"

"What? I know I am being presumptuous and this is crazy ... and please forgive me, but may I audition? If I must say so, I am a skilled guitarist ... no, I am a gifted guitarist. Geez Brad and Brie, I would love to audition I have my guitar at Uncle and Auntie's house. I apologize for being overly ambitious, but I need this new beginning. If its okay, perhaps we can swing by the house, I will grab my guitar, and come to audition with the others. Will that be okay?"

Laughing, Brad replied, "Wow, you are not modest."

"Hmmm," laughed Brie, "Tom you are a lot like my favorite cousin, Cullen."

"Why sure, Tom," answered Brad, "you can audition. This is my youth group, and the group has been praying for the right guitarist. God answers prayers His way."

Woody stood back, listening. *So this is Cullen's cousin Tom.* Woody's phantom thought. *I have heard about him. Salvation? We will see. If I couldn't use Brie or Cullen, I will use Tom. And if that doesn't work out, then he may just meet up with an accident, like his cousin Sally and her husband.*

Grandpa watched Woody watching Tom from a distance. He came over to Woody and agitatedly said, "Woody, you will stay away from that boy. I still believe you killed my daughter and her husband. I have no proof, but one day the truth will come out and you will pay for it. I also believe you killed Anderson."

Grandpa Jeremiah's constrained dam erupted, and his heavy voice boomed, "You are nothing but a murdering scumbag, stay away from Tom!"

Woody inner phantom spewed, "Old man, one day I will close that mouth of yours!"

Woody grabbed Grandpa Jeremiah by his suit collar, pulled out his pistol, his phantom order him *to ram it into Grandpa Jeremiah's mouth,* and he shouted. "Windbag, say something now!"

George and Jason heard Woody's threat and saw the pistol he had shoved into Grandpa Jeremiah's mouth. George and Jason started to run towards them and Grandma Vetta saw Luke Allen, Red, and Pete pointing their guns.

Grandma Vetta hollered, "No! Stop! Jason, George, Woody! No!" Grandma Vetta adamantly shouted, "All of you, stay here, and all of you put those guns away now!"

She rushed over to her husband and to Woody. She said "Let go of him and shame on you Woodrow, dishonoring your mother like this at your cousin's homecoming. Take that gun out of my Jeremy's mouth and look around Woody."

Woody lowered his gun and looked around; he saw all eyes were on him. Grandma Vetta shouted, "Jeremiah Sullivan, what has gotten into you?"

Seizing hold of her husband's arm she forcibly dragged him away from Woody. "Come on. Let's go."

As Grandma Vetta walked away, she stopped to look back at Woody and told him, "Woody, You and Jeremy need to monitor this rage you both have toward each other … and Woody, put that pistol away and learn to respect your elders!"

Grandma Sullivan turned back around and pulled her traumatized husband to their car.

Woody quickly walked to his van and signaled Harry to come out of hiding. Luke sat behind the wheel ready to drive. Harry came and opened the passenger side. As Woody was about to get in he stopped and smiled at those who were staring.

Woody shouted, 'Harry, get behind the wheel, and Luke, come here."

"Yes, Boss."

Woody's mind seeped revenge on Jeremiah Sullivan

and anything or anyone even remotely related to him in any form. He thought about that geezer's words. *You are nothing but a murdering scumbag, stay away from Tom!*

Luke came and stood in front of Woody and Woody whispered, "I am going to visit MJ. I want you, Harry, Red and Pete to go into hiding. Before coming here, I was told by my informants that things are heating up with the investigation against us. And Luke, see that kid with Brie?"

"Yes, Boss."

"His name is Tom. I want him dead, but I want to torment him before he dies. Go to our friend and get yourself a disguise and I will do the same. I want you to keep tabs on Tom until I think of a way to get to him, and when it's time I will kill the boy."

Snickering, Woody said, "The beauty of my plan is I want Harry to take the fall for his death and then you be sure to take Harry out."

"With delight, Boss."

Ida Parks, rushed over to Woody's van and grabbed his arm. Through clinched teeth, she hissed, "Woodrow why are you acting this way?"

He answered with a low raspy whisper, "I will tell you why when you tell me. Have you seen Jada?"

Ida recoiled. She slapped his face and asked, "Who are you?"

"You are about to find out who I am if you are hiding Jada, Ida!"

Gloria come rushing over, she screeched, "Did you kill Anderson?"

Woody glared at Gloria and his mother. He looked

around and saw the others nearby watching and waiting for an answer.

Woody chuckled. Not responding to Gloria's question, he got into the van, slammed the car door shut, the door and shouted, "Drive!"

As Harry drove away, through his open window, Woody heard Anderson's small son's question. "Mommy, did Uncle Woody kill my daddy?"

Chapter 27, Brunch with Friends

Several weeks later Ida Parks met with Lovetta and Cate for coffee at her restaurant.

"Where did I go wrong with my boys, Lovetta? As you and Cate well know, Michael was a faithful worship leader throughout his late teen years. Then along comes Woodrow, with his smooth and deathly overtures, persuading him into leaving the church and working for him.

"Then," Ida took in a short sip of coffee. "A short time later, I heard rumors that Michael had started selling drugs. Once Jada came back, Michael stopped pushing Woodrow's drugs to manage his bar. But the decision to accept his brother's lifestyle was Michael's choice." Ida paused, she took longer sips of coffee then released a loud sorrowful sigh.

"Michael, worked full time with his brother and he immersed himself into a lifestyle that I disapproved of. It was against God's laws and my moral values. I gave Michael a choice to either change or move out. Woodrow sanctioned his moving out of my home and Michael chose the latter." Ida shifted her weight, took another sip of coffee and continued, "Michael moved into that fancy expensive apartment and right away Michael started emulating his brother's lifestyle.

He was buying expensive clothes, driving fast cars and had women coming and going in and out of his life. He became

ensnared, in his brothers' sinful, showy, seducing, lifestyle.

Michael, just like Woodrow, pushed God completely out of his life."

Ida Parks savored her last sip of coffee and noticed her friends' cups were also empty. She raised her arm, and wiggled her pearl-red manicured fingers to get their waiter's attention. The waiter took Cate and Vetta's cups and poured their coffee, and then he poured coffee into his boss's cup. Ida Parks nodded her head, indicating she was pleased, she smiled and said, "Clarence, I thank you."

"You're welcome Mrs. Parks, and is there anything else any of you ladies need?"

Cate shook her head, indicating no, and Vetta answered, "No, Clarence, and I thank you."

Ida smiled and replied, "Thank you for asking."

After a few sips of hot coffee, Ida told Vetta and Cate, "I thank my church family and both of you for praying for Michael." Ida shook her head and told them, "He's been in that coma much too long." A smile spread across her 80-year-old, wrinkled free, face and she told them, "Last week, a new expensive neurologist was assigned to Michael. I'd scheduled an appointment with the billing department to ask how much this neurologist will cost, and they told me Michael's neurologist' finances were all taken care of by a few anonymous donors."

Ida smiled and said, "After some investigation I found that once again you, my dear godchild, and Vetta, along with George, Jeremiah, and the rest of my church family spared no expense in finding this doctor. My words can never express how appreciative I am."

Ida began to laugh.

"Why are you laughing?" Vetta asked,

Ida leaned forward and whispered, "Vetta it has been rumored that this new doctor only been here one week and already, he's praying with the nurses.

"Well Ida, Vetta said, "That's God. He always has His plans."

"Amen." Cate replied.

Vetta noticed Ida's joyous facial expression change. She suddenly had a look of concern and Vetta asked, "What are you thinking about Ida? Tell us."

"Vetta, Michael is unconscious, but I still talk with him about his soul. I believe God will open the eyes of his heart. I believe Michael hears my songs and he hears all of our prayers. I believe God will give Michael a second chance and I have pushed all my doubt aside. I trust God to fulfil the promises that were spoken into Michael's life. I have to believe. I can't pray with faith in the power of God without something happening in Michael's spirit, soul and body. God's power works from the inside out.

"Lovetta?"

"Yes, Ida?"

"Will you continue to fast with me on Mondays, and Wednesdays, and pray at our appointed times, and continue to stand in agreement with me for Michael's miracle.

"You know I will."

"Thanks, Lovetta."

"Mom Parks?"

"Yes, Cate?"

"I have been praying for Jada. Have you heard from her?"

"Cate." Ida reached across the table and held Cate's hands. She smiled and inhaled and exhaled as she prepared her mind to disclose a well-hidden secret. "Don't worry anymore. Jada is with me and she's safe."

"What? Oh no, Mom Parks. Woody will be."

Vetta interrupted Cate and asked, "Where are you hiding her? In the basement's secret room? Ida, Woodrow knows about that room."

Ida replied, "Heaven no, Vetta."

Ida's soft brown eyes leaped with joy, she leaned in closer to her friends and whispered, "I have Jada inside a secret place, a very spacious place inside my home that no one else knows about. The only other person, besides me, who knew the entrance to the place Jada is hiding is Samuel. Cate, let me reassure you and Vetta, Jada is very safe."

"Has Woody contacted you?" Vetta asked.

"No, but it's my understanding that Harry was shot and was left in the woods to die, but a hiker found him and called an ambulance. Chief Jones hopes Harry will pull through his operation. Then he will question him concerning the deaths of Anderson and Tom."

"Tom." Vetta hesitated and said, "When our Tom came to live with us, he told us he had a feeling something bad would happen to him, but not this. Tom is dead, and once again, Woody is involved."

"Ida, I pray Harry pulls through and gets a chance to repent again and get his life right with God. He tried to help Tom when Woody was threatening his life."

 Cate reached out and touched her mother's hands.

"Up until now, I have only told my family this." Cate said, "When Anderson was in the hospital, Harry came into Anderson's room to check on his progress. Harry said to me. 'I heard Anderson asking God to forgive him for his sins and I am happy for him. Harry started to walk away, then Harry turned around and said to me, 'Evangelist Cate, please keep my name in your prayers. Your words at church Sunday keep turning over and over in my mind and I know I want to change. I know you have heard these words so many times I will give my life to God tomorrow. But each second in my day with Woody causes me to believe my tomorrow may not come, and my death could happen any moment. Take care, and I know what I'm going to say may mean nothing to you, but I am really happy for Brie..., but I'm afraid for Cullen, your dad, Anderson and myself.'"

I prayed for Harry and Harry gave his life to Jesus. I stood and I watched as he left the room."

"God's will will be done," said Ida. "It's my prayer that Harry will come out of his coma, give a confession about Woodrow's involvement in all his murderous acts, and Harry will be free in his spirit. Ida looked down at her watch and she observed the time. She rapidly tapped the face of her watch with her fingers and shouted, "Oh my, the time! Lovetta, and Cate please stay and have lunch on me. I wish I could stay longer to talk, but I'm off to the hospital to get updates on Michael's new security guard."

Ida stood and motioned their waiter to come over. Ida took him aside and gently shoved $40.00 into his hands. She told him that was his tip, and to take good care of her friends. She instructed him to give them whatever they ordered, and charge their meals to her.

She walked back to Cate and Lovetta and said, "My friends, I love you."

She motioned for their waiter to come over. Ida gently held his elbow and she told Lovetta and Cate, "As you already know, this is Clarence, and he will take care of you. Order whatever you like, your meals have been taken care of."

"Ida, we can pay."

"Hush, nonsense Vetta, this is my restaurant, and you are my friends. Eat, have dessert, and I will see you both soon."

Vetta smiled and said "Alright Ida, take care and call me later with an update on Michael's progress."

"I will do just that." Waving, and rapidly moving out the restaurant Ida shouted, "Love you both, bye."

Lovetta and Cate watched Ida rush out the door to her car. Cate said, "Mom, let's pray for God's blood covering over my godmother, Jada, and Michael."

And Woody..." Cate pondered a moment and said, "We all know how desperate, out of control and vengeful Woody has become, and ..." Vetta placed her hands over her own heart when she interrupted Cate's words. She whispered, "Oh my, Cate ... Woody ... if he finds out that Ida has had Jada all..."

"Yes, Mom." Cate answered back. "We all saw that unplugged rage in him at Anderson's graveside. We heard the words Woody spoke to dad, and the vulgarity that spewed from his mouth surprised me."

"And Tom, our precious, precious Tom. Cate, I know all the evidence points to Harry as Tom's killer, but I believe Woody killed him."

"Mom, let's continue to pray for Harry and his recovery, and the truth will be revealed."

"Woody … his eyes that day at the cemetery … when I stared into his eyes, they were dark, void of light, and foreboding. Cate, oh dear ... I now fear for Ida and Jada's lives ..., if Woody finds out Ida has been hiding Jada all this time... Oh, he will ... Oh my ... Cate."

"Mom, we must always remember we serve a mighty warrior, an awesome God. Woody's corrupt actions will be God's opportunity to show His greatness. We have to believe this is God's plan for all of us who are involved in Woody's revengeful saga."

"Yes, dear you're right. This is God's plan, and we just have to pray and watch God's plan unfold."

Chapter 28, Masquerade

A short time later, Ida Parks arrived at Jane Case Hospital and met with the security administrator. Afterward, she went directly to Michael's room. At the entrance, she was greeted by Michael's newly assigned security officer and once inside, she saw Nurse Angela.

Nurse Angela smiled and pointed to the monitor, "Hi, Mrs. Parks, I know it's been almost a month and it seems to you and us that Michael's condition hasn't changed. But with God's help, the new doctor, and your constant presence each day, Michael has been very good. Today, Michael's heart beat has improved. Your singing and prayers are doing the job, keep it up."

Ida clasped her hands, laughed, and said, "Praise be to God. He is the healer."

"Amen to that," said Nurse Angela as she walked to the door. Suddenly, she stopped and turned saying, "Mrs. Parks?"

Ida turned and answered, "Yes, Nurse Angela, what is it?"

"I want you to know the other nurses on this floor are with you in believing that God will provide Michael's miracle.

"I really appreciate that. I thank you and please thank the other nurses for me."

"I will do that," she said.

Ida, leaning over the bed railing, whispered, "Michael, please open your eyes, son, open your eyes."

Ida pulled her chair beside her son's bed, and sat down and told him, "Did you hear Nurse Angela, Michael? She said the nurses are believing God for your miracle. Cate, George, and Pastor Wilson, have been coming daily to pray for you. Vetta and I have been on a continuous fast, praying for you to wake up. Our prayer is that you will allow God to open the eyes of your heart to receive His healing power. God's word says, 'If you have faith the size of a mustard seed, you will say to this mountain, 'Move from here to there,' and it will move; and nothing will be impossible to you.' 'And he said unto them, this kind of miracles can come forth by nothing, but by prayer and fasting.'"

Ida's soft brown eyes stared down on her son's sleeping body and she asked, "Now, Michael, where was I when I left you? Oh yes, baby, I remember. I was talking to you concerning the transforming and renewing of your mind. Son, you know your mind becomes renewed with God's Spirit only when your spirit, soul, and body align with His Spirit. When His spirit activates your soul, your soul stirs God's mind and His mind activates your body. That's when God's healing balm, His oil will start flowing and you will be healed.

"Michael, you must believe that the battle has been fought, and God has already won the battle for your soul. Right now, you must push. You must push past all obstacles that are trying to prevent you from coming back into God's open arms. With the eyes of your heart, believe in Him.

"With your mind, start speaking His words that you

are hearing in your spirit. That's God's Holy language you are hearing. Jesus has prayed for you. He is interceding for you right now. His Spirit is telling your spirit what you need from God. Trust His voice, speak His words and live.

Ida, placed her hands on Michael's head and spoke with confidence, "Your body, soul, and spirit are covered by the Blood of Jesus. In the Name of Jesus, and with His authority that He has given to me, I command all demonic forces to leave Michael *now!* I speak life! Come alive Michael, in Jesus' name. Come alive!"

Instantly, she heard, "Beep, beep, beep, B-e-e-p!" The monitor begin to hum!

Michael stirred. The nurses and doctor rushed in. Ida scooted her chair away from his bed and walked to corner of the room. She stood, silently thanking God and observing with tears flowing.

Just before the door closed, Ida's peripheral vision saw Cate, George and Pastor Wilson standing outside the door. She rushed to the partially closed door, swung it wide open and shouted, "God did it! Michael woke up!"

Moments later, Michael's doctor stepped into the hallway, smiling. He said, "Mrs. Parks, we had our audio monitor open for a few days, and we were able to hear your conversations with Michael. I was able to listen and as you spoke to Michael, God changed my heart. I grew up in a saved home, but during my college years I walked away from God. For the last two nights my duty list has been light, and I was able to listen to your conversations with Michael. He hesitated then asked, "Mrs. Parks, may I call you Mom Parks?"

"Yes, you may."

Dr. Phillip said, "Mom Parks, tonight I asked God to forgive me of all my transgressions." His smile broadened as he motioned for the nurses, who had been silently listening, to come out into the hall. Once they were all there, he continued "These two nurses are believers. They sat with me while I listened to you, and then they prayed for me."

Ida, hugged them and said to the doctor, "Welcome home."

"Thank you." Dr. Grace turned to Cate, George and Pastor Wilson and said, "I thank all of you.

Now about Michael, he is alert and his vitals are getting stronger. You all may go in for a short visit but his body is healing and he will need proper rest."

Cate, George and Pastor Wilson thanked the doctor and went into Michael's room.

"Dr. Phillip."

"Yes, Mom Parks."

"Is the audio monitor still on?"

"Yes, Ma'am."

"I am curious. It may be against hospital rules to talk about this, but weeks ago my nephew was in this exact room and he died."

"Mom Parks, my condolences to you. I was informed that a gentleman was beaten severely, and was doing well. I was told that they were understaffed that night and when the nurse went in to check on him, she found him dead. His death is being investigated and the investigating officer is looking at all our security cameras.

As a precautionary backup, since you talked with them, this hospital has placed video surveillance cameras on all visitors, and also audio monitors for those in our trauma units. It's my understanding that you asked for front door security for Michael, and the hospital administrators believed having a monitor in his room at all times would be included in our safety measures."

"You are right, and I am elated with this precautionary measure. Ida laughed and said, "I thank you doctor."

"May I ask why are you laughing?"

"I see your last name is Grace?"

Ida reached out for his hands. As she held them, she said, "I laughed because all this time, I've been calling you Dr. Philip. This is the first I have seen you in your white jacket with your name badge. I can officially call you Doctor Philip Grace. Dr. Grace, I thank you."

Dr. Grace responded, "I thank God for His great grace and for sending me here to Jane Case Hospital to you."

Dr. Grace turned and walked down the hall whistling "Grace, grace, God's grace. Grace that is greater than all our sins."

"Ida walked back into Michael's room. Michael saw his mother through his one open eye and weakly said, "Mom." She reached through the railings, held his hand and said, "I love you, Michael."

"Mom, is Pastor Wilson here? I can only see shadows with my one eye, but I can hear very well."

Pastor Wilson answered, "Yes, Michael, I am here."

"Pastor Wilson, I know you have heard these words so many times from those who are incarcerated or near death's doors.

'If God gets me out of this mess I will come to church, or I will give my life back to Jesus.' Well, I am going to say those same words, but with a vow to God, in His presence and all who are listening, as well as all of heaven as my witnesses. I surrender my body, soul, and spirit to God."

Michael's head turned towards his mother and he said, "Mom, God has opened the eyes of my heart and I welcome Him in to stay forever."

With tears flowing, she responded, "Michael you heard my prayers."

"I did, Mom."

"Brother Michael," Pastor Wilson said, "I am so happy that you listened to our prayers with an open heart and heard God's voice."

Cate leaned over the railing, kissed his forehead and said, "Welcome back home, Michael."

"Apparently, there's no brain damage," said George. "This young man is thinking clearly and that's miracle one. Well y'all, God has done His work, I think we had better leave and let Michael get some rest."

"Michael?"

"Yes, Pastor Wilson?"

"I will be back first thing in the morning."

"Okay, Pastor Wilson."

"Mom"

"Yes, Michael?"

"Stay, don't go, I have to tell you something that you need to know."

She patted her son's hands, and placed her finger to his lips, and whispered, "Wait a minute, Michael, I will be right back."

Ida walked George, Cate and Pastor Wilson to the elevator. As the elevator door closed, she turned and swiftly walked past the security guard sitting at his small desk outside Michael's door. She continued around the corner to the nursing station, where she saw Nurse Angela.

"Excuse me, Nurse Angela."

"Yes, ma'am?

"Is the monitor still on in my son's room?"

"No, Mrs. Parks, it isn't. But when you leave, please let us know, and we will turn it back on."

"Thank you. I will do that."

Once again, Ida hurried past the security guard. She went back into her son's room and closed the door. Standing next to him she said "Now, son, we are alone. Tell me what is it you wanted me to hear."

"Mom, it's about Woody."

Startled, Ida jumped when she hear a heavy knock at the door. Turning, she asked, "Who is it?"

"Mrs. Parks, its John, Michael's security guard. I have a man standing here with me saying his name is Samuel Parks. He said he's your nephew and Michael is his cousin."

Ida turned and glanced at Michael. He moved his head slightly back and closed his eyes.

Through the closed door, Ida heard Woody's treacherous voice shouting, "Man, let me in."

"Yes, Officer John, he can come in."

The door opened and Ida saw Woody was in a disguise. He had short curly hair, a black moustache, and a well-trimmed black beard with almond color eyes, and the only recognizable trait was his coffee colored skin. He entered and asked with deceitfulness, "Is there any change?"

Not responding to his question, Ida said, "Officer John, please close the door."

Samuel cautiously walked over to Michael's bed, lifted Michael's limp hand, and cried. Michael heard his brother's voice and recognized his pretend crying.

Concerned for his well-being, Michael laid very still, with his eyes closed, pretending to sleep.

Ida quickly pulled Michael's heart rate monitor from the wall and an alarm sounded. Immediately, the nurse rushed in.

"What's happening?" shouted Samuel, "Is Michael dying?

Oh my, no, no. No!" Samuel became inconsolable.

Ida shoved Samuel out of Michael's room and down the hall into a corner far away from all the activity.

With tears soaking into his moustache and beard, Samuel asked, "Ida is Michael dying?"

"Drop this sham, Woodrow. Michael is a fighter and his doctors and nurses will take care of him. You've been hiding out for weeks and you come here wearing a disguise and using your dead father's name. I can't forget your behavior with Pastor Wilson and the vulgarity you used with Jeremiah Sullivan at Anderson's funeral is inexcusable."

Not desiring to hear his mother's chastisement, Woody turned away and removed his black handkerchief from his back pocket. As he dried his fake tears, he stared down the hall. He was aroused by the possibility that his brother may be dying and the rattling activities surrounding Michael. His inner phantom's thoughts were, *Die brother die!*

"Don't turn away from me, Woodrow."

"Shh Ida, keep your voice down, I am Samuel."

He quickly, but gently, grabbed his mother's shoulders. With controlled emotions, he told her, "To be honest, Jeremiah Sullivan, I have never cared for that ... that, cranky, old, bent-over nosy man. I really hate him."

Hearing his harsh remarks, Ida pulled away from his hold. Once again, she saw his eyes were without light and his eyelids were black.

She asked, "Who are you?"

"Why, Ida Jackson Parks all of your life, you have been delusional about me.

Who am I? I am Samuel's son. The son whose father kept telling his wife, 'Ida, that boy needs help. We need to send him away before he hurts someone or himself.'"

"Woodrow, you heard your father's conversations concerning you? How? We were so careful not to say anything around you?"

"Obviously, not careful enough."

"Did you kill Jeremiah and Lovetta's nephew, and your best friends Mike and Sally?"

Choosing not to answer her question, Woody stared at his mother and the corners of his lips spread. He snickered when he told her, "Ida, if I told you, then you would have to die too."

"What do you mean, 'too?"

"Oh, you too will die in the fiery furnace,"

Woody's head sagged when he said, "Ida, I'm not joking … my master will order me to kill you. Everybody, but you, knows I am a killer. I love my Mom. To be able to kill you; you must become Ida Jackson Parks. My master has taught me how to separate you both. For, you see, I could never hurt my mom unless ..." Woody moved in closer to his mother's face and stared into her tear-filled brown eyes and said, "Unless my mother betrayed me and has been hiding Jada." He tilted his head and looked into his mother's eyes and asked, "Are you, Mother, hiding Jada?"

"What?" She shoved him and shouted, "Why are you acting like this?"

Woody gave Ida a sinister look and he answered, "I am my master's son and we are asking you, have you seen Jada?" He cackled when he said, "Ida, oh Ida, it's obvious to us that you are hiding her."

"Us? ... Woodrow, who's us?"

"My only friend and me."

"You have allowed this thing you call a friend to destroy your life. You have been brainwashed and, that so called master of yours hates you. His job is to kill your hope, and destroy your life, and he has already done just that ...."

Woody gave his mom an unsettling look and answered, "Yep, I have been brainwashed and I am not concerned."

He chuckled and continued, "We have called Cate and George many times and they wouldn't answer their house phone nor their cell phones. Jada's been missing for weeks and she didn't come to Anderson's funeral service. We asked you if you had seen her and you would never give us a direct answer. Nevertheless, we will ask for the umpteenth time; Ida, have you seen Jada?"

"Whatever that thing you are housing inside of you is, it is messing with the wrong woman. As far as Jada is concerned, if she desired to leave you, and needs my help, know this much Woodrow Hugh Parks, I would be more than willing to help her get away from you. What I witnessed that Thursday night at Gloria's made me ashamed to call you my son, and your rudeness with Cate. Woodrow, your actions and your callous remarks were uncalled for."

"Ida, Ida, your words, your words, they are not breaking my heart. I have this inner rage, this frightening spirit that controls me. It comes out of nowhere, and it forces me to hurt those I love. Especially if they have betrayed our trust."

"Our trust? How many times have you allowed that thing inside you to betray others' trust they have had in you, Woodrow?"

"Excuse me, Mrs. Parks, do you need my assistance?"

"No," Woody answered for her, "Ida doesn't need

your assistance!"

The officer placed his hand on his revolver and angrily shouted, "I am not speaking to you. I am addressing Mrs. Parks." Not averting his eyes from the disguised man, the officer repeated, "Ma'am do you need my help?"

"Ida," Woody hastily responded, "Ida, we will finish this conversation later. I see a nurse is motioning for us to come back."

Woody grasped his mother's elbow. She jerked away from his grip and preceded to walk in front of him. She was stopped at Michael's door by Nurse Angela and Woody went into Michael's room. The security officer stood behind him.

"Can I have a few minutes alone with my cousin?"

"No sir, you can't," replied the officer.

A few curse words were hurled towards the officer and he hissed, "I own you John, now get out!"

"You own me? ... Woody?"

"Yes, get out! NOW!"

Officer John backed away and stood near the open door. Woody turned away, bent down, kissed Michael's swollen lips and whispered, "Little brother, please don't come back to us, please don't wake up."

Michael's one undamaged eye opened and he spoke in barely a whispered. "Woody why?"

Startled, Woody's legs buckled.

Ida walked in and she shouted, "You need to leave."

"No, I am staying. You tell Officer John he can leave, and you, Ida, take a break, go to the cafeteria to eat, or to the lounge, and take a nap. I will stay here with Michael."

"What?" Ida sighed heavily. She hissed through clenched teeth, "Boy, I'll knock your head off. I am not one of your slithering, timorous bodyguards. You telling me what to do?"

Seemingly apologetic, Woody turned towards her with his bogus sobbing. Sniffling, he cried, "No, Ida ... I was thinking, you look tired and need rest, that's all. It's my fault that I didn't watch over Michael and Anderson. I am the reason why Michael is here, I just want to spend some alone time with him, Ida. Can't you understand that?"

"Oh cut the act. I understand all of this, and much more, and it is all your fault." Ida pulled a chair up to Michael's bed and plopped down. She shouted, "And I will stay here as long as I please. Why don't you go!"

"I will when I am ready." he retorted. "And besides Ida, all this loud talking isn't helping Michael."

Woody gave Ida a cast-iron look, studied her expression, and he said, "Ida, Ida, Ida you have Jada. Don't you? I am asking you as my momma for the last time… he whispered, "and as your son, are you sure you haven't seen Jada?"

Ida stood, lifted her chair and took three steps toward her son with intentions to hit him. She yelled, "Get out of here. I do not want to see you, nor talk with you, ever again, just go! Leave now!"

"It doesn't matter now ..." he replied.

"Guard!" shouted Ida.

Officer John entered with three more officers. They

heard Mrs. Parks shouting, “I have had enough of you.”

She stepped closer, gave Woody a quizzical glance and asked, “Who do you think you are? You are no match for my God.”

She leaned in and whispered in his ear, “Goodbye, Woodrow Hugh Parks, I never knew you. You are now in the hands of the living God, and may God have mercy on your miserable soul.” She kissed his forehead and turned away.

“Ida!” he screamed.”

Ida covered her ears with her hands. She stood with tears staining her distressed face. Not turning, she shouted, “No! Not one more word. Just go!”

“Come on!” Growled one of the officers. “Let’s go; she doesn’t want you here.”

“Ida, please, nooo. Ida...!”

Ida Parks slowly sat the chair back onto the floor. With sorrowful tears flowing, she stood, turned and stared at her vanquished son, locked in the arms of the guards. Not averting her eyes from his, Ida courageously walked to the open door, seemingly undaunted by his plead. She looked intently into her son’s fiery red eyes and closed the door.

She walked back to Michael’s bed, and whispered, “Michael he’s gone. Open your eye.”

Opening his one eye, Michael said, “Mom, I heard you and Woody. Mom, Woody is beyond dangerous. He’s the one who beat me and poor Anderson. He bludgeoned him with his aluminum baseball bat … is Anderson okay?”

She released a deep, remorseful heavy sigh and said,

"Michael, my heart is being ripped apart. Anderson died."

"Woody did it mom. He hit Anderson over and over with his aluminum baseball bat. He also beat me, his own brother, and after he finished beating me, he had his bodyguards beat me, while he sat and watched."

"Why, Michael why?"

"Mom, think. What has it always been about with Woody? It's all about money, control and power. He became irate when he found out what Anderson had done."

"How did he find out? And what did Anderson and you do?"

"He found out by looking at the hidden video recordings he had installed without telling us about it. The surveillance recordings showed Anderson taking money. Anderson was taking money because his family needed food and he had past due utilities bills. He asked Woody for help and Woody refused. He told Anderson that the only way he would help if he became a dope pusher."

"Michael, why did Woodrow beat you, then leave you to ..." She stuttered, "to die in your apartment?"

"He watched the video and saw I gave away drinks to my friends and talked with his working girls too much.

The only reason he called an ambulance is because… let me see… how did he put it? He said to me; 'The only reason I am saving your sorry butt of yours is because of Momma.'"

"While I was laying on the floor in my apartment, Woody cursed and kicked me over and over. Then he lifted me off the floor and tossed my body on the sofa. He sat back on his heels and slapped my face very hard and said, 'MJ, I wanted you to die just like all my trusting friends; Sally, Michael, Anderson, and my…' he paused then continued to say, 'so, so many more.'

"Woody told me, 'I went against my master's orders. I was to kill you, but something inside me wouldn't allow that. Our Momma sent me to check on you. She's the only one I can trust and if she crosses me, then all hell will break out.'

"Then I heard this cunning evil laughter coming out of Woody and he said..."

Michael suddenly stopped talking.

"Michael, Michael what's wrong son, you need help?"

"I am remembering it all, Mom. Woody, told me Anderson was dead. He told me at my apartment. He said, 'Before I call 911, I will tell you a secret that only three people know. You will make four and I know you aren't going to make it so I have no reason to fear you will let this secret out of the bag.'

"He came over to the sofa and with an eerie whisper he said, "MJ, I could put a pillow over your head, like I did Anderson, or I can put bullet holes in your head like I did to Sally and Mike.

"Oh my God!" Ida covered her mouth to keep from screaming. After a long wait, she said, "Michael, Woodrow is a psychopathic killer ... Michael."

"I know, Mom. Harry told me Woody beat poor Jada, then he had him and Luke Allen to tossed Jada's body on the street corner like you would have done to a dirty bag.

Harry also told me Woody was planning on doing something bad to Brie and Cullen because they won his money gambling and he wants it back."

Ida grasped Michael's hands and told him, "Well, that's not going to happen."

"Why do you say that?"

"Because Brie and Cullen gave all of their money to Gloria, in front of Woody, the night before Anderson's funeral. And when the hospital staff returned Anderson's clothing to Gloria, I found $10,000 in Anderson's pants pocket."

"Woody put it in Anderson's pocket."

"And he had all of us believing Anderson won it at another gambling house…" her voice trailed, then she said, "Michael, I asked Woody to give her an additional $25,000 to help with burial expenses. However, Gloria refused to accept his money, because she suspected Woody killed Anderson.

"Cate and George gave Gloria a check for $290,000 which included $90,000 of money Cullen and Brie won at Woodrow's club. The other $200,000 was a gift from Cate and George and Senator Rock and Julia. Gloria had enough money to pay for Anderson's' funeral and to move back to her hometown to make a new life for herself and the kids."

"Mom?"

"Yes, son?"

"Woody? He's looking for Jada. Is Jada missing?

"She's not missing. I have her hidden away."

"Mom, I know Woody will be even more violent

when he finds her. He considers anyone that worked for him as his property. He wants Jada dead because she knows too much. Please, Mom, if you are hiding her, be very careful. And please keep me safe. He has informants on the police force. One of them is Officer John."

"What!" His mother reached for her cell phone. She said, "I'll call Chief Jones."

Michael weakly whispered, "Mom, sit down and listen. I have nothing to worry about from John. Woody has mistreated him badly over the years and he has confided in me about his animosity toward Woody."

Michael motioned with his finger for a drink of water. His mother inserted a straw into the cup. After taking a few sips, he continued.

"Woody has never been right. As kids he would snatch legs and wings off insects and laugh while he watched them die. As long as I can recall, he has carried a plastic bag inside his back pocket. When we walked, he would captured small rodents or frogs, put them inside. Then he would suck out the air from the bag and watch, with delight, as they struggled to live.

"Woody has always been a user. He plots and takes from others." Michael slightly tilted his head and said, "The guard who's outside the door detests Woody?"

"Why?"

"Because Woody is blackmailing him for something his dead brother did. Woody killed Officer John's brother. Woody has many enemies. He is a cold-blooded, calculating serial killer. Over the years, he has become more unstable … he talks with an unseen, mysterious inner spirit that controls him. Mom … Woody… is…"

Beep, beep, beep, b-e-e-e-e-e-p. Michael slipped back into a coma.

When the doctor came out he told her Michael's brain was healing and they had no way of knowing when he will wake up.

Ida returned to her son's room and watched him sleep. She leaned over and kissed his forehead as bitter tears dropped onto her son's hospital garment. With her trembling fingers, she stroked her son's curly black locks and whispered, "Mom is here Michael. You will be protected from Woodrow's poisonous tentacles. I will put you where you will be safe."

Chapter 29, No Love for Momma

One month later, Mom Parks was at home when the house phone rang.

"Hello."

'Hi, Ida."

"Woodrow?"

"I have a new disguise, and I have decided to come out from hiding and come over for breakfast."

"I am not cooking. And you aren't welcome at my home anymore."

"Ouch! Ida, Ida, the sound of your voice and your words, they have pierced what little I have left...." Woody released a quick bizarre laughter and said, "... of my heart.

"Ida, what about all that love you have preached about? I am not feeling it. Oh, oh, oh, I know, your love for me has ran out."

Woody, not waiting for a reply, said, "Since you aren't cooking and my friend and I aren't invited into your house, could you meet us at your restaurant?"

"By us, are you referring to that demonic phantom you are housing? Then my answer is no. Woodrow, the police have warrants for the arrest of Luke, Pete and Red. Once they have arrested them, the police will be moments away from capturing you. You murdered Anderson, you attempted to kill your brother, and you killed Jeremiah's and Lovetta's nephew. Woodrow you aren't welcome here at my house, or my restaurant. You need to turn yourself in."

"Ida, I am a suspect. Believe me there's no conclusive

evidence against me."

"Woodrow, that thing you are housing has made you delusional. You aren't a suspect? Really, and how do you know this?"

"I am a businessman, Ida. I owned of a successful gambling casino. Police like to gamble, and I have several police officers who are indebted to me and they have kept me informed. Besides poor, poor MJ, I heard he relapsed, and he's in a deep coma. That investigation, led by that stupidly named Chief, can't pen anything on me. If he had evidence, he would have grabbed me by now."

"Woodrow, you are telling me that your informants on the police force have contacted you, and told you to come out of hiding? Is that the truth?"

"Ida, Ida, enlighten us! Tell us, what's your definition of truth? Aren't all men liars?"

"Woodrow, my Bible says, 'Let God be true, and every human being a liar.' As it is written: 'So that you may be proved right when you speak and prevail when you are judged. It was David's fear or anxiety that provoked him to say, 'all men are liars.'"

Ida, we don't need a Bible class and Ida, will soon feel anxiety and fear of death. She's hiding Jada in the secret room.

"Oh forget that bible teaching, Ida. I've been thinking about the basement at the house. I am coming there. You can hide us in your basement You have quarters in the basement that was used by the owner's great-great grandparents, the slave sympathizers. I could cook and sleep and can hide for years."

 Woody said with a loud chuckled, "Ida you can be

my sympathizer, you know, and hide us in the secret room?"

"What? You are talking crazy. You want me to hide that lying, destructive, murderous, slanderous imp you are delightfully housing in your mind? Absolutely not. Woodrow, turn yourself in."

"Please, Mom."

"Oh now I'm Mom? I will not play your devil's games, and I will do no such thing as to let you inside my house or hide you in my basement. You need to turn yourself in, and do it now. You are talking crazy, and need God's help. You have the boldness to ask me to help you when I know you killed Anderson and Tom, and then attempted to kill your brother and Harry? Woodrow you are very sick, and need professional and spiritual help."

"Ida, I have nothing more to say to you."

"Nor I to you. Goodbye Woodrow."

"Mom!" Woody shouted.

"Goodbye, Woodrow."

"Mom, wait! Wait! Mom. Please don't hang up."

"Woodrow, I am hanging up.

"Ida?"

'Woodrow, I haven't time for your nonsense.

I have errands to run, and you need to turn yourself in.

"Ida?"

Click.

Woody's inner Phantoms thought, *Ida cut us off., and Harry, and he's snitching. The secret room. Ida said no to us. Jada … Ida has hidden her there.*

Woody's phantom spoke. *For months Ida has had Jada with her. Ida never cared for you, she hates you. When you find Jada in her house, then hell will be released on them. Hell's fiery fury will fall on Ida Jackson Parks. I, in you, will become her worst nightmare. She must be punished with fire. You must obey my commands and do all that I order when that time comes. Do you understand me my son?*

Woody responded, "Yes, I understand, I am your obedient servant my lord."

Then park your car several houses away from Ida's. Do not call anyone else.

Woody obeyed his phantom's orders and parked Jada's car several houses down from his mother's home and waited. While waiting, his cell phone began to ring.

Answer, we need to hear this.

His cell phone screen showed the caller's name

Ring, ring, ring, and on the fifth ring, Woody heard himself saying, "Hey Luke."

"Woody, we have been worrying about you man. Where are you?"

"Right now, we're parked down the street from my mom's house."

"We? Oh, your inner phantom in you."

"Do you want us to come and get you?"

"Us? Red with you?"

"Yep."

"What about Pete?

"Don't know where Pete went."

"Where are you now?'

"At the club in your office."

"You and Red need to get out of that club, that's the first place they will look. I am glad my informant, Officer John, scrubbed the videos showing us beating Anderson and MJ. MJ is still in a coma, and Harry…"

Luke interjected, "You haven't heard?"

"What?"

"Officer John was working as an undercover agent and he didn't destroy the videos. Harry woke up, and ratted us out. Harry told things from when you killed Sally and Mike, and took out the owners of the club you once worked in and more. Woody, anytime now, the FBI will be coming for us. That's why we are here. We have disguises but we need money and we don't have the combination to your safe."

"Luke tell me, trust, what happened to trust? Officer John was also a traitor." With a heavy sighed Woody said, "Luke the combination is my mother's birth month, date and year. 961936. Go ahead take it all, I will never use it."

"Woody, our faces are plastered on all the major television stations.

The only reason why Pete, Red and I can move around is because of our disguises."

"That's why I am able to drive Jada's car. I went back and got a different disguise after leaving the hospital. Luke, hindsight is always 20/20, we should have killed Michael, Harry and Jada. Loose lips sink ships and our ship is sinking faster than the Titanic.

I also believe my Mom is hiding Jada."

"No way, where?"

"Luke, Mom has a secret room inside her basement

and in that room behind an old cupboard is another room where slaves slept. When I asked her if she would let me hide there, she told me no."

"Woody, your mom being a Christian and all, I can understand her not wanting you there. But if Jada has been withher all this time ... oh man, what are you going to do?"

"If my dear wife is there with my dear mother, then I will kill them both.

"Both? That's dark man, killing your mom?"

"Yeah, it's dark alright."

"Hey Luke, speaking of dark, I never told you this, but your name means, light."

"What? And all this time I have willingly let you lead into darkness."

Woody laughed and said, "Well, my old friend, this may be our last ..."

Their conversation came to an abrupt halt. Through the cell phone, Woody heard pounding on the club's door.

"Open up! Federal Agents!"

Woody heard, Red cursing and shouting, "What the..."

Then he heard the door to his office being knocked down.

Again, Red was shouting, "I'm not going back to prison!"

Gunshots rang out and Luke shouted, "Don't shoot, don't shoot"

The next voice Woody heard was Officer John's. He screamed into Luke's cellphone, "Woodrow Parks, we're coming for you next."

Click. The phone went dead.

Chapter 30, Unauthorized Entry

With intense irritation, Woody sat parked inside Jada's car a few houses down from his mother' house. While waiting, his mind was being agitated by his phantom. "I heard you. "You want me to burn my mom's house down. I am to destroy Jada, my mom and myself in the mansion." Minutes later, he saw his mother's car pull out of the garage. He dialed her cell phone. His special ring tone alerted her that Woody was calling.

"Woodrow."

"Mom, they've captured Luke Allen and Red."

"Good, then it's just a matter of time before they have you."

"Mom, I need your help!"

"Woodrow, my answer is no."

"Mom, I am not feeling your love and you are not listening. I am telling you that I need your help right now.

"Woodrow, I will always love you and what you are feeling is my heart's pain, my shame, my non acceptance to your father's wishes, and my regret for my years of denying that you had a problem and needed professional help. Woodrow, from here on out, you will only speak the truth; no more lies, secrets, and deceit will come from your mouth when talking to me, and that's what you will hear and receive from me."

"Truth, Ida? Truth? Ah, déjà vu." He continued slowly and sarcastically, "I've been there and heard that.

Truth? You have told me umpteenth times that you never saw Jada, isn't that true Ida?"

Woody heard silence, and shouted, "Ida!"

"Woodrow, when you called me Ida, I heard the tone in your voice change. Why are you calling me Ida?"

"Because Ida is a liar. And my mom is a saint, incapable of doing wrong. Ida, is a traitor, and to me, Ida is already dead."

"Woodrow, you are very disturbed. And Jada? Woodrow, I am happy she got away from you and that insane spirit you are housing. You need God's help, son. Goodbye."

"Wait! Mom, mom, wait! Please don't hang up."

"First, I'm Ida, and now I'm Mom. Can't you see that spirit you are housing has caused you to become unstable? And I am talking directly to that thing you are housing when I say, devil, you are messing with the wrong woman."

"Momma!"

"Goodbye."

Click.

Mom Park's cell phone rang. The screen revealed the caller's name.

"Hello, Chief Jones."

"Mrs. Parks, the videos from Anderson's hospital room, and the fingerprints lifted from the utility closet's trays and stairwell are all conclusive. Woodrow Parks and Harry Brown are our men.""But Chief, I thought you told Gloria that the surveillance camera inside Anderson's room was malfunctioning."

"I did, and I lied. I didn't want Woody to run. We have had undercover officers posing as Woody's informants for months. They have been feeding Woody false information to get him comfortable, especially Officer John. When Michael was conscious, he told me Officer Jones worked for Woody, but he could be trusted.

"The surveillance cameras that Woody installed in his office show him assailing Jada, Anderson, Michael and many more. Luke Allen and Harry, Pete and Red, Woody's henchmen are seen helping him beat Anderson and Michael. We also saw Jada cleaning up Woody's mess, under duress.

"The $10,000 in marked bills that George Hayes gave to us along with Harry's testimony will ensure that Woody will never experience freedom again. An APB, all-points bulletin, is out for Woody's arrest."

"Harry came out of his coma last night and provided us with more information on the death of Tom Redding, and other unsolved murders involving Woodrow."

"Did you say other unsolved murders?"

"Are you saying Woodrow is a serial killer?"

"I'm sorry, Mrs. Parks, but it seems Woody has been killing for years. We have already captured Luke Allen, and Red Goodman was killed in a gun battle when he refused to surrender. Pete is on the run."

"I just talked with Woodrow, he's driving Jada's car."

Mrs. Parks, keep alert. Your son is a desperate man without a conscious, and he will kill anyone, even you, to achieve his psychotic phantom's needs."

"Yes, Chief Jones, I now know that to be true. Unfortunately, I am too late to help Woodrow. Thank you for calling me. Bye."

Woodrow, Woodrow, where are you? She thought… *Woodrow is in my house.* Ida quickly turned her car around and headed back home.

Meanwhile, Woody stood in his mother's driveway debating with his phantom. *I order you to go inside and do what I have spoken.*

Woody hesitated, then turned to walk away. Suddenly, he began fighting his phantom, flailing his head and hands. *Stop! Ida has changed the back and front door locks but her bedroom window is unlocked. Go and gain entrance.*

From inside, Jada covered her squeal with her hands when she heard an unexpected, loud crash coming from downstairs. Woody had opened Mom Parks' bedroom window and it hit hard against the wall. Jada felt the house's vibrations. She heard the kitchen door that led into the basement being slammed. She heard heavy walking back up the steps and through the house. He heard Woody calmly sang, "Jada, my Jada, come out, come out wherever you are." Then he screamed, Jada! I know you are here! I also know every inch of this house even its hidden secrets."

In a frenzy, he shouted, "Jada, we order you to come out now!"

Woody waited for a response, and hearing none he screamed like a small child throwing a tantrum. "Jada!"

Jada cautiously crept to the window and looked out. *Woody is driving my mother's old car.* She tentatively crawled to the corner of the attic, and sat trembling, and praying that what Woody said about knowing the house's secrets wasn't true.

She heard him walking around in his mother's room. "Jada!" he stormed. "I know you are here, I smell your perfume. I know you are hiding somewhere!" He moved around his mother's room and sang, "Somewhere in Ida's house my Jada is, oh where can my little traitor be?"

She heard his heinous sniggering as he continued his search, singing, "With her brown eyes so bright and her full lips so sweet, where, oh where can my traitor be?"

She heard what sounded like glass being thrown against something hard and it shattered. She shuddered when she heard his heavy footsteps inside his mom's closet. *The door!* Jada remembered she had left the hidden door that led up the steps to the secret room cracked. She heard him shouting and ranting as he moved his mother's clothes aside. He screamed, "Where are you woman? You are here somewhere, I smell your perfume."

He slammed his mother's bedroom closet door shut. Jada scurried across the floor and listened as Woody continued his ranting while he searched the house.

Jada heard Mom Parks' valuable antiques breaking in her front room.

She heard more breakage as he ransacked the other six bedrooms, the den, the parlor and the living room. Then, silence.

Jada found herself lying flat on the floor praying and daring not to move. She heard Mom Parks' voice inside her head. *Stay here, do not come out.*

She heard Woody once again opening the kitchen door which lead into the basement, she heard his heavy feet as they clumped down the twenty-two steps, and then again, silence. Moments later, she heard what sounded like scraping noises of heavy equipment being moved.

In the basement, Woody pushed against a heavy cement block, the doorway opened and he walked into the hidden room. He groped until he found the hanging string and he yanked it. The room illuminated.

He screamed, "Jada! I smell your perfume!"

He looked at the cupboard. His phantom shouted, *Move it!* Woody removed the heavy cupboard and saw a door leading into another room he knew nothing about. He removed his cigarette lighter and looked around. He thought, *this must be where the slaves slept, so those conducting searched would not suspect a room behind a cupboard.*

He, laughing hysterically, no Jada! Repeating Jada's name while chanting, "we will, we will, find you."

Driving towards her home, Mom Parks noticed Jada's mother's car parked a few houses away from hers. She rushed out of her car and hastily up the steps. She inserted her door key, pushed the door open and yelled. "Woodrow Hugh Parks, where are you, and why are you here in my home?"

He answered back, "I'm in the basement, Ida."

"Get yourself up here now! I have told you I would not hide you in my home."

Ida heard a loud grunt. Woody had fallen over a wooden crate and scraped his hands and knees. While on his knees, he searched for his cigarette lighter with his hands. He stopped his search when he heard Ida's footsteps in the kitchen. He heard the anger in her voice when she shouted, "Woodrow, I told you that you weren't welcome in my home, nor could you stay in my basement. Why are you down there?"

I'm looking for Jada. I thought perhaps you were hiding her in the basement's secret room, and that's why you told me I couldn't stay there."

"So Detective Sherlock Holmes, what makes you think she's here in my house?"

"Her perfume, Ida. I still smell her perfume. Take a sniff. Do you smell her perfume?

Where is she hiding Ida?"

Looking down the steps to her son, she yelled, "Woodrow, come up here and follow me!"

Woodrow climbed the steps and he followed his mother into her bedroom.

She looked at her furniture in disarray and the many broken pieces scattered around. She asked, "What have you done to my house?"

"What difference does it make? After all they're just things."

"Come!"

She opened her bedroom door and saw her lamps and antiques shattered. The phantom within ordered Woody to laughed. Hearing his loud uncanny laughter, Ida kept her composure, and told him, "Look on my dresser, what are you seeing":

"Perfume bottles."

"Find the fragrance called, "Deception."

"Yes, Ma'am."

He picked it up and with his free hand. Woody heard his phantom's command. He obeyed with pleasure and shoved all her perfume bottles onto the mahogany floor.

"Oops… They're just things."

"Yes, Woodrow, they are, just things, now open the one you are holding and smell it."

He sniffed and looked at his mother with unfavorable restraint.

She said, "Now come over here and sniff my scarf."

He sniffed her scarf.

"Well, isn't it the same fragrance Jada wears? Do you remember giving me a bottle on Christmas?"

"Yes. I'm sorry for destroying your things, Mom."

"Woodrow, you have a lot to be sorry about these days.

Ida turned in circles, looking with disbelief and said, "Look at my room, and the other rooms, the antiques that have been in this house for centuries. In only seconds, you have destroyed so much."

"What difference does it make, Ida? If we find Jada here, I have been ordered to set all us on fire ... right here in this old house."

Chapter 31, Derision

"**Your master is a liar**! Woodrow, you were told by that consummated liar who controls you to burn this house down to the ground and you are going to willingly obey him? That will not happened. This house will remain intact. And tell me Woodrow, why are you so sure Jada is here with me?"

With scorn he answered, "I can't find her, Ida. I have called everyone who knows her. I even went to Jada's sister Sharon more than a few times, and she wasn't there."

"You visited Sharon, what happened?"

Jada tiptoed down the attic steps leading into Mom Ida's closet. She cautiously pushed against the partially open door and heard chairs scraping against the floor. Jada sat on the bench inside Ida's closet and listened to their conversation.

"When I arrived at Sharon's home, Sharon's husband, Ray, met me at the door and told me I wasn't welcome. We exchanged many not so admirable words. He told me he heard rumors that I like to beat women, and he would get much satisfaction in beating me down to a pulp. He told me, 'then you can feel the pain that you have inflicted on Jada and other helpless women.'

"I pulled my pistol on him and I demanded to come inside their home. But he, being muscular, quicker and more powerful than me, did an Ali punch on me."

"An Ali punch, I don't understand. What's that?"

Woody whooshed his fists in the air and chanted, "'float like a butterfly, sting like a bee. The hands can't touch what the eyes can't see.'

"Pow, pow, Ray hit me in both eyes. He knocked me flat on my butt, and my pistol dropped from my hands. Like a wounded animal, I struggled to get up. I was woozy and trying to get my bearings as I watched him remove the clips from my pistol and toss my gun on the grass. He lifted me like I was a shot-put and hurled me onto the grass. I heard his door slam and he locked his door.

"I struggled to stand. I was hurting really bad. That was the first time anyone had inflicted pain on me. Slowly, I picked up my pistol off the grass and stumbled over to open my car door. That's when Sharon drove up and Ray opened their house door and came outside. He shouted, 'That bully came here looking for Jada and this time I was home.'

"Sharon's youngest daughter, who looks so much like Jada, blurted, 'Mom has been worrying about Aunt Jada, she keeps calling and Aunt Jada isn't answering her phone. Mom told dad that you may have killed her. Did you Uncle Woody, did you kill Aunt Jada?"

Woodrow, what was your answer to the child?

"I said nothing. Sharon sent the children into the house. Sharon called the littlest child Sally Michelle.

"You know Ida, Sharon's little girl's looks haunt me, she looks like Jada. She has Jada's full lips, curly brown hair, my dad's high cheekbones, and your soft brown eyes. If I didn't know better, I would think she was my child." *Is she? No way.* He stopped, and said aloud, "No way, what am I thinking?" He shook his head to clear the cobwebs and said, "Jada, she was not with Sharon and when I asked you if you've seen her, you never give me a straight answer. Then I thought about the basement's secret slave quarters. I figured you must have hidden Jada in the secret place."

Ida folded her arms and said, "hmmm, in the basement ... inside the secret quarters. Well, Mr. Watson, I guess you've figured wrong."

"Have I, Ida, figured wrong? ... You know this house is very old, and could hold more secret rooms that I was never told about. That's why my master wants it to be burned down."

"And again, that will not happen, this house will remain intact."

With mockery he repeated, "This house will remain intact."

"Woodrow, stop! I am tired of hearing that poisonous viper's voice coming out of your mouth. Woodrow, CJ called my cell phone minutes before I came back here."

"CJ? Oh, you mean, Chief Jones? Are you two best friends now?" Not responding to Woodrow's ridicule. Ida continued. "Chief Jones called just moments before I came here, and he informed me your brother has four additional police bodyguards protecting him. They have captured your two remaining bodyguards, Luke Allen and Pete. Harry Brown gave them information about Sally, Mike, Tom, Anderson, and others you have killed…"

Woody stopped listening. He looked at his mother

with intense contempt and thought. *That louse, I should have poisoned Harry a long time ago.* He heard Ida say, "... and Red, he's dead."

Ida Parks stared into her son's dark black eyes and saw no reaction to the news she shared. She said, "Woodrow, you knew this.

"Yes I did Ida."

"Since you said I am going to die Woodrow. I have often wondered, what's your fascination with the number 75?"

"You really want to know?" He chuckled, and said, "We will go right to the heart of the matter, that number 75, has always been my number of bad fortune."

"Bad fortune? What do you mean by that, Woodrow?"

"The number 75, that's the number that ignites all my killings."

"All your killings?"

"Oh never mind, Ida. I will tell you about my killings after you finish telling me what you wanted me to know about the conversation you had with your friend Chief Jones."

"Woodrow, as you already know, the hospital had a hidden video camera over the entrance door and one hidden inside Anderson's room that records all visitors."

"Ida, don't you remember? I was there at Gloria's house with all of you when the investigator called and told Gloria they were malfunctioning."

"That was a lie told to Gloria by Chief Jones to trick you."

"Where are you going with this, Ida?"

"I believe you already know, and if you would quiet that overactive mind of that murderous evil imp you are housing, you will find out where I am going."

Woody smiled, and put his mouth close to his mother's ear and whispered, "You know, he doesn't like you, Ida."

Ida laughed and shouted, "Newsflash and I have no admiration for it."

"Forgive us, Ida, please go on. I must warn you, each word you speak will add additional nails to your coffin." With mockery he laughed and said, "Oh yes, I forgot, there's no coffin for you because you will die in this house when we burn it down. But by all means, go on, Ida, tell us more."

"Oh Woodrow, Woodrow, that phantom has no power in my house. Anyway, Anderson's doctor became a renewed Christian by listening to my prayers and worshiping with Michael on their nursing station's monitor."

"What are you expecting from us, Ida? Are you expecting us to shout, hallelujah?" With loud snickering, Woody jumped out of his chair, moved closer to her and shouted, "That will never happen!
And to be frank Ida, we aren't interested in hearing any more of your story."

"Woodrow, stop! I am God's property. My body houses God's Spirit and that spirit you are housing will shut its mouth and listen."

 Woody smiled. He pulled his chair closer, and

straddled it, and scornfully said, "Speak."

"Michael's doctor became a Christian, and he and his family visited my church. After church, we had dinner and talked. During our conversation, I told him I was Anderson's aunt, and I thought of Anderson like a son. The doctor told me he had heard Anderson was doing well and was expected to live. The floor Anderson was on was understaffed the night he died. When the nurse went to check on Anderson, he was already dead, and his pillow was on the floor.

"The killer tried to cover his presence by erasing his finger smudges, but the police found fingerprints on trays inside the supply closet across from Anderson's room, as well as the banisters in the stairwell leading to and from Anderson's room. The hidden camera in Anderson's room caught the killer's face, and heard the killer's final words.

"They've known it was you for a long time. Even when you visited the hospital, the officers heard me calling you by your name. They were told to keep you there as long as possible while your informants who worked as double agents went into your Casino office to find your surveillance videos.

"The police now have evidence that shows Luke Allen and Harry Brown assisting you in beating Anderson and Michael. The hospital video saw you laughing while you held the pillow to Anderson's face. They know that while you were smothering Anderson, you said to him, 'Now I lay Anderson down to sleep, I will see your face in hell.' Perhaps those weren't yours exact words. "By the way, Woodrow, would you like to unsay those words you quoted over Anderson? He will not be with you in hell. He's in heaven. The only reason Chief Jones couldn't arrest you that day in the hospital was they didn't have then conclusive evidence against you. But now they have your own surveillance tapes. And, Woodrow, your snitch, Officer John, he was an undercover informant."

Woody became unglued after hearing his mother's remarks. He stood to pace. He suddenly stopped, leaned his body against the refrigerator and said with charred bitterness, "Ida, please continue with my diabolical story map."

With calmness Ida continued, "From the hospital video, they saw you. Now the television stations know Woodrow Hugh Parks is a serial killer. And by the way, Harry Brown, your puppet, went into Anderson's room while Cate was there and told her you sent him there to see about Michael, and that he was afraid for his life, her father's, nephew and for her.

"The day you came to the hospital, Michael was awake and alert. He told me you kissed his lips, and told him, "Die, brother die."

He opened his one good eye and asked you why? Michael told me and Chief Jones how you beat Anderson and him. He also told us that $10,000 was planted on Anderson by you. Jada recognized the small green dots, and told us that's how you mark all your money. Gloria gave the money to George and George turned it over to Chief Jones.

"Woodrow, I didn't want to believe my own flesh and blood, my son, was capable of doing something so, so heinous! You killed your cousin for your greed of money? Then you and your thugs beat your own brother, almost to death."

Ida Parks stood and walked over to the large kitchen window overlooking her garden. She noticed the beautiful vibrant colorful flowers, nestled on lustrous emerald grass; she then turned and looked at her son and saw his grotesque appearance, shrouded in darkness.

Gloom was all around her son, and a heavy sorrowful burden clouded her mind; tears begin to fall. Between heavy sobs Woodrow's mother unlocked her secret with a confession. "Woodrow, I should have listened to your father. He said you needed help, but I let my love for you blind my eyes. I thought my love and support would be enough, but it wasn't and I helped create what you have become."

Woody put his hand on his pistol inside his coat. His mother asked, "Son, who drove you to kill Jada's precious poodle, and then force her into prostitution? Who drove you to kill your cousin? Why did you beat your brother almost to death? Why did you kill your best friend Sally and her husband?" Disgust over her son's actions caused her to explode.

"Woodrow!" she screamed, "Many innocent people are dead because they trusted you. A very small part of me still wants to believe you aren't capable of murder, but they have proof. You did it all. Harry said you have bodies buried under your club! Who are you?"

Woodrow, stared down into the kitchen sink, he turned the spigot on and off. *You have to kill Ida.* He lifted his head to stare out the window, onto the street where he saw carefree happy children playing.

He recalled those days he played with Anderson and MJ on the same street; the days when everything in life seemed to be simple. Then he turned 12 and he met "his special phantom friend" when playing a forbidden board game with a friend and his mother. That's when everything changed.

Time for truth, now we know Jada is here!

Woodrow turned towards his mom. With disrespect he said, "Ida, how would you have known I killed Jada's poodle while she was in college, and about Sally and Mike? Unless... unless!" He released a deep wail, and shouted "Jada!"

He began waving his pistol erratically, bang! The bullet hit the wall, and again he shrieked "Jada, Ja-daaaaa!" Bang, bang! Pieces of plaster fell onto the floor, Woody screamed, "Come out, or I will shoot Ida. Please, please come out!"

Jada, heard Woody pleading. She also knew in his twisted mind, he believed he would have to kill his mother because she knew the truth about him.

Sobbing hard, Woody turned and fell into his mother's' arms. He said to her, "Ida, you know the truth and everybody who finds truth..." He hesitated, then said, "about me ... dies."

Ida Parks gently lifted her son's chin, and cupped his unshaven face into her tender, strong hands. With empathy and kindness, she said, "Woodrow, you could kill me, but you can't kill God's memory. God sees, hears and knows everything you have done. It is written Woodrow, 'God will bring every judgment, including every hidden thing, whether it is good or evil.' Son, you can run from God, but your evil deeds will follow and you can never hide."

Woody lifted his head. The phantom within him was provoked by her truth. *Slap Ida.*

His hit was so forceful that Ida's head hit the mahogany kitchen table and she fell from her chair onto the floor.

Woodrow stood over Ida and showed no remorse. As he looked down on her, he stooped and shoved his revolver into his Ida's chest and said, "You are no longer my mom, I have been instructed to call you Ida. The spirit that controls my mind forced me to hit you. I have been ordered to kill you, set this house on fire, and stay here and to burn with you."

"Woodrow, can't you see that evil spirit that controls you can't love? Even if you kill yourself and me, it will not erase what you have done from God's memory. What you have done is nothing other than pure evil. God will not permit that to continue. You will live and not die. You will stand in man's court to be judged, and you will be found guilty. Even when you are given the chance to ask God for His forgiveness, will you be sincere?"

God can forgive, however you will still pay man's penalty for what you have done."

Woodrow watched without remorse as Ida crawled over to a chair. She pulled her body erect, not sitting. She turned and walked herself into the revolver.

"Son, I love you." She said, "But my heart aches heavily for what you have become. I repent here and now and ask God for His forgiveness for denying you help, and I also ask you for yours. And Woodrow, if God desires me to die by my son's gun then shall it be."

She showed no fear as she watched her son put his hand into his pocket and remove a silencer. He slid the silencer onto the barrel of another firearm. He pulled back the trigger, and smiled. Then he heard a door opening and out stepped Jada.

Ping! The kitchen's tiffany pendant chandelier crashed onto the floor, shattering into thousands of tiny pieces. Woody looked and saw Jada, and then he looked at Ida and he pounded his chest, and wailed, "Why?"

Immediately, his facial expression changed. With an unnerving smirk, he said, "So Ida, all these weeks when I was looking for Jada, you were hiding her. That' the reason why I could no longer call you Mom, because my Mom is a liar.

"Before you die, do you need to ask God for His forgiveness for hiding Jada, and lying to us about it? I believe that good book you love so much says, 'All liars will have their part in hell's fire.'"

Jada stood in the doorway entrance trembling.

Ida walked over to Jada, wrapped her arms around her and looked at her son. With boldness she said, "Shhh, Jada, don't be afraid. God got this."

"Woodrow?"

"Ida?"

 "I never told you a lie; because I never answered your

questions."

Jada broke from Ida's embrace and rushed to Woody. She grabbed hold of his arm and pleaded, "Woody, please no. She's your mother. You can't kill her!"

He shoved Jada and said, "Jada, you are right." I can't kill your Ida, you will."

Jada shook her head and repeatedly shouted,

"No, no, no. I will not!"

Agonizing, she screamed, "Woody, this is your mother!"

He mimicked her, "Woody, this is your mother!"

"No she's not. I have no mother, her name is Ida."

"Jada," he bellowed, "obviously, you and your dear mother-in-law don't care about me, nor did my dear cousin and brother. I should have killed MJ that night, just like I did Dad!"

His dad? Stunned, Ida slowly turned. Trying not to believe what she heard, she questioned his remarks. "Did you just say you killed your Dad?"

"Yes, you heard right, Ida. I killed your beloved Samuel."

Ida's body shook as she tried to process what she heard, and she again repeated, "You killed your Dad! How? I don't understand?"

"Well this time you will need to sit down, my dear Ida, and I will enlighten you.

Brokenhearted, Ida Park's turned to walk to her chair, but stumbled. Jada rushed over to support her. As they walked, Ida's ears heard and her heart felt the crunch underneath her shoes of the jagged pieces of stained glass that were scattered all over the mahogany wood. In a state of confusion, combined with disbelief, Ida leaned on Jada, not taking her eyes off her son. Jada said, "Sit, Mom."

Feeling with her trembling hands for the chair's seat, she sat.

Woody, pulled a chair out and straddled it; he rested his chest on the chair's back as he brandished his pistol. Menacingly, he shouted, "Jada, you get yourself a chair and sit next to your dear, overprotective Ida.

Jada slowly pulled a chair over, sat down, and held her mother-in-law's hand.

"Now, Ida, you want to hear my story?

"Oh you are in shock and can't talk, can you? Well, Ida… it all started because of you. I couldn't believe you would let Dad sleep with all those women during the weekend, and then preach on Sunday."

Not understanding nor believing what she was hearing, she asked, "What? What are you talking about Woodrow? Your Dad never slept with any woman but me."

"I wanted that to be true, but the real truth came too late for me and my victims." "Victims? Woodrow, you were only twelve years old. Victims? Too late."

"Yes, you heard me, I said victims. You see Ida,

I found the truth on the night I killed Dad's twin brother."

"Woodrow, no! No! I'm not understanding. We never told you your father had a twin. You're aren't saying you killed your Uncle Milton, and your father?"

"Bingo, Ida! Plus another unfortunate unknown

person. At the age of twelve, I killed five people, my school friend Willie and his mom, I set their house on fire and watch it burn, and yes, I was only twelve years old."

Woody stood, walked over to his mother's chair, squatted down, and looked undaunted. With delight seeing her stunned face, he smiled chillingly and without pain gloated when he said, "Yes Ida, to my pleasure, I killed both Milton, his lady friend. Three swings with my aluminum bat. Whack, whack, whack!"

Woodrow's face felt the sting from his mother's hand. He stood, rubbed his face and said, "I deserved that one."

"Woody are you even capable of loving?" Jada asked. "Did you ever care about Mike and Sally? Or was she like me and the others who were just convenient pawns that you used? Here you stand, apparently without remorse, telling your mother you killed your childhood friend and his mother,

your dad, and your uncle and his woman. Woody, again I ask, have you ever been capable of loving anyone?"

His response came as a bone chilling voice of truth from his inner phantom. It hissed, "I love no one. I delight in killing, stealing and destroying lives."

God give me Your strength. Ida prayed and then she spoke, "The enemy in you speaks truth. Did you hear him? He hates you too, Woodrow. Were you really listening to his words? There is no love in him. Woodrow tell me, why did you kill your Uncle, that woman and your dad?"

"I thought Dad was fooling around with other women. No one ever told me he had a twin brother."

"That's because he was a derelict Woodrow. He was always in trouble, he was just release from prison, and came back to his hometown to live. Many of the church members also mistook Milton to be Samuel and they were ready to dismiss your father as pastor for misconduct. Your Dad searched and found Milton and brought him to the business meeting. It was then when they realized they had made a horrible mistake, and after that day your father never spoke of him again."

With teary eyes, and distress, Woodrow said, "Ida, you and Dad didn't tell me. You didn't tell me. I believed Milton was Daddy.

I would slip away from home many nights and go to the place I thought was my Dad's hiding place. I saw him there with a different woman each Saturday night but he had one woman he really liked. I watched them for weeks, and one

night I waited until she left his old shack and I followed her. She turned down a dark alley and I screamed 'Leave my daddy alone.' She stopped, and stumbled towards me, she stooped down and gave me this drunken smirk, and asked, 'Who's your daddy, baby?'

"I didn't answer her, I just rotated my aluminum baseball bat I held in my hands and hit her. She fell to the ground and I kept hitting, and hitting. I couldn't stop myself because it felt good, and when I did stop, she was dead. I rolled her dead body over to the nearby swamp. I pushed her down the hill and watched as her body was consumed by alligators.

"I returned to the alley and found her purse. I opened

it and removed her money. I still remembered the amount $75.00. I tucked it into my pocket and tossed her purse into the swamp. Then the strangest thing happened, it started to rain, and washed away all her blood. But I wasn't finished. I walked to that shack where the man I thought to be dad, and my timing was right. The man, who I now know to be Milton, was walking out from the old outhouse, he was drunk and he didn't see me. I crept behind him, I swung and hit him on his head and he fell. I kept hitting him over, and over, with my aluminum baseball bat. I wanted to stop, but again, I couldn't. After resting for a short while, I went into his pockets and removed his money. To my surprise, he had the same amount as his girlfriend, $75.00. To this day, when I see the number 75, I know I will have to kill and take whatever my phantom tells me.

"After killing and taking his money I left his body by that stinky outhouse, and returned home. As I was climbing into my bedroom window, I saw Dad and I thought Dad was a ghost. I started screaming and he muffled my mouth with his hands so I would not awake you.

"After my thrashing about was over, I told him what I saw him do, and what I had done. I remember crying, and daddy held me and told me he would take care of it all.

Daddy took me out to the barn and washed the blood off of my body and took my clothes. He told me to go inside and take a good bathe and to clean up after myself. He told me when I was done with my bath, he would wait for me to come to my bedroom window and to wave as a signal that I had done what he told me. I watched Daddy from my bedroom window that night. I remember it was a full moon and I saw Daddy put my clothes into a bag and he left the house carrying burlap bags. I guess he went over to his brother's house and..."

Ida Parks finished her son's sentence for him. "He buried his brother.

"Bingo once again, Ida."

"Woody?"

"Jada?"

"Did you tell your dad about the woman?"

"No, I never told dad about the woman I killed."

"Why did you kill your father?"

"Well, my dear wife, after Dad's brother's death, my dad became sick, and I was afraid he would make one of those deathbed confessions about how Uncle Milton died. One evening, that old geezer, Jeremiah Sullivan, visited him and Daddy was feeling well enough to walk to the barn. I followed them, and I heard Daddy telling Jeremiah that he feared me, but he couldn't tell him why. Eventually, Jeremiah left and Dad stayed. Dad was on his leaning an old wooden milk crate on his knees praying, and I surprised Daddy. I put him out of his misery. I smothered my dear, weak, father with a plastic bag, and everybody thought he had a heart attack. Everybody except that nosey Jeremiah Sullivan.

"After my dad's funeral, that old geezer pulled me aside and he told me he believed I was responsible for my own father's death."

Woody squinted his dark black eyes and said, "You know that hunched back old man hates me just as much as

I hate him and one day, even if I die here in this house in the fire, I will find a way to get to him."

Ida shouted, "Who are you?"

Jada jumped from her chair, picked up a glass and threw it at his head. He dodged the glass and laughed as he watched it hit the wall and shatter.

Woody walked over and tried to hold her. She pushed him away. He grabbed her arm and pulled her towards him. She jerked away from his grasp and rushed into Ida's arms.

Jada said, "Mom Parks, since we are going to die, I need to tell you something. Woody sent me to his office to clean. Once I was there, Luke Allen took away my cell phone and he locked me inside. In the darkness I groped for the light switch. Finding it, I clicked the switch, and was horrified by all the blood I saw over the walls and on the floor."

Jada slowly put her left hand into her dress pocket and she pulled out the crumpled tissue that Cate gave back to her. Opening it, she dumped out its contents. With her trembling fingers, Jada picked up two teeth and held them in her hands. "Mom," she said, "you talked about Anderson's front teeth missing. Here they are. I found them with Woody's bloody aluminum baseball bat inside Woody's office.

"Mom ..." tears erupted when Jada said, "Woody bludgeoned Michael and Anderson that night. I was forced to clean their blood from the walls and floor; while cleaning I found Anderson's missing teeth, and I also found this..." Jada reached into her sewn in bra pocket and showed Anderson's pocket watch.

"So, my dear supportive, loving wife, you kept them to blackmail me?"

"No, Woody, not to blackmail you; you have nothing I want. I kept them to show Cate, George, Mom and Grandpa what a cold-blooded calculating killer you are.

Woody aimed the gun at Jada's head. *Shoot, kill, shoot! I order you to shoot.* Instead, he walked over to Jada, removed the teeth and pocket watch from her hand, and flung them across the room. The he struck her like a swift bite from a rattlesnake's fangs. Jada's quivering body hit the floor and her face burned like fire. He put the gun into his pocket, then walked over, lifted her tiny body into the air, and flung her across the room. Her body hit hard against the wall and Woody shouted, "My, that felt good! Once again Jada, your God didn't catch you. He still must be asleep."

Ida rushed to her side. She heard Woody bark, "Pick her up!" He reached into his side holster and removed another pistol. "Let's take a walk down into your tomb."

Once they reached the basement, Woody's body started to vibrate.

The phantom within hollered, "Hey, Ida, we will see if your God can deliver you and Jada from your basement tomb and fiery mansion that's soon to come? Ida, Ida, my master has ordered me to burn your house down."

Ida let out a faint chuckle and said, "Woodrow, my God is my deliverer. My God is greater than that thing you are housing in your mind. With the authority of Jesus and in the name of Jesus, I proclaim that spirit you are carrying is powerless.

My God has given me His Spirit to overcome all the fiery darts of your enemy, and nothing will harm us. I command that spirit in you to leave this house, and you, intact."

"Ida, you are so funny. Once you are sealed inside that secret room, there's no help for you. You know, just as well as I, that there's no escape from that room. Come on, Ida, hold Jada's hand and move."

An unnatural laughter spewed from Woody's mouth. He shoved both Jada and his mother into the secret room and walked out, leaving them alone. He reached up to the top cement block and proceeded to count aloud as he moved his hand down each block. "1, 2, 3, 4, 5," and he bellowed, 'Push."

Woody stepped back, grinning as the cemented door closed, sealing Ida and Jada in forever.

He stood on the top step that lead back into the kitchen. Woody shouted down, hoping they could hear him, "I knew that hidden room would come in handy one day! Goodbye, Ida and Jada."

Woody hastily closed the door, and walked into the kitchen. He opened and closed kitchen drawers until he found a box of long stem wooden matches. Woody's phantom spoke, *Burn this house down.*

Woody's phantom, through Woody, laughed triumphantly as he held the match box erratically in his hands. Woody heard his own aching heart pulsating against his chest and his chaotic head pounded as he argued with his inward phantom's voice.

He heard his mother's voice shouting, *Son, stop! You have gone too far.* He stopped walking. Outside, he heard the downpour of heavy rain, the roar of the blustery wind and the explosive sound of thunder. From his mother's large mansion kitchen window, he saw yellowish red flashes of lightning against the black ominous sky. He thought about the scripture, *out from the throne come flashed of lightening and sound and peals of thunder*. Immediately, he heard a loud boom that shook the foundation of the mansion.

Woody heedlessly opened the wide double doors that lead onto his mother's large back porch. He walked to the edge and momentarily paused near its railing to look up into the foreboding darkness. He felt heavy rain water soaking his face. He lifted his hands to touch his unshielded eyes, and for the first time in his life he felt genuine tears mingling with the rain.

He recalled ... the rain and his mother shouting, *Son you gone too far*. He looked at the match box in his hand and suddenly he hurled the box into the air, the box open; its contents spilled and fused with the heavy rain. From the railing, he looked down and saw mud covering the matches.

He turned to sit on a wobbly wooden chair that his dad had built for his mother more than 60 years ago.

He thought, *I murdered my daddy and now I'm killing my mother*.

The wind blew and the thunder roared and the lightning shone like a fearsome blast of brilliant light flashing around him. He sat unsteady and panic-stricken. Woody put his head back and soaked up his and the stormy sky's tears.

The End of book 1

REQUEST:

After reading Lies, Secrecy & Deceptions Unlocked, and if you purchased online please rate & write a review of the book. Also, please recommend my book to your family members, friends, Twitter and Facebook followers and go online or to your local bookstores to order.

Thank you.

ABOUT THE AUTHOR

Theodora Collier Higgenbotham is a retired public school teacher. She graduated from Ohio Wesleyan University, (B.A). The University of Phoenix, (M.Ed.); She is married and has two children

Preview of Book 2. Coming December, 2016

"Cullen," said Grandpa, "the government put an enormous bright red sign on the grass of our house. While listening to the radio I learned that the signs indicate what houses will be used by our new world order government as headquarters. I haven't been outside since they all were caught up. I've been living in our basement. As you know, Vetta stored plenty food and water down here."

"Grandpa, I know Grandma, Aunt Cate and Uncle George were caught up. And when driving to the airport. Brie told me she went to see Woody. Why would Aunt Cate go to see Woody?"

"Cate said God told her to go.

"Cullen, yesterday, I heard footsteps in our house. I heard a voice that sounded like Woody and I remembered too late that I had left the basement door cracked. I rushed to turn off the lights and hide, but I wasn't quick enough. Woody opened the door and our eyes locked. Although it was dark, I saw his smile. I saw his teeth, they were covered with sparkling diamond studs."

"Grandpa, Woody had that done before he killed Anderson." "Yes, I know. I also know the new government has mandated that all citizens worldwide receive self-absorbing patches on their arms or hands. Their CEO's and their appointed overseers to the people will have diamond studs implants on their teeth."

"When you and Woody saw each other, what happened?"

"Woody quickly closed the door and I heard him say, 'See, Bryan, I told you they were all Christians.' I heard him laugh when he said, 'All those living in this house were followers of Jesus."

Then Woody laughed louder and shouted, 'No Jesus followers will be found here.' "Then I heard the man he called Bryan say, 'On our TA's take possession list, this house, the Hayes' home, and Senator Jason Rock's house, as well as a house belonging to a woman with your last named, Ida Parks, her home will be used as permanent headquarters for the new government and its upcoming election.' He then said to Woody, 'This Senator Rock, I heard he is giving them a hard time. He will not relinquish his home; however, we have the means to get what we want?'

"I heard Woody questioning Bryan about Jason. He said, 'Bryan, you mean to tell me that Senator Rock didn't make the rapture?'

"Bryan retorted, 'Woody, we do not use the word rapture anymore. You are to say, the transportation."

"Woody, said, 'Yeah that word, transportation. Is that what they are calling it now? If so, then let it be.'

"Woody asked, 'What about the Senator's wife and their son and daughter-in-law, were they transported?'"

"Bryan answered, 'Obviously, his wife was. I heard his son and wife lived out of state.'

"I heard Bryan snicker when he told Woody, 'Jason Rock is a career politician, he didn't stand a chance of being transported.

Everybody knows politicians lies.'

"Get this, I heard with my own ears when Woody responded to Bryan's remarks with a quote from the Bible. He said what the Bible said, *the fearful, and unbelieving, and the abominable, and murderers, and whoremongers, and sorcerers, and idolaters, and all liars, shall not have their part in the lake which burns with fire and brimstone: which is the second death.*'"

"What? Grandpa. Woody misquoted that scripture?

"Grandpa, the devil can quote scriptures too. But from what you just said, Woody's quote wasn't accurate. He inserted the word 'not.' And the scripture says, "*shall have their part in the lake which burns with fire and brimstone: which is the second death.*'"

"Ummm, Cullen that means the verdict is still out on that one.

We know Woody is a chameleon, and he can't be trusted." "What happened next?"

"Bryan's response to Woody was, 'ah ... Woody, that's another thing you should know, no references will be given from biblical scriptures. Let this be a warning, any words pertaining to God are forbidden. If you keep it up, I will report you.'

"Woody said, 'I hear you and would you mind dropping me off at the station?'

"Bryan told him, 'I can drop you off at your mom's house.

You are Woodrow Parks, son of Ida Jackson Parks, and why aren't you staying there?'"

"Woody said, 'You are a nosy one Bryan. No thanks, I

have Cate Hayes' luxury, BMW, at the station.'

"Bryan asked, 'How did you get that?'

"When Woody answered, he raised his voice so I could hear. He said, "She was visiting me in prison when... now what's that name we are calling the rapture? Oh yes, I remember, let me rephrase my answer, Cate Hayes was visiting me in prison when the transportation happened. I watched her face glow bright as the sun and her clothing changed from head to toe into beautiful gemstones. On her head she wore a magnificent golden diamond crown and she disappeared. I took her money, her ATM cards, her car and I am now living in their beautiful house. I guess I will continue to live there until the government tells me to leave."'

"Praise God, Grandpa. Woody saw it." "But did Cate get to him in time to repent?"

"Obviously not, he's still here."

"When Cate left, she reminded George what God told her when she arrived home several years back. *No more trips, return home, preach two times at your church and complete a coming assignment in a city not far away.* God sent her to Woody and only God and Woody know the truth."

"So afterwards, I heard Bryan say, 'Oh, my patch data is working now. I see your full name is Woodrow Hugh Parks, you are a serial killer, with a long list of murders you have committed and you were sentenced to die last Wednesday.'

Bryan hesitated and said, 'But they have you listed as dead.'

"Woody shouted, 'Yep, that's me. And surprise, I'm

not dead.' "He then asked Bryan, 'Why is that important to you?' Then I heard Woody say to Bryan, 'Do I have to kill you?'

"Bryan responded, 'No man, you don't have to kill me, we are playing on the same team. It's just that your mother's house is on the list to be occupied by high-ups, so I was wondering, why aren't you living there?'

"Woody told him, 'I have my reasons. You know man, you ask too many questions. Where I live and where I go shouldn't be any concern to you. Let's go."'

"Bryan said, "Not so fast, Woody! I have been told to keep you here, someone from TA is coming to talk with you.'

"Woody asked Bryan, 'What does the TA stand for?'

"Bryan laughed and told him, 'Ironically, it stands for Transportation Agency.'

"Soon, I heard another set of footsteps and a woman's voice. She asked them if the house had been swept, and Bryan told her, 'Yes.'

"Then she said, 'Mr. Woodrow Hugh Parks, our records show you were scheduled to die before the transportation. Now I have been authorized by the President of the World Transportation Agency to offer you a top level job.

We are in need of men such as you to carry out our plans for those who refuse to insert the patch or chip.

'Our records show you haven't received your patch, but obviously we were wrong, because your teeth are covered with our diamond studs. Which is an indicator that you are all in!

'Mr. Parks, George Allen is one of our agents' saw you name on our list and he highly recommended you to our Transportation Agency. TA is offering you a top level executive job. Being a self- made entrepreneur and with your educational background and your criminal record, you will be very valuable to us.'

"Woody asked, 'Will I be Bryan's boss?'

"She replied, "Yes, you will."

"Then I heard Woody say, 'I am your man.'"

Book 1: Lies, Secrecy and Deception Scriptures

Prologue
John 8:44
Chapter 1
John 3:9;
Matt. 7:23; Rev.14;1
Thess. 5:2;
1 Corinthians 11:14-15
Rev. 5:3
James 2:19;
Psalms 88:3-5
Isaiah 14:16
Gen. 28:15;
Isaiah 32:6-7
Chapter 2
Jeremiah 29:11 Rev.3:16
Chapter 3
1 John 3-9
1 Corinthians 13:4-8
Chapter 4
Proverb 11:27
Change Me ` Lyrics written by author
Chapter 5
Job 38:15
Chapter 6
Proverbs 16:15-8
Chapter 7
Ecc. 3:1, 4-5
Chapter 8
James 3:17
Chapter 9
Chapter 10
Job. 11:13-15
Chapter 11
Proverbs 6:17-19
Chapter 12
2 Thess. 2:8-12; Ps. 136:4
Hebrews 2:3-4, 4-16; Roman 3
Ps. 51:7 ; John 4:23-24
Psalm 16:11 ; John 1:17; 2 Timothy 3:1-7
Zephaniah 3:17 'Psalms 85:10: Lyrics to Change Me; You Are God;
John 8:44

Chapter 13
Hebrews 4:13
Ecc. 3:1
Chapter 14
Chapter 15
Ecc. 3:1
Chapter 16
Chapter 17
Eph. 4:22-24
John 8:31
Rev. 6:12
Psalms 91:11
Luke 4:10
Gen. 1:2
Isaiah 14: 13-14
Luke 10:18
Ezekiel 28:14
Rev. 12:3-4
Chapter 18
Psalms 17-13
Ecc. 11:3
Chapter 19
Chapter 20
Numbers 32:23
Matt. 6:4
1 Cor. 7:14
2 Cor. 9:6-7
Chapter 21
Genesis 50:20
1 John 4:4
1 Timothy 3:8
James 4:27
Acts 10:40
Genesis 1
Luke 8:58
Proverbs 13:22
Ezekiel 7:19
Luke 6:21
James 1:2
2 Corinthians 1:46
Chapter 22
Psalms 91
Chapter 23
Proverbs 6:17

Chapter 24
***Romans 6:23**
***Psalms 139:12-14**
***Jesus Love me Lyric, Writer unknown**
***John 7:38; *Isaiah 28:11; *Acts 2:11**
***1 Cor. 14:14; Acts 2, 5, 6, 11**
***1 Peter 1:2**
***Luke 9:58**

Chapter 25
Luke 12:2; John 14; Ezekiel 28:6
Isaiah 14: 12-14; Rev. 12:4; John 8:44

Chapter 26
Luke 8:17; John 8:32

Chapter 27
Ephesians 1:18-19; James 5:16

Chapter 28
Isaiah 65:24;
Matt. 9:29; Matt, 17:20
Mark 9:29
John 16: 13-16

Chapter 29
Ephesians 5:6

Chapter 30
John 17:15

Chapter 31
Mark 11:23
Ecc.12:14; Rev. 21:8; Luke 10:18
Rev.4:5
Quote from Muhammad Ali

Never, ever give up on God, because He will never give up on you. He loves you! Have faith in The Foundation.

New International Version

I pray that the eyes of your heart may be enlightened in order that you may know the hope to which He has called you, the riches of His glorious inheritance in His holy people. **Ephesians 1:18**

Book 1: Lies, Secrecy and Deception Scriptures

Prologue
John 8:44

Chapter 1
John 3:9;
Matt. 7:23;
Rev.14;1
Thess. 5:2;
1 Corinthians 11:14-15
Rev. 5:3
James 2:19;
Psalms 88:3-5
Isaiah 14:16
Gen. 28:15;
Isaiah 32:6-7

Chapter 2
Jeremiah 29:11
Rev.3:16

Chapter 3
1 John 3-9
1 Corinthians 13:4-8

Chapter 4
Proverb 11:27
Change Me ` Lyrics written by author

Chapter 5
Job 38:15

Chapter 6
Proverbs 16:15-8

Chapter 7
Ecc. 3:1, 4-5

Chapter 8
James 3:17

Chapter 9
2 Thess. 2:8-12; Ps. 136:4
Hebrews 2:3-4, 4-16; Roman 3
Ps. 51:7 ; John 4:23-24
Psalm 16:11 ; John 1:17; 2 Timothy 3:1-7
Zephaniah 3:17 'Psalms 85:10:
Lyrics to Change Me; You Are God;

He's a God Who Forgives, written by author

Chapter 10
Job. 11:13-15

Chapter 11
Proverbs 6:17-19

Chapter 12

Chapter 13
1 Cor. 13:1
Hebrews 4:13
Ecc. 3:1

Chapter 14

Chapter 15
Ecc. 3:1

Chapter 16

Chapter 17
Eph. 4:22-24
John 8:31
Rev. 6:12
Psalms 91:11
Luke 4:10
Gen. 1:2
Isaiah 14: 13-14
Luke 10:18
Ezekiel 28:14
Rev. 12:3-4

Chapter 18
Psalms 17-13
Ecc. 11:3

Chapter 19

Chapter 20
Numbers 32:23
Matt. 6:4
1 Cor. 7:14
2 Cor. 9:6-7

Chapter 21
Genesis 50:20
1 John 4:4
1 Timothy 3:8
James 4:27
Acts 10:40
Genesis 1

Matt. 8:20
Luke 8:58
Proverbs 13:22
Ezekiel 7:19
Luke 6:21
James 1:2
2 Corinthians 1:46

Chapter 22
Psalms 91
Chapter 23
Proverbs 6:17

Chapter 24
*Romans 6:23
*Psalms 139:12-14
*Jesus Love me Lyric, Writer unknown
*John 7:38; *Isaiah 28:11; *Acts 2:11
*1 Cor. 14:14; Acts 2, 5, 6, 11
*1 Peter 1:2
*Luke 9:58

Chapter 25
Luke 12:2; John 14; Ezekiel 28:6
Isaiah 14: 12-14; Rev. 12:4; John 8:44

Chapter 26
Luke 8:17; John 8:32

Chapter 27
Ephesians 1:18-19; James 5:16

Chapter 28
Isaiah 65:24; matt. 9:29; Matt, 17:20
Mark 9:29; John 16: 13-16

Chapter 29
Ephesians 5:6

Chapter 30
John 17:15

Chapter 31
Mark 11:23
Ecc.12:14; Rev. 21:8; Luke 10:18; Rev.4:5
Quote from Muhammad Ali

Never, ever give up on God, because He will never give up on you. He loves you!
Have faith in The Foundation.

<u>New International Version</u>
I pray that the eyes of your heart may be enlightened in order that you may know the hope to which he has called you, the riches of his glorious inheritance in his holy people. Ephesians 1:18

Made in the USA
Charleston, SC
06 July 2016